A Villa in Portofino

Evonne Wareham

Where heroes are like chocolate – irresistible!

At its core this book is about family – the things you know about them and the things you don't – the unintended secrets. It's dedicated to the memory of my mother and grandmother for the inspiration and the questions I can no longer ask.

Acknowledgements

As always, many thanks to the Choc Lit team and, of course, the Tasting Panel for their crucial input: Lynda Adcock, Zoe Rippon, Yvonne Greene, Shone Nicolson, Sharon Walsh, Ruth Nägele, Rosie Farrell, Nikky Whittaker, Michele Rollins, Lorna Baker, Kirsty White, Jo Osborne, Jenny Mitchell, Honor Gilbert, Hilary Brown, Helen Maddison, Gill Leivers, Charlotte Whittaker, Celia Bourgi, Amy Nordon and Alma Hough. Also to members of the Cariad Chapter for support and friendship.

Very special thanks to Angela Garofalo for taking me through some of the finer points of Italian law and to Kath for introducing us. Thanks also to Katie Hutton/Katherine Mezzacappa for her help with some essential Italian spelling. Their assistance was invaluable and any errors that remain are mine.

Chapter One

'I didn't think people really got letters out of the blue like this from solicitors.' Megan Morrison pushed the single sheet of headed paper across the table. 'Do you think it's some sort of scam?'

Cassie Travers scooped the letter up from between the coffee cups, quickly scanning the contents. Megan tried not to fidget as she waited for her friend's verdict. She knew she was on edge. Everything was uncertain enough at present, without something like this making it even more complicated. She needed all her energy to focus on rebuilding her life and sorting out her future. *If you have a future.*

Rather than watch Cassie as she read, she gazed around the room. At the height of the tourist season in Bath the Pump Room Restaurant buzzed with visitors. Now, on a wet Tuesday morning in October, it was quieter, but there was a low hum of conversation from groups of women enjoying coffee and cake.

Taking a deep breath, Megan consciously relaxed her shoulders and her jaw. Cassie had suggested meeting at the Pump Room because it was half way between the office of her concierge business and the hotel where Megan had a temporary job as a chambermaid, but she was sure her friend had also thought of the subtle effect of spending time in elegant surroundings. It was working. Megan could feel muscles that had been tense for days – weeks – relaxing. She jumped slightly when Cassie put the letter down on the table again. 'What do you think?' she asked.

Cassie tilted her head in a characteristic gesture. 'Well, I've never encountered anything like it before. It doesn't actually say "Please attend our offices where you will hear something to your advantage," but that's clearly how you're supposed to read it.'

Megan nodded. 'That's what I thought. It must be some sort of scam.'

'Mmmm.' Cassie looked at the letter again. 'If it is, it's an unusual one. Most scams these days are e-mails promising money in exchange for your bank details.' She ran her finger over the letter. 'Good quality paper and the letterhead is embossed. And the address.' Cassie wrinkled her nose. 'EC4 is the area around the Temple and the Inns of Court, suitably old school and reassuring. Trueheart Alley sounds like something out of Dickens.'

'I couldn't find it in the A-Z of London, and I Googled the firm – Grampian, Gifford and Guardida. There were entries in those business

1

directory things, but nothing more than what's there.' Megan gestured to the letter. 'Just the name and address. I didn't ring the number. If it *is* a con, I thought it might encourage them.' She picked up the letter, weighing it in her hand. Cassie was right; the paper was good quality, cream-coloured, thick and smooth. 'Anyone could get letterheads printed,' she pointed out.

'True,' Cassie agreed. 'A bit of an investment for your average con artist though, and they've researched you.' She pointed to the opening salutation. 'Dear *Dr* Morrison.'

Megan blinked, taking in a sharp breath. She hadn't noticed. *Too tired to think straight.* Her doctorate was only a few weeks old. She didn't even have any paperwork yet. 'I didn't notice. That's why I knew I should show it to you.'

Cassie shrugged. 'Not surprising. When you get a letter, you're looking at the contents, not the tops and tails – the Dear Mrs Bloggs and Yours Sincerely bits aren't the interesting part.'

Megan could feel the analytical segment of her brain slowly cranking into gear. 'It was sent to the hotel too, not the cottage.' She shivered suddenly – the creepy feeling that someone had pried into her life mixed with the cold stab of loss. *Home, job, fiancé, hopes and dreams for the future. All gone.*

'If it had gone there, Ellery would be sniffing around, especially if he thought there was money involved,' Cassie said briskly. She'd never liked Ellery.

Dr Ellery Peters, Head of the Modern Languages Department at the University of Aquae Sulis – *ex boss, ex lover, ex fiancé.* Megan gave a deep sigh. Six weeks ago – was it only six weeks? – she would have defended him, but now ... well, even with everything that had happened, she still had difficulty in thinking of Ellery in that way. *Calculating and mercenary?* She pushed away the question and the pain of memories to concentrate on the matter in hand. 'Someone has gone to a lot of trouble to send me this,' she said slowly.

'Which means that it might even be genuine?' Cassie grinned suddenly. A waiter, seeing this as a signal to approach, came up to offer more coffee. Cups refilled, Cassie settled into her chair and gave Megan a speculative look. 'So – who is the mysterious benefactor who might have left you a fortune? Any obvious candidates?'

'No.' Megan was sure about that. 'There's no money in my family. The bit Gran left paid my fees for my doctorate, which was what she wanted. Other than that, there was only some jewellery.' She touched the gold locket at her throat. 'I don't *have* any relatives.' She closed her mind to an old familiar sadness. 'Certainly no mysterious ones. I—Oh!' She stopped, putting down her cup with a clatter.

'Yes?' Cassie encouraged. 'Who?'

'Well ...' She really didn't know what had put the idea into her head, and it wasn't possible anyway. 'No.'

'Who?' Cassie persisted. 'Who did you think of?'

'Well – I just remembered wicked Aunt Olwen – Great-Great Aunt Olwen.'

'She sounds like an interesting possibility.' Cassie looked intrigued. 'Who was she and why was she wicked? Mistress to royalty and left you a fortune in not-quite crown jewels?'

'Nothing like that.' Despite herself, Megan laughed. Knowing that had been Cassie's intention didn't detract from the lift to her spirits. 'She was my gran's aunt. She ran away – eloped, just after the Second World War, with an Italian soldier. He was a prisoner of war. I don't know how she came to meet him. She was barely eighteen and he probably wasn't much older. Of course, he was a foreigner and an enemy and I assume a Catholic. Olwen's father was a very strict Nonconformist. He was a lay preacher, no shops or cinema on Sunday, all that stuff. He effectively erased her from the family. Her name was never to be mentioned.'

'Yet you still know about her.'

'Yes.' Megan thought for a moment. 'Gran talked about her occasionally. She was her mother's younger sister and they were very close growing up. There were a few old family photographs that must have been hidden away or overlooked – young girls in white dresses and pudding basin haircuts. I have a couple of books with her name in, given as Sunday school prizes.' Megan spooned sugar into her coffee, then stopped abruptly in the act of stirring it.

'What else?' Cassie leaned forward.

'It's just ...' Megan shook her head. 'It can't be. There's no way there could be a connection.'

'What with?'

'Nothing, just a stupid idea.' She stopped stirring the coffee and picked up her cup. 'I never told you how I found Cosimo, did I?'

Cassie raised her eyebrows at the change of subject, shaking her head. Megan's heart was beating a little fast, which was really quite silly ...

That letter *had* to be a scam.

'What has your mysterious poet got to do with wicked Aunt Olwen?'

3

'Nothing,' Megan said decisively. 'There can't be anything.'

'Well tell me anyway,' Cassie encouraged. 'I'd like to know.'

Megan could see from Cassie's expression that she wouldn't let it rest. She huffed and then gave in. 'I was about ten – it was the summer holidays and it was raining – so I was helping Gran clear out her old family home, after her mother died. Eluned was my great grandmother – Olwen's sister. I don't really remember her that well. She'd been in a nursing home for several years before she died. There was a box of papers in the spare room – mostly letters and bills and stuff. I remember Gran going quiet when she leafed through them, but I was more interested in some old board games I'd found – Cluedo and something called Scoop, which was about reporters. I thought at the time I might like to be a journalist.' Memories were coming back that she hadn't thought about in years. 'There was an envelope too, with books inside.'

She shut her eyes, remembering the faint smell of faded lavender and mothballs, and a beam of sunshine, full of dust motes, falling like a spotlight on the battered old box stuffed with papers. And Gran, sitting back on her heels with the manila envelope in her hands, and the books falling out on the floor when she upended it. Two slim volumes, beautifully bound in blue leather. Megan caught her breath as she remembered the first experience of that smooth binding under her fingers when she picked one up off the floor.

'They were the poems?' Cassie prompted.

'Two volumes. Twenty-four poems in Italian and the English translations.'

Megan rested her elbows on the table, deep in recollection. The "Cosimo" poems; the product of a young Italian Romantic poet, a near contemporary of Byron and Shelley. So little was known of him, he was almost a ghost – except for a few obscure manuscript references and the fragile genius of the poems themselves – the subject of her doctoral thesis.

'The "Cosimo" poems,' Cassie said it now, and Megan nodded.

'Gran gathered up the papers to sort through later. She probably burned most of them, but she wouldn't destroy books. It just wasn't done, so she gave them to me. At ten I wasn't very impressed with poetry, even the ones in English that I could read. I stuck them in my bookcase, next to my Enid Blytons and forgot about them, until, well you know ...'

Another house clearance in the last term of her first degree, following the death of her parents in an earthquake on an archaeological site in Turkey. 'When I found them again, I asked Gran about them, but she didn't know

4

where they came from, or how they got into that box.' *She wasn't well, and devastated about losing her daughter and son-in-law.* 'Of course, I read them and was stunned by how lovely they were.'

In an effort to get her mind back onto her academic studies while still on compassionate leave from her degree, she'd gone to a lecture by a visiting professor. A lecture about some newly discovered fragmentary verse from a young Italian poet known only as "Cosimo", hailed as a lost genius on a par with the English poet Thomas Chatterton. She'd gone home, almost too frightened to look at the books …

And a slim ray of sunlight had opened in the darkness of bereavement.

With a start, Megan jerked back from her memories, to find herself sitting in the Pump Room, with Cassie watching her. 'Sorry. I drifted.'

'I noticed.' Cassie smiled. 'You think the poems could have come from Aunt Olwen?'

'I can't see how. I don't know why I suddenly remembered finding the books. The only connection is the poems being written in Italian and Olwen eloping with an Italian. No one knows what happened to her afterwards – there was no contact with the family after she ran away. I've just connected one family mystery with another and with *that*.' She nodded to the solicitor's letter. 'It seemed most likely that their brother, Tom, brought the books back from Italy.' That was what she'd suggested in her thesis, acknowledging that it was speculation.

'He was an older brother who served there during the war. There's some internal evidence linking the poems to Rome, and there were British troops there. I never found a definite location for the tower that's mentioned in the longest poem. It might have been imaginary. There were some of Tom's wartime letters and photographs in the box and folders of old postcards of various places in Italy – tourist type stuff that he must have brought home and given to his sister. It made sense that the books came from him too. When Gran went through the papers later, she kept his letters and the postcards. She thought I might be interested in them when I got older.'

'Which you were.'

'Which I was,' Megan agreed. 'Tom died in an accident on Coronation Day, but he did teacher training after the war and ended up teaching English in a posh boys' school. He could have had an interest in poetry – enough to bring the books home – and then they got put away with his other stuff.'

Cassie narrowed her eyes. Megan could see she was fascinated. 'Where did Olwen's soldier come from?'

'No idea. I think he came from farming stock. Olwen told her sister she wanted to be a farmer's wife.'

Cassie was calculating. 'How old would Olwen be, if she was still alive? Early nineties?'

Megan nodded. 'She was the youngest. There were four brothers and two sisters, I think, all older. The family broke up – lost touch before I was born. I imagine the others are all gone by now, but yes, I suppose it's possible Olwen could still be alive.'

'Or only just have died.'

'That too.' Megan digested the idea. It made something inside her clench into a knot. She'd become used to having no close family, no relations that she knew about. The idea that she might have had an elderly aunt, still living …

Cassie was looking at her with concern in her eyes. With an effort she pulled herself back into the moment. 'I know this much – if the letter is about her and she's left me something, it's not going to make me a millionaire. Maybe it's old photographs or a few more bits of family jewellery. All the sisters had a locket. This belonged to Eluned, my great grandmother.' She touched it again. 'Maybe it's something like that.'

'A lot of trouble for a few trinkets.'

'Which makes it more likely that it's a scam? I expect they'll want fees or something.' Megan tapped the paper. 'There are probably hundreds of these floating about. If they get one or two hits, it's probably worth it.' She grimaced. 'They're wasting their time with me. I don't have any money to pay them, *or* anything worth stealing.'

'Do you want me to ask Jake to put someone on it?'

Megan looked the letter for a moment, then shook her head. 'I don't think it needs a detective on the case.' Cassie was married to the owner of a detective agency, and the idea was tempting, but she didn't want to impose on friends any more than she had to. 'If I can get a cheap train ticket, maybe I'll go and have a look for myself. See if I can find Trueheart Alley.' She picked up the paper. 'Really, that has to be made up.'

She dropped the letter into her bag, bringing out her purse to pay her share of the bill, putting the money down on the table so Cassie couldn't refuse to take it. 'Thanks Cass, for coming out this morning. The letter – well it's just a bit weird. I needed to run the thing by someone.'

Cassie's expression told her that she understood. *And that hurts because it should have been Ellery.*

'I never say no to a trip to the Pump Room,' Cassie said, standing up and leaning over to give Megan a hug. 'Let me know if you're going up to London or if you change your mind about letting Jake investigate. You know he loves pretending he's a real detective, not just the owner of the firm.'

Megan laughed. 'I will,' she promised. 'If I do go, I won't be parting with the details of my bank account.'

Megan strode purposefully over Pulteney Bridge. She felt different. Freer. Lighter. She had something to focus on now that wasn't about what she had lost. Taking time out to meet Cassie had put a brake on the hamster wheel of her thoughts. *Ellery, Ellery, Ellery.* She'd begun to feel better simply getting ready – warming her pale skin with blusher, blotting out the dark smudges under her eyes with a dab of concealer and tying a scarf through her hair to bring it into some kind of order. On a chambermaid's wages she could no longer afford the expensive salon Ellery insisted was necessary to keep its wildness under control. *And you're thinking about him again.*

She tilted her chin defiantly. Going forward, if her dark curls wanted to riot, she would let them. A pedestrian coming in the opposite direction on the narrow pavement abruptly jumped aside to give her right of way. For a moment she was confused, then she realised that she'd been glaring at the poor man. She suppressed a giggle, murmuring what she hoped was gracious 'Thank you' as she glided past. *And it's been a while since you felt the urge to giggle.*

As of this morning she had a plan. Not a world-shaking one, but still a plan. The letter, scam or not, had given it to her. There was no time now to put it into effect. It was nearly check-out time for the hotel. There would be rooms to be turned for tonight's incoming guests, but as soon as her shift was over, she would walk down to the station and buy herself a ticket for London. A cheap advance day return might be five or six weeks away but that didn't matter. When she had a date, she would write to, not telephone, Messrs. Grampian, Gifford and Guardida to tell them when she would be available to visit them. She grinned. She really didn't think that the offices in Trueheart Alley existed.

The money for the train ticket would not be wasted. She would spend a few hours in the British Library, trying again to find an elusive reference to a meeting between Lord Byron and Cosimo that she'd been unable to track down. Then she could look up some old contacts who might know about job vacancies she could apply for. It was positive. She would be moving forward.

The fog that had been clouding her brain since *that* day, when her world fell apart, had finally begun to lift. She had a *plan* – something to look forward to.

She crossed the road, hurrying down the long street of Georgian townhouses towards the hotel. The letter was the impetus she needed and she was grateful for it, but once she'd written back, she would put the whole thing out of her mind. *Don't start hoping for anything. You know that it's probably a con.* She had to start thinking about the future. Grampian, Gifford and Guardida weren't part of it.

She was pretty sure she wouldn't be hearing any more from them.

Chapter Two

The last rays of the late afternoon sun cast a brief golden glow over the high-ceilinged room. In its corners, shadows were already gathering. Down below in Portofino, subject of countless photographs and paintings, yachts occupied the choicest berths claimed by mega wealthy owners. The shops and restaurants housed in the narrow pastel-coloured buildings were busy, even this late in the season. Up above, in the palatial palazzo on the tree-swathed hillside, it was quiet.

'*Buona sera*, Signor Brown.' Gabriella De Stefano sat before a low table, empty except for an old and battered leather-bound photo album. She addressed the speakerphone that had just announced an incoming call. 'You have news for me?'

'Er, yes, Signora De Stefano.' The disembodied voice echoed in the cavernous space, but the woman could still hear the note of unease. 'Edwards found the young woman. The niece ... er ... the great-great niece. I couldn't stop—'

'It is of no matter.' She dismissed the attempted excuse with a casual tone, belied by the twist of meticulously outlined and tinted lips. 'Who is she?'

'Oh ... Well ...' Cut off mid justification, Brown took a moment to regroup. 'Her name is Megan Morrison. *Dr* Morrison. She just got her PhD.'

'Interesting.' The woman gently fingered some loose photographs that had been tucked into the front of the album, spreading them out, along with an envelope. 'And what is Dr Morrison an expert in?'

'Huh ... er ... Italian poetry.'

'Indeed?' Immaculately shaped brows rose. 'How apt. What else do you know?'

'Well, until a couple of months ago she was engaged to a Dr Ellery Peters. He's Head of the Department of Modern Languages at the University of Aquae Sulis. That's near Bath, in Somerset,' Brown explained. 'It's a new place – a small campus, but it seems to have a good reputation,' he offered doubtfully. The puzzlement of the non-academic was clear. 'It looked like she was all set. She had a job at this university. She was a junior lecturer in Italian and English Literature. Only on a short-term contract, but she was going to get tenure.' Brown hesitated. 'That means, like, a permanent job,' he qualified. 'She was all set to marry this Dr Peters. They'd been living together for a few years in a cottage in one of the villages near Bath.'

'A few years?' She let the words hang as a prompt to continue, but she hadn't disguised her distaste for the mundane sordidness of a relationship between tutor and student. *One preying on youth, the other looking for easy advancement.*

'He's a young bloke, well, youngish – late thirties, maybe – and he wasn't her supervisor, or mentor, or whatever it is.' Brown seemed to understand her disapproval. 'That was a professor from Oxford. Morrison was lucky to get him apparently. He's quite well known. Lectures and writes books.'

'Quite. But something happened to the engagement?' Gabriella smoothly drew her caller back to the matter in hand.

'Yeah. This guy Peters finished it – everything – engagement, job, the lot. Put someone else in her place – niece of some big knob connected to the University, Vice Chancellor or something. Morrison lost everything.'

'Harsh,' Gabriella commented. *But perhaps the penalty of choosing the wrong man to set your hopes on?* 'And now?'

'She's working as a chambermaid in one of the Bath hotels, living in. The report on her went to the solicitors two weeks ago …' There was an uncomfortable pause. 'I didn't find out until today. Edwards always keeps stuff close to his chest.' The bitterness was audible, even over the telephone. Edwards was the head of the heir-finder firm tasked with tracing the old woman's English relative. 'The solicitors have probably written to her by now.'

'No matter.' Again, the woman dismissed Brown's uneasy self-justification. She was pleased with what he reported. An impoverished, jobless, homeless and no doubt naive academic? How hard would it be to convince her to have nothing to do with a dubious legacy in a foreign country? A semi-derelict house, grounds running wild, a folly on the brink of collapse. With the right offer, a generous one, she would be easily persuaded to sell. It would all do very well, provided that there were no other impediments. 'You are sure there is no one else, only this Dottoressa Morrison? She has no family?'

'None. Her grandmother and her mother are both gone. Her parents were killed in an earthquake. They were archaeologists.'

Better and better. The academic daughter of academic parents – she would undoubtedly settle for sufficient money to make her comfortable while she chose a new life away from the disastrous ex-fiancé. It would do very well. An offer from a stranger to a stranger, with no reference to the past …

'Is that all, Signor Brown?' Gabriella enquired abruptly.

'Er, yes, um … My fee—'

'Will be dispatched to you. Thank you for your time, Signor Brown.'

'Oh.' Brown sounded surprised to be thanked. *But good manners cost nothing.* 'If there's anything else—'

'I will be sure to be in touch.'

Gabriella ended the call, looking thoughtfully at the items on the table. Brown's cheque was already prepared, along with a small bonus to guarantee discretion, waiting in the envelope. She would ensure that it was posted discreetly when she was next in Genoa. The stark white of the envelope contrasted with the rubbed and faded lettering of the photo album and the equally faded photographs spread alongside it. The woman sifted the pile with a fingertip, the nail tinted a delicate shade of peach.

She was content. More content than she had been since first learning that Agnello, the fool of a solicitor from Genoa, had instituted a search for the missing British heirs to Il Giardino delle Rose. Now the heir, just one, was found. She would instruct her own solicitor to make an offer on the estate and it would be hers. *At last.* Now that the interminable old woman was finally gone, the villa would return to its true owner.

She teased out a photograph, smiling when she saw the image. A fairy-tale view of the tower – a folly decked with roses and behind it the blue glitter of the sea. She pulled out another photograph – a middle-aged couple standing either side of a young man of about seventeen with a wide smile and a tangle of blond curls. With a wince of dismay, she pushed it quickly back into the pile, focusing instead on the picture of the tower. It no longer looked as it did in this image. It certainly didn't look like the idealised paintings on display in the gallery down in Portofino. Her mouth twisted in disapproval. She would have prevented that ... but what was done was done. She picked up the photograph, tapping it gently against her lips. Did she need to do something alongside the offer to purchase – something to plant the idea in Dottoressa Morrison's mind that her unexpected inheritance would be nothing but a burden to a struggling academic?

Gabriella returned the photograph to the pile, considering. An estate run wild, a house with only a few rooms still habitable, a derelict folly in danger of falling into the sea? Even so, there *was* beauty. The thought constricted something close to her heart. Others could see the beauty. The artist had, although it pained her to acknowledge it.

Megan Morrison must not.

The manicured hand clenched into a fist. Carefully, Gabriella released her grip. The beauty of the estate would take money to reclaim. Money she was sure Dottoressa Morrison did not possess ... and as for the old woman – hopefully her niece would not even bother to visit before disposing of a costly encumbrance.

Gabriella shifted restlessly in her seat. She could not be *sure.* Even with the old witch dead, she could not see her way clearly. Perhaps if there was a profitable distraction for this Megan Morrison? An attractive job offer somewhere well away from Portofino? She still had contacts she could call on. She had found Brown that way. Something might be devised.

She fanned out the photos – views of the house, the garden, a loggia, a rose smothered arbour, more views of the tower and the sea. Her finger hovered over a shot of a marble statue – a goddess half hidden in ivy – Justitia, arbiter of justice and judgement, her scales at her feet and her sword by her side.

Justice brought in by time.

An inheritance coming home.

Completion.

Chapter Three

Gideon West stood in the shadows of the restaurant awning, scanning the waterfront scene before him. His job was simply to stand around and look imposing in shades, a sharp black suit and the standard bodyguard prop, a fancy earpiece. *No problem with that.* All he had to do was look the part.

When he was a student, he'd supplemented his student loans with door security work around Bath and Bristol for Jake McQuire's agency, capitalising on being a fraction over six-foot-six, with shoulders to match. He'd kept up his licensing certificates. The money from occasional security jobs was still welcome. *Even more so now.* It was financing his trip here to Liguria, but he wasn't really a bodyguard. That would be the other three of Jake's operatives stationed around Portofino harbour. They were waiting for an out-of-this-world hen party to leave the swish restaurant which had been exclusively reserved for them to enjoy an early dinner before moving to a fancy yacht moored a few hundred yards away. He was just here to make up the numbers. He'd had enough training to act if he had to, but it wasn't likely. The group didn't really need the protection of four operatives, even though the bride was a top Hollywood star, Skylark France, celebrating with her A-list friends and her sister, a bestselling novelist. Faced with a hissy fit of massive proportions her besotted groom had upped the security detail to keep his bride happy. Portofino in early November was hardly bristling with threats, but Ms France had apparently considered it beneath her dignity to make do with just *three* protectors.

With all Jake's small staff of personal security operatives otherwise deployed, Gideon had been drafted in. Jake, who had a phenomenal if selective memory, had recalled a casual conversation a few months ago, when Gideon mentioned his interest in researching gardens on the Riviera. And now here he was, earning enough money to finance a couple of weeks' stay, with the chance to leave behind the painful mess back home.

He winced slightly at the thought, pushing it away to concentrate on the job in hand. Once the transfer was complete and the women were safely aboard the yacht, then the thing was done and they were stood down. When the yacht reached its destination, the port of Livorno, security would be in the hands of the wedding planner who would supervise the onward journey to an exclusive Tuscan estate for the romantic ceremony.

The receiver in Gideon's ear crackled slightly – Liam's voice. 'And they're on their way out. We're nearly done here, dude.'

Gideon straightened up and looked as menacing as he could manage as the hen party spilled out of the restaurant, flanked by Liam, Jason and Caro. As long as no one broke a heel or fell in the water, it was all good. He stepped forward, scanning the waterfront as the others shepherded the party towards the yacht. The weather was mild, but in November the resort was nowhere near as crowded as it would be at the height of summer. Patrons at some of the open-air restaurants looked up curiously. He saw a few phones raised to take pictures, but nothing that set off alarm bells.

The group had reached the yacht and were going aboard. The crew were already making ready to sail. In a very few moments the stately craft eased its way out of the harbour. Gideon could see champagne being opened on deck. The sound of music drifted back over the receding noise of the engine.

And relax.

Liam came over, clapping him on the shoulder. 'Good job, mate'

'All I had to do was stand here.'

'And look good filling out a fancy suit.' Caro joined Liam, teasingly pretending to check Gideon out. He knew she was teasing. Her wedding to fiancée Gemma was set for next May. She nudged him. 'How many of them asked for your phone number then?'

'At least three, that I saw,' Liam chipped in. 'He didn't give it to them though. Professional to his fingertips.' He looked out over the water, where the yacht was rapidly making way towards Livorno. 'They weren't a bad group. No one sniffed anything they shouldn't and no one puked on anyone's shoes, which is pretty much a result. And we got all twelve of them on the boat.' He caught Caro's eye. 'We *did* get all twelve of them on the boat,' he confirmed, clearly sensing a potential wind-up. 'I counted them. Twice.'

'So did I,' Gideon agreed.

Caro held up a hand in laughing surrender. 'Now we're officially off duty, did someone mention wine?'

'I heard beer,' Jason suggested.

Gideon hesitated. He'd seen the prices in the local bars. Liam saw his hesitation. 'Tonight's on Jake. Bonus-in-kind.'

'Perk of having a boss who is also a billionaire,' Caro put in, grinning.

Gideon grinned in response. It would be good to get out of the suit. And the earpiece, he remembered, touching the device in his ear. 'If Jake is paying, I can definitely drink a beer.'

Gideon was alone when it happened. *Right place, right time.* Liam and Jason had lingered, attempting to identify a bar that was rumoured to have a back room with a snooker table. Caro had peeled off to stalk a pair of shoes in one of the upmarket boutiques, trying by the deadly application of concentrated willpower to get them transferred to the "Sale" rack. Gideon headed past the shops and waterside diners towards their hotel, his mind already moving to the two-week stay that the pay from the security job would fund.

In the morning, when they all checked out, he'd be moving to a smaller and cheaper hotel in Genoa. He'd be depending on trains and buses for transport, but the trip was more than he could have imagined before Jake's phone call last week. He had a programme of garden visits worked out. He'd do the big names like La Mortola and Villa Ephrussi on the French side of the border, but he'd also set up some visits to private gardens that weren't normally open to the public through his old tutor at horticultural college. He was hoping to get material for an article or two in the trade journals, maybe even something he could pitch to one of the popular garden magazines. *If they'll take stuff in your name.*

He exhaled deeply as he negotiated one of the restaurant tables that was protruding into the footway, still bearing the debris of a late and large lunch party. Six months ago, he would have been hoping to identify a specimen plant with commercial potential that might be propagated and sold at Brickhaven Nurseries, but now that the business was gone … he dragged his thoughts away from *that* rabbit hole. There was nothing to be done. When he got back, he'd check out landscape gardening firms who were hiring and who might still be willing to take him on. Before that he had two weeks of freedom. He had to make the most of it.

Pulling himself out of the depressing way his thoughts were heading, he focused on his surroundings. Portofino was beautiful, if a little too rich for his blood – or make that his wallet. The shops and galleries featuring designer goods and high-priced art didn't have a lot to offer him. All he needed was for his watch and his steel-capped boots to do their job and survive the occasional bash with a spade. It didn't really matter how they looked. Now, if you were talking about a rose or a rhododendron—

Even so, a display in one of the smaller galleries caught his eye as he passed. He'd noticed it yesterday, mainly because the pictures were of gardens, or maybe one garden. The prices would be way out of his league but the images, mixing the real with the fairy tale, still attracted him. He was pretty certain they were based on an actual garden – one that was wildly overgrown. The pictures had a haunting, other-worldly quality to them. He was contemplating turning back for another look, perhaps even going in to ask if they'd been painted locally, when it happened.

The outcry behind him, yells of '*Al ladro*! Stop thief!' made him turn. A man was bulleting towards him at a dead run, clutching a bag. The hue and cry in pursuit – some of the shop and restaurant owners – was too far behind. The thief, if that's what he was, was going to get away.

Without even thinking, Gideon stepped into the man's path. As they both went down the fugitive let go of the bag. Wallets, a small painting, and a glittering tangle of watches and jewellery spilled across the paving stones.

The next hour was crowded. Attracted by the noise, Liam, Jason and Caro pelted over. Liam summoned the police, Jason stood guard over the thief and Caro took charge of his haul, dissuading shop owners and restaurant patrons from reclaiming items before the authorities arrived. Gideon sat in a chair commandeered from one of the restaurants. Liam had shoved him into it, after checking that he wasn't bleeding anywhere and hadn't hit his head.

The thief was alternately demanding to be let go, loudly protesting his innocence, calling for medical attention for his supposed injuries and threatening to sue Gideon for assault. At least, that's what Gideon thought was going on. His evening class Italian wasn't up to some of the finer and more colourful bits. He'd angled the tackle so that he'd gone down first, breaking the thief's fall at the expense of a few bruises. He was pretty sure the guy wasn't too badly damaged. In the end, Caro barked something at the man in what Gideon guessed was *not* evening class Italian and he mercifully shut up, except for the occasional sullen muttering and attempts to free himself from Jason's hold.

Then the police turned up and everything moved indoors and onto an official basis. Finally, with statements made, the man was removed, the goods taken into custody and the show was over. Gideon stood up wearily from another chair in the back room of one of the bars, which the police had requisitioned as a temporary office, and inspected the damage to his good suit. *Nothing the drycleaner can't sort out. I hope.*

'Come on.' Liam put his hand on Gideon's arm, navigating him over to the bar proper. 'I think you've earned that beer.'

As the evening wore on, the gathering turned into an impromptu party with what seemed like half the population of Portofino and a heavy

16

smattering of tourists wanting to slap Gideon's back, shake his hand, kiss his cheek or buy him drinks. One of the policemen turned up just before the bar closed, discreetly letting them know that the man in custody was wanted for theft and picking pockets in resorts all along the coast, on both sides of the border. Relief unknotted tension in Gideon's shoulders that he'd not been aware of carrying – he hadn't made a mistake and the man's protests had clearly not been genuine. Incautiously, he knocked back a shot that had been pressed into his hand and grabbed the back of a chair as the room suddenly gave a sharp lurch.

'Steady on, old son.' Laughing, Caro gave him a push, to shift him upright. 'If you go over, it'll be like a tree going down in the forest – we'll never get you up again.'

'Probably.' The room stopped swaying, but Gideon knew better than to nod. He wasn't much of a drinker these days – he'd got that out of his system in college. Everything was telling him that he'd had enough. There was a sinking feeling in the back of his mind that he would be paying for this in the morning. 'I think it's about time I called it a day.' He was pleased he wasn't slurring.

'Yeah, and me,' Caro agreed. 'Our flight is at eight tomorrow. God knows what time we have to leave to get to the airport. *Hoi!*' She yelled across the bar at Jason and Liam, jerking her head in a "time to go" movement that Gideon could only envy. He was being *very* careful what he did with his head. Liam grinned and began to weave his way over to them. Jason, having clearly had some success in chatting up the waitress, made a "later" gesture over his shoulder.

'Come on.' Liam reached them. 'Leave him. He can walk to the airport in the morning.'

'You're a hard man.' Gideon returned the grin.

'Someone has to be. It's all right for you, you're not flying home.'

Gideon was profoundly grateful about that.

A few of the locals were getting ready to leave as well. They made a merry and somewhat noisy party crossing the square, but no one seemed to mind.

There was sunlight coming in through the edges of the shutters and his head was killing him. Gideon lay on his back, staring at the ceiling and thanking God profusely that he was not on his way to the airport. He reached out, gingerly, to pick up his watch from the bedside table. Eight o'clock – the others would be on the plane by now. He'd said his goodbyes to Liam and Caro last night. He wondered if Jason had made it. *Probably.* Not his problem anyway. Today he had to pack up and find himself a cheap hotel.

He sat up carefully. There were still men with pickaxes mining his brain, but the room wasn't moving. *So far so good*

Ten minutes in the shower and a bottle of water from the mini-bar and he was ready to climb into his clothes and stuff his belongings into his rucksack. His decision to let his beard grow meant that he didn't have to test the steadiness of his hands by shaving. He checked for damage in the mirror when he got out of the shower – some interesting black and blue patches and stiffness in his shoulder. *Probably more than the thief has on him.*

Gideon bundled his wash bag into the rucksack and picked it up. He'd grab breakfast and be on the train to Genoa as soon as he could get to the nearest railway station. Food would settle his stomach. Provided he kept that goal in his mind – getting to Genoa – he could cope with an aching head. Letting himself out of the room, he closed the door very softly. Descending the stairs didn't make him feel too chipper, but it didn't kill him either, so he was calling that a win.

He made it as far as the hotel foyer without incident, although the weight of his pack made him wonder if the staff had deposited rocks in the bottom. Once he got to the foyer, things got a little confused.

There was a reception committee waiting for him.

He recognised the owner of one of the shops and a couple of the restaurateurs. He watched them approach, slightly alarmed and fuzzy from his hangover. The shop owner, a tall woman with sleek black hair, stepped forward, clearly urged on as spokesperson by the others. *What the hell do they want?*

'Signor West, last night we spoke with your colleague, Signor Carter.' Through the post-alcohol haze, Gideon recognised Liam's name. 'We wish to make some acknowledgement of your brave action yesterday in apprehending the thief.' For a moment the tranquil face shifted to an expression of disgust. 'Signor Carter, he said that you are making a stay here, on the Riviera, to study gardens.' She stopped, clearly checking that she understood this correctly.

Totally confused now, Gideon agreed. He wasn't sure what this was, but it didn't seem as if it was anything bad. 'We have spoken, my friends and I—' She indicated the reception committee '—about the best way of showing our appreciation.' Suddenly, a smile lit up her whole face. 'I would like to offer you the use of the small apartment above my shop and these gentlemen, and several others who are not able to be here, would like for you to eat at their restaurants for the winter months, until the new season begins. We hope it will help you look at many more of our beautiful gardens.'

Chapter Four

Trueheart Alley *did* exist. Megan stood at the entrance and stared down. It was dark and narrow and looked like a film set, or maybe a portal that would take her back to the time of Charles Dickens. Two black-and-white, timber-framed buildings leaned together, their overhangs almost meeting, so that the sky was only a narrow strip of wintry blue above them. There were shops at ground level: an antiquarian bookseller, a dealer in coins and stamps and an emporium – there was no other word for it – that proclaimed itself as a purveyor of sporting goods to the discerning patron. In the window, life-size mannequins displayed waterproof jackets, leggings and hats, surrounded by a formidable display of shotguns and fishing tackle.

The alley was empty and very quiet. Not a lot of passing footfall. *Definitely destination shopping.* Beyond the black-and-white buildings was a terrace of Georgian townhouses, and beyond that a glimpse of a section of the Embankment and the Thames. The solicitors' offices were in one of the townhouses. Megan walked cautiously down the alley. The setting might have looked Dickensian at first glance, but the shop fronts were freshly painted and the multi-paned windows of the bookshop gleamed. There was a small Christmas tree in the corner of the window alongside a stuffed raven, sporting a jaunty tinsel collar. *Maybe it is a film set?*

The letter from Grampian, Gifford and Guardida, answering hers by return of post and fixing an appointment for three weeks hence, had surprised her. The meticulously hand-drawn map, showing how to reach the offices from the Temple tube station even more so. Megan was meeting with Mr Gifford (Junior) at 11.30. It was now 11.25. She took a deep breath and mounted the steps, aware of her heart beating a little fast. *Don't expect anything.*

Entering through the open outer door, she found herself in a small vestibule. A door to the right had a brass plate beside it, announcing consultation times for two medical specialists. The building was breathlessly quiet.

Her footsteps echoed on the narrow, uncarpeted staircase that led to the solicitors' office on the first floor. Once through the partly glazed door, the dark panelling and heavy furniture also looked like a film set. A grey-haired woman in a heather-coloured twinset and tweed skirt, who looked to be in her late fifties, was sitting behind the reception desk. Her face lit up with a smile when she saw Megan.

'Dr Morrison, I'm so pleased to meet you at last.' She rose and came forward, and Megan found herself shaking hands. 'My father has been so looking forward to this meeting.'

Her father? Deciding she must have misheard, Megan was ushered into another pleasant, dark-panelled room. Bookshelves were lined with weighty legal tomes. There were more stacked on a low table in front of the window, beside a tall vase of bronze chrysanthemums.

Megan took a deep, steadying breath. The man rising to greet her was old, with sparse white hair and heavily wrinkled skin, but the eyes that considered her, over a pair of half-moon spectacles, were bright blue with a definite twinkle.

The receptionist, who could indeed be this man's daughter given the clear age difference, bustled off to arrange for coffee. It was served from a silver tray, in bone china cups. There was a matching china coffee pot. *If this is a scam, then the set dresser deserves an Oscar.* Bemused, Megan sipped excellent coffee. Mr Gifford made polite conversation about her journey for a few moments, then pulled forward a blue folder, regarding her now with an assessing expression.

'I regret that you may have been somewhat confused about the purpose of this meeting today. Please accept my apologies, but I did not feel that the news to be conveyed was suitable for a letter.' *He's wondering what you know... or have guessed?*

He opened the folder, still watching her with that assessing expression. *He might be ancient but he's a wily old bird.* Megan started slightly. The inner voice sounded remarkably like her gran. 'I was unsure if our firm's name would be known to you,' he continued. Seeing that it clearly wasn't, he tapped the bundle of papers in the folder. 'It has been customary for the senior member of this firm to handle the Marchesa's affairs in this country, but we have not been called upon to act for her for some time. Until we were contacted by our colleagues in Italy, I was not aware that the Marchesa had any remaining family here. Or, indeed, any remaining family at all.'

'The Marchesa?' Megan put the cup down, very carefully, on its delicate saucer. Her thoughts were turning somersaults. 'Um … are we … are we talking about my Aunt Olwen?'

Mr Gifford inclined his head. 'We are.' He paused, letting the information sink in. 'I regret to inform you that your aunt died in March of this year.'

Megan swallowed, aware of a surge of emotion rising in her chest – confusion, a thin thread of excitement and an overwhelming wash of regret. *You still had an aunt – family – and you never knew, and now she's gone.* A desolate tide of loneliness succeeded the regret. It was all she could do not to shiver. She picked up the coffee cup again, taking a large gulp. Its strength and heat bolstered her.

Mr Gifford was still speaking, 'We were instructed to seek out the lady's heirs. The Marchesa was very specific that this should be her twin sister, Eluned, if she was still living, and if not her sister's descendants. Enquiries were put in hand immediately.' Suddenly the solicitor smiled. 'We found *you,* Dr Morrison. You have probably already realised it. You are Olwen Rossi's heir.'

Megan gripped the wooden arm of the chair she was sitting in, thoughts and emotions in freefall. *Am I dreaming?* Had she fallen asleep on the journey? Would she wake up with a start when the train reached Paddington? She could feel the smoothness of the wooden arm of the chair under her fingers. Could you feel things like that in a dream? *No. You're awake. This* is *really happening.*

Mr Gifford had stopped speaking, waiting for her reaction. With an effort she pulled herself together 'I... wondered ... it seemed so unlikely.' Her speculation with Cassie in the Pump Room seemed a world away. 'I didn't ...' She paused and tried again. 'Olwen ran away with an Italian soldier – a POW. I don't know much about her other than that. I didn't even know that she and my great grandmother were twins ...' Something else surfaced, a tiny sliver of fact. 'She said she was going to be a farmer's wife. But you say she had a title?'

'Courtesy only – but I believed it amused her ... and maybe satisfied her to use it?' he suggested. 'This firm began to act for her and her husband in 1990. I know little about her life before that. She did once mention that she met her husband at the end of the war. I assume some sort of family rift?'

Megan nodded. 'She was cut out of the family when she eloped.' Her mind was working again now. She could understand an errant and cast-off daughter finding amusement and satisfaction in her despised husband's status. Olwen had made a choice for love – and earned a lifetime of exile, left without a family. For a breathless second, Megan felt the pain rise again. The consequences of that rift had echoed down the years, all the way to her. *Up until March, I still had a living relative.* 'I wish I could have met her,' she said softly.

Mr Gifford nodded as if she had passed some sort of test. 'Had I been aware of your existence and had we been actively handling Signora Rossi's affairs, I believe I would have counselled her to seek you out.' He looked away, as if staring into the past. 'The Marchesa was a woman of decided opinions, and for the last decades of her life I understand that she lived more or less as a recluse. This firm has not done business for her for many years.' He shrugged, his gaze coming back to the room and to Megan. 'As it is, I can only give you details of your inheritance.'

'Oh. Yes.' *That's the reason you came here.* She picked up her cup, draining the last of the coffee, finding her hand was trembling slightly. *Oh – for heaven's sake.* She cast her eyes around the well-appointed room. *If there is any money, most of it will be eaten up in legal fees.*

'There are certain formalities to be completed, proof of identity and so on, before any property is released.' Mr Gifford looked at her over his spectacles, before delving into the folder again. 'However, I am sufficiently confident of your identity to disclose the main terms of your aunt's bequest.' He'd found what he was looking for. A photograph. He passed it across the desk.

It was old. *Seventy years old?* A young woman in a simple white lace dress, holding a posy of roses and clinging to the arm of a tall and handsome dark-haired man. Both were beaming at the camera. A wedding photograph. *She has my hair. Or I have hers.*

'There is also this.' Mr Gifford opened a wooden box with an inlaid lid that was standing on the end of the desk, selected an item and laid it on the old-fashioned blotter.

Automatically Megan's hand went to her throat. On impulse she had fastened her great grandmother's locket around her neck before leaving the hotel this morning. Now she was looking at its perfect double. She put out her hand tentatively to touch it. 'That was Olwen's?'

Mr Gifford nodded. 'And you are wearing Eluned's – Olwen's older sister by, I understand, twenty minutes. They were twins, but not identical.'

'I didn't know that. I did know that my grandmother inherited the locket from *her* mother – from Eluned.' Emotion was threatening to swamp her again. A sense of belonging and a sense of loss – this had been her family. 'My grandmother's has pictures of my grandfather and of my mother.' She'd never had the heart to change them. The thought that she might have put Ellery's picture there made her shudder.

'Olwen's has her husband and her son as a baby.'

'Son?' Megan's head jerked. 'But—'

'I understand that he died a few weeks after his eighteenth birthday,' Mr Gifford said. 'He had no siblings. The Marquis was the younger of two brothers, but his elder brother died in the war. His father, grandfather and great grandfather were only children. It was not a … prolific family.'

Megan nodded silently. She could see now how she had come to be Olwen's heir, but even so ... 'Surely – there must be someone else, from my uncle's family?' The idea of an uncle felt strange. 'Cousins, or something?'

Mr Gifford shook his head. 'As I said, not a prolific family, and the depredations of two world wars and the Spanish flu epidemic....' For a moment, he appeared to be looking into the past again. He came back to the present on a breath that might have been a sigh. 'As you have not been in touch with your aunt, you will not be aware of the property she has left you.' He delved for another photograph. Pulling out several, he selected one and passed it across the desk. 'Il Giardino delle Rose. The Rossi villa in Portofino.'

'The Rose Garden.' Finding herself slightly breathless, Megan picked up the photograph. 'Oh!'

The building in the picture was white stucco with tall windows and gothic style shutters that gave it an air of something out of a fairy tale. Wide front steps were flanked by rose beds.

Mr Gifford passed over the other photographs. One was clearly the back of the house. There was a colonnade, with what looked like marble pillars, twined with climbing roses. Other pictures were of gardens, statues, more roses and finally an image that totally made her catch her breath. A tower set on a cliff and beyond it a view of the sea. Her heart started to thump. Could this be …? *La Torre* – Cosimo's tower?

Mr Gifford was still speaking. With an effort, she pulled her thoughts back to the panelled room. 'The Rossis devoted much of their time to the gardens after the loss of their son. These pictures were taken some time ago. Sadly, neither house nor grounds have been kept up. In her later years, after the death of her husband, I understand your aunt lived only in a few rooms, with the rest of the building unused and the gardens sadly neglected.'

'Oh … Of course.' Megan looked up from the photographs. For a few seconds she had been transported into the fairy tale. *You own this?* But, of

24

course, it wouldn't be like that. With a painful thump, she settled back to reality. The magic of the photographs mustn't distract her from reality, or practicality. She'd inherited what was probably a semi-derelict building with an overgrown garden in a foreign country. *A white elephant.* She wouldn't be able to keep it. Dismally, she wondered how much it would cost to bring the place into good enough order to sell. Maybe she could get a loan?

Mr Gifford was still speaking – something about her aunt's jewellery and the keys to the villa. With a shock, she realised he expected her to travel to Italy to meet with more lawyers there.

'I'm sorry—' she interrupted abruptly. She had to stop this *now*. 'I can't ... I'm afraid I won't be going to Italy. It's out of the question.'

'Oh. I had assumed ... I apologise.' The solicitor straightened up, back stiffening, his expression settling into professional indifference. 'I was obviously in error. Naturally, if it is not convenient, matters can be dealt with by correspondence.' He leaned forward, gathering up the photographs to return to the folder. 'You may wish to instruct your own solicitor—'

'It's not ...' she interrupted, then stammered to a stop. She had offended and disappointed Mr Gifford and she hadn't meant to. The wooden arm of the chair bit into her hand. Megan hadn't realised how hard she'd been gripping it. An embarrassed flush crept up from the neck of her dress. She couldn't let him think ... 'It's not that I don't want to go.' She definitely *did*, with an intensity that startled her. 'I can't afford the fare,' she admitted with blunt misery. 'That's why I had to wait to come here – for a cheap train ticket.'

'Ah!' Mr Gifford's expression suggested that a small mystery had been cleared up. 'My dear Dr Morrison, I must again beg your pardon. I should perhaps have begun the meeting at a different point. I thought that you would like to see the photographs of the house and the gardens.'

'I did. I do.' *Enough to already be falling in love?* 'But ... perhaps it's better that I don't visit, as I'll undoubtedly have to sell.' A horrific thought occurred to her: what if Olwen had been living in poverty? 'I should have asked before, are their outstanding debts that have to be paid?'

Now Mr Gifford was smiling, almost grinning. 'I can see I really should have explained.' He was sifting the folder again, pulling out more paperwork. 'In her later years, your aunt spent very little – I believe that she may have formed the notion that she was somehow impoverished, so both capital and revenue continued, largely untouched. The solicitors in Italy will be taking care of all the liabilities of the estate – some other bequests, legal requirements and taxes. The remainder is the bulk of your inheritance.' He passed over the papers he had extracted from the folder. 'The details of the various investments and holdings are here. An advance can be arranged, to permit you to make arrangements to travel.'

Megan took them, looked, and then her brain abruptly closed down as she scanned the figures. 'This … you mean …?'

Gifford nodded, still smiling. He spoke for a few moments more. Megan caught something about wealth management; she didn't really take in what he was saying. On autopilot, she agreed to a further appointment, was congratulated and wished well and found herself back on the pavement in Trueheart Alley.

The chill air of a clear November day brought her back to herself sufficiently to walk away, instinctively turning her steps to the Embankment and the river. Walking along blindly, trying to unscramble her thoughts, the insistent buzzing of her phone jerked her out of her daze.

A text from Cassie. *Hi hon. How's it going? Are you a millionaire?* The message ended with a laughing emoji.

Megan found there was a bench in front of her, looking out over the water and the boats. She sat down, or her legs gave way, she wasn't quite sure which. With shaking fingers, she texted her response. *Yes.*

Chapter Five

He was pretty sure he was trespassing. *Come on, you know you are.*

Gideon jogged along a narrow path, fiercely guarded by sprawling bushes and rampant unpruned roses – a leafless tangle of branches and thorns. Although overgrown, the place had to be private property. He was only skirting the edge, the interior being pretty much impenetrable. He just couldn't seem to stay away. Three times since he'd discovered it last week, he'd found himself routing his early morning run to take in the edges of what seemed to be a large estate, where the path was still passable.

What were clearly once formal gardens were wild and neglected, and the house, just visible through stands of trees, seemed to be unoccupied, which was a crying shame as the place was amazing. The bones of something magical were still here, waiting to be reclaimed. *Like Sleeping Beauty's castle.* His fingers itched to clear the undergrowth, bring the trees and shrubs back to order and penetrate deeper to uncover the centre of the garden. Light glinted off something that might have been a domed metal roof, and pale glimmers hinted at statues. The place even had a tower, visible out on the headland. The front drive was still relatively clear, although threatened by overhanging trees and bushes, with weeds encroaching onto the gravel. Ornate metal gates sagged from brick pillars, propped half open by two boulders.

If he could find out who owned the place, he'd be tempted to tell them what he thought of letting so much beauty disintegrate. He'd asked around but no one seemed to know anything. The place had been neglected for some time. Mostly he got characteristic head shakes and shrugged shoulders. The thing was a mystery. Before it was left to nature it must have been magnificent, but he'd found no mention of it in guidebooks or online. He'd got a name from a stone plaque on the gatepost – *Giardino delle Rose* – Rose Garden. That was a fair description from what he'd seen. There were roses everywhere, but other shrubs and bushes too, and swathes of mature trees. Time, money and love had been spent on the place.

He jogged on the spot, trying to see a way through the undergrowth. It was very quiet. There was a path, crossing the one he was on, that still looked as if it might be passable. So far, he'd resisted the temptation, knowing it would take him deeper into the garden. But this morning …

Abruptly, the sun emerged from behind a cloud, throwing a beam of light along the overgrown way. Almost as if he was being invited. *Well, if you want to believe that ...*

Of course he did. He headed into the sunlight.

It was still very quiet, with only birdsong, his footfalls and the distant susurrus of the sea. His run slowed to a walk and a scratchy scramble in places. Some clearance had been done, but it wasn't recent. The loudest thing now was his own breathing. He was pretty sure that there was no other human life anywhere close.

The sun, which had invited him in, was coming and going behind high scudding clouds, fitfully dappling the path with light, then patches of dense shade that seemed faintly ominous. *That's just your guilty conscience.* There was no way that he was being watched from the shadows; the undergrowth was too thick.

Picking his way around a massively spreading rose with very long and enthusiastic thorns, that he thought might be a *Henri Martin*, his heart nearly rocketed out of his chest as he came face-to-face with a ghostly white figure. Trapped by the embrace of the bush, he staggered to a halt, stuttering words of apology, '*Scusi*. I'm sorry. Oh!'

Realisation hit him in a burst of laughter. He was apologising to a statue. He was eye to eye with a life-size nymph, or maybe a goddess, leaning forward over the path with her draperies flowing around her feet. The smooth marble of her hair was crowned with a coronet of ivy. Her plinth was choked with dead grass and weeds.

With a small salute Gideon edged past her. He was coming nearer the house. The planting in front of him was thinning. Instinctively, he slowed his pace once more. The building, like the gardens, was neglected but beautiful. He was approaching from the back, where there was a covered walk – a loggia – lined with pillars of pale veined marble. The strip of grass at the bottom of a shallow set of steps had clearly been mowed and edged, though again not recently. There were straggling bushes of lavender and rosemary ringing the lawn. The place looked sad enough to make him shiver.

Looking up at the sky, he could see that the scudding clouds had lowered and grown dark, threatening rain. He crossed the grass and skirted the building along a narrow tunnel-like path, overhung with bushes. The crunch of gravel under his feet told him that he'd hit the drive. He sprinted away as the first raindrops began to fall.

'Giardino delle Rose? Near Portofino? That's the old Rossi place.' Gideon nodded encouragingly, conscious of his heart beating a little faster. *At last, someone who knows something.*

He was touring a private garden outside San Remo with its owner, a British ex-pat who was a friend of his college supervisor. The contrast between this immaculately kept space and the overgrown villa of his morning run could not have been greater and had prompted him to say so. The ex-pat owner preened, proud of his display. 'Big estate that, history too – legends and airy-fairy stuff.' His turned down mouth indicated his views on airy-fairy stuff.

'I was trying to find out more about it,' Gideon probed. 'There doesn't seem to be anything in any books or guides.'

'No, probably not,' the garden owner agreed. 'Old family, very private – although, of course, *she* wasn't Italian.' He frowned, screwing up his eyes in thought. 'I seem to remember that there was a book – more like a pamphlet really, in English – but that was decades ago.' He shook his head. 'Sad that it should have been let go. Takes a lot of work to keep a place up to scratch.' He rubbed his hands together, his self-satisfaction obvious. 'Now you must come and look at the greenhouses. Then can we offer you a spot of lunch?'

The sun was going down and twilight was settling over Portofino. His evening meal finished, Gideon sat in a quiet corner of the harbour-side restaurant, enjoying the contrast between the mysterious pools of shadow created by the gathering dusk and the golden warmth spilling from lighted shop windows and eating places. Although it was late in the season, the weather was mild and there were still tourists about. Out on the water a cruise ship stood at anchor. An off-shore breeze and a choppy sea had limited the number of passengers risking the ship's tenders to come ashore, but the tables around him were filling up and it was time for him to leave. With a wave of thanks to the proprietor, he gathered his backpack and slung it over his shoulder.

He wandered down the parade of shops, their windows dressed for the Christmas trade, until he came to the gallery. He hadn't realised that he was going in, until he pushed open the door and a wind chime tinkled softly just over his head. The paintings of the gardens had drawn him.

The click in his mind as brain and sight connected was almost audible. This was not just *any* garden; it was the garden of the deserted villa, painted when it was already overgrown but not quite as wild as it was now.

29

He looked around the space. There were fifteen large paintings on display and several dozen smaller ones. Discreet posters suggested the pictures as suitable for Christmas gifts. *If you've got that kind of money.* Obviously, some did. There were other people browsing. The owner or manager, a slim brunette in a simple black dress that screamed expensive, was helping a couple who looked to be serious buyers. *Which you are definitely not. Not even for one of the smaller canvases,* he realised ruefully. There were sufficient potential customers for him not to look out of place though.

The larger pictures seemed to be a series – first simply plants and flowers, then views including belvederes and statuary. He recognised his nymph with a grin. Possessive, much? *Well, she did scare the daylights out of you.* The depiction wasn't quite as he remembered. She was leaning out of the picture towards the viewer, a much more flirtatious cast to her eyes than in the blank cold marble of the real thing. *Inviting you into a secret.* She wasn't wearing her crown of ivy either. That was confined to a straggle of leaves around the plinth. Artistic licence or an indication of the passage of time?

Gideon looked around, wishing that he could ask more about the garden. Could he do it without revealing himself as a trespasser? He moved further into the display. These pictures were slightly disturbing. Nothing distinct, just the choice of more ominously saturated colours, denser shadows and the tinge of threat in the cloud-filled sky. The tower featured in the background of several. Some depicted human figures—

'Creepy, aren't they?' The gallery owner had approached him without his realising. He'd decided she was the owner on the basis of the dress. He'd been too engrossed in the artwork to notice that the buyers she had been attending to had completed their purchase, triumphantly carrying off a small wrapped parcel. The wind chime on the door softly marked their departure.

The woman indicated a row of six paintings. 'This group was inspired by the work of Giambattista Basile.' She looked up at him, with a question in her eyes.

'Fairy tales,' he suggested.

'Yes.' Her face lit with pleasure at his response. 'Written in Neapolitan dialect in the fifteenth century – not quite bedtime stories for children though, some are quite gruesome.' She gave a theatrical shudder.

'They are creepy,' he agreed. 'There's nothing you can really put your finger on. It's just … atmosphere.'

The woman was nodding. 'Very talented, my sister.' She grinned. 'But don't tell her I said so.'

'Your sister?'

She gestured to a side table with a pile of publicity postcards. Gideon saw the name of the artist – Alcinda Zabarella. 'I'm Bianca Zabarella.' The woman held out her hand.

Gideon shook it and introduced himself, wondering if he dared ...

'It was the setting in particular that attracted me.' He indicated the paintings with the fairy-tale elements. 'I'm a landscape gardener.'

'Really?' Perfectly groomed brows rose in surprise. 'I thought you were something in security – a bodyguard? You were the one that took down the thief.' Her expression told him that, as usual, his height gave him away.

'Yes, that was me,' he admitted. 'But it's not my regular work. I help out sometimes, that's all.'

'Well, you did a good job with that guy.' She nodded to the display of smaller canvases where there was a gap. 'He took the picture that should have been there.' She made a face. 'It was slightly damaged, so it has to be repaired, but it could have been gone for good, so my sister and I owe you our thanks.'

Gideon shrugged awkwardly. 'I was in the right place at the right time. He ran straight into me.'

Bianca gave him a sceptical look but didn't comment, just gestured. 'You have a favourite?'

'Maybe the one with the nymph, goddess, whoever she is.' He took a quick breath and a risk. 'Where were they painted? Somewhere local?' He put effort into sounding casual and was pleased with the result. *Just a gardener, talking shop.*

He didn't miss a slight narrowing of Bianca Zabarella's eyes before her equally casual reply, 'Somewhere near here, I believe. You need to ask my sister.' She leaned forward to pick up one of the cards on the table. 'We're having a small reception on Saturday, so buyers can meet the artist. Alcinda will be here from 6 p.m. I'm sure she'd love to meet you. You can talk to her then.'

Gideon accepted the card with thanks. With a last look at his nymph, he left the gallery, thrusting the invitation into the pocket of his jeans. Signora Zabarella had evaded his question with an easy smoothness – but she *had* evaded it. *Is that because her sister was also trespassing when she did the painting?*

31

Chapter Six

'It's not really millions.' Megan was sitting with Cassie and their friend, Nadine Wells, in the bar of one of Bath's most upmarket hotels. Christmas carols played softly over the sound system and a heavily decorated tree, swathed in white lights, sparkled in a corner. A bottle of champagne nestled in an ice bucket on the table. She'd already regaled Cassie and Nadine with the story of her trip to Trueheart Alley. 'I was a bit afraid it would be like Brigadoon, disappearing into the mist once I walked away,' she confessed. 'But it was still there when I went back last week. A lot of the money is only on paper, because it includes the value of the villa and jewellery and antiques, and there's a small olive farm – which might be why Olwen said she was going to marry a farmer. There's a vineyard too. I think that was more of a hobby for—' she hesitated '—my Great-Great Uncle Eduardo.' It still felt strange to say that.

'Even if it is on paper and in property, you're now a wealthy woman,' Cassie pointed out, sipping champagne.

'Do you have any idea how your uncle made that kind of money?' Nadine asked curiously.

'Apparently he was an ace at investments. Mr Gifford only began acting for him and my aunt a few years before Uncle Eduardo died. He was already a rich man and he was stream-lining his assets, selling property that he owned in London. It's a bit of a mystery where he and Olwen went when they eloped and where they were for the twenty or so years afterwards. They built the villa in the 1970s and their son was born there. He's a bit of a mystery too. I don't even know his name. He would have been about the same age now as my mother.' For a second, the room darkened at the memory of loss. 'He died when he was a teenager.'

'That's so sad. Maybe you can find out more? His name at least. You're going out there, of course?' Nadine helped herself to a handful of nuts from a bowl on the table.

'Of course,' Megan answered. The thought made her heart trip. She knew it was mostly excitement, but it seemed there were so many questions and family secrets. 'The formalities are still being completed, and I'm working over Christmas and New Year. I don't want to let the hotel down.'

'Better to keep everything low-key anyway,' Cassie suggested. Nadine raised her eyebrows in a question. 'Ellery,' Cassie said succinctly. Now the feeling around Megan's heart was a squeeze of pain rather than excitement. It must have shown on her face. 'He dumped you, hon.' Cassie grimaced. 'It hurts, but you shouldn't give him a chance to worm his way back in.'

Nadine shot Cassie what might be described as an old-fashioned look. They all knew that her marriage to Jake McQuire was the result of a second-chance romance.

'Yes, all right,' Cassie answered the look, topping up their glasses again. 'But in my case, *he* was the one with the money.' She grinned, then her face sobered. 'Your heart is your own, honey. You have to make your own decisions, but if he came looking for you and you took him back, wouldn't you always wonder?'

'I know.' The pain of betrayal had lessened, but it was still there. 'I don't want him back.' She was *almost* sure that was true.

Nadine nudged her with her elbow. 'Maybe you'll find yourself a hunky Italian to sweep you off your feet?'

'I'll drink to that,' Cassie seconded the idea, raising her glass. 'Whatever you do, make sure you have a little fun. Italy – food, wine, sunshine.' She sighed.

'I'm not sure about sunshine in January, but the rest sounds good,' Megan agreed.

'What else?' Ever astute, Cassie picked up something in her expression.

'I'm not sure if you'd think it was fun, but Mr Gifford said that the villa has a library. It's been put into safe storage, but there are a number of old and antique books.'

'And you're wondering about the "Cosimo" volumes.'

Nadine looked blank, so Megan quickly described the background to her thesis, explaining about "Cosimo" and finding the poems. 'My supervisor first unearthed a clutch of verses and some other material in the late 1990s, in an archive in Oxford,' she added. 'There was a brief note that *might* have been written by Lord Byron, saying that the author was a boy of about seventeen or eighteen. There was a lot of excitement in academic circles. The general opinion was that they were something special for such a young man – a bit like Thomas Chatterton.'

'Boy genius,' Cassie supplied, in clarification. 'Like you, he lived in Bristol – in a house not far from Temple Meads station.'

'I'll investigate,' Nadine promised. 'And you think now that the books you found came from your Aunt Olwen?'

Megan gave a half shrug. She knew that the insistent whisper in her mind was irrational. 'I really can't see how there can be a connection.'

'But you can't help hoping that there might be,' Nadine suggested shrewdly.

Megan shrugged again, then nodded. 'I know it's ridiculously wishful thinking, but you're right – I *can't* help hoping that there might be something in the villa's library. The Oxford material was only found by accident, in a place no one would have expected,' she said. 'What we have so far is so sparse – there should be more out there to find. There's no indication of who the translator was, or where they got the material. The only name we have for the poet is "Cosimo". There's precious little in the way of biographical information and no definite locations. All we really have is the verses themselves, with the main source being my books. Three of the poems my supervisor found are very close to the printed ones – they were probably first drafts.'

Cassie gestured with her glass. '*Dr* Morrison proved they were all from the same writer. Linguistics.' She gave a don't-ask-me shrug and rolled her eyes. Megan stuck out her tongue in retaliation. It felt so good, after months of pain and stress, just to be here, like this, with friends.

She hesitated. 'There is something else ...' She stopped. She'd begged the photograph from Mr Gifford, and so far had not shown it to anyone. She pulled it out now and laid it on the table. 'In the grounds of the villa, there's a tower. *This* tower.'

'And one of the "Cosimo" poems features a tower.' Cassie leaned forward to look.

'There's absolutely *nothing* to say that there's a link,' Megan pointed out carefully.

'But it's another mystery. Your kind of mystery.' Cassie grinned. 'I recognise that expression – the academic scenting the hunt. We should drink to that – and to your trip.' She waved to the waiter, signalling for another bottle.

He'd never been to an art event like this before. He knew a little about Victorian and Edwardian art, courtesy of a girlfriend at college who'd dragged him around Tate Britain, but nothing about contemporary painting, or how you judged if it was good. The pictures on the walls, which included a number that were new to the display, looked good to him. Other people seemed to think so too, going by the crowd in the room. Gideon accepted a glass of something pale and bubbly from a uniformed waitress and wandered to the back of the space, where the smaller canvases had been repositioned. He was glad that he'd worn his posh suit. He fitted in well enough with the paying patrons not to look or feel out of place.

He sipped the wine, watching Bianca working the room. This evening was about selling the larger canvases to art lovers with a taste for the unusual. *And very deep pockets.* He'd done a bit of online research. Alcinda Zabarella was making a name for herself with those who wanted something "decorative but different" to hang on their walls. Gideon grinned; he was definitely from the "I know what I like" school of art appreciation, but he *did* like these. *Or maybe it's just because of the garden?*

The thing that had really brought him here tonight was the chance of speaking to the artist. Now, seeing the crowd, he wasn't sure if he'd actually get to talk to her after all. Signora Zabarella was leaning beside the table in the centre of the room, chatting to prospective buyers as Bianca deftly cut them out from the herd and brought them forward for introductions. The sisters didn't resemble each other. Alcinda was small and blonde. Her hair, piled up in a messy topknot, and high-heeled, Victorian-style, lace-up boots gave her a few precious inches, but she was still tiny. Miss Havisham might have coveted the tattered silk and lace of her white dress, which he suspected was the work of some big-name designer. Fingerless open weave gloves partly concealed paint stains on her hands. Her nails glittered silver and gold. She looked as if she'd stepped down from one of her own paintings.

Intrigued, Gideon watched her interact with people who might buy her work – charming, mildly flirtatious, enjoying herself. He was curious. How much was an act and how much the real deal?

Turning his attention back to the paintings, he accepted another glass of wine and studied the detail. Alcinda had taken trouble with the depictions of flowers and bushes, even when they were simply background. He could almost sense the smoothness of a leaf, smell the scent of tangled jasmine, feel the sting of a bramble …

A large number of the paintings bore discreet red stickers on the corner of the frame, indicating that they were sold. As he watched, dividing his attention between the paintings and the interaction at the centre of the room, Bianca crossed over to add another red dot to the picture he was looking at.

Her face lit up with a smile when she saw him. '*Ciao*, Signor West. Glad you could make it.' She cast a glance back over her shoulder. The crowd was thinning, the keen buyers having made their purchases. For the moment,

Alcinda was standing alone – relaxed, sipping her drink and seemingly people watching. With a quick check on the state of the room that amused Gideon, although he tried not to show it, Bianca held out a hand. 'Let me introduce you to my sister. She is looking forward to meeting you.'

Doubting that, but willing to play along, Gideon followed her. They'd almost reached the table when Bianca's attention was drawn by another guest, and Gideon found himself taking the last few steps alone. Alcinda looked up, with a glance that transformed her rapidly from a member of the fey to a mischievous street urchin. *Does she know how much of herself she's put into that wicked nymph, I wonder?*

'Fee-fi-fo-fum,' she recited with an evil grin. 'I think I'd like to paint you.'

'Let me guess – Jack and the Beanstalk. And a shade over six-foot-six, to save you asking.'

'I bet you get that a lot.' Now she was laughing.

'Occasionally,' he agreed blandly.

'I feel I should be standing on the table to have this conversation.' She narrowed her eyes and Gideon realised, with a slight shock, that she really *wa*s sizing him up as a possible subject. It was a strange sensation.

Bianca joined them and reminded Alcinda about the rescued canvas.

'I should do something, to show my appreciation,' Alcinda declared. 'And persuade you to sit for me,' she added irrepressibly. 'I'll paint you something.'

Gideon swallowed, afraid he might blush. 'I didn't ... I mean ...'

Alcinda waved a hand. 'Consider it done. A garden,' she decided. 'Bianca said that's what you do for a living. Gardens.'

'Landscaping and garden design,' he agreed. *Although once the next few weeks are over, it will be jobbing gardening, if you're lucky.* He pushed the unwanted thought away. 'I'd be very honoured to have a painting,' he said, with a slightly formal nod. It was the right thing. Alcinda's eyes glowed and Bianca gave a quiet purr of approval. Gideon took a breath. If he was going to do this, it had to be now. 'Actually, I wanted to ask you ...' He turned slightly, towards the paintings and one in particular. Not the one with the nymph; he had something subtler in mind than that. 'There's a very lovely magnolia in the background there – quite a rare one – I wondered where it was painted. Somewhere near here?'

The pause was brief, but it was there.

Bianca picked up a bottle of wine to top up their drinks. Alcinda waved her hand again, this time in a vague, dismissive gesture. 'Oh, I paint in a lot of places. Sometimes here, sometimes there,' she said airily. 'If you like that one, I'm sure I have initial sketches. I can paint from those.'

'That would be awesome,' Gideon said, with perfect sincerity. The tree was beautiful and unusual, and he would treasure any painting of it, but unless he was very much mistaken, he'd already seen the original. It was planted in the overgrown tangle behind the statue of the nymph in the garden of Il Giardino delle Rose.

Chapter Seven

This was the most luxurious hotel she'd ever stayed in. *Quite a change from the one where you were making beds and cleaning bathrooms just the week before last.* Her aunt's Italian solicitor, Signor Agnello, had arranged it. *And now he's your Italian solicitor.* Realisation was still a shock. The formalities had been completed much faster than expected and here she was, in late January, staying in one of the best hotels in Genoa and trying to look as if she belonged in a place populated with antiques, exquisitely faded rugs and frescoed walls.

At least she looked the part, which gave her confidence. Cassie, whose declared speciality was holiday shopping, had herded her to the hairdresser and for a makeover in the cosmetic section of Bath's biggest department store, then to several of the city's most upmarket boutiques and a couple of vintage shops. She'd supervised packing the results in fancy new suitcases, with the instruction that Megan should relax and enjoy herself. *And here I am doing just that.* It wasn't exactly a holiday but … a fascinating Italian city, new clothes, this hotel – Cassie would undoubtedly approve of the hotel.

Signor Agnello's secretary telephoned while Megan was unpacking. The lawyer was desolate but he had been called out of town urgently and would be unable to meet her tomorrow. He would not be available to take her to view her inheritance until the following day. A company from Genoa had cleaned the villa. Her aunt's elderly gardener had kept up minimal work on the gardens while she was still living there, and contractors were now dealing with urgent items. It was for Dottoressa Morrison to give further directions of what she wished done. In the meantime, the secretary would send over an information pack on the sights of Genoa to occupy her until Signor Agnello was available.

Disappointment segued into impatience as Megan returned to emptying her suitcase. Genoa was an interesting city, but she *wasn't* a tourist. She didn't want to wait to be shown around Il Giardino delle Rose like a guest. She *owned* the place.

Hurriedly cramming the rest of her clothes into the capacious wardrobe, Megan took herself down to the elegant foyer. She found what she was looking for discreetly located at an antique desk to the side of the reception area. The uniformed concierge greeted her, 'Dottoressa Morrison, welcome to our hotel. May I assist you?'

'I'd like a map of the coast, including Portofino, if you have it.' She gave him her widest smile. 'And can you arrange car hire?'

'Maps we have.' He gestured to a small information stand behind him. 'Please take what you need.' He picked up the phone. 'I will speak with the car rental agency. Do you wish the vehicle to be delivered this evening?'

The compact dark blue Fiat arrived half an hour later, while Megan sat in the lounge studying the map and sipping an exotic mocktail constructed for her by a good-looking bartender. After a careful test drive for a few blocks around the hotel, Megan headed to the restaurant for dinner. She ordered a room service breakfast in a takeaway bag for the morning, and prepared for an early night. Tomorrow she would be on the road to Portofino before traffic got too heavy.

The photograph album was again displayed on the table, released from its hiding place in the painted cassone that had been in the family for generations. *Generations – these things matter.* Gabriella De Stephano caressed the leather cover of the album, tracing the worn corners with a delicate fingertip, tinted today in the palest shell pink. *A shade favoured by the Queen of England*, her manicurist assured her. She had no reason to doubt it. Caring for one's hands was the mark of a lady.

She flinched at a sudden sound – the bang of a door. Someone in the apartment? Instinctively leaning forward to protect the album, she waited tensely, listening. No footsteps, no voices. Gradually she relaxed again. She was too jumpy. The noise was from elsewhere in the house. This … business … played on her nerves.

She focused again on the album, savouring the moment when she would open it. She was the only one who really cared. She knew what they thought. She heard the sighs, saw the sideways glances and suspected the knowing looks behind her back. They humoured her, indulging what they considered her eccentricities. Even darling Frederico, who was almost a son to her ...

They did not understand. They did not see the necessity for restitution – for justice.

She had waited, striving for patience, during the holiday celebrations, waited for the news that the villa would be offered for sale. Instead, the niece, Megan Morrison, had arrived here in Genoa, thanks to that fool of a solicitor. Gabriella's mouth twisted. Even watched as she was, she had her sources of information. Agnello had installed Dottoressa Morrison in one of the best hotels and had people working at the villa, no doubt trying to impress her.

39

Running through what little money the old woman had left. Heaven knows that could not be much, given the way the usurper had lived for her last years, crouched in a corner of the house while brambles grew all the way to the doors …

Shifting to get more comfortable, Gabriella cast a complacent glance around the room made golden by the setting sun. Soon she would light scented candles. No doubt Dottoressa Morrison now considered herself a great lady, but in truth she was simply another usurper. For a second, the fingers resting on the warm leather spasmed into a fist. *She* was the rightful heir to Il Giardino delle Rose, but the inheritance – the *rightful* inheritance – must be *purchased*. The estate would be offered for sale. *Then* it would be hers.

Reclaimed.

With a satisfied smile, Gabriella opened the album.

The morning light was soft, faintly pearlescent, promising sunshine later, even though the air now was chilly. Megan made good time after successfully navigating out of Genoa and onto the correct road for Portofino. She had planned her route the night before, with the concierge's map, figuring out that she had to turn some way short of Portofino itself to reach the villa. Setting off before it was properly light had been a good move. Now she was getting close.

There was nothing to prevent her visiting the property without waiting for Signor Agnello to escort her, but she didn't want to run into any of the work people and have to account for herself. Ellery would have dismissed her attitude as stupidity, given that she was the one paying them. *I am not spoiling a beautiful morning by thinking of Ellery.*

She couldn't explain the impulse that had sent her off into the early morning like this, except that she wanted to be alone for her first encounter with Il Giardino delle Rose. She wasn't expecting there to be anything left of the spirit of her aunt, except for a sadness that they'd never met. It just felt right that she should be alone the first time she saw and explored the place that had been her last relative's home. Something in those old photographs in the faraway lawyer's office in Trueheart Alley called to her.

She made the final turn. The road was narrow and climbing. An unkempt hedge leaned over the roadway. *Somewhere here ...*

And there it was – a pair of drunken looking gates and two weathered pillars, half smothered in ivy, with the simple legend, *Giardino delle Rose*, carved into the right-hand one. Megan stopped the car, leaning over the steering wheel to peer at the driveway. It was weedy but passable, Piles of cut branches with wilting leaves stacked on the verge suggested that some clearing had been done. There was no view of the building. With her heart thumping in her ears, Megan started the car and nosed cautiously through the gates.

Gideon was late. He probably should have skipped the morning run, and he *definitely* shouldn't have given in to the impulse to come this way. The damn garden seemed to have put a spell on him. He'd even *dreamed* about it last night. *Which is probably why you're here today, even though you know you shouldn't be.*

As he ran, he could see distinct signs of work going on in the house and grounds. He'd managed to stay away over Christmas and New Year, helped by a patch of bad weather that kept his morning run short and brisk. But now here he was, thanks to the dream – the details of which he couldn't even remember clearly. If he wasn't careful, late as he was, he'd be powering straight into the arms of a workman or a gardener. Deciding that discretion was the better part of valour, he diverted away from the path that would have taken him past the goddess, cutting through to hit the lower end of the drive.

Someone had been busy with a chainsaw, he noted critically as he emerged onto the gravel. He jogged on the spot for a moment, assessing the work. It was clearance rather than pruning – but it really wasn't any of his business. He hoped the owner, whoever they were, would get someone who knew what they were doing for the main garden. *Again, not your business.*

And this really must be the last visit. This was goodbye, even though he felt a pang for the loss of his private enchanted space. Someone was putting the place in order; his time here was over. He took off again, moving faster when he saw the small blue Fiat parked ahead of him in the drive. If there were people about, it was high time he disappeared. He moved up to a sprint, heading for the gates.

It was like something out of a fairy tale – literally Sleeping Beauty's castle. Briars and overgrown roses scrambled everywhere, yet Megan could see the bones of beauty underneath the mad riot of thorns. She moved quietly around the perimeter of the house, resisting an irrational urge to tiptoe. She was no expert, but the place looked sound, if rather bedraggled in the early sunshine.

41

She ducked under a rose spray that someone had made an effort to restrain, but which had triumphantly broken free, to slip around the back of the building, glad for her thick jeans and jacket and stout boots. There was a small green lawn, recently mowed, and the marble colonnade from the photographs. Dead leaves piled in drifts in corners and spider webs sparkled with rain drops. She trod carefully up the steps to peer through the French windows, shading her eyes with a hand but seeing only humps of shrouded furniture. She turned, looking back towards the garden. If she went that way …

She moved very slowly, feeling each step before she made it, working her way carefully through the vestiges of an old path until the tangled undergrowth began to clear.

She emerged onto a headland where the edge of the garden met the scrubby ground of poorer, uncultivated soil. Beyond that was the pale crystal-blue of the sky and the grey and white of a heaving sea. And there it was – *La Torre* – the tower. A shiver of excitement ran along her spine. It might have come straight from the "Cosimo" poems – the tower where the poet and his secret love stole sleepy afternoons and moon-drenched nights, before their tragic end.

Megan jumped, letting out a muffled shriek as a missile hurtled over her head, before resolving itself into a screaming gull. She stood for a moment, letting her heart settle back into its regular rhythm. The bird had broken the spell, which was perhaps a good thing. To walk any further over the uneven ground could be disastrous. *And no one actually knows you're here.* A different kind of shiver ran over her. She turned to retrace her steps.

Dusting leaves off the steps of the loggia, she sat down. It was very quiet. Living in the centre of Bath with the noise of traffic and people, she hadn't realised how much she missed silence.

An idea was growing, like a little ball of light. Excitement thrilled through her, making her breathless. Could she … might she actually be able to *live* here? The idea was majorly scary and majorly exhilarating, both at the same time. She folded her hands around her upraised knee, frowning. She hadn't really thought about what happened after she got to Italy and saw her inheritance. She'd vaguely expected to sell the place and settle back into academic life. She'd assumed that was the sensible thing, what the solicitors would advise. She dropped her hands and sat up. That picture wasn't quite true. Mr Gifford had shown her those photographs. He'd been disappointed when she told him she wouldn't be going to Italy ...

Abruptly her thoughts cleared. She could see her way perfectly. She wasn't going to sell. She was going to *live* here. Elation and a little fear fluttered under her ribs. She didn't want to let the place go. Her aunt hadn't simply willed her an estate; she'd given her a *home.*

Megan laughed, still hearing the edge of surprise and trepidation. It was the right thing to do. Mr Gifford, she acknowledged with respect, *was* a wily old bird. He'd known she wouldn't be able to resist the pull of all this beauty. She belonged here. She could feel it.

She rocked a little, exploring that edge of fear. Was she falling for the soft-focus dream, the one presented in so many books and films, where the lone English or American woman finds the derelict house in Italy and settles into an idyllic life? Megan shook her head, although there was no one to see. Living here *would* be a dream, but it was the *right* dream.

A new life.

She and Il Giardino delle Rose were going to start a whole new chapter. Together.

Chapter Eight

Gideon had decided that his last possible source of local gossip was his self-appointed landlady, who had nearly lost a valuable brooch to the thief he had intercepted. He'd kept his promise to himself. No more early-morning running in the enchanted garden. Unfortunately, that didn't stifle his curiosity, which seemed to be growing.

He'd be leaving Portofino in a matter of weeks.

He'd completed a healthy quota of garden visits, filled three notebooks and pitched articles to professional journals and a new mass-market gardening magazine. His stay had been even more productive than he'd hoped, but Il Giardino delle Rose still hovered on the brink of his consciousness. He'd been meaning for ages to properly explore the shop on the ground floor of the building that housed his borrowed apartment. Tonight was as good a time as any.

He opened the door and ducked inside, down two steps and into an Aladdin's cave of books. Bookcases lined the walls and extended into the room. The lighting was soft and atmospheric. Comfortable leather chairs invited browsers. The front of the shop had international bestsellers prominently displayed, but beyond that the racks were entirely given over to books about the Riviera. Everything you could ever want – art books, glossy guides, memoirs and novels. It was nearly closing time, but a few people still wandered around the shelves.

Gideon nodded to his landlady, who was packing a pile of books for a customer, then drifted into the interior, drawn inevitably by the section on gardens. He took down a few books, riffling through the pages before returning them to the shelves and prowling further into the shop. In an alcove at the back was a heavy bookcase of dark wood. The books here were second hand, with battered spines and well-worn bindings. Most were in Italian, but there were a few volumes of Dickens, Austen and the Brontës, as well as a couple of battered and well-loved children's classics.

On the bottom shelf was a row of paperbacks – American authors from the fifties and sixties. He could see Steinbeck, Burroughs and Kerouac. Reaching for a copy of *East of Eden*, which he hadn't read, Gideon dislodged a small parcel of books bundled together with fraying silk ribbon. They were slim leather-bound volumes and there was something else too. Aware that his pulse had speeded up, Gideon lifted the bundle into the light. The books seemed to be poetry, one in English, one in Italian, but the thing that had caught his notice wasn't a book. *Not much more than a pamphlet* – he could hear the voice of the ex-pat gardener from San Remo loud in his head. The paper cover was torn, but the title on the page was clear – *Il Giardino delle Rose* – and there was a picture of the garden, the statue of the nymph almost buried in a mass of flowering roses. With a hand that he was alarmed to note had a slight tremor, Gideon gathered the bundle and the Steinbeck and carried them over to the sales desk.

'Signor West,' Signora Bertolo greeted him with a wide smile. 'You found something you like?'

He nodded, putting the paperback down on the desk, but keeping hold of the others. 'I'd like these too – I was wondering, do you know anything about this place – Il Giardino delle Rose?'

'Ah.' The woman looked at the books in his hands with a sigh. 'I don't know that those ...' She looked up. 'You found them in the case at the back?' she queried.

Gideon nodded again, with a sudden urgent stab of concern. 'They are for sale?'

'I suppose ...' She gestured for him to put them down, pulling at the ribbon, freeing the books to spread them apart on the desk, muttering something in Italian that Gideon didn't catch. Then her back stiffened, as if she had made up her mind. 'Yes, they are for sale. But, of course, you are interested in the garden.'

'I am,' he agreed quietly, slightly alarmed at the strength of his relief that he was going to be able to buy the bundle. *Obsessive much?* 'I ... er ... passed the gate one morning while I was running. The place looked very overgrown ...' He let the observation hang, but she didn't respond.

Her fingers were still running over the bindings and teasing the ribbon. 'You wish to take all of them?'

'Please,' Gideon confirmed. 'It seems as if someone felt they belonged together.'

'It appears so.' Signora Bertolo almost visibly shook herself, gathering the books back into the fastening and producing a paper carrier bag from behind the desk. 'It is very sad – the lady who owned the villa – an American lady, but married into an old local family – she recently died. She was very old. Now there is no one of the family left. She and her husband created the garden – it must have been in the 1970s.' She tapped the pamphlet. 'The history is here. There was a visitor who would come, from England, I think.'

She shrugged. 'You see, it is in English. She wrote this. I am sure you will find it interesting.'

'I'm sure I will.' Gideon had no doubt of that. He had to swallow hard to hold down his excitement at finally getting some of the story. 'And the other books – they're poems?'

'Some other member of the family? A private printing?' She shrugged again, then continued with a soft laugh, 'Poetry. It is not a big seller.' She dropped the books into the bag and accepted Gideon's credit card. 'There.' Signora Bertolo pulled the handles of the bag together and offered it to Gideon. 'It will be an unusual souvenir of your stay in Portofino.'

Chapter Nine

Megan dressed carefully for her meeting with Signor Agnello, in a slim cashmere camel coat, black leather boots and an oversized scarf in a smudgy leopard print, and was glad that she had. The lawyer's stylish modern offices, as well as the man himself, could not have been in greater contrast to Trueheart Alley. In his mid-fifties, she guessed, with a distinguished sprinkling of grey in thick dark hair and a handsomely proportioned nose and chin, he was brisk and efficient, taking her speedily through the necessary paperwork and setting out the possibilities for disposing of the property. Megan sipped excellent coffee, brought in by his secretary immediately on her arrival, and listened.

'The present condition of the estate—' he made an eloquent gesture '—is not the best to attract suitable purchasers. It would perhaps be wise to put some resources into restoring the house and grounds, to bring them into a more marketable state.' He stopped, looking questioning, waiting for her reaction.

Illogically, her heart was thumping. *This is it. When you* say *it, that makes it real.*

'I do want to put resources into the estate,' she agreed quietly. 'But not as preparation for sale. I want to restore the house and garden so I can live there. I want to make it my home.' Even as she uttered it, the word *home* sent a strange, breathless shiver through her.

'My dear Signora Morrison!' With a smile that completely transformed his rather severe features, the lawyer surged to his feet, leaning over the desk to shake her hand. 'This is excellent news!' He released her, sitting back in his chair. 'Il Giardino delle Rose.' He shrugged. 'It is a special place,' he said simply. 'Signor Gifford told me that if anyone was to bring it back to life again, you were the woman to do it. I am glad he is not to be disappointed.' He beamed at her. 'Now! We will go and see your new home.'

They spent a pleasant and amicable morning going over the villa, starting with the few feet of the garden that were accessible to a sharp-suited lawyer and a client with a new cashmere coat and shiny black boots. Megan confessed to her clandestine trip and Signor Agnello expressed his understanding for her impatience, particularly as it resulted in a decision not to sell.

'An absentee owner, or a developer? No.' He shook his head. 'This place …' He waved his hands at the untended garden. 'It needs … someone who has sympathy with its spirit.' He looked slightly puzzled and maybe a little embarrassed to be expressing such an un-lawyer like opinion, until Megan assured him that she quite understood.

That was exactly how she felt. 'It kind of grabs you. Like the brambles.' She bent to dislodge one that was trying to tangle around her foot. They both laughed. A bird hidden somewhere in the thicket let out a long trail of song.

Something inside Megan settled. *This place is yours. A place to belong.*

Signor Agnello had commissioned a surveyor's report that confirmed that the fabric of the villa was sound, barring some small repairs. Once the front door was opened, with an imposingly massive key, Megan was pleasantly surprised by the interior. The contract cleaners had done a good job. Although there was a great deal of updating needed to the kitchen and bathrooms and general decor, all the rooms were habitable. The larger pieces of her aunt's furniture were still in place, covered in dust sheets. Smaller and more delicate or valuable items were in storage, including the majority of the volumes from the library that Megan was delighted to find at the end of the hall. She could envisage her own collection of research books lining the shelves. To be able to sit here, completely surrounded by books …

The bookcases had been positioned to create a deep window seat, which Signor Agnello thought might have a view of the front garden. At the moment, foliage covered the glass, casting a dim greenish light over the interior. *You're going to need professional help for that. A lot of it.*

Having inspected everything that was possible, they returned to Signor Agnello's office. Over a lunch of focaccia and fruit, they put together a checklist of work, Agnello entering entirely into the preparation. Megan was amused at the change in the stiff and formal lawyer. Now that she was intending to live in the villa, he was entirely invested in the scheme for renovations. The work on the villa itself was easy to quantify – refitted kitchen and bathrooms and redecoration throughout, but the garden … Megan felt a tiny flicker of panic.

'I assume there must be original plans and maybe plant lists?' she asked hopefully.

'That I do not know.' Agnello frowned. 'The Marchesa lodged very few papers here with us – her will and some official documents only. There may be records amongst the volumes that were removed from the library – or in the house itself.' His frown deepened. 'I have to say that towards the end Signora Rossi had Tommaso burn a large quantity of her papers.'

Megan's heart sank a little to meet the rise of the panic. 'Tommaso?' She latched onto the name. *Who was Tommaso?*

'He was head gardener at the property for nearly thirty years.'

Megan fell on the information with a new burst of hope. 'Then he would know about everything. Will it be possible to re-employ him?'

'I am sure it would. In fact—' the transforming smile lit Signor Agnello's face again '—that is something I was wondering about. The villa is somewhat isolated, for a woman living alone.' The lawyer had already delicately determined that there would be no partner joining Megan from England, and for a moment Ellery's presence had intruded into the stylish office. She had been pleased how firm her voice sounded when she said no. Now she leaned forward, curious. What did Agnello have in mind?

'It would, of course, be for you to decide. There is no reason for any concern, you understand, but it would perhaps be more … convivial … if there were others also on the estate. And to provide some help in the house.'

Megan wondered if her eyes widened. They had viewed a compact and much more modern staff apartment at the back of the garage block. Was the lawyer about to suggest live-in help?

It seemed that he was. 'Tommaso and his granddaughter resided at the villa until the Marchesa's death. Maria took care of the house and the Marchesa herself, towards the end. She is a capable girl and devoted to her grandfather. Tommaso …' Agnello spread his hands. 'He is old, nearly eighty. Healthy and still active, although his memory …' The lawyer gave an elegant shrug. 'He is, in turn, devoted to the garden.'

Megan drew in a long breath. 'He is the one who has been tending it?'

'To the best of his ability, yes, although contractors were brought in to clear the drive and to cut back some of the hedges.'

'When my aunt died, Maria and Tommaso must have lost their home and their livelihood. Where are they now?'

'Signora Rossi left a generous bequest to both. Maria has a job at a nursing home here in Genoa and shares a flat. Tommaso lives with his married daughter in Santa Margarita.' He gave a huff of laughter. 'I know he tries the poor woman's patience, always sneaking off back to the garden instead of dozing quietly in a chair. It is the place he feels that he belongs, where he can still be useful, even if he cannot tend it as he once did.'

'You think they would come back?' Megan wasn't quite sure how she felt, having people working for her. *Servants?* But she did need help, and if it meant Maria and Tommaso had their home back … She nodded her head. 'Could you ask if they would meet me? I'd like to thank them for taking care of my Aunt Olwen anyway.'

Signor Agnello agreed with a smile. 'Meet them, and think about it.'

When Megan shook hands with the lawyer at the end of the meeting, she felt as if she had made an ally. Agnello would put matters in hand to engage contractors and organise the necessary formalities for her to make an extended stay. For the moment, the only thing she had to think about was decor and soft furnishings. She didn't have much experience of that, but she knew someone who did.

'Cassie?' Megan dodged a passer-by as the call connected. 'It's me. Yeah, everything is fine.' Striding towards her hotel, she filled her friend in on the details of her trips to the villa and her decision to live at Il Giardino delle Rose.

Cassie assured her that while she would be missed in Bath, a fresh start sounded like a good choice. 'And you know Jake and I *love* the Riviera.'

Megan recognised a heavy hint when she heard it. She laughed. 'You'll be welcome to visit when I have the place straight. Talking of which, I have a commission for you. A paid commission, good cash money, but I won't say no to mates' rates,' she offered cheerfully.

Now she could hear Cassie laughing. 'You're catching on, hon. That's how the very rich do it. Keep your eye on the pennies.'

'You'd know, married to a billionaire.'

'Ha! He makes it, I spend it.'

Megan knew that was the image Cassie liked to convey, going back to the events in San Remo when she and Jake had rekindled their old romance. In fact, she was a very successful businesswoman in her own right. Her concierge business organised everything from dog walking to house renovations. She had plenty of experience to offer on the subject of home furnishing.

Megan joined a sprinkling of people enjoying the bright but chilly afternoon at the outside tables of a small café. She ordered a hot chocolate and chatted to Cassie while it was prepared. 'I don't quite know what I want yet – I need a better idea of the place and to see my aunt's stuff when it comes out of storage, but I've always had a hankering for the beach house look.'

'Hmm. Maybe a variation that includes some sort of nod to the garden setting? Florals rather than shells and boats?'

'I knew you were the right person to ask!'

'Let me think. Other than decorating, is everything else okay?'

'There's no rush … and it's fine. It's just that it's all a bit strange. The big house, live-in staff …' Disconcertingly, her voice faltered.

'Don't worry, hon. You're the woman to do it, just like your Mr Gifford says. Ellery knocked the stuffing out of you – but you don't have to defer to him now,' Cassie insisted. 'The villa might be grander than a cottage in Bath, but it isn't Manderley and you're not the second Mrs de Winter. You're an intelligent, respected academic, remember? You've got this.'

An intelligent, respected academic. Megan grinned, cheered by her friend's confidence and the sight of the hot chocolate covered with whipped cream that was being carried towards her. She rang off, with a promise to send Cassie pictures of the villa, and turned her attention to her drink.

Cassie's remark about Ellery and the second Mrs de Winter came back to Megan later as she sat in her hotel room making lists. Cassie was right about Ellery. Somehow, she'd got into the habit of deferring to him. He was always so sure of his judgement that he managed to subtly diminish hers. Megan could see that now. *You were fading out of your own life. Then, when he dumped you, he took away everything.* Even with the one thing that Ellery had no part in, her doctorate, she'd sat at the feet of her supervisor, in awe of an eminent expert. *But you were the one who brought him the poems; the one who began to unlock the secret of Cosimo.*

And maybe now there was more to find?

Signor Agnello made good on his promise, arranging for Maria and her grandfather to join Megan for tea at her hotel. Maria was a tall, statuesque young woman with curly dark hair and calm brown eyes. Her grandfather resembled a garden gnome – there was no getting away from it – small, wiry and whiskery, with bowed legs and grey hair that stuck up straight like a scrubbing brush. After they'd talked for a while, Megan found she had no hesitation in offering them their old jobs back. A voice in her head, that sounded a lot like Ellery, muttered about references and "elderly hangers on" but she ignored it.

The light in Tommaso's eyes when he realised he would be returning to his beloved garden and Maria's smile as she watched her grandfather told Megan everything that she needed to know. It was easily agreed. They would move back into the villa the following week. When they rose to leave, Tommaso took her hand in both his calloused ones. 'We will do it, Signora. The roses of Il Giardino delle Rose will bloom again.'

Chapter Ten

The next day Megan took a picnic lunch with her to the villa. This time *she* had the massive key to the front door. She let herself in and crossed to the kitchen, depositing a bag with a new electric kettle and toaster, then moving to the salon with the French windows, pulling dust covers off furniture and looking critically at what she had uncovered. The stuff was good quality but dated – 1970s at a guess. It took only a few seconds to decide that it was all going on eBay – there was probably a collector somewhere who would adore it. She was already imagining squashy sofas in soft sludgy colours, floral cushions, some simple modern pieces, mixed with a few well-chosen antiques …

By late morning, she'd prowled the rooms, taking pictures for Cassie and sending her links to ideas that had caught her notice on decorating sites. At noon she fetched the picnic and, unlocking the doors onto the loggia, dragged out a chair. She sat quietly eating cheese and a large ripe tomato with focaccia that was studded with rosemary. This afternoon a new mattress and a large fridge-freezer would be delivered. All she had to do was wait.

Silence hung gently around her, punctuated by birdsong and the occasional burst of whirring wings – which was surprisingly loud. A faint and distant pulse might have been the sea – or the traffic from the main road. She knew that it was her imagination – but it almost felt as if she could see … *something* … just out of the corner of her eye. Not her aunt's ghost, but maybe … her spirit?

'It will be beautiful again, Aunt Olwen, I promise,' she said softly into the silence. 'This is my home now. Thank you.'

The sound like a sigh had to be a sudden breath of wind in the cypress trees.

Megan scattered breadcrumbs on the steps for the birds, and then went to look for a broom to brush the dried leaves off the loggia.

Gideon's feet hurt. He'd spent the day scrambling around the terraces of a villa down the coast beyond La Spezia and the Bay of Poets. He had returned very late and was glad to remove his boots and flop onto the bed. The lamps were lit and the windows were open to the gathering dusk. The hum of music and voices and the scent of cooking drifted up from the harbour.

Gideon stretched out, then moved to adjust the lamp so that the light illuminated the pamphlet he'd picked up from the bedside table. He'd glanced at the two books, but poetry wasn't really his thing. He *wanted* to read about the garden, but a strenuous day in the fresh air was making his eyelids heavy. Yawning, he hitched himself higher against the head of the bed. *Getting soft, my lad. When you go back to jobbing gardening, you'll be working at least eight hours a day*. The unpleasant thought, not of the work but of the circumstances, made him grimace. He had two weeks left of his unexpected holiday. He needed to make every minute count.

Giving up on the faded print, he turned the pages, squinting at the scattered black-and-white photographs of the garden as it had looked fifty years ago. The booklet was the story of the initial creation of the garden, back in the 1970s, written in English by someone who appeared to have been a regular visitor, but not the owner. There was a picture on the next to last page of a vista over a mass of roses. Two women, tiny indistinct figures, stood close together in front of some small cypress trees. The owner and the author? There was no caption. He knew the trees were still there, although very much closer to the sky now.

On the last page was a detailed plan of the garden. Across the corner was an intriguingly scratchy signature, probably made with an old-fashioned fountain pen. The letters weren't clear, but Gideon thought the name might be Eleanor or Enid and the second name was Holmes. Was she one of the women?

Yawning again and giving up the struggle, Gideon put the pamphlet down on the bedside table, smoothing the cover so that it lay flat. It was a tantalising trifle – written to be given to visitors when the garden was open for viewing, perhaps? Tomorrow he'd buy a folder to protect it. Then he could take it out with him and read it in better light.

No! Gabriella De Stephano paced around the room in agitation. Instead of putting Il Giardino delle Rose on the market, the niece was engaging contractors to work on the house and gardens. Such gall, thinking that *she* could make herself at home there!

Gabriella crumpled the note from the investigator she had hired to keep her informed about what the fool lawyer was doing. This was major work, not simply cosmetic touches. *She intends to stay.*

Slightly alarmed to see that her hand was trembling, Gabriella dropped the note. She needed to be calm. Her physician warned her often, but this was enough to infuriate a saint. She had waited too long. She had been wary of swooping in too soon and her lawyer had urged caution, but now she could see her mistake. And it was not just the girl, with her misguided plans ...

Gabriella bent to retrieve the note. The investigator had found that there were at least two other offers to purchase already submitted. His source in the solicitor's office – probably some cleaning woman – had seen the papers. There was no way Il Giardino delle Rose would become a holiday home or a hotel! She crumpled the note again. She had been remiss. She had not expected the estate would attract so much interest so fast. Her approach must be made tomorrow. Her legal man would see to it. She would top anything that had already been offered.

She breathed in deeply. This idea of engaging workmen – how was the Morrison girl going to pay? Meagre savings? A loan?

If things were to become ... difficult.

Gabriella put her hands to her face, smiling slowly. A casual word in the right place – the merest hint, carefully dropped, that there was no money? She tapped her finger against her lips. It needed to be subtle. *Rumour soon spreads.*

She circled the room to pick up the phone. 'Signor Matarazzo? *Ciao.* I am well, thank you.' She turned, considering her reflection in a mirror on the wall, watching her smile grow. 'You remember we spoke about some redecorating? Would you be free to visit tomorrow? Ah ... That would be most kind.'

'It is quite inexplicable!' Signor Agnello was as affronted as he was confused. Affronted enough to bang his hand on the desk. 'All except one of the contractors I requested to estimate for the work on the villa and gardens inform me that they do not wish to tender for the work.' Agnello's expression showed what he thought of workmen who saw fit to decline an invitation from *him* to work for the Marchesa's heir.

'Er ...What about the one who didn't say no?' Megan asked. *Someone* had to be practical.

Signor Agnello's expression became even darker. He almost visibly puffed up with indignation. 'Ha! *That* gentleman will undertake to bid for the work, but requires an advance payment of half the estimated price before he will move onto the site!'

'Oh.' Megan was in uncharted waters, never having engaged tradesmen before. Clearly this was not the lawyer's idea of correct behaviour. 'Um ... this firm ... are they builders or gardeners? Are they any good?'

'Builders. And they are very good.' Signor Agnello was clearly pained to admit. 'They are the ones I would have recommended.'

'In that case, why not give them what they want?' Megan suggested gently. 'In the interests of progress?'

The lawyer considered for a moment, then nodded, visibly calming. 'That would be possible. But I will look *closely* into the contractor's financial situation, if he's in *such* need of money,' he cautioned grimly.

'I know I can leave it in your hands,' Megan said soothingly. It was all a bit odd, but maybe the contractors just didn't like the idea of working for an incomer? She frowned. 'I'm more worried about the garden, to be honest. Tommaso will do what he can, but I can almost *see* everything waking up and starting to grow in front of my eyes.' A week of mild weather and rain showers was turning her undergrowth into a jungle. 'None of the landscape people wanted the job?'

'No.' Signor Agnello was looking thoughtful. 'It is strange, considering the villa's pedigree.' He seemed to find something interesting on his desk for a moment, then he snapped back to attention. 'There would be no difficulty in retaining the contractors who did the clearing on the drive again. It is a very large firm with many maintenance contracts all along the coast,' he explained. 'But for the kind of work that is required? That needs the direction of someone who has skills and understanding – a true feeling for the garden.' He grinned suddenly. 'It is like the opera – there must be sympathy for the art.'

Megan made a mental note that Signor Agnello liked opera. She would get tickets and invite him and his wife, as a thank you for all that he was doing for her. She didn't know much about opera, but Ellery had said ... she squashed down quickly on Ellery's opinion that she needed to widen her interests and understanding. *That was when you were going to be the wife of the Head of Department and prospective Vice Chancellor.* The fragrant Julia, niece of the current Vice Chancellor, undoubtedly already knew about those things. Megan snapped her mind away from the past. No time to indulge her inner bitch. She had a jungle to tame.

She weighed up the options. The garden contractors had clearly been good with chainsaws and brush cutters, but even *she* could see that their achievements lacked finesse. Their speciality was clearance rather than restoration. Tommaso made his views known in heated mumbling. But if that was all she could get … thinking of the tangle around the villa, she made a snap decision. 'We'll try them, but we need someone who knows what they're doing to supervise. Can we get someone?'

'I will make further enquiries about freelancers, but the two companies I approached were recommended as the best in the area for this kind of work. I wonder …' He paused.

'Yes?' Megan prompted encouragingly.

'If there is a local difficulty, perhaps someone you know from England would be prepared to travel? It is, after all, a prestige project.' His face clouded yet again with the memory of being turned down by the local experts.

Megan chewed her lip. 'I don't know anyone personally. But I know someone who might.'

'Cassie.' She'd waited until she got back to her hotel room to phone. Her bags were packed. She would be checking out at noon to move to the villa. 'I need help – concierge service help – *again*. Yeah, I know.' She paced across the floor of her room and back again. 'At this rate you'd better set me up an account.' Quickly she outlined the problem and Signor Agnello's suggestion. 'You can get someone?'

'There are plenty of firms I can contact and I'm sure there will be someone,' Cassie responded briskly, all business.

Megan felt the flood of relief as tense muscles relaxed, but she really needed to stop running to Cassie for help. *On the other hand, this is how she earns her living.*

Cassie was still speaking, 'I have another idea though. I need to check with Jake and he's in London at meetings all day. Leave it with me. I'll ring you tonight about seven.'

At Signor Agnello's request Megan dropped into the office before going out to the villa, to sign some documents his secretary had prepared. At the bottom of the pile was a list of names and sums of money. Quite large sums of money.

'Offers to buy,' Agnello explained. 'For your information.'

'All developers?'

The lawyer nodded, then hesitated. 'The first three are.' He tapped the paper. 'These two are ambitious locals, trying their luck. This one—' he tapped the paper again '—the agent for a large global conglomerate. I understand they are assembling blocks of land in a number of prime locations.'

'And the villa is a prime location, even under a ton of undergrowth.' Megan sighed. 'What about the last one. A legal firm?'

Signor Agnello nodded, looking thoughtful. 'Acting for a client. It only came this morning. I am wondering ...' He broke off, waving his hand. 'It is no matter, as you are not intending to sell. I will inform them all.' He looked up with an astute glance. 'I don't think this is the last we will hear. All are respectable offers, but they will undoubtedly be expecting to improve them. They will assume that you are waiting for that.'

'Well, they can assume all they like. I'm not selling.'

Chapter Eleven

Megan spent most of the rest of the day transporting and unpacking her luggage and arranging delivery of her new car. She'd played safe and gone for a more upmarket version of the hire car she'd been driving. She tried not to think about landscapers or designers, and to stop wondering why Cassie had to talk to Jake. It wasn't easy.

In the late afternoon she walked the grounds with Tommaso, scoping the work that needed to be done. The old man was resigned to the return of the contractors. 'They're not so bad if you get someone to tell them what to do. They're hard workers,' he admitted. He showed touching faith that Dottoressa Morrison and her business friend from England would solve the problem of a designer. Megan wished she had his conviction. Even if Cassie found someone, would they be willing? And would they be the right fit?

Her stomach churned as she surveyed the grounds once more. She was an academic. She knew nothing about plants. Staring at a towering rose that seemed to be just a mass of thorns and dead leaves, she raised her chin, glaring at the spiky tangle. *You are a rose bush. You are not going to beat me.* If she had to, she'd work it out for herself, one bush at a time. The old gardener had shown her some of the weeding and pruning that he was doing and she'd got the basics, although the local accent sometimes made it difficult to communicate the finer points. *I am not giving this up.*

Pacing the salon at 6.45, waiting for the phone to ring, her resolve wavered. Outside the shadows were rapidly lengthening, making the garden a collection of darkly menacing shapes. *You really have no idea what you're doing.*

She paced some more and took a deep breath. She'd ferreted out facts about an unknown poet and chased down texts in libraries that no one expected her to find, including the eminent professor who had mentored her. Now she had to transfer that determination and persistence to this. *Bushes, trees, how hard can it be?* It would be better and easier with an expert, but if she had to go it alone, she would.

When the phone rang, it startled her into nearly dropping it. *Come on woman, get a grip.*

'Right.' Cassie sounded amused and triumphant. 'All sorted.'

'Yes?' Hope rose in Megan's chest.

'Obviously you'll want to talk to the guy, but Jake vouches for him.'
There was something that sounded suspiciously like a sigh. 'Gorgeous
Gideon, the answer to a maiden's prayer. Makes me wish I was still a
maiden.'

'Cassie!'

'Hmm. Yes, Gideon West. Tall, dark and handsome. Actually, make that
big, dark and handsome. Very big. Makes Jake look like a ten-stone
weakling.' Megan blinked. Jake was over six-foot with a physique to match.
'He does security work for the detective agency.'

Megan's heart, which had begun to lift, abruptly plummeted. 'Cass,' she
almost wailed. 'I need a gardener, not a bodyguard.'

'That's it. Gideon *is* a gardener. The security work is just a sideline. I
checked it all out with Jake. He has a shed-load of horticultural diplomas.
Used to work in the family business – horticultural nurseries – and they've
won gold medals all over the place, including the Chelsea Flower Show, but
there was a *very* nasty family bust-up and he's on the market. He needs a job.
Like I said, Jake vouches for him, *and* he says he's got a bit of a thing for
Riviera gardens.'

Megan began to hope again 'He sounds as if he might be okay,' she said
cautiously. 'I need to talk to him though. Would he be prepared to fly out to
see the place?'

'I'll give you his mobile number.' Now Cassie was laughing. 'But that's
actually the best bit. He's already in Portofino.'

Megan stretched luxuriously on her brand-new mattress. Light was coming in
at the edges of the shutters, but she could tell it was still early. The clock on
the bedside table said 6.10. The sun was coming up over the garden. A flicker
of apprehension shifted under her breastbone. *The garden.* As soon as it was
a civilised hour to do business, she would ring Gideon West. She looked at
the clock again – 6.11. She wouldn't be going back to sleep now, so she
might as well get up. She threw back the duvet, reaching for the long robe of
scarlet silk that Nadine had given her as a going away present; part of an
exclusive line stocked by her company that made designer beds.

Gathering her hair into a messy topknot and skewering it with a pencil
she found on the dressing table, she padded downstairs, hesitating at the
bottom. The first cup of coffee of the day was in the kitchen – that way – but
the early morning sunlight was calling her into the salon and the loggia

beyond. She chose the sunlight, unlocking the French doors and stepping out into a cool, clear morning.

She took a deep breath – the heavy fragrance of growing things. *Many growing things.* The undergrowth was creeping closer. She was being engulfed with thorns, like in some sort of fairy tale. She braced one hand on a marble pillar and leaned out to look, afraid that the path that Tommaso had cleared, so that they could at least walk the perimeter, was already in danger of being obliterated.

No, the path was still visible, although there were short tendrils of bramble encroaching onto it. She straightened up, suddenly alert to an unfamiliar noise. Something was moving on the path. Something much bigger than a bird. There was a blur of movement. One hand convulsed on the pillar. The other lifted involuntarily to her throat.

There was a giant running out of the undergrowth, straight towards her.

Chapter Twelve

Gideon's skidded to a stop at the sight in front of him.

A woman, standing next to a marble column engulfed with rampant ivy. She might have stepped out of a Victorian painting – some sumptuous canvas by Reynolds or Alma-Tadema. Luxuriant dark hair curled down around her face from a messily fastened top knot, framing delicate features. The flame-red silk robe clung around her, hinting at curves beneath—

Ahh! Abruptly Gideon jerked from fantasy to reality, cursing the mad impulse that had drawn him down a newly cleared path. This was *not* a painting.

You're trespassing. And you've probably scared the living daylights out of her.

Steadying himself with a deep breath, he took a slow pace forward. 'I'm sorry ... er ... *Mi scusi* ...' His tongue felt like it had swollen and stuck to the roof of his mouth. The woman's eyes, dark blue, were the size of saucers. She'd stepped down from the loggia, carefully gathering the folds of silk to avoid the eager rose thorns. A totally inappropriate part of Gideon's brain that was apparently still functioning just fine noted that the hint of curves had become more pronounced. *Do not go there!* '*Mi dispiace.* I really am sorry. I know I'm trespassing ...' His voice faltered. Unbelievably she was shaking her head … and laughing?

'Don't be.' Her smile was as glorious as her words were confusing. She held out her hand. 'I'm Megan Morrison. I think you must be Gideon West?'

'Mrs McQuire left me a message with your name and number, but she didn't explain why. I was going to ring you this morning.'

'And I was going to ring you too.'

He was sitting in a large, slightly shabby kitchen. His Victorian vision had changed into a much more practical hoodie and jeans – which still looked good on her – and offered him breakfast – a welcome mug of coffee and some crisp pastries delivered by a local girl called Maria who was now doing something with vegetables at the sink.

He'd apologised yet again and explained, with a degree of red-faced embarrassment, how he'd been drawn to the garden for his morning run, confirming that his presence *wasn't* as a result of a conversation with Cassie McQuire. Cassie had obviously described him, he reflected ruefully. Ms

Morrison led him through the house to the kitchen before hurrying off to dress, but she still hadn't enlightened him further about what she wanted.

Now she was nursing a mug and looking at him speculatively across the table. Her eyes really were a fascinating dark blue. From a distance, they almost looked black. He jerked himself away from his mental rambling and back to the shabby kitchen. 'Er ... why exactly did Mrs McQuire give you my number?'

She took a deep breath. It occurred to him that underneath the cool composure she might be a little anxious. He wasn't sure why that would be. *What the hell does she want?*

'Well, Mr West ...' She seemed to gather herself. 'It's like this – I just inherited this place from my great-great aunt. I'm a university lecturer, not a gardener. I need assistance with the jungle out there. Cassie suggested you.'

He listened as she explained, excitement rising. *She's offering you a job.* And not just any job – restoring, redesigning, replanting – the specialist work he loved. Handing him back his career. *All the stuff you thought you'd lost ... now she's letting you loose on that incredible garden.* His tongue was sticking to the roof of his mouth again, which was a good thing as it stopped him blurting out the only words that were in his head. *When can I start?*

She was looking at him expectantly. *Hopefully?* 'Cassie seemed to think you would be interested.'

'I would ... I am.' He got his tongue working enough to respond with something that sounded more or less coherent. Her face lit with a smile that could have made roses bloom in January. With an effort, Gideon dragged his mind back from fantasies involving red silk. *This is work. Concentrate.* Hard on that thought came another one – *you have to make sure she knows ...*

Realisation came with such a sense of loss that the mug in his hand wobbled. He put it down quickly. 'Mrs McQuire told you, about what happened with the family business?' he probed cautiously. 'I *can* get you references—'

'Cassie said that Jake vouched for you. She checked with him.'

Relief that he didn't have to pick over that pain with this woman hit Gideon with such force he felt momentarily lightheaded. *Thank you, Jake.* He reached for the coffee mug and took a sustaining swig. *And you will work your bloody socks off to prove that Jake was right to trust you. And that she can trust you.*

She was running through the proposed arrangements for contract labour and confirming that he had enough Italian to be able to supervise. She'd been candid with him over the puzzling reluctance of local firms to tender for the work. *Their loss. This is the job of your dreams.* He'd seen enough of the garden to know what he was taking on. *And to know that you can do it.* Even so, she was hiring him blind, on the recommendation of friends. She'd been honest and she deserved something in return. 'Why don't we try it for a month – see how things go?' he suggested.

A very slight frown between her straight brows melted away and he was glad he'd made the offer. She was proposing an official contract. He quashed a flicker of unease when she mentioned a solicitor. *Jake vouched for you.* His mind had been turning over practicalities. He would be freelancing. He'd need to find out any legal requirements for that and talk to his landlady about staying in the apartment. The sum that Ms Morrison proposed to pay him made that possible, as well as hiring a car.

Excitement and anticipation powered through him. He hadn't felt like this since … since the day he finally realised what was happening to the Nurseries. And everything that followed …

He pulled his mind back to the present. All of that was over. *Focus your mind on the here and now.* Ms Morrison was looking at him uncertainly. Had she seen something in his face? He rearranged his expression to look encouraging.

'There is one thing.' She swallowed, as if she was nervous. 'Um … I would like … as part of the job … I want lessons. I want to learn about gardening,' she finished in a rush.

'Oh.' He hadn't expected that. For a brief, confusing moment, he had the impression that Megan Morrison hadn't expected it either, which was absurd. It made sense. She was an academic who'd become the owner of a notable garden. She'd want to know more about caring for it. He respected her for making the request. 'I can do that,' he confirmed. He nodded his head towards the window. 'Seeing that lot out there, the more hands to help, the better.'

There was a pause before Ms Morrison nodded. He knew he was imagining it, but there was the suggestion of a flush at the base of her neck. *Imagination. No way is this cool, composed woman blushing.*

'Good. Fine.' She braced her hands on the table to stand up and Gideon rose quickly to follow suit. 'I think we have an agreement.' There was a muffled noise from the sink where Maria had finished preparing vegetables and was leaning against the drainer, sipping from a mug. The two women exchanged some sort of look and Ms Morrison smiled. 'Of course,' she confirmed, as if a conversation had taken place. 'Before you go, I need to take you to meet Tommaso.'

Gideon felt something in his stomach drop. It was jarring and unwelcome. *Naturally this glorious woman will have a man in her life.* 'Er … Tommaso … your husband?'

'Oh, no.' She turned to him with a wide grin. 'I'm not married. Tommaso was my aunt's head gardener. Shall we go and find him?

Megan led the way to the kitchen garden. She could feel Gideon West's large presence looming behind her on the path. *Gardening lessons! What the hell were you thinking?* She needed someone to tame the wilderness, not a tutor. *And this tutor?* Gorgeous Gideon. Cassie had not been wrong. *Since when is Cassie ever wrong about devastating men?* And now she'd asked him to teach her about gardening.

Megan dodged an incoming bramble, slightly disconcerted when a large and well-muscled arm reached over her shoulder to hold it out of her way. *Muscles – No!* She had to remember that, good-looking or not, Gideon West was *not* her type. She was all about brains not brawn – someone like Ellery was her ideal man. *And look how well that turned out.*

She concentrated on keeping her footing on the slightly slippery path. Mr West was an impressive specimen, *but* really, *gardening lessons?* She straightened her spine. It was a good idea. She needed to learn, *wanted* to learn. *Nothing to do with how good Gideon West looks in his casual running gear. Nothing at all.*

They found Tommaso in the dilapidated greenhouse at the end of the garden. After a cautious exchange of courtesies between the two men, it was agreed that Mr West would return in the morning to talk further. Today he had an appointment to keep. After that, they would both confirm that they wanted to go ahead.

Megan felt a small flicker of apprehension. *Come on, the guy admitted he was drawn to the place. He's not going to turn you down.*

Arrangements made, they retraced their steps, Gideon to resume his run and Megan to go back to the kitchen. She resisted the temptation to watch as he jogged away. She needed more coffee. *Strong coffee.*

When she got inside, she found that Maria had brewed a fresh pot. Megan fell on it gratefully.

'Signor West.' Maria gave a saucy giggle. 'He is very ... dishy.' She rolled her eyes suggestively. Megan tried to look disapproving but couldn't manage it.

'Yes, he *is* dishy,' she admitted. She'd noted that a lot of Maria's English slang was rather dated, picked up from Olwen no doubt. 'But I think these days the expression would probably be "fit".'

Maria shrugged. 'That too. Like the actor Chris Hemsworth.' She rolled her eyes again. 'Except Mr West is so very dark. Also, he is very big.' She gestured with a soapy hand.

'As long as he knows his way around a garden, it doesn't really matter what he looks like.' When Maria treated her to a sceptical glance, Megan picked up her mug and stalked off to coax hot water out of the elderly shower in the main bathroom.

Megan spent the rest of the day in the library, sorting through the first of the cases of books that had been delivered from storage. She'd hoped there would be plans and history of the garden, but there were only novels, biographies and memoirs.

She sat back on her heels with a frustrated sigh, glaring at the remaining boxes. Whoever had packed them – the storage company, she assumed – had not labelled the contents. Any one of them could hold the records ... *or none of them.*

She was trying to find her way through fog. Both sets of lawyers had worked for her aunt for decades, but neither firm had been in place when the villa and its garden were created. Maria was too young to know. Tommaso had not come to work at the villa until after Olwen's son died, but he had recalled the young man's name – Cosimo. *Another Cosimo?*

'Who were you, Olwen? Where did you go when you ran away if it wasn't here? How did you come to make this place? What happened to your son? Is there really a connection between the "Cosimo" poems and the tower?'

Megan shivered a little as she realised she'd spoken aloud. The questions hovered in the still air of the dimly lit room. Outside the sun had gone. It was getting difficult to see and the room was growing cold. She reached for the sweater that she had removed while shifting books onto shelves. A new heating system was high on the list of renovations. She'd been here with the books long enough for today. *Only six more cases to go.*

She grabbed the last bundle of sorted volumes, selecting *The Enchanted April* and *Under the Tuscan Sun* to take up to her room, to read about other women and their Italian villas. She carried the remainder over to the shelves, running a finger over the spines. Her aunt's life was a mystery, but maybe there was someone local who knew something?

Chapter Thirteen

Gideon dressed carefully for his date with Megan Morrison. *Not date – business meeting.* His suit was OTT but the dark jeans, blue shirt and tie, and black jacket struck the right note. *You hope.*

He'd put together a small portfolio of the work he'd done since arriving on the Riviera – it was only photographs and drafts of a couple of articles, but it would be something to show that he knew what he was doing. His qualification certificates were with his other belongings in storage. The medals and trophies had gone with the Nurseries. He could no longer lay claim to those anyway. For a second a twist of bitterness took his breath, but he pushed it away. *No sense in dwelling on what's gone.* This job was something new.

Collecting the items for the portfolio, he hesitated over the brochure about the villa garden, then left it where it was. Ms Morrison would undoubtedly have copies and probably the original plans. Realising that he had bought this while trespassing on the estate … well, it might look just a little bit creepy.

Arriving at the villa by the front door this time, he was admitted by a grinning Maria who led him to a room at the end of the hall, opened the door and ushered him in. The space was clearly intended to be a library, although it was currently mostly empty shelves and packing cases. Ms Morrison was on her knees, scrabbling in one of the cases. She looked up when he stepped into the room, irritation clear on every line of her face, and made to get to her feet. Without thinking, Gideon held out his hand to help. Their fingers connected with a jolt that ran up his arm. Her skin was warm and soft, and her hand felt small in his calloused paw. Taking a deep breath, he made sure she was steady on her feet before letting go. 'I'm sorry, am I too early? Only Maria brought me in—'

'No, it's okay.' She looked around the room and he realised, with relief, that her irritation *wasn't* directed at him. 'I was hoping that there were records of the garden in this lot, but I haven't found anything so far. I thought maybe this box … there are gardening books, but they're old.' She pointed to a side table. Gideon went to look and she followed him. 'That one talks about statues and structure – not so much about flowers. The other one is a "how to" guide. Lots of plant lists.'

Gideon picked the books up – Edith Wharton's *Italian Villas and Their Gardens* and Cecil Middleton's *Mr Middleton Suggests*. 'These are vintage – classics. The Wharton might be useful for the hard landscaping, if your aunt used it as a reference. Mr Middleton was a popular gardener in the 1930s and 40s. He did broadcasts and articles in the Second World War about Dig for Victory.'

Ms Morrison nodded. 'That makes sense, something dating from the war.' She reached up to push her hair off her face. Gideon tried not to notice the interesting things that did to the clinging qualities of a fine wool sweater. The implications of what she'd just said abruptly filtered through. 'You're looking for records? You don't have anything?'

'If I have, I haven't found them yet.' She gave her hair a ruthless shove and let out a long, frustrated breath. 'I'm going to have to tell you the whole story, Mr West. Shall we go to the salon and I'll rustle up some coffee?'

It wasn't quite the formal meeting that he'd been expecting. He'd hoped for coffee, but he hadn't expected the slice of family history that Megan Morrison related. 'Wow!' He shook his head, when *Dr* Morrison finished her recital of how she came to inherit the house. 'That's … amazing. And you don't know anything about your aunt's past?'

'Very little. I didn't even know that she was still alive … until after she wasn't.' For an instant, a desolate expression crossed her face. 'And I don't have anything to guide us over what the hell is out there.' She waved towards the window.

Gideon grimaced. He *should* have brought the pamphlet with him. He was going to have to come clean about what he knew. 'Er ... actually ... I have.'

The blue eyes widened – astonishment mixed with a trace of something that might be suspicion. Quickly he explained about the books and the pamphlet, managing, he hoped, to gloss over the stalker-ish elements. Surprisingly, it was the books that she fixated on, a spark of excitement in her eyes.

'Poetry, in Italian and English, blue leather binding, about this big?'

He nodded. *What is this?* When she explained about her thesis, he understood. 'It's a link between the poems and the tower.'

'Yes and no.' She frowned, clearly thinking. 'The fact that they were bundled together suggest that they came from the same place – *this* place, but it's not conclusive. Do you think the bookseller, your landlady, knows more?'

'She might. She seemed to accept that they belonged together – but she said that your aunt was an American and she wasn't, so I don't know how reliable any information would be.'

'I'd like to talk to her, even so.' She gestured, as if refocusing herself. 'The garden comes first though. Can we use the plan and the booklet for renovations?'

'If it's all we have. It's quite detailed.' *And written with love.* He didn't voice that thought. *She really would think you were weird.* 'Have you paper and pen – I can draw a rough outline.'

Once the necessities were found, he sketched what he remembered. 'There were a lot of roses but also other shrubs and bushes, and statuary and a couple of follies – a little round temple like the one at La Mortola. It would be good to get an expert to look at the statues. Some of them might be old and possibly valuable. They might want repairs and cleaning. And the estate is circled by chestnut trees. Some of them are older than the garden and some near the road need attention.' He indicated on the plan. 'You could get an arboricultralist to inspect.'

'We'll have one of those. What else?'

'Well …' He considered the plan. It was something he thought that *he* would do if he ever had the chance, and now he did. 'I know you want to restore, but a garden moves on – it *ought* to move on. There will be things that have died or are not worth saving. You might want to try something new.'

'Like?'

'New plants and new groupings. Maybe leaving some parts a little wild.' He grinned. 'Not as wild as it is *now*, but you could create habitat for wildlife and insects, pollinators.'

'That sounds good.' She was leaning over the plan, looking completely absorbed. Gideon caught a hint of her perfume – lily of the valley? He gritted his teeth and forced himself to concentrate. He hadn't felt an attraction like this since Lucy – the memory acted like a shower of cold water full in the face. *Boundaries.* He had to set them and keep them. *This is the chance to be part of something awesome. Do not screw it up.*

Megan watched Gideon lope off in the direction of the kitchen garden to talk to Tommaso. He moved well for such a big man and the rear view was … enticing. When he'd taken her hand to help her up from the packing case, there had been a distinct frisson over her skin. She was pretty sure he'd felt it too.

She blew out a breath. Gideon West was an attractive male. It was a relief, after Ellery, that her hormones were sitting up and taking notice. *But Gideon West has something you want more than you might want his body.* He was the key to restoring her inheritance. And he was committed. He'd been tentative, but it was obvious that the garden had worked its subtle magic on him too. And now there was that tantalising connection to the "Cosimo" poems. Reluctantly, she pushed the quiver of academic excitement into the compartment of her mind marked "later". Her academic career was currently on hold. She hadn't yet decided how she was going to revive it, but right now there were more pressing concerns, most of which had thorns.

And there were five more boxes waiting for her in the library.

When she walked around to the kitchen garden two hours later, sent by Maria to call Tommaso to lunch, she found Gideon too. Minus jacket and tie, with what looked like a piece of clean sacking protecting the smart blue shirt, he was helping the old man do something with tiny plants in the greenhouse.

She stood for a moment unseen, watching them work together efficiently and companionably. Tommaso made a remark and Gideon laughed. Megan felt something low in her stomach contract. *Just hormones.* She dropped her eyes from his face to watch his hands. Large hands, teasing out the seedlings – long, deft fingers … an embarrassingly strangled sound came out of her throat that she just managed to turn into a cough before they both swivelled round to look at her. 'Uh … Lunch. You're welcome to join us, Mr West.'

'Oh!' He looked at his watch. 'I didn't realise. I should have left ages ago.'

Megan made a never mind gesture. 'We can talk some more after we eat.'

The meal – pasta with a vegetable and herb sauce of Maria's own devising – was a casual affair, taken around the kitchen table, with Gideon and Tommaso attempting to identify the individual herbs that had gone into the dish and Maria teasing and pretending not to understand – *just like family.* The thought came to Megan with jolt. She hadn't had a family meal since her gran died.

Disconcerted, she caught Gideon's eye across the table and something inside shifted again. *Brawn not brain?* After their discussion this morning, it was becoming clear that Gideon West possessed both. She clenched her fist a little harder around her fork.

Beard. You don't fancy men with beards.

Once the meal was over, the men disappeared again. Gideon was accompanying Tommaso, in his disreputable old truck, to buy the old man a new wheelbarrow. Megan went out to the loggia, listening until she heard the truck leave before returning to help Maria finish the washing up.

'They do well together,' Maria observed as she passed over a plate to be dried. 'This is good,' she decided. Megan waited for some remark about the dishy Mr West, but it didn't come.

With a sigh, Megan went back to the library.

She'd just emptied another box when Gideon tapped on the door and handed over a brown paper parcel. 'For me? What is it?' Gideon just grinned. She unwrapped it, uncovering a pair of heavy-duty gardening gloves and a set of secateurs in an eye-popping shade of Schiaparelli pink. 'Didn't they have anything brighter?' The taunt was out before she even thought.

'Nope.' He shook his head. 'Method in the madness – if you put them down in the jungle out there, you stand a chance of finding them again.' He leaned casually against the door frame. 'If it's okay with you, I'll come back tomorrow with the pamphlet and we can plan how you want to organise everything.' He gave her a reassuring smile. 'It's going to be a lot of work, but it's doable. You can see the skeleton there.'

'You might. To me it looks like something out of Sleeping Beauty.'

'We'll dial down the fairy-tale elements,' he promised. 'And tomorrow you can have your first gardening lesson.'

'That … that would be … great.' It *would*. There was no reason for that thought to make her face match the colour of the gloves.

Chapter Fourteen

She'd been working for an hour and had pruned a large chunk of a rose
growing near the house, carefully cutting it back so it no longer overhung the
path. Determined to prove to … someone – *herself?* – that the gardening
lessons were not a way of seeking Gideon's company, she'd resisted the
impulse to pounce on him as soon as he arrived, waiting for him to suggest it.
He'd chosen this rose for her to start on, patiently indicated the right place to
snip, until she got the hang of it. He said it was an old variety with pink
blooms called Fantin Latour. To her, it was a jumble of branches with a few
scabby leaves and old desiccated buds. Sad and sorry for itself.

'Will it really revive and grow again?' she asked doubtfully.

Gideon shrugged. 'We'll see what happens. If it doesn't perk up it can be
replaced.'

Megan pouted. Now that she'd invested time and care she wanted the
rose to recover. With the old wood cut away she fancied it *did* look better.
Almost as if the branches were heaving a sigh of relief to be freed from their
congested tangle. She grinned. Never mind identifying with the garden, now
she was getting emotionally involved with a rose bush! She stepped back to
assess what she'd achieved and where she was going next, when a large
raindrop flopped onto a dead leaf in front of her, then another.

Gideon looked at the sky. 'Heavy shower on the way. Good idea to stop
now anyway. Too much too soon will give you blisters, even with gloves.'

Now that he'd drawn attention to it, she could feel the first tingling
soreness and see that the rain was about to come down in earnest. They ran
for the loggia, just making it, breathless and laughing, as the heavens opened.
Megan slipped off the gloves and inspected her fingers, seeing patches of
slightly reddened skin. Gideon held out his own hands, showing her the
work-worn calluses. 'You can do some more tomorrow,' he suggested. 'You
know what to do now.'

'I will. Thank you.' They stood for a moment in the dimness of the
loggia, with the rain pelting down outside. Megan knew she was smiling.
Something that she recognised as contentment was stealing through her. *And
something else?* Gideon was watching her face, gauging her expression. Her
chest suddenly felt constricted. Here, sheltered by the marble pillars, with a
curtain of rain obscuring the garden, everything seemed strangely suspended,
cocooned in an enclosed, breathless space.

Megan let out a long, slow sigh. Gideon West was like no man she had ever known before. She'd never been so close to anything this *big*. She was a tall woman; with most men she was virtually eye to eye. Gideon made her feel small and fragile. The muscles in his arms, bunched under the short sleeves of a black T-shirt, were hard and solid. His eyes were dark brown; warm and serious, with the envy-making eyelashes that seemed to be obligatory for any attractive male. He was smiling and it was doing something strange to her stomach. She had a crazy urge to put up a hand and touch the smiling mouth, to test the softness of the neatly trimmed beard. *Never kissed a man with a beard.* For a second, she had a dizzying sensation of what it would be like if she just leaned forward … Her hand was reaching up; she really wasn't sure what for—

Maria stuck her head out of the French windows. 'Your special delivery has come.' She disappeared again.

Megan felt a full body shiver run through her. *What the hell?*

'You're cold.' There was concern in Gideon's voice and warmth in the brown eyes. 'You should go in.'

'Yes,' she agreed shakily. 'Er ... I ordered some gardening books.' She hoped she wasn't blushing. Wanting to gain skills was nothing to be ashamed of and books were her thing. *Although there is a lot to be said for hands-on lessons.* She pushed the idea away. There had been absolutely *no* hands-on, and she was *not* giving headroom to regret over that. She'd spent most of yesterday evening on her laptop, searching and ordering, and had paid the premium to have the results sent by express delivery. 'I realised yesterday, when you said about making changes in the garden. I'm not just a caretaker here.'

'It's your garden now. You can put your stamp on it.'

'I know.' She hadn't thought of it though, until he'd put it in front of her. 'I need to know what my stamp is. Books are one way of finding out. Do you want to come and see?'

They were in the salon, surrounded by cardboard wrappers and empty mugs, leafing through the books Megan had chosen. 'This one is good.' Gideon held out a coffee-table size volume. 'It's got a lot about taking on an established garden, with pictures and plans.' It was a new publication. He'd read the glowing reviews but hadn't had money to buy it himself.

He watched now as Megan's dark head bent over the glossy pages. He hadn't sat like this, looking for inspiration – that spark that would set off a chain of ideas – since Lucy. The sharp indrawn breath caught at the thought. *This woman is not Lucy.* He wouldn't, *couldn't*, go down that road again. The pull of attraction he felt for Megan Morrison was getting confused in his mind with emotions that were dead and buried. For a moment out there, on the loggia, he'd wanted to kiss Dr Morrison. The idea that she might have been leaning towards him for that very same purpose was absurd. This was *Dr* Morrison and his employer. He was tangling her in his mind with Lucy, and that was a disaster waiting to happen. *You need this job too much to screw it up.*

'This plan.' The woman who was employing him looked up, showing him the open page. 'It's not unlike the one you drew yesterday, for what's out there. Maybe there are some ideas here.'

'Could be.' He looked around for the document case he'd brought with him and stood up to retrieve it from a console table near the door. 'Talking of plans, I brought the book.'

He extracted it carefully and passed it over. Megan took it as if he had handed her a rare Fabergé egg. She slid it out of its protective folder, carefully turning the pages. 'This is amazing. Descriptions, plant lists.' She stopped at the picture of the two women standing by the trees, running her finger over the image with a slightly puzzled look.

'I think that might be the owner – your aunt – and maybe the other woman is the one who wrote this?' Gideon said. 'It's not clear enough to make out their faces. The plan is at the back and there's a signature.' He pointed it out as Megan turned the page. 'I was wondering if that was the name of the writer – Eleanor, or maybe Enid – Holmes?

Megan turned the page and read the signature. She looked up now, face drained of colour. 'It's not either of those – it's Eluned. Eluned Holmes was my great grandmother.'

Chapter Fifteen

'I'm sorry.' Gideon wasn't sure exactly what he was apologising for, or why, but the shocked and confused look in Dr Morrison's eyes seemed to make it necessary. 'I didn't realise—'

'How were you to know?' She brushed his words aside. 'I don't understand.' She was clutching the booklet with what looked like an iron grip. Gideon couldn't help himself; he leaned forward to gently disentangle her fingers. 'Oh!' She looked down at her hands. 'Thank you, I mustn't damage it.' She laid it carefully down on the table beside the books, visibly pulling herself together. 'This is weird. How did this get here, with my great grandmother's signature on it? Does it mean that she was here?' She shook her head. 'As far as I know she never travelled abroad. She'd never been out of Wales.'

'As far as you know.' He shifted a little, leaning slightly closer to where she sat on the floor. 'When did she die? Do you remember her?'

'Not clearly. I was about ten, but she'd been in a care home for a while – dementia. It was a nice place. My grandmother used to visit. She took me with her sometimes, but Eluned didn't really know who I was.' She leaned back, brow furrowed in thought. 'If she did come here to visit her sister, I'm sure my grandmother didn't know, but that might explain something that was a bit of a puzzle. When Eluned died, I helped my gran clear the house – that's how I got the poems. It was the family home, but it was never sold to pay care fees. There was a health insurance that covered everything. Gran assumed it was something to do with her father's job.'

'You think your aunt set it up?'

'She had the money and they *were* twins, though not identical.' She pushed her hair away from her face in a gesture he was beginning to recognise. 'I don't understand any of it.' She puffed out her lower lip.

'If it's capable of being unravelled, you'll do it – in the meantime, we have the plan and the description of the garden.' He tapped the pamphlet, forcing himself not to think about that lower lip. 'We need to decide how to use it.'

Yawning, Megan looked over at the clock. Ten p.m. She reached to switch off the lamp beside her chair. Gideon had left the precious booklet with her when he left for an appointment to view a garden further down the coast.

She'd read the whole thing. It felt strange to hold something in her hands signed by her great grandmother, which might have been written by her – the visitor from England. She peered at the photograph of the two women. The features were too indistinct to be sure of anything, even when looking through a magnifying glass that she'd found in a drawer. The pamphlet was an account of the making of the garden in the 1970s. She'd done some calculations. Her great-great grandfather was still alive then. He'd died four days before his ninety-fifth birthday, and by all accounts was still as stiff-necked and unrelenting as he'd always been. He would have been a good reason to keep visits to Italy a secret. Not for Olwen's sake but maybe for her sister – who still had to live with him?

Megan returned the brochure to its folder and laid it carefully on the table to return to Gideon when he started work – which would be as soon as the contractors could be organised. It had been a surprising and tiring day. She flexed her fingers, aware of the slight stiffness from holding the secateurs too tightly. The sense of achievement was partly overlaid by that strange interlude on the loggia. Had she *really* come close to kissing Gideon West? If she had, then it wouldn't happen again. Nothing could mess up their business arrangement. It was too important.

He gave her a confidence that she hadn't even realised she was missing, but now she felt she could really make something of the place she'd inherited. She'd been *happy* pruning that rose, doing something that was productive, something that mattered, even if it was only half a rosebush. She still felt the residue of that happiness, despite the puzzling uncertainty that followed. Working together they could restore the garden. It was a strange feeling but reassuring.

Il Giardino delle Rose is yours now.

Chapter Sixteen

Megan sat on the lawn, carefully clipping overgrown stalks from the lavender and rosemary bushes that edged it. The sun was warm on her back, and bees were buzzing around the plants, heralding spring. Snipping away, Megan wondered if Olwen had tended the plants like this. On impulse she'd telephoned Mr Gifford. Under the pressure of a direct question, he'd admitted knowledge of the health insurance. That was all he could or would admit. Megan suspected it was both. Client confidences clearly went to the grave – theirs and his – but he wouldn't have known the things she really wanted to find out – the personal things. For now, her curiosity had to be confined to what they were uncovering in the garden.

In the three weeks that Gideon had been supervising a small crew of the contractors' most experienced men, he'd already worked wonders. Lopping, pruning and grubbing out bramble roots and dead bushes were already opening up the paths leading to the centre of the garden. Glimpses of statues and a small round temple – a folly – were tantalisingly visible. She'd got in touch with a university contact, and an authority on sculpture was standing by to make an inspection if and when they turned up something that looked suitably old. Under advice from the arboriculturalist, specialist workmen were attending to the chestnut and hazel trees. A large wood chipper had been installed at the bottom of the drive, dealing noisily with debris. Tommaso *loved* the wood chipper.

Spending her evenings between library packing cases and her new books, which now had their own shelf, the garden was on her mind almost 24/7. If they could—

She jerked out of her thoughts when a large bee almost blundered into her face. Megan waved it away, laughing. With the arrival of the builders inside the house and the weather improving, Megan found herself increasingly taking refuge in the garden. The space simply called to her. She had to resist the temptation to shadow Gideon as he worked. *Like an overenthusiastic Labrador pup.* She tried to have more dignity, but if she could find somewhere out of the way and unnoticed to sit and watch …

When she asked, and sometimes when she didn't, Gideon showed her what he was doing and explained why. Mostly it was basic clearance, with barrow loads of branches making their way to feed the chipper. She sighed. Gideon West had rapidly made himself indispensable. Maria and Tommaso were complete fans and, at Maria's insistence, he usually ate lunch with them. Mr West had established his very large booted feet very firmly under the kitchen table. Megan resolutely ignored the mocking voice that whispered about boots under the bed, bending again to the lavender bush.

Gideon watched the dead branch come down exactly as it was meant to, in a smooth, controlled glide. There was a ragged cheer from the work gang as it reached the ground with a soft but satisfying thud. Gideon grinned, nodding congratulations as hands reached to unfasten ropes. Leaving the crew to finish tending to the tree and the clear-up, Gideon headed back to the main garden, relieved that the job was done. He'd noticed the branch overhanging the road, threatening vehicles passing underneath, and had pulled the gang off their systematic progress through the woodland belt to deal with it.

Once he emerged from the shadow of the trees, blinking slightly, he headed back to the place he'd been working yesterday – the path with the nymph. When he got there, he found that Matteo, the gang foreman, had taken up where he'd left off, and was standing with Megan, looking at the newly uncovered statue. Her plinth had subsided a little more, giving the nymph an even tipsier look.

'I can see what you mean.' Megan greeted him as he came up behind them. 'She does look as if she might have had a glass too many.' Matteo roared with laughter then, one eye on the boss, excused himself and began work on one of the cross paths.

'It's the way she's tipped forward. When she's straightened up, she should get her dignity back.' Gideon moved closer, reaching to carefully peel off a small strand of ivy. 'It would be good to get your expert to take a look at her, but I don't think she's old – not an antiquity.'

Megan was considering the statue with a critical eye. 'She's a goddess, not a nymph,' she decided. 'I wonder which one?'

'Flora?' Gideon suggested.

Megan was still studying the statue. 'There's no coronet of flowers. And look.' She pointed to an object nestling at the statue's feet. 'I think that's an old-fashioned scale.'

Gideon peered closer. Now he could see the classic beam and chained pans of an old-style balance scale. 'I think you're right. And that's a sword, half hidden by the drapes. I think she's Justitia, the goddess of justice.' He frowned. 'Unusual choice for a garden.'

'It is.' Megan turned to look at him, her eyes troubled. 'If she's not old, maybe she was commissioned? But why?'

For a second, the light dimmed as a cloud skidded over the sun.

Gabriella De Stefano paced across the room. Outside the windows spring sunshine sparkled on a deep blue sea, but the view meant nothing to her. Now, as well as that fool employed by the Morrison woman, her own lawyer had proved himself an idiot. Instead of making a generous offer for the property, as instructed, the imbecile had taken it on himself to substitute what he claimed was a reasonable sum ... and seemed puzzled when it met with a flat refusal! Of course it was refused. The man had no concept of value that made price irrelevant, but the Morrison woman clearly did. She was holding out for more. She would get it, but now there was delay and muddle while the lawyers did their dance of negotiations.

Gabriella looked down to find that she had a crumpled flower in her hand. She had removed it from the display to reposition it just before the lawyer telephoned. The limp petals and broken stem were of no use now. Impatiently, she dropped the wreckage into a waste bin. She circled the room, skirt swishing. Not only had the Morrison woman turned down her offer – she had also enticed workmen to the villa. The builder would no doubt regret his greed when he found that the money he had demanded up-front was *all* the money. It had to be, but the Morrison woman was obviously adroit. Gabriella paused in her pacing to consider that. Much cleverer than she had expected – clever and devious. She had found labour for the garden and another foreigner to oversee it. She had even set in train a rumour, no doubt via her lawyer, that she actually intended to *live* there.

Gabriella slowed her step, conscious of her fast-beating heart. Her doctor would complain ... another idiot, but even so ...

She sank down onto a gold brocade sofa, folding her hands in her lap and breathing deeply until her heartbeat calmed. Maybe it was no bad thing. Let Dottoressa Morrison expend her time and money. Both would run out soon. She would need to return to work. A small smile lifted Gabriella's mouth. What was the saying – Catch-22? With no job and no money Morrison could not keep working on the villa. To get money the villa must be sold. Unless the woman tried to trammel herself with loans ... Gabriella shook her head. She would not contemplate that. Her offer to purchase would be too generous to be resisted. Il Giardino delle Rose *would* be sold.

Gabriella smoothed a crease from the fine fabric of her skirt. She was too impatient. All would be well. Megan Morrison would go back to England to her university and to the errant fiancé, who would no doubt soon return to a wealthy woman.

Gabriella tapped her steepled forefingers against her lips. *The fiancé.* Could that be encouraged? Did the man realise the extent of the inheritance?

She reached for the phone.

'Ur ... I don't know, Signora De Stefano ...' The doubt in Brown's voice was audible, even over the telephone. 'I can't just pitch up to the bloke – I mean approach him – and ask him if he knows his ex-girlfriend has come into money.'

'You don't have to.' She took a deep breath, searching for patience. Was she entirely surrounded by idiots? 'The man may already be aware.' *But not perhaps the* amount *of money involved.* 'You are more subtle than that. You tell him you are a freelance reporter, trying to contact Dottoressa Morrison about her wonderful legacy – inheriting a *very* valuable estate in Italy from an unknown relative – it is a good human interest story. It will serve, whether he knows or not.'

'Well ...' She could almost hear the cogs turning in his brain. 'I suppose I could do that. Yeah.' He brightened up. 'That would work.'

'I'm sure it will,' she reassured with gritted teeth. 'Stress the value of the estate. You don't have to do anything else. I believe we can trust Ellery Peters to do the rest.'

'And payment?'

'The same rate as before. Let me know when it is done.'

Gabriella put the phone down gently, ending the call and leaning back against the sofa cushions. When it was brought home to Peters that his former fiancée was sitting on a fortune, would an ambitious man let a chance like that slip through his fingers? Especially if certain *opportunities* were put his way? And when Megan Morrison realised that she had the means to get her fiancé back ...

Gabriella smiled. A simple and workable plan. All that was required was the right setting and that little extra incentive.

'Good evening, Signor West.' Alcinda Zabarella darted across the cobbled square to fall into step beside Gideon, narrowly avoiding two skateboarders who bucketed noisily out of a side alley. Today she was the complete street urchin in paint-stained dungarees, her hair piled up under a baseball cap. 'All finished for the week?' She grinned as they strode between the lines of shops. The streets were more crowded now that the weather was warming. 'Signora Bertolo said you have a job at Il Giardino delle Rose.'

'Yes,' Gideon agreed. His landlady was obviously spreading the word.

'And you will bring the garden back to what it was.'

Gideon laughed. 'Well, not single-handedly, but that's the general idea.'

Alcinda made a gentle humming noise, slanting a sideways look up at him. 'You know, don't you?'

'Know what?'

'The garden in my paintings is the garden at the villa.'

'And that you must have trespassed there?' He nodded. 'I do.'

'Mmmm.' She hummed a little louder, exchanging a wave with a woman standing in the doorway of one of the shops. 'And now you will spoil it.' She pouted. 'You will make it all manicured and tame again, for the old lady.'

Gideon was too diverted by the last part of the sentence to question the manicured and tame bit. 'What old lady?'

'The new owner, of course.'

'She's not an old lady,' he protested. 'Late twenties, I think. What made you assume she was old?'

'Oh.' Alcinda was clearly reassessing the new information. 'She's the niece, yes? Of the former owner? She was *very very* old. We thought it would be another old American lady.'

'She's not old and she's not American. She just wants to restore the garden to what it was. And maybe make it even better.'

Alcinda looked sceptical. Clearly in her view brambles and thorns were "better".

They were nearing the gallery. Alcinda darted away again, walking backwards to call out, 'I haven't forgotten that I'm going to paint you, Gideon West. You can come here, to my studio in Camogli at 10 a.m. on Sunday.' Gideon reached up quickly to catch the business card she threw to him. 'Be there.' She pointed a demanding finger before swinging round to disappear through the door of the gallery.

Grinning, Gideon carried on down to the harbour and along the narrow street lined with shops and restaurants, to reach his building. It was early, but there were already diners at water-side tables. Friday night brought weekenders off the sumptuous yachts moored in the harbour, early-season tourists and locals celebrating the end of the working week. It had been a shock to find that it was Friday – he was not expected at the villa for two whole days. Tomorrow he would shop for essentials, do laundry, catch up on neglected emails and make up his notes

On Sunday it appeared he was going to Camogli.

He found the place quite easily. It was at the very top of a narrow building with six floors. Pausing on the last flight of stairs, he could hear raised voices from above. He halted at the open door of the studio space – a big open room spreading across the whole of the top floor, with wide north facing windows. Alcinda was sitting cross-legged on top of a battered metal filing cabinet, with hunched shoulders and an expression like a sulky kitten. Her sister was shrugging herself into her jacket with short, jerky movements. The raised voices had clearly been an argument.

'Er ... Should I—'

'Oh!' Bianca turned, forcing a smile. She snatched up her handbag and slung it over her shoulder. '*Buongiorno*, Signor West, please come in. I was just leaving.'

Despite the invitation, Gideon remained awkwardly in the doorway, disconcerted at the uncharacteristic emotion in Bianca's face and voice.

'Running away.' Alcinda taunted from her perch. 'I don't care what you think, sister dear. I'm going to that party.'

'Not if you can't behave yourself,' Bianca shot back. She made a repudiating gesture. 'There's no way that you're going to get those paintings back. Cousin Gabriella *bought* them.'

'Bought them to hide them away, so no one would see them!' Alcinda uncoiled herself and slid to the edge of the cabinet. Resting one foot on a drawer handle, she jumped down with practised twist of her body, stalking towards her sister. 'It's not just those canvases. You *know* what that woman did.'

'Alcinda! For heaven's sake! You can't still believe that Gabriella De Stefano *murdered* her secretary.'

Chapter Seventeen

There was a long moment of silence while the sisters faced each other down. Bianca broke the spell, gathering herself together and moving towards the door. 'I'm not even trying to talk to you in this mood. My apologies, Signor West.' She brushed past him on her way out. 'Perhaps this is not a good time for you to sit for my sister.' She clattered off down the uncarpeted stairs, leaving Gideon and Alcinda staring at each other.

'Well.' Gideon tried not to sound confused, judgmental and curious as hell. 'Is it? Shall I go?'

'No!' Alcinda shook her head. Now that Bianca was gone the anger had drained out of her face. She looked tired, her eyes heavy with the suggestion of unshed tears. She scooped up a sketch pad and dropped it and a couple of pencils into a small backpack, dragging a battered leather flying jacket off a peg. 'Let's go and walk on the beach.'

It was a dank and murky morning, with a haze of fog lying over the sea. The beach was almost deserted. They walked together for a while, crunching over the pebbles without speaking, until Alcinda broke the silence. 'You can ask, you know.' She slanted a sideways glance up at him in a way that he was coming to recognise.

'O-kay.' He took a breath. 'Why do you think your cousin murdered her secretary?'

'I don't know.' Alcinda's voice was flat without its usual teasing note. 'No one else does. It was written off as an accident.' She waved a hand. 'Long story.'

'I have plenty of time.'

Alcinda was looking up at him again. She crossed to a large rock and sat on it. Gideon followed to lean beside her.

'You're a patient man, Gideon West. Remarkably restful.'

Gideon wasn't quite sure that it was a compliment. Alcinda looked out at the foggy sea.

'You could start by telling me who Cousin Gabriella is?' he suggested.

'Hmm.' Alcinda narrowed her eyes. 'Our grandmothers were sisters – so we're cousins removed, or something. Gabriella is the posh side of the family – or thinks she is. She married old money. Second wife – he was *much* older. Widow now, mid-fifties. They lived for a long while in the Caribbean, but he endowed a cultural institute in Genoa before he died, so he has a big local reputation. She lives in a huge palazzo outside Portofino, also old – she likes to pretend it's historic, because a Russian princess is supposed to have slept there. Gabriella behaves as if *she's* royalty.' Alcinda made a face. 'She doesn't mix much locally, or at least not in the circles I travel in. About twice a year she holds a big reception – reminds everyone how grand she and the house are.'

'And you and your sister are invited.'

'Even though I disgraced myself the year before last? Yeah. She likes to give a good impression, and I'm sort of famous these days. She also hopes to set one of us up with Frederico, her stepson. Keep all that lovely money and direction of the Institute in the family.' Alcinda gave a short, sharp laugh. 'Not going to happen on several counts. Not least because Freddie is gay and living happily with a very nice architect and two French bulldogs in Milan, at a suitably safe distance from step-mama.' Alcinda paused. Silence fell between them. The sea washed against the pebbles.

'She bought some of your pictures?' Gideon prompted.

He saw the shadow cross his companion's face – loss and anger. 'I'd just begun to paint the garden.' Alcinda gestured. 'She's another one with a thing about it – the tower, especially. It used to be family land or something, back in the dark ages. I don't really keep up with her obsessions.' There was a flicker of the old sardonic grin that abruptly faded. 'The tower is in the paintings. I put the first three into an exhibition at a gallery in New York and they sold almost at once. Then I found out that Gabriella was the buyer and that her New York agent had *instructed* the gallery that paintings featuring the garden were not to be offered to anyone else. I managed to put a stop to *that*, but she still has the first three squirreled away in the family mansion. Not on display, just locked in a room somewhere.'

Gideon was quiet for a moment, thinking. 'The secretary who died was your friend,' he guessed.

Alcinda nodded. 'Battista wasn't one of her regular secretaries – she has two, God knows why. She was hired as extra help from an agency, to assist with organising the party.'

Noticing Alcinda's expression – grief and guilt – Gideon had a sudden whispering flash of intuition. 'Were you and Battista—'

'Lovers? No – not yet – only a few kisses – but it was going to happen. Until I had the mad idea of going to the party and stealing back the paintings, with her help. While the guests were guzzling canapés and champagne, we were going to snatch the paintings and ride off into the sunset. Except that

Cousin Gabriella had hired special security for the occasion – you know – a man mountain in a sharp suit.' She gave him a slanted look, unable to resist the jibe. 'I was escorted off the premises before we'd even got one of the canvases off the wall. Then the next day Battista fell down the main stairs of the palazzo – her neck was broken.'

She shrugged, but he could still see grief and guilt etched on her face. 'Officially, it was an accident. I can't prove otherwise. Gabriella made all the right noises, paid Battista's family the salary she would have earned, attended the funeral. There was just a second, at the funeral, when I saw my cousin's face ... satisfaction. She was *satisfied.*' Alcinda shrugged again. 'Bianca didn't see anything. She says I imagined it. Maybe she's right.'

The foggy silence enfolded them. Gideon found that he believed Alcinda. Maybe not that the cousin was a murderer, but that she'd not been much concerned over the death of her secretary. *Simply keeping up appearances.* Alcinda's artist's eye was no doubt tuned to expressions and body language. She'd probably caught an unguarded reflection of indifference.

Beside him, Alcinda braced her arms on the rock. 'Will you come to my cousin's party with me, Gideon West?'

For a second Gideon felt as if he'd been sucker punched. 'Uh, er ... I ...' he stuttered.

Alcinda squinted up at him. 'I'm not expecting you to help steal the pictures.' She scuffed a pebble with her toe. 'I'd just like to see them again. If you come with me there's a reason to ask, as you're the person restoring the garden. I think she might agree to show them to you.'

'Uh ... when is it?' Was he mad even to think about it? Could he trust Alcinda? Would posh Cousin Gabriella want to show her treasures to a *gardener*?

'Three weeks Wednesday. You can wear *your* sharp suit.' She pushed herself off the rock. 'Shall we walk some more?'

The fog was clearing. They walked the length of the beach and back. Alcinda got him to sit on the rock, then stand beside it, while she did some quick sketches, entirely focused on her smoothly moving pencil. At last, she looked up before glancing around. 'We'll have to get here early, before it gets busy. Just as it's getting light. Can you do that?'

'I can,' he agreed. Before work would suit him fine. 'This is where you want me to pose?'

'To start. We can do more in the studio later.'

'Will there be ... you know ... costume involved?'

86

'Jerkins and stripy socks? Seven league boots?' Now she was laughing. 'No. I've moved on from fairy tales.' Gideon let out a breath of relief. 'I'm thinking superheroes.' The confusion and alarm she'd caught on his face *really* made her laugh. 'Don't panic – classical ones – Achilles, maybe Hercules – Perseus … yes.' She sucked the end of a pencil that had already been comprehensively chewed. 'Medusa's head,' she muttered softly. 'You can wear your own clothes. In fact, do you have a long coat?'

Chapter Eighteen

Megan fingered the stiff, heavily embossed card that had arrived in the post.

She was hiding in the library, away from the workmen who were currently upgrading the downstairs cloakroom. Gideon had organised a gang to clear the overgrowth from the window and Tommaso and his son-in-law had moved in an antique desk from one of the small reception rooms. She looked up when Maria ambled in bearing a tray of coffee. 'Oh, thanks.' She leaned over to clear a space on the desk. 'Do you know anything about Signora Gabriella De Stefano?'

Maria put down the tray and took a mug, pushing the other and a plate of biscuits towards Megan. She waved her free hand. 'Snooty,' she decided. Megan recognised another word that was probably from Olwen's vocabulary. 'Owns a villa on the other side of Portofino – more like a palazzo – thinks that makes her important.' Maria leaned over to look at the card. 'Oh – one of the Signora's parties. You must go,' she said decisively.

'To meet Signora De Stefano?'

'To meet lots of people. And to show Signora De Stefano that you are important too.'

Megan studied the invitation again. It was certainly elaborate, with what looked like a family crest in the corner. Normally she wouldn't be interested – brown-nosing at university parties was bad enough, although it was Ellery who liked to brown-nose. He called it networking, she remembered with a grin. But arriving as the owner of Il Giardino delle Rose was very different from being just a girlfriend and junior lecturer ... and if it was a chance to meet some local people ...

Maria had caught the grin. 'You will go.'

'I think so.'

'You must wear something ... high-class ... and *expensive*. And hire a car service,' Maria said sternly.

Megan's grin widened. Obviously her best jeans and her little Fiat were not the thing for meeting snooty Signora De Stefano.

Alcinda was right about the security guard. Bulging muscles and a sharp black suit and stationed, discreet but visible, in the lee of a magnificent staircase, scrutinising the guests as they entered.

Alcinda appeared to be completely relaxed, grinning and looking smug as they crossed the echoing hall. *I'll see your security detail and raise you my own.*

And that would be me, he thought.

Gideon pulled in a breath and straightened his spine. The worst that could happen would be that they were asked to leave. Although, actually, maybe that wasn't the worst – in a rush Gideon realised that this was *the* staircase; a high sweeping curve with a hard tile floor below. Alcinda's step hesitated, just for a second. Gideon braced himself. If she turned tail to run, he would make sure that they went with a semblance of dignity. He had no doubt that Bianca, walking alongside them with her escort for the evening, would cover any exit with her commendable coolness. He heard Alcinda's tiny smothered gasp and then she was gliding on to meet the woman coming forward to greet them. Gabriella De Stefano.

In the flurry of hand clasps and air kisses between the cousins, Gideon's respect for Alcinda rose. Feeling as she did, entering this place took courage. Seeing her sister's hand pressed into her back for support he knew he wasn't the only one to pick up on this. Despite her disapproval, Bianca was there for her sister.

Gideon hung back, watching the interaction. Observing Signora De Stefano the phrase "well preserved" rose in Gideon's mind. The pink dress with fussy detailing at the neck, the immaculately arranged helmet of dark hair and careful maquillage made the woman seem as if she had been lacquered – encased in a moment in time that epitomised her idea of good taste. Bianca was introducing her escort, a consultant surgeon from Genoa, and looking sleek and sexy in a sleeveless green dress. In contrast, Alcinda looked like the result of a riot in a ribbon factory. Her multi-coloured dress was clearly out of the same stable – presumably the same designer – as the Miss Havisham creation. Her hair was gathered in a messy knot on the top of her head and her red snakeskin boots had sharply pointed toes. The lacquer cracked, just for a second, when her cousin took in the full force of the ribbons. Then it was his turn to be introduced.

'Gabriella,' Alcinda almost purred the name. 'I know you will want to meet Gideon – Gideon West. He is the garden specialist who is overseeing the restoration at Il Giardino delle Rose.'

Gideon had expected to be greeted and passed over quickly for someone more important. Cousin Gabriella hadn't been much interested in the Genoese consultant. Instead, the lacquer cracked again in a version of a smile. He was given a cold, delicately manicured hand. 'I should like to speak to you about your work,' she offered. 'Once I have greeted the rest of my guests.'

'I look forward to it,' Gideon managed to respond, concealing his surprise.

'I wonder—' Alcinda was clearly striking while the iron was hot '—if later in the evening we might show Signor West my paintings? Possibly they will help him with his work,' she suggested silkily.

There was a heartbeat of silence while the women stared at each other, then, amazingly, Cousin Gabriella nodded. 'An excellent suggestion. I'm sure another of my guests would also be interested in seeing them.'

Gabriella moved off to greet new arrivals. Behind her back Alcinda punched the air, her sister hissed at her to behave and the consultant looked confused. A waiter with a tray of champagne provided a diversion while Gideon regained his bearings. When he'd first seen Cousin Gabriella, painted and perfected, he'd agreed with Bianca – the idea of the woman as a murderer was absurd. But there was something in her eyes as she took his hand, something dark and cold. Now he wasn't quite so sure.

Megan slid out of the hired limo in front of the brightly lit doorway of the palazzo. Maria had been right on several counts. The place was very grand and the town car had been the right choice. Her little Fiat would have been sadly out of place amongst the limousines and Ferraris queuing on the drive for the parking area at the rear of the building. She took a moment to collect herself before starting forward over the raked gravel in unfamiliar heels. She was also pleased with what she'd chosen to wear. She'd resisted Maria's urgent directions to go to Genoa or even Milan to buy a new designer outfit. Instead, she'd selected one of Cassie's finds; a dark blue vintage Jean Muir. Superbly cut, its simplicity was the perfect foil for her aunt's diamond and sapphire earrings and a delicate white-gold cocktail watch with diamond chips circling the face.

Taking them from the small safe in her aunt's bedroom, Megan had weighed the earrings in her hand. Had they been a gift of love from her husband, to mark some special event? The style of the watch in particular made Megan think it might be American. Gideon's landlady had suggested Olwen was American. It was confusing and tantalising in the extreme. Slightly breathless, Megan fitted the earrings and slipped on the watch. The air around her in the room offered no chill or resistance, just a sigh of warmth and approval. 'And you have an overactive imagination.' She'd picked up her evening bag and gone to await the car, feeling like something out of a glamorous old Hollywood movie.

Now she entered the wide doorway and stood blinking for a moment in the brightness of the hall. The building was magnificent. *But not really welcoming?* High ceilings, shiny hard surfaces, gilding and marble statuary in niches around the walls. And Gideon West, visible through the open doorway of an inner room, looking edible in an amazing dark suit with a tiny blonde woman, in an even more amazing dress, laughing up at him.

Of course a guy like that would have a beautiful girlfriend, although he'd never mentioned that he would be here with her ...

The thought, along with an inexplicable feeling of hurt, made her blink as much as the lights. Something inside her seemed to shift. Before she had time to analyse it, a dark woman in a pink chiffon dress was bearing down on her. 'Dottoressa Morrison, welcome.'

Stepford wife. The thought rose instantly in Megan's mind; stuck in some sort of time warp, with a bland expression of welcome and not a hair out of place. Had Megan imagined the woman's eyes widening a fraction though, when she spotted Olwen's earrings? It had only been for a second, before they'd settled back into polite blankness. *Probably decided that they're paste.* Quite where that thought came from Megan didn't know, and the silence was stretching.

'Thank you for inviting me. You have a ... memorable home,' she offered quickly. It was the right thing. The woman's shoulders straightened as she preened.

'You are welcome.' Gabriella stood to one side, giving Megan a better view of the space, clearly waiting for more compliments.

'It's very ... impressive.'

'It is,' Gabriella agreed complacently, beckoning a waiter with a tray of glasses. Megan took one and found herself ushered forward. 'I believe there is someone here that you know, and I must introduce you to my cousins, Bianca and Alcinda.' She looked around, with the barest suggestion of a frown. 'Also, my stepson Frederico is here somewhere. He will be enchanted to meet you.' Megan allowed herself to be led into the main room – more gilt, statues and magnificent chandeliers. Gideon didn't quite do a double take when he recognised her, but there was certainly surprise. His smile was slightly bashful, as if he'd been caught out in something. He hadn't said anything about attending the party, but thinking about it, she hadn't told him either. *Why shouldn't he be here with a girlfriend?* The tiny blonde was even more stunning close-up, with a heart-shaped face almost swamped by dark-lashed blue eyes. Megan made suitably pleased-to-meet-you noises, aware that Alcinda was studying her closely

Megan didn't have a chance to consider the reasons for that before she was drawn into a conversation about painting. Alcinda was an artist. Two British guests who had recognised her were admirers and were clearly trying to discover what she was currently working on. She was pretending to misunderstand, acting coy, with wicked sideways glances towards Gideon. He wasn't giving anything away either. *But he does know.* There was absolutely no reason for that to cause a pang in her chest. Megan sipped her drink carefully as her stomach was empty, and listened.

After hovering for a moment, Signora De Stefano drifted off to greet more arrivals. Waiters were circulating with trays of finger food. Megan watched out of the corner of her eye. Maria had ruthlessly vetoed a meal before she left, issuing strict instructions that Megan was to take note of all she ate.

'Everything that Signora De Stefano serves is of the highest luxury. It is her signature.'

Megan was sincerely hoping that some of that signature would come her way, and soon.

She belongs here. You don't. The thought created a slightly uncomfortable feeling in Gideon's gut. It hadn't occurred to him that Megan Morrison would be one of the guests tonight, but it should have. She was part of local society now, the owner of Il Giardino delle Rose. *And you're just a drifter, passing through.* Seeing her so unexpectedly had been a jolt. She looked amazing in a plain dark dress that clung subtly before sinking to swirl around her calves. She was poised, cool, sophisticated – *out of your league.* She was also eyeing the platter of food that a waiter was bringing in their direction in the way a lioness might contemplate a plump gazelle. He couldn't help himself. 'Hungry?'

'Starving! Maria wouldn't let me eat before I left. Thank God, he's coming this way.'

It seemed she wasn't the only one. With an imperious gesture Alcinda commandeered the whole platter, setting it down in a convenient niche, at the feet of a rather rotund Cupid, and sending the grinning waiter off with instructions to bring another. 'I'll say this for Cousin Gabriella, she picks the best caterers.'

Gideon knew better than to get between lionesses and their prey – if the delicate bite-size offerings could be called that. For a swift painful second, he could hear Phillip West's voice in his head. *'That'll only make a fool of your mouth, son.'* It hardly mattered as it didn't look as if his mouth was going to get the opportunity to be fooled. Alcinda and Megan had moved in as if choreographed. Bianca remonstrated briefly with her sister before stepping aside, laughing. Another waiter sidled up with a smaller tray, to serve the neglected members of the group.

Gideon sampled a twist of smoked salmon, which melted on his tongue in a few seconds, then stood back, surveying the room. The male half of Alcinda's admirers, who was something in antiques, came to stand beside him, providing a running commentary on the palazzo's decor. More acid than approving, Gideon noted. The magnificent chandeliers and a few of the smaller statues did get commendations.

'The best pieces were bought by her late husband, of course, and it all goes to his son when our hostess passes on. She only has a life interest. If Frederico has any taste he'll rip out all this old tat.' Antiques Man gestured to the gilt and gloss. 'He's here somewhere, usually drifts in for these affairs. Keeping an eye on the inheritance.'

Gideon found that he didn't much care for Antiques Man, whom he suspected had drunk rather too freely of his hostess's champagne. He gave a noncommittal grunt, glad that Gabriella De Stefano was not close enough to hear. Not getting an encouraging response, the antiques expert moved on to a complicated story about a deal he'd just done for a house clearance.

Gideon let the words wash over him, watching their hostess flit from group to group, never pausing long with any of her guests. Although she'd invited these people into her home, did she actually want to spend time with them? *Are they simply here to admire and envy?* That unexpected thought rocked Gideon for a second before an even more disturbing idea overtook it. Was it that Signora De Stefano didn't want to spend time with her guests, or that they didn't want to spend time with her? The room was full of sophisticated people enjoying superb food and drink, networking and gossiping. No one seemed to be seeking out Gabriella's company or including her in their conversational groups. Memories of Alcinda's accusation and those cold, dark eyes flitted through his mind.

As he watched, he realised that, despite the perfectly presented exterior, Signora De Stefano was emanating a banked down nervous energy. *She's waiting for something. Or someone?* She glanced at her watch, then at the door, then at her watch again. *A guest who has not yet arrived? Someone important?*

Gideon sipped excellent champagne and wondered.

Confusingly, Megan found that she *liked* Gideon West's girlfriend. *And, really, it's no concern of yours who he dates.* Alcinda's personality matched her amazing dress. She'd fallen on the platter of delectable morsels with the same enthusiasm as Megan, and she'd been willing to share. Now the contents of the second platter, brought by the obliging waiter, were gone too. Bianca had clucked a little at her sister's blatant greed, but Alcinda had not been in the slightest bit daunted. She popped the last bite of a canapé into her mouth, eyes closed, letting out a long ecstatic sigh. When she opened them again, licking her fingers, her face was lit with what Megan could only identify as mischief. The unexpectedly blue depths of her eyes brimmed with laughter, but also with a hint of challenge? They fixed on her.

'Now, Dottoressa Morrison, you can tell me what you and Signor West are planning to do to my beautiful garden.'

Chapter Nineteen

'Alcinda!' Bianca's remonstrating exclamation was loud enough to turn a few heads. 'I must apologise for my sister, Dottoressa Morrison,' she continued more quietly, turning an irritated eye on her sibling. 'Just because she has trespassed on your late aunt's garden to paint, does *not* give her any claim to it.'

'You painted Aunt Olwen's garden?' Far from being annoyed, Megan found herself intrigued. The two art admirers were pressing closer also, avidly listening. Alcinda, having issued her provocative challenge, was happily registering the reactions. *Collecting faces and expressions, perhaps?* 'I'd love to see them, are they on display somewhere?' She waited for a second as Bianca's annoyance warred with something else, inwardly amused as the "something else" won – the instinct of a born saleswoman. Swiftly, Bianca sketched the pedigree of the paintings – fairy-tale themes in the background of the overgrown garden.

'My sister believes brambles and thorns are preferable to restoration and order.' She shot Alcinda a barbed but indulgent look. 'The paintings, those that are not already sold, are on display at the family gallery in Portofino. You are most welcome to view them.' *And, of course, to buy one.* Megan heard the unspoken comment as if it had actually been said. Now she really was intrigued and really *did* want to see them.

'Dottoressa Morrison does not need to wait to visit the gallery.' A stocky young man with dark curly hair and a round, amiable face, wearing a three-piece suit with a watch chain, joined the group. 'We can go and look at Mama's collection.' He was grinning at Alcinda. 'Like the originator, small but perfectly formed.'

'Freddie!' Alcinda threw herself into the young man's arms with an enthusiasm that made Megan cast an involuntary glance up at Gideon. He wasn't showing any signs of concern – or surprise. *He already knew about this too.*

Bianca was greeting Signora De Stefano's stepson with pleasure only slightly overlaid with irritation at having her sales pitch thwarted. Megan promised herself that if these pictures appealed, she *would* visit the gallery and she *would* buy one. It was high time she visited Portofino.

Frederico was dispatched to find his stepmother and get the key to the room where the paintings were kept. Alcinda was clearly excited, her blue eyes dancing with glee and cheeks delicately flushed. Both Bianca and Gideon were watching her, Megan realised. *Something's going on here.*

Freddie was soon back, brandishing a ring of keys. 'I gather you'd already asked, sweetheart.' He offered Alcinda his arm. With a cheekily triumphant glance over her shoulder at the rest of the group, Alcinda took it and they led the way to an archway giving onto a side room. The rest of the party, including the two art fans, straggled behind. Megan found herself walking beside Gideon, glancing up at him. It wasn't so far to look up at him tonight, when she was wearing high-heeled Jimmy Choos, not trainers.

'You knew about this,' she said softly. 'What's the story?'

'What Bianca said. Her sister used the garden as a setting. Another trespasser. That garden has one hell of a drawing power.'

'I know,' Megan agreed. She shivered slightly, although the evening was mild and the palazzo was not chilled by air conditioning. Il Giardino delle Rose had its own energy.

They had passed through to the back of the hall and an uncarpeted staircase of a much more modest appearance than the one near the front door. Megan looked doubtfully at the sleep risers. *Her heels ...*

Without speaking Gideon offered his arm. She put her hand on his sleeve and they started up the stairs. Megan swallowed. Gideon West's arm was warm and firm and reassuring under her fingers. It felt right to be holding onto him, to the point of being disturbing. What the hell was the matter with her tonight? Awareness shimmered over her. She swallowed, groping for a question to ask as a distraction. 'You've seen Alcinda's paintings. Are they good?'

'Very. I think you'll like them. I did,' he said. 'The ones at the gallery, that is. I gather Signora De Stefano bought these some time ago. Alcinda herself hasn't seen them for quite a while.'

Which might explain her air of suppressed excitement?

'Did ...' she hesitated, but she had to ask. 'Is that where you met? At the gallery?' *Or maybe it was somewhere in the garden?* She didn't know why that should give her such a hollow feeling.

'Yes.'

Megan waited. She sensed that he was going to say more and her breath was catching in her throat. 'She and I ... we're not an item. She invited me tonight because she thought I'd like to see the pictures, if she could persuade her cousin. I understand Signora De Stefano does not show them often.'

The sense of relief that flooded through Megan was almost enough to make her lose her footing. *She's not his girlfriend.* And on top of that thought – *why does that matter?* She wobbled a little on the heels, clinging tighter to Gideon's arm. She didn't know why it mattered, but elation was crowding her chest as they made their way up the stairs. The paintings might be hideous, but now she really didn't care.

At the head of the little procession Alcinda and Freddie had stopped in front of a stout looking door.

It seemed they had arrived.

Chapter Twenty

Gideon tensed as the party halted. Why had he felt the need to explain that he wasn't dating Alcinda? And it had been a need, bound up with the warm pressure of Megan's hand on his arm, a subtle awareness of the movements of her body as she climbed the stairs beside him, and the delicate, tantalising trace of her perfume, in such contrast to the dramatic fragrance that Alcinda wore. He hadn't been thinking, when he'd offered her his arm. It was an automatic gesture, seeing her hesitating at the sight of the stairs. Now his libido was raising its head and laughing.

Hey! Yeah! Look at me, I'm available!

Megan hadn't said anything in response to his declaration. Maybe tightened her hold, but that was probably the stairs, or his imagination. Now Freddie and Alcinda were making a performance of opening the door. Megan had dropped his arm, jostled by the art admirers who were crowding in excitedly. Stepping away, he let Megan and the admirers move in front.

Opening it actually *was* a performance. There was more than one lock, which also meant more than one key. With that level of security, Gideon wondered why the guard hadn't been instructed to accompany them. Perhaps the stepson was considered enough? Then the door was open, and Freddie was ushering everyone in with a flourishing bow. The room was dark. Alcinda giggled, with a slightly frantic edge, patting along the wall for the light switches. In the instant before she found them, Megan was back at his side with her hand back on his arm. His heart, or something else in his chest, gave an uncomfortable jerk. He opened his mouth. 'I ...'

Abruptly the room was flooded with light, everyone was exclaiming and whatever he had been about to say was lost in the commotion. Which was good, as he had no idea what he had been about to say.

The room was high, square and painted white. The canvases were mounted one to a wall, with display lights above them, like in a gallery. Gideon realised that he had half expected them to be piled on the floor, facing the wall. Alcinda darted to the middle of the room, pirouetting to survey each of the walls, then letting out a long, enraged hiss. There were not three canvases, as had been expected, but four. With everyone else still bunched close to the door, she stalked towards the painting opposite it. Clearly that was the one she had not been anticipating. *If she had a tail, she'd be lashing it.*

With a startled and slightly anguished glance at her sister, Bianca moved forward to take charge of the admirers, who were reaching for mobile phones, gaping at the spectacle. She quietly vetoed the idea of photographs, provoking some pouting disappointment. Freddie backed her up, while drawing Bianca's bemused escort into the room, talking and gesturing to the pictures. This left him and Megan. She was looking up at him. 'Alcinda is angry. You know why.'

'Yes.' He took a swift glance at the other occupants of the room. Bianca was okay, but everyone else ... 'Can't really explain now. She has cause.'

'Should you be helping her? As a friend.'

He took another quick glance. Alcinda stood in front of the fourth painting. Her hands were bunched into fists and she was rocking on the heels of her red boots, but he sensed that she was better left alone for the moment. 'I think it's okay. Shall we look at the other paintings, and speak to her when we get to that one?' *The one that's different.*

Megan nodded and they crossed to the wall where the largest of the paintings hung. Behind them, Bianca was shepherding her charges towards another canvas with a low-voiced commentary. Gideon heard Megan's quick intake of breath. 'It's beautiful. Wild.'

It *was* wild. This, and the two others that were the original purchases, were scenes of the garden in winter. They had the breathtaking impact of a punch. Almost but not quite monochrome, briars and thorns twisted through bare branches. The occasional shrivelled bud or leaf gave a hint of colour in the foreground, while a tower loomed darkly behind. It was Sleeping Beauty's Castle gone to the bad – the disturbed and disturbing edge where the fairy tale tipped into nightmare. He could almost imagine himself trapped, caught in the thorns as he searched for something that he couldn't find.

Megan shivered beside him, and he knew it affected her too. He had to resist the impulse to pull her close. Her hand still rested on his arm. In the picture the tower brooded over two distant, entwined figures. The man's cloak of deep blue and the woman's red dress were simple slivers of colour in a black-and-white landscape. In the next painting there was snow on the ground and the figures were even more distant, appearing to walk hand-in-hand towards the cliff beyond the tower. In the third, a few green shoots were visible on the branches and the figures were mere smudges of faded colour on the horizon, beneath a low hanging cloud-covered sun. 'They're stunning.' Megan murmured.

'Thank you.' Gideon started at the soft voice behind them. Alcinda had stepped away from the fourth painting. Her face was impassive, although there was still a hint of fire in her eyes. Gideon nodded without speaking.

He agreed with Megan – the pictures *were* stunning, but he wasn't sure he'd want to live with any of them. The thought that maybe Gabriella was right to hide them away rose in his mind for a brief treacherous second. He smothered it. Paintings like these *could* live in the light, but in a museum or gallery, not in someone's home. Here, together, they were overpowering in intensity. His respect for Alcinda as an artist notched up a few more places. As a human being, she was still a first-class PITA.

Alcinda's slanted smile made him wonder if his thoughts were visible on his face, but she was looking at Megan. 'I was working something out in my head when I did these.'

Megan seemed to understand. 'It's the story of the lovers and the tower.'

Alcinda nodded, throwing an irritated glance over her shoulder at the noisy exclamations from the interlopers who'd attached themselves to the group. 'Come to the gallery. We'll talk.'

They moved on to the fourth painting. Gideon heard Megan catch her breath again. The last canvas was different, much more like the ones on display in Portofino. It was the garden in spring, in burgeoning, writhing life. At first, it seemed to be only the garden – green shoots and unfurling flower buds – but as he stood before it, Gideon could see the suggestion of a male and a female face rising out of the canvas. He wasn't sure whether the faces were hidden in the leaves or emerging from them

'I bought that one for Mama. Christmas present.' Freddie spoke from behind them. 'It's the last in the series.' He looked at Alcinda with a slight challenge in his eyes.

'It is,' she agreed calmly. 'I wondered what had happened to it.' She turned to Megan and Gideon. 'This was the bridge that took me to the paintings in the gallery – the commercial ones.' The mischief was creeping back into her face as she looked over at her sister. 'Easier to sell fairy tales than tragic old legends.'

'I have to say I like the fairy tales better.' The female half of the admirers had joined them. 'These are brilliant but … different?'

'Different,' Alcinda agreed, with a half-smile.

'I'm glad we've seen them though. Privileged.' The woman turned to Freddie to gush at him. Antique Man was quizzing Bianca on what the pictures were worth.

Alcinda jerked her head in a gesture that was complete street urchin. 'Shall we go back to the party now? Before Cousin Gabriella sends someone to find out if we've bopped poor Freddie on the head and stolen her treasures?'

Gabriella De Stefano paced slowly through the rooms, smiling benignly at her guests. She paused here and there to exchange a gracious word, sharply calling forward the waiting staff when she saw an unfilled glass or an empty plate, accepting compliments on her home and hospitality. She stopped for a moment, surveying the gathering she had assembled. *Fools and social climbers, here to gawp and gossip, but serving their purpose.* With an effort, she resisted the impulse to look once more at her watch. The surprise that she had arranged for Megan Morrison should have been here when the woman arrived, but some stupid delay with flights …

Everything would be well in a very few moments, and Dottoressa Morrison was occupied in the meantime. Gabriella would have liked to have accompanied the party to view the paintings, but she could not miss the arrival of her last guests. Freddie was a dear boy and would take care of everything. A small quiver of satisfaction ran through her – Alcinda had expected an argument over the paintings. It had been pleasing to see her surprise. Bringing the gardener here was intended as a snub – Gabriella was aware of that. Her cousin could call him a consultant and any other fancy name, but a gardener was all he was. It would be interesting, nevertheless, to talk to him before the end of the evening. Gabriella's mouth formed a careful smile. Welcoming him had taken the wind from Alcinda's sails, and the man was passable and well enough dressed.

So, surprisingly, was Megan Morrison. A frown succeeded the smile. She had expected an academic to be dowdy or inappropriately attired, aping her students. The frown blossomed at the recollection of Alcinda's outfit. Megan Morrison's dress was plain but well cut. For a moment, she had thought the jewels were real. Of course they were not. Excellent imitations, but they could only be paste, undoubtedly belonging to the aunt – and what could the old woman have left but cheap costume jewellery? Everything had been sunk into the estate and then abandoned to decay when the money was gone.

Realising that she had been standing for too long and had drifted too far into her thoughts, Gabriella gathered herself to circulate. Rumours were old and few here would remember them, but there was no need to invite speculation. Her heartbeat quickened as she approached a clump of gossiping guests who had retreated to the quieter environment of the hall. She signalled a waitress to bring more champagne. The girl jumped with gratifying speed when she beckoned. That was the kind of service she expected. The double doors stood open, letting in a cool evening breeze. And yes – the sound of a car on the gravel drive. She hurried forward.

At last!

Chapter Twenty-One

Megan stepped carefully as she descended the stairs, grateful for the continued support of Gideon's arm. In front of them the art admirers were attempting to pump Alcinda and Bianca for information on the paintings. Behind them, Freddie and the hospital consultant had abandoned art in favour of discussing football. The consultant sounded happier.

Megan tried to concentrate on keeping her balance and not on the confused and excited thoughts bubbling in her head. The most exciting and confusing was walking right next to her. Gideon was … she really wasn't sure what Gideon was. That crazy sense of relief, when she'd understood that Alcinda wasn't his girlfriend – what was that telling her? *Oh, come on girl, you know what it's telling you. You're interested in Gideon West and not just because he's renovating your garden.* Gideon was a powerfully attractive man. *And he's attracting me.* There, she'd admitted it. Her fingers were tingling just resting on the sleeve of his jacket.

They reached a small half landing. Already the noise of the party could be heard drifting up from below. And now it wasn't just her fingers that were tingling. She swallowed, hoping her face wasn't flushed. *The paintings, think about the paintings.* The art admirers were blatantly fishing for details on the theme of the pictures. Alcinda, clearly irritated by their insistence, was pretending to misunderstand the questions.

Megan *knew* what the paintings were about.

Alcinda had brought to life the last and longest of the "Cosimo" poems, melding the story of doomed mediaeval lovers in their tower with the wildness of the abandoned garden.

What does Alcinda know and how does she know it?

Megan's heart was thumping against her ribs. She wasn't naive enough to think that it was only academic excitement. They'd almost reached the bottom of the stairs. In a few seconds and a few steps, she'd have to let go of Gideon's arm and go back to the party. Really that was no big deal. She'd see Gideon tomorrow.

But that's not it, is it? That's not here, now, with the awareness running through you and the man warm and close beside you.

They'd reached the ground floor. Gideon's heart dropped with a disconsolate plop as his feet hit the tiles of the hall. Megan would let go of his arm any second. Then they'd be out of the dimness behind the main staircase and he'd lose her to the buzz and brightness of the party. Alcinda and Bianca had already rejoined the crowd, followed by the art admirers, keen to crow about their private view. Freddie and Bianca's escort had stopped on the landing, caught up in some obscure question about penalty shootouts.

For the moment it was just him and Megan.

The tantalising fragrance of her scent teased him, even as she relinquished her hold on his arm. She'd half leaned towards him, wobbling a little on those crazy heels. He put out his hand automatically to grab her elbow and steady her. The movement drew her closer than he'd intended. She had her free hand up, splaying her fingers on his chest. For a breathless second, she simply stood, looking up at him. There was enough light for him to make out the flush of her skin and the glitter of her eyes. Heat and need skittered through him. He could see the throb of the pulse in her throat, in time with his own. As he looked down, hardly daring to imagine, wanting to ask, not knowing how … her mouth formed the single word. *Yes.* She moved then, brushing against him, reaching up on her toes to bring her mouth closer to his. The world hung suspended for a heartbeat – and then he was kissing Megan Morrison.

Yes. The word was a soft hiss of pleasure, sighing softly through her brain. Gideon's lips pressed against hers, hesitant at first, as if he couldn't believe … then seeking and confident as she gladly opened to him. He pulled her into his arms and her breasts, tingling and needy, were crushed against the solid wall of his chest. She'd never felt like this in a kiss before, surrounded by power and strength.

And his mouth …

His mouth was heat and demand and heaven. Joy and laughter and excitement and *need* poured through her as she held on, swirling and giddy. The only reality was that hot, demanding mouth. She could have stayed there forever, cloaked in the shadows, except that the other urgent need to breathe broke them apart. Gideon was still holding her, hands under her elbows. He was laughing and so was she, and she was just about to reach for him again—

'Dottoressa Morrison? Ah! There you are,' Freddie spoke from behind them. Gideon somehow managed to move her away from him, so they weren't caught by the hostess's stepson snogging like teenagers in a dark corner.

'*Uff*! Shoes,' she said, wagging one of her feet as if to show him that there had been some problem that had kept them here in the hall.

'Ah, yes,' Freddie agreed, as if he understood when he clearly didn't. He was holding up his phone which glowed in the dark. 'Mamma was wondering where we were. Apparently, there's someone just arrived who she wants you to meet.'

'Oh.' Megan smoothed down her dress, taking a couple of beats to steady herself. She would have liked a moment to check that her hair wasn't tangled and her lipstick not smeared, but Freddie was clearly expecting her to hurry at his stepmother's bidding. She took another pass over her dress, turning towards the noise of the party. Gideon had tactfully melted into the gloom under the main stairs.

'They're in the entrance hall.' Freddie smiled, indicating the other direction.

'Thank you.' Megan gathered herself together to walk past him. *Who the hell could Gabriella be rolling out to meet her?* Some academic from the University? An elderly inhabitant who remembered her aunt? In normal circumstances, either would be interesting, but with her thoughts bouncing around and her body vibrating, would she be able to muster the brainpower to hold a conversation? *You're going to have to try.*

She reached the foot of the main staircase. Signora De Stephano was standing near the front door with a burly man with thinning grey hair and a baggy suit, who looked pleased with himself. There was another man, shorter, slimmer, clearly younger, with his back to her. Gabriella spotted her and held up an imperious hand to wave her forward, clearly also pleased with herself. *Actually, she looks positively triumphant ...*

'Here she is now. Come my dear, see who's here.'

The younger man turned and Megan felt a shock as if a pit had opened up in front of her on the shiny tiled floor.

'Ellery!'

105

Chapter Twenty-Two

Gideon had walked the whole length of the beach and was on his way back before Alcinda appeared beside the rocks, setting up her painting gear. The sun was just coming up, tinting everything pale pink and gold. He pushed his hand through his hair, tugging at the roots. Last night … last night … one minute he'd been holding Megan Morrison in his arms, the next some other guy was there in his place. *A guy with a prior claim.*

Gideon had faded discreetly into the shadows when Freddie interrupted them. He wasn't made of stone and kissing Megan had had a glorious but visible effect. He hadn't wanted to embarrass all three of them. Then all he could do was watch and feel like a voyeur as the big reunion scene played out beside the front door. Gabriella De Stefano, jubilant, a big bloke, obviously well pleased with himself, and a younger man – good-looking if you liked the foxy type – forming a welcoming committee for Megan. Foxy made straight for her, taking her hands, calling her darling, pulling her into a kiss. The guy did everything but sweep her into an old-style Hollywood dip. Staking his claim in front of an audience of interested partygoers. *Look at me – I'm the fiancé.*

'He's the *ex*-fiancé.' Gideon had reached Alcinda and she was reading his mind, or his body language, *again.* She'd cottoned on fast last night that something was going on between him and Megan, despite his best efforts to disguise it. She'd introduced him around, dragging him into conversations and throwing herself into diverting him and saving his face, staying within earshot when a smirking Signora De Stefano interrogated him over Il Giardino delle Rose. And it had worked – well, the saving face part anyway.

'Your lady made the "ex" bit as clear as she could, given that our hostess seems to have gone to a lot of trouble to produce him.' Alcinda looked thoughtful as she squeezed paint on a palette and studied the sky. 'I wonder how and why she did that?'

'Trying to be helpful?' Gideon suggested. 'She found out through that artistic institute thing.' *Coincidence and sheer bloody bad luck.* 'The guy is giving a lecture for them. And I don't think you can say that Dr Morrison is my lady,' he added.

'But you want her to be.'

'Well – yes,' Gideon admitted dolefully. *But do you really stand a chance against the smooth, good-looking academic – the guy from her world?* Megan had fallen for Ellery Peters once. And he quite clearly wanted her back.

'I say again, *ex-fiancé*,' Alcinda emphasised. 'I suggest you talk to Dottoressa Morrison about it. Find out where you stand. And in the meantime—' she gave him one of her evil grins '—I have to say it's making you most *delightfully* dark and brooding.' She nodded her head at the rock. 'So go and stand over there and brood for *me*, while I paint you.'

Megan was sitting on the loggia, trying to order her thoughts … and there were a lot of thoughts to order. She sighed and looked at her watch. It was only 11 a.m. *Much too early for gin.* She'd survived her breakfast interrogation from Maria by concentrating on describing the palazzo, what everyone was wearing and the food – especially the food. Maria had listened carefully with the light of battle in her eyes. Megan had a feeling that once the building works were done and a significant part of the garden was finished, there would be pressure to open the house for entertaining. *And why not?* The big salon, which ran the width of the house and was currently unused, would be perfect for parties.

Megan jerked away from the diverting distraction. She had too much else on her mind to wonder about parties. First, there were the paintings. What did the artist know about the legend of the tower? She needed to meet up with Alcinda again and talk to her. That was an easy decision.

And then there was Gideon. She could still feel the strength of his arms around her and the pressure of his mouth. She moved restlessly, crossing her legs, then uncrossing them again, before she started to laugh. Right – she wanted more of that. Hopefully Gideon did too. The big SUV that he'd rented was parked in the drive, but he hadn't come near the house today. Was he being tactful or was he simply avoiding her? Whatever, she needed to know, which meant she had to go and look for him.

She screwed up her eyes and pursed her mouth. Given that Ellery was history, would this be a rebound fling? *Does it matter if it is?* Gideon would be gone once his contract was over, but they could both enjoy whatever this was in the meantime. She'd been stupid falling for Ellery. She wasn't doing *that* again in a hurry.

And, of course, there *was* bloody Ellery back on the scene. She huffed crossly. *Why the hell did he have to turn up?* The only emotion he stirred in her now was anger. Her attempts to rebuff him last night had been severely hampered because Signora De Stefano and Dottore Marchiano, who was the director of some sort of cultural institute that had invited Ellery to deliver two guest lectures, had been so pleased with themselves for producing him. She'd done her best to get the message across that Ellery was her *ex*-fiancé, but no one was listening.

Her composure had already been shaken by the impact of the paintings and the encounter with Gideon. She'd passed the rest of the evening in an unhealthy state of heavily suppressed fury. Ellery had come out of nowhere, spoiling her excitement at Alcinda's art and at the bone-melting delight of kissing Gideon, acting as if they were still a couple and Julia Metcalf had never existed. Guests at the party had been intrigued by his romantic gesture – coming straight off the plane to repair what Ellery had managed to convey was merely a lovers' tiff.

She'd asked him point blank what had happened to Julia, when they'd briefly been left facing each other, alone in a lull amongst the swirl of conversation. He'd waved the question away without missing a beat – Megan had overreacted to a little campus gossip. Somehow being eased out of her job and chucked out of her home hadn't felt like campus gossip, and she'd told him so. He'd looked a bit sick at that, muttering something about knowing he'd have to win her back. Then a waiter had offered more champagne "to celebrate". Someone had asked a question and they'd been swept back into the party.

She thought that he'd at least got a glimpse of the suppressed fury, when later he'd manoeuvred her into an alcove in the shadow of a large statue and attempted to take her in his arms. For a second, something like panic spiked under her ribs. She breathed it down, putting her hand firmly on his chest to hold him off.

'What was between us is *over*, Ellery. You made that quite clear when you dumped me. I've moved on. You are not part of my new life.'

'Darling, don't exaggerate, please. You know you need me. We can be great together – this is such a huge opportunity for both of us.' He reached around her restraining hand to touch her cheek.

She'd shut her eyes for a frustrated second, wondering if he'd *ever* really listened to her. 'There is no *us* any more, Ellery – and that was *your* choice.'

They'd been interrupted then because the party was breaking up. Dottore Marchiano, radiating bonhomie and good nature, had come to escort Ellery to the hotel the Institute had arranged. She'd managed to limit his goodbye to a kiss on the cheek. She scrubbed absently at it now, dropping her hand when she realised what she was doing. At least he hadn't expected to stay here at the villa. *Or maybe he had?* If so, she'd got some sort of message across.

She rocked back a little in her chair, thinking of the party as a whole. She'd gone in the hope of meeting local people, knowing she'd been concentrating too narrowly on the villa and the garden. It had been going moderately well too, until Ellery had made the evening all about *him*. She still wasn't sure why she had received the invitation in the first place. She'd assumed Gabriella was curious and wanted to find out more about her, but the woman hadn't made any real effort to speak to her. *It was almost as if you were invited in order to meet Ellery there.*

Megan shook her head at the absurd thought. The woman had gone to some trouble to orchestrate a reunion that she thought would please her guests. The impetus *must* have come from Ellery. He'd probably found out about the inheritance. Megan could hear Cassie's voice, predicting that he'd come running at the prospect of money. He'd probably engineered the whole thing, wangling both the invitation to lecture and to the party in order to stage a dramatic re-entry into Megan's life. It was so typically Ellery, inventive and devious in the extreme. *You just never realised.* Making a flashy public appearance would appeal to him. He'd expected her to be over-awed with gratitude that he'd come back, all ready to fall under his spell again. Yes, his ego was *that* big. *I have news, buddy. It didn't work.*

It wouldn't have worked even if she hadn't just kissed Gideon West, but now …

She knew that Ellery would turn up here at some stage. She was sure he hadn't taken in what she'd told him last night. She would have to make it quite clear that there was no longer anything between them. She put her hands on her knees, setting her feet firmly on the floor. Now she had a plan of action. She knew what she was going to do on two fronts – rebuff Ellery and make a trip to Portofino to the gallery and the bookshop – which just left Gideon West …

What if he'd decided that kiss was a mistake?

The possibility sent a chill rippling over her. Looking down, she found that she'd scrunched up her hands. Uncurling them, she saw dents on her palms from her fingernails. *Please don't let Gideon's absence be that.* If it was about bloody Ellery … irritation drove off the chill. If Gideon thought she was going to let that bastard back into her life, maybe even that he'd spent the night, well, that was easy to fix. *And when it is fixed, what do you want?*

A repeat of that kiss would be a good start.

Megan stretched her hands above her head and stood up.

Chapter Twenty-Three

Gideon was standing on a cleared path looking at a wooden arbour that was leaning drunkenly to one side under the pressing embrace of a *La Mortola* rambling rose. This section of the garden was the heart of the estate, entirely given over to roses in a sunken enclosure. There were shallow steps on one side and a belvedere surrounding the other three, allowing viewers to look down over a sea of colour from the massed plantings below. On a warm day the scent would be heavenly. The stonework at least was in good order, which was more than could be said for the arbour.

'It'll have to come down, won't it, boss?' Matteo prodded the side of the structure, revealing rotten wood at the base.

'Afraid so.' He'd done sketches so if Megan – Dr Morrison – wanted to replace it exactly as it was, they would have a blueprint. Gideon turned to look back over the space behind him. The beds had been cleared of weeds and many of the roses on the edges were capable of being saved, but the square in the centre ... it would be Dr Morrison's decision, but he'd been wondering about a knot garden, with beds of herbs. *Even more English than the roses*. He turned back. 'We'll get the rambler pruned. We can train it over an arch for the moment, until Dr Morrison decides what she wants to do.'

Dr Morrison ... *Megan*. Memory floated up, although he'd been trying to repress it. He could almost taste her on his lips. *Going to have to see her sometime*. He'd avoided the house this morning, afraid he might find Foxy – Dr Peters – having breakfast. Alcinda might be convinced that Peters was *ex*-fiancé and wouldn't be staying, but his proprietary air last night had grated on every one of Gideon's nerves. It had been impossible to judge from Megan's polite social mask whether it was concealing "Get lost" or "I'm angry but open to persuasion". Perhaps she'd already decided to return to the UK. The guy had certainly jumped through a few hoops to get her attention ...

Gideon was jerked out of his depressing reflection by Matteo, greeting someone behind him. '*Buon giorno*, Signora Megan.'

'*Buon giorno*.'

Gideon swung round. Megan was making her way towards the steps, smiling at Matteo ... and him.

'Hello' Suddenly, Gideon felt stupidly self-conscious, aware that his T-shirt had a rip in it from a vicious thorn, his heavy work boots were muddy and he couldn't remember if he'd combed his hair that morning, except with his fingers. Megan looked great of course, in narrow white jeans and a loose

111

pink top, if a little heavy-eyed. *Late night, after the party.* He tried not to speculate on other reasons for too little sleep.

'Hi.' She arrived beside him, a little breathless. Or maybe he was just hyper aware of her breathing. 'I've been sitting on the loggia this morning, thinking.'

'Oh?' Gideon's stomach contracted. *This is where she tells you that kiss was a mistake, that it should never have happened, that she's giving Foxy another chance.*

'I'm sorry about last night. I really didn't expect Ellery to show up like that.'

He tried a nonchalant shrug and was pretty sure he had succeeded. *Nothing to see here. No big deal.*

She tipped her head and her dark eyes met and held his. His throat constricted. *Here it comes.* 'It was a really good evening until then. Really good,' she repeated.

'It was?' He wasn't sure he was hearing right.

'It was.' She took a breath. 'And whatever Ellery says, or thinks, he is and will *remain* my ex-fiancé,' she said quietly, although Matteo had moved back to examine the arbour again and was out of earshot.

'That's … that's good to know, I think? Is it good to know?' Now he was babbling.

'It is.' She'd started to laugh. God knew what his face looked like, but suddenly he didn't care. He wanted to snatch her up and kiss her again – except that Matteo was still poking about in the arbour, there were two more of the gardening crew within sight and she *was* the one who was employing them all.

Her laughter faded into a resigned sigh. 'He'll turn up here sooner or later. I'll have to talk to him.' She gestured, as if brushing something away. It was a small, eloquent movement, revealing and reassuring. Something in Gideon's chest warmed. 'Anyway, as I said, I was thinking,' she went on, 'I'd like to go to Portofino, to meet Alcinda and the owner of the bookshop.'

The warmth grew. 'I could come with you, to make introductions?'

'I'd like that.' She'd been looking towards Matteo, distracted by whatever the gardener was doing. Now her focus came back to him. 'And I'd like you to kiss me again.'

'*Uff!*' He knew he sounded like he'd been punched. *Oh, smooth, West.* His eyes were riveted on her lips and his blood was rushing all over the place. 'Um … not now?'

She was smiling. He could feel his own mouth shifting into a grin. 'Not now. But soon,' she agreed, mock-gravely.

'Soon,' he echoed. *Oh hell, he wanted—*

'Boss!' Matteo's voice dragged Gideon away from totally inappropriate thoughts. He was walking towards them with his hand outstretched. Something metallic glinted in it.

'Hell!' Gideon registered the look of the metal. 'Is that a bullet?'

'Yeah.' Matteo's normally smiling face was sombre. 'I just dug it out of the back wall in there.' He nodded to the arbour. 'There are two more holes as well. Someone, sometime, has been letting loose with a gun.'

Chapter Twenty-Four

'Dr Peters!' Ellery turned to see Frederico De Stefano coming towards him. 'I'm glad I caught you before you go to the Institute. I wanted to invite you to have dinner tonight with me and my partner, Giancarlo.' He indicated a tall man in heavy-framed glasses who was crossing the hotel foyer at a slower pace. 'Would you join us at the restaurant here? I'd like to speak about the work of the Institute. It was a cause very dear to my father's heart.'

'I would enjoy having dinner and discussing it.' Ellery inclined his head in his most gracious gesture. 'It would be very interesting to hear about your father's work.'

With the details settled, Ellery left the two men, striding off to find his hire car while mentally punching the air. *Yes!* Luck had really turned his way in the last five weeks, starting with finding out from that reporter about Megan's inheritance. For a moment, his elation dipped. Her "friends" had certainly kept *that* quiet. Of course, he'd never intended the break in their engagement to be anything more than a simple timeout, for both of them to explore other options. Megan had taken the whole thing much too seriously. Unexpectedly getting offered a lecture spot here during the Easter vacation, so close to where Megan had hidden herself away, had been pure serendipity. He would make the most of it. He'd lectured in Italy before, so they'd obviously picked up on his reputation, but this was a distinct step up. The chance to talk to Freddie De Stefano tonight, without the rather gruesome stepmother fluttering around, was the opening he needed. Frederico was the power behind the Institute. He controlled the money.

Ellery slowed his pace for a moment, thinking of the previous night. Was the villa Megan had inherited as hideous as the palazzo? Presumably there were ways in which it could be tarted up to sell. He'd got the impression last night that there was work going on. The girl was showing some initiative. Maybe it would only need his touch here and there to take it to the right level.

He reached the car but hesitated for a moment before unlocking it, his eyes caught by the florist's shop across the road. Emerging ten minutes later, carrying an extravagant bouquet of flowers and having arranged for a small thank you gift to be sent to his hostess of the previous evening, Ellery unlocked the car, put the bouquet on the back seat and slid behind the wheel.

He was aware of a deep sense of satisfaction. The sun was shining and things were going well. Dinner tonight was real progress. It would be good if

Megan could join them – a reminder of how well he operated in this kind of milieu. She could no doubt be persuaded – the flowers would help; he was glad he'd thought of them. She couldn't stay on her high horse forever. He grinned indulgently. He'd packed the ring that she'd left on the table in a fit of pique when she'd flounced out. With the way his luck was running, it would be back on her finger before tonight.

He started the car and pulled out into the traffic. It was a hassle, having to put his mind to smoothing Megan down when there were important things that needed his attention, but it really shouldn't take too long to get her back in place – not now that she needed him. She was intelligent enough to understand that. There was a whole new life opening up for them. He had to strategise, and dinner tonight was crucial. If he could get a regular lecture spot at the Institute other doors would open. The place was small at the moment, but it had prestige and potential above its size.

He navigated the car onto the right road for this place of Megan's. Was it on the market yet? He'd need to talk to agents and solicitors, whoever Megan had working for her, to let them know that he was taking over. He moved the car into the correct lane. Would it be better to soft pedal a little on the sale? Having a property in the area could be a lever. Dr Marchiano couldn't have long to go before retirement …

'Three bullet holes.' Gideon ran his fingers over the splintered wood. 'But how did they get here?'

'Hunting?' Megan looked around doubtfully. 'If there were deer or something marauding in the garden?'

Gideon squinted at the ragged line of holes. He didn't know much about firearms, but it didn't look like the sort of damage left by a careless hunter. 'Someone messing about with a gun without realising it was loaded?' he suggested. Seeing Megan shiver, Gideon tapped lightly on her arm, to indicate that they should step back into the sunshine. 'Probably going to remain one of life's mysteries,' he continued. 'There's no way of knowing how long they've been there. I suppose forensics might tell you, but I don't really think you can call in the police.'

Megan shook her head. 'I don't expect they'd thank me for dragging them out here when it was probably done years ago.' She straightened up, looking around the garden, visibly putting the matter behind her. 'You've done wonders here already – but the centre bed needs to be replaced.'

'I've got some ideas.' Despite the brave stance and the determined change of subject, Gideon could see she was still disturbed by what they'd found. He made a snap decision. 'Look, how about we go down to Portofino today? Now. I don't know if Alcinda will be there but Bianca probably will be, and you can see the other paintings and the bookshop. We can talk on the way.' He waited while she considered the idea, then she smiled.

'I'd like that. We can have lunch? My treat.'

He laughed. 'An offer I can't refuse.' He looked down at his work clothes. 'I need to change. I've got some spare gear in the SUV, if you want to go and get ready. I'll see you at the car in ten minutes.'

He watched her walk up the path before turning to Matteo, who was considering his approach to the pruning and propping up of the rambling rose. The gardener looked up with a shrewd expression in his eyes. 'What do you need, boss?'

'Before you knock that thing down, can you dig out those bullets and put them in a bag? Try not to handle them too much if you can help it.'

'Got you.' Matteo tilted his head. 'You're going to get them analysed?'

'Maybe.' Gideon shrugged. 'I don't know. Probably wouldn't tell us anything useful. But it feels wrong to just ignore them.' Unable to define his unease, he wasn't even sure *why* he was uneasy. But if anything should happen in the future … he'd have something to show Jake at least.

Matteo looked back at the arbour and nodded. Gideon felt relieved that the man agreed with him. 'Something happened here,' Matteo said thoughtfully. 'I'll dig out those bullets.'

Gideon retrieved the bag of smarter clothes and quickly changed in the downstairs cloakroom, currently empty of workmen. They'd replaced the avocado sanitary ware with modern white pieces, but the floor and walls were still unfinished. He had to check that his hair wasn't standing on end in the mirror in the hall. Megan came up behind him as he was dealing with a cow lick and rested her hand on his back. The warmth of her palm through the cotton of his shirt sent a tremor of awareness through him – a simple gesture but a connection. Suggesting a day out had been right. Her shoulders were relaxed now and her expression full of anticipation.

'Ready?' He met her eyes in the mirror.

'Ready,' she confirmed.

Gideon led them to the SUV, pausing before getting in to look across the bonnet at Megan. Her eyes were lively with a promise that sent heat skittering through him. He wanted to take her into his arms *now*. The way she was grinning indicated she knew exactly what he was thinking. *And she's thinking it too. But not in front of an interested audience of gardeners and builders.* He swung himself into the car and reached to start the engine. It was going to happen soon.

He couldn't wait.

Ellery parked his hire car on the gravel space before the front door. He had to acknowledge a degree of surprise. He'd known Il Giardino delle Rose was an extensive estate, but he hadn't expected something this impressive. And there was work going on – a lot of work – in both house and grounds. He frowned. The reporter had implied that the value of the inheritance was only in the property. He hoped Megan hadn't been talked into taking out loans against the sale by some so-called adviser.

He got out of the car, collected the flowers, straightened his tie and took a deep breath. At the very least he would get Megan to agree to dinner tonight. He'd tried phoning her, but the number seemed to be unobtainable – probably some technical glitch from international connections.

He'd started for the door when he was hailed by a workman ambling around the side of the house. The man wore a faded T-shirt with a gardening contractors' logo. 'You looking for someone?'

'I'm calling on Dr Morrison,' Ellery said stiffly. Really, he didn't see why he should justify himself to a gardener, but he was glad to have the flowers as his reason for calling.

'She's gone out. With the boss.'

Ellery hesitated. Who exactly was the boss, and why was Megan with him? He would have liked to know, but he wasn't about to question a workman. 'I presume I can leave these in the house.' He indicated the bouquet.

'Yeah.' The man gave a careless shrug. 'Maria'll take them.'

The young woman who answered the door, presumably Maria, confirmed that Megan was not at home. She agreed, somewhat reluctantly, to let him enter to leave a note, showing him into a small library and standing by the door while he wrote. The room was very pleasant. He could envisage a desk near the window, something big and antique, suitable for composing papers for journals and lecture notes …

The sound of hammering brought him back to the matter in hand. Finishing the note, he made a carefully casual remark about the scale of the building work, but the girl just looked at him with blank eyes. *Clearly not too bright.* He sealed the envelope and handed it to her. 'Make sure Miss Morrison gets that as soon as she comes in,' he emphasised. He hadn't given up hope that Megan would make it for dinner at the hotel. 'Have you any indication when that will be?'

'Don't know. She didn't say. Maybe she will be out all day.'

'Well, make sure she gets it immediately. And if she should return soon, I intend to look around the garden before I leave. I've heard a great deal about it.'

Another careless shrug, before she ushered him to the door.

When Ellery returned to the car, an hour later, he was slightly stunned. The grounds were huge, gardens within gardens, glasshouses, stands of trees, statuary. He'd found a more amenable gardener to quiz and discovered that there were vineyards and an olive farm in addition to the main estate, before an old man with an execrable accent came to escort him back to his vehicle. He'd seen enough by then. *Enough to completely revise his ideas.* He started the engine, raising his hand to the old man who was standing on the steps watching him. *Making sure he left.*

He would be back, and there would be some changes.

The idea of keeping the property as local base was growing. Just the villa, with a much smaller garden – something manageable where only one or two part-time gardeners would be needed to assist Megan. The rest of the grounds could easily be divided into small plots for buyers to construct holiday or retirement homes. Properly marketed in the UK, he was sure they would sell well. And the promontory, when that ramshackle eyesore of a tower was bulldozed – that was ripe for larger villas with amazing sea views. Schemes danced in his mind. A divided career, here and in Bath, with money to distribute in the right places – endowments and bursaries, buildings even – the Professor and Mrs Ellery Peters' Graduate Library?

He'd reached the gates. He turned the car into the road. If Megan didn't show up for dinner, he would be back here in the morning.

Chapter Twenty-Five

The second kiss happened on the terrace of the Rossi vineyard, looking down over the neat rows of vines.

As the vineyard was on the route that would eventually take them into Portofino, Megan suggested an early lunch in the restaurant that was part of the visitor centre. She'd not been to the place since a short formal introduction, accompanied by Signor Agnello; a quick and confusing glimpse on a day heavy with rain. Now they had leisure to look around and properly meet the manager and staff who ran the enterprise for the estate, producing wine and also staging vineyard tours and running catering facilities.

On a private tour with the manager, Megan was impressed that her unannounced arrival had not fazed the man. His enthusiasm shone as he conducted them around all the components of making a light but excellent white wine. He was just as keen for them to sample the food that was on offer, taking them to the entrance of the empty restaurant terrace before darting off to find one of the waiting staff. Megan caught her breath. The place was lovely. A wide flagstone area, dotted with simple rustic tables surrounded by arches supporting bougainvillea – and there was an amazing view.

Walking ahead of Gideon, Megan stopped at the top of two shallow steps shielded by the entrance arch. She let Gideon almost walk into her, knowing his arms would come around her to steady her. Laughter bubbled up inside her for no reason other than that the sun was shining and that this man, who smelled so good and felt even better, was going to kiss her. It was so easy simply to turn in his arms with the laughter and the invitation in her eyes.

He was smiling as his mouth came down on hers. Her breath hissed out in a sigh as her lips parted.

The second kiss.

Totally different from the first, full of light and sunshine, a kiss of daylight and anticipation rather than surprise and shadows. *But every bit as good.* The sound of a discreet cough drew them apart. A waitress in jeans and white T-shirt, enveloped in a stylish dark blue apron, was grinning at them from the restaurant, waiting to show them to a table. Megan's hand, which had been on Gideon's shoulder, drifted down his arm. When he offered her *his* hand, palm up, she took it, pulling him up the steps and through the arch.

Their table was close to the retaining wall that protected the drop to the vineyard below, giving them the full advantage of the view. Within a few moments, several other couples arrived and the place was soon busy with a low hum of conversation and the enticing scent of food. The waitress brought focaccia and dishes of olive oil, also the product of the Rossi estate, and a single small glass each of the estate wine, in deference to the fact that Gideon was driving. It was delicately chilled, condensation clouding the glass. Megan ran her finger down the cold surface and inhaled deeply, savouring the sensation.

'Mmmm.' Gideon dipped a piece of focaccia in the oil. 'This is good. Your uncle ran this place and the olive groves?'

'So I'm told. That was about twenty years ago.' Megan sighed softly. 'It's so frustrating, knowing so little – just bits and pieces from the lawyers and scraps of family gossip. They had a life here, built a home and raised and lost a child.' For a moment the darkness of that loss squeezed her heart. Gideon stretched his hand over the table and their fingers briefly entwined.

Megan helped herself to a piece of bread and dipped it. It was a very tactile way of eating. She watched Gideon putting torn pieces of bread in his mouth, knowing he was watching her licking oil off her fingers. It was gently teasing, the mildest of flirtations, without pressure. *So different from everything with Ellery, where it was all about appearances.* Had it always been like that? In the beginning, surely it was different? She couldn't remember and she didn't want to think about Ellery when she was *here*, in the moment, with a man who was everything that Ellery wasn't.

The sun was warm. Gideon's presence was both restful and enticing. She wouldn't have expected that combination. He was intriguing her without trying at all.

The focaccia was succeeded by a dish of pasta with basil pesto. When the waitress came to take their empty plates, Megan agreed to her suggestion of panera, a strong coffee ice cream, for dessert. Gideon just opted for the coffee. He was frowning a little. 'Don't get your hopes up too high about this trip to Portofino. We might not find out anything more than you already know,' he warned.

'I understand,' she confirmed. 'But I have to ask.'

When they reached the gallery, Alcinda was not there, but Bianca gladly showed them the paintings and told them what she knew about the legend of the tower. 'It was something our grandmother told us – a local folk tale, I

120

assume. I didn't know it had been turned into a poem – or maybe it was the poem first and that's where the story came from?' she suggested.

'That might be right,' Megan agreed. 'It was written about the time that Byron and Shelley were here on the Riviera.' They'd wandered twice around the display. Megan stopped in front of one of the canvases. 'I would really like to buy this painting.' She turned impulsively to Bianca, whose face lit up at the prospect of selling one of the largest pictures. 'Can you keep it until work is finished at the villa – and maybe advise me on the best place to hang it?'

Bianca grinned. 'For a chance to visit the gardens Alcinda would probably come personally to supervise.'

'That would be lovely.' Megan realised, with a slight surprise, that it would. 'Will you both come?'

'Yes. I'd like that, and I'm sure she would.' Bianca also looked slightly surprised, then she smiled and bustled off to put together sales paperwork.

'What do you think?' Megan turned to Gideon to ask. He had stood back, letting her make her way around the exhibit with Bianca, but she'd been conscious of his presence the whole time. *You're more aware of him than you ever were of Ellery.* The thought was mildly disturbing. *And there was Ellery again.* She pushed away the intrusion.

'I think it's a good choice.' Considering the picture, Gideon answered her question. The one she'd chosen was simply of the garden. No figures, just the rampant undergrowth and the tower in the background, surrounded by gulls. *Just as you saw it that first time, when you went to the villa alone.* It seemed a very long time ago. She realised, with a small shock, how much had happened in the interim. *How much you've changed?* She didn't have time to unpack the idea, or the deep sense of rightness that came with it. Bianca was ushering her to the desk to complete the purchase.

Gideon led the way along the narrow space left between the arcade of shops and the harbour-side restaurants. The building housing the bookshop and his small apartment was two-thirds along. Thoughts of inviting Megan up to the top floor, and of what they might do there, passed quickly through his mind – and were just as quickly discarded. It was too soon. He tried to ignore a tiny nagging doubt, but he had to acknowledge it – the time might never be right. They'd shared a couple of kisses – heat juddered through him at the memory – but maybe that was all there would be. Megan was an academic and the wealthy owner of a magnificent estate – who had just dropped thousands of

Euros on a painting. He ... he wasn't anything. He was just ... that drifter. A year ago, when he was a stakeholder in a family business, or thought he was, things were different. Now he didn't even own his reputation. Even if Megan didn't decide to go back to Foxy, and he really hoped she wouldn't, the gulf between them was huge.

He was jerked out of his thoughts when a waiter from one of the restaurants greeted him by name.

They'd reached the bookshop.

Chapter Twenty-Six

Gideon pushed open the door and stood aside for Megan to enter, relieved to see that Signora Bertolo was in place behind the desk, and that the shop was relatively empty. Since the Easter holidays Portofino had been steadily filling with visitors. *If you hadn't been paying rent, you would have been gone by now.* The sense of loss was powerful and unexpected. He swallowed. *Didn't happen. You're still here.*

He drew Megan forward, introducing her and explaining as briefly as he could what they wanted. Signora Bertolo's eyes widened with surprise and something that he thought, confusingly, might be a trace of guilt. '*You* are the owner of Il Giardino delle Rose.' Signora Bertolo held out her hands to take Megan's. 'I believe I have some things that belong to you.' Megan shot him a questioning look. He could only shrug and shake his head. Signora Bertolo had let Megan go and was beckoning them to the back of the shop, to the bookcase where the second-hand volumes were housed.

'This is where Gideon found the poems and the booklet about the garden.'

'It is,' Signora Bertolo agreed. 'And you see these books.' She indicated the row of paperbacks that had first attracted Gideon's attention. 'I think they too came from the villa. I do not know for certain, but they are all American editions. Your great-great aunt, she was an American.'

'Well, no, she wasn't.' Megan shook her head. 'She was Welsh.'

Now Signora Bertolo was looking confused. 'I was so sure …' She gestured to a seating area in the middle of the shop, currently unoccupied. 'Please sit – I must explain.' There was a small but efficient looking coffee machine on a shelf beside the seats. Signora Bertolo set it going and they sat down. 'I do not know quite how the shop came to acquire those books and the ones that Signor West purchased.' She was clearly perturbed by the admission. Gideon leaned forward, interested and curious. Megan's face reflected the same feelings. 'I visited my daughter in Padua for a few weeks about eighteen months ago. They were here when I returned. I had left my assistant in charge. She is very reliable, but there was a young man helping out here also, just for a month; a student. He left before I returned. He was the one who bought the books.' She grimaced. 'When I checked the inventory later there were one or two – discrepancies, should we say? – and these books. There was paperwork to support the purchase, at somewhat inflated prices, but it was more or less in order. It was the origin of the stock that concerned me. They had been acquired from his friend, who worked for a while in the gardens at the villa.'

'You think the books were stolen?' Megan queried.

'I believed that was possible, but they had both moved on without leaving an address. After a few days of hesitation, I wrote to Signora Rossi to enquire if they were missing. I never received a reply. In the end, I put them on display. The paperwork was, after all, in order and the other boy was an American. They *might* have belonged to him. There was nothing obvious to say that it was not so. I looked. There are maybe six or seven that have been sold, and of course the poems and the garden guide.' She sighed. 'That was what made me think that the books came from the villa. I really should have called to see your aunt.'

Megan gestured, dismissing the suggestion. 'I think by then she was quite ill. She probably would not have agreed to see you.' The coffee machine made a gentle beeping noise. Signora Bertolo rose to pour coffee. Gideon took his cup with thanks, watching Megan's face. She was clearly thinking. 'The books were bought in good faith. I'm not expecting you to return them, but would it be okay if we looked through them again, to see if there *is* anything personal in them?'

Signora Bertolo agreed, with visible relief, before going back to the desk to serve a customer. Gideon fetched the books from the shelf and divided them into two piles, passing one to Megan. She looked at him, slightly shamefaced. 'Sorry, I seem to have disposed of the rest of your afternoon.'

He grinned. 'You really think I'm going to miss out on a treasure hunt?'

Megan smiled back. 'Well, if you put it like that!'

He reached for a book. *Really, I'd spend all night here, just for that smile.*

It took them an hour and a half and another round of coffee to go carefully through the volumes. There was some excitement when Megan found handwriting in a dog-eared copy of *For Whom the Bell Tolls,* but it proved to be only margin notes on the text.

'Unless it's in code, it's just notes.' She put the book on the completed pile.

Gideon was the one who found the small clue. He held out a hardback copy of Truman Capote's *In Cold Blood.* On the inside of the back cover there was a small sticker with the details of a bookstore in Boston,

Massachusetts, and the ragged remains of a bookplate. A stylised swirl of roses around what might have been part of a capital letter "R".

'For Rossi?' Megan suggested when he showed her.

'So maybe the books *did* come from the library at the house.'

Megan took the book. 'Maria says that Olwen had the contents of the library put into storage a few months before she died. She was afraid of the books being neglected and damaged. Perhaps the student who was working in the garden helped himself to a few when the boxes were left unattended somewhere.'

'Sounds plausible. It doesn't get us very much further though.'

'It suggests they were in America at some stage.' She checked the publication date of the book. '1966 – if that's where they went after the war, it might fit with the idea that Uncle Eduardo made money on the stock market.'

They finished the last few books, but nothing else turned up.

'No old letters being used as bookmarks, or tell-tale inscriptions on a flyleaf.' Megan sat back with a disconsolate air. 'I started off wanting to know about the garden. Now I want to know about *her*. And her son – Cosimo.' She looked at the book with the margin notes. 'Maybe that was schoolbook of his?' she speculated. 'He must have gone to school somewhere, had friends, girlfriends even. There should be records – maybe people who remember.'

Gideon studied her face, watching her sort through the possibilities. This was her family she was trying to reach into the past to find. *That sense of connection.* Something cold flitted across his chest. He knew about that rootless feeling. For a second he thought about his apartment on the top floor. He could take Megan up there, and for a short time that would be all that mattered. He could take that desolate look from her face; without arrogance, he was sure of it. And wipe out the chill around his own heart,

But it's too soon. He didn't need the voice in his head to remind him.

And Megan had come to a decision. He could see that in her expression. 'I'm going to ask Signor Agnello to make enquiries, get an investigator if necessary, to see what they can find out – put all the half-truths and mysteries to rest. Maybe some of the people at the party last night could have helped, if I'd known who to ask – maybe Signora De Stefano herself. I was focused on the paintings, but now I want to know about my family.'

The determination in her eyes twisted his heart in a different way. 'It sounds good, to try to find out.' He stood, stretching out a hand to pull her up from the chair. 'I'll put these books back and run you home.'

When they reached the house, Gideon departed to check on the demolition of the arbour and Megan let herself in, balancing the book with the bookplate, which Signora Bertolo had insisted that she take, and two bottles of wine, acquired at the vineyard, on her hip. The first thing she saw was a large bouquet resting on the side table.

'Wow!' Pleasure was succeeded by realisation as Maria appeared in the doorway of the kitchen. 'From Ellery, I presume?' She handed over the wine and went to look at the blooms. 'I can't remember him ever giving me flowers before.' Maria's expression told her that she was not surprised by this. *You never owned a villa in Italy before.* Amused, Megan deduced that Maria had met Ellery and had not taken to him. 'He brought them himself?'

'This morning.' Maria jerked her head. 'There's a note on your desk. He came in to write it. You are supposed to read it *immediately.*' She grinned. 'He was trying to get a look at the house, and he did get a look round the garden, until Grandpapa saw him off. *Snooping,*' she pronounced with disgust.

'Probably.' Megan sighed. It was inevitable that once he knew about the villa, Ellery would want to see it. It was an annoying ending to a lovely day. *A perfect day?* 'I'd better put them in water.' She wasn't going to take it out on the flowers because of the giver.

They rounded up a selection of vases and distributed them to the rooms that were in use and not inhabited by the builders. The bouquet really was lovely. The delicate fragrance from a vase crammed with dark pink stocks filled the hall.

Megan was tempted simply to open the wine and share a glass with Maria, leaving Ellery's note until the morning. *But it will only keep hovering in the back of your mind.* She had other more pressing things to think about. With another sigh, she headed to the library.

Ellery was inviting her to dinner with Freddie De Stefano and his partner. The chance to ask Freddie whether his stepmother might remember her aunt would be good, but she knew it would not be a pleasant evening with people who might become friends. It would be about whatever agenda Ellery had going on. The note was more like a command than an invitation, including instructions about what she should wear. The dress code was a red flag. She'd experienced many similar encounters, so was aware of what would be expected. She would sit, demure and supportive, while Ellery demonstrated who was the smartest man in the room.

'I don't think so, Dr Peters.' Even if it had not gone six and too late for her to get ready and make the trip to Genoa without being fashionably late – drawing attention to herself, in Ellery's terms – she wasn't going back to playing those games. If the invitation had just been to meet him, she might have made the effort – their final confrontation. She wasn't going to a business meeting. Since coming to Italy, she'd changed her phone, with a new number. Ellery was no longer in her contacts list. He hadn't put his number on the note and she certainly couldn't remember it, so she couldn't text him and he wouldn't be able to text or call her. *He'll find out soon enough that you're not coming. Maybe that will tell him something?* She dropped the note into the wastepaper bin. It landed with a satisfying clunk.

She was crossing the hall when Gideon emerged from the kitchen, looking a little uncertain. 'Maria said you had flowers delivered.' He indicated the stocks and another large display on the hall table.

'Rather a lot of them. And an invitation to dinner. I'm not going,' she said evenly.

Gideon's face cleared. There was even a trace of a smile. 'The flowers *are* lovely.'

'You're giving me a whole garden of them.' Suddenly, that seemed important. She swooped across the hall, pulling Gideon into a small room beside the front door, where the floor was stacked with paint tins and tools.

Kiss number three was toe-curlingly good. *We're getting the hang of this.* Almost as good was lingering in Gideon's arms afterwards, her head on his chest, listening to the thump of his heart. She'd never stood like this with Ellery, holding and being held. 'Thank you for the day.' She looked up to meet his eyes. *Such dark brown, reassuring eyes.* Something pulsed along her spine. It was nonsense, but with Gideon she felt *safe.*

Gideon pulled her close in a quick hug, then released her. 'I'd better get going.' His lips on her forehead were warm and brief. 'I'll see you tomorrow.'

Chapter Twenty-Seven

Ellery sat in the hotel bar, restlessly checking his watch. He'd told Megan to meet him here, and with only half an hour to go, she was cutting it fine. He took a careful sip of his Aperol Spritz over ice. He needed to keep a clear head. He did *not* need Megan rushing in at the last minute, late and flustered, making herself the centre of attention. He sipped again, aware that the man sitting two stools along at the bar was watching him. He returned the man's look with a frown. The man seemed to interpret that as an invitation. He leaned over, offering his hand. 'Antonio Cascione. I saw you at Signora De Stephano's last night, but we didn't get to speak.'

'Ah.' Ellery relaxed a little. Networking – that was good, although the man didn't look like an academic. *So, what is this?*

Cascione handed over his card. 'I'm in property – a developer. Put in an offer for that place of your fiancée's.' He gave a rueful shrug. 'Her lawyer turned me down flat.'

'Oh, well, lawyers.' Ellery returned the shrug, man-of-the-world style. 'To be honest, Megan and I haven't made any firm decisions on the future yet.' He gave the ice in his glass a casual stir. 'It's a big chunk of land. Out of interest, what did you have in mind for it?'

Ellery walked towards the restaurant entrance. Ahead of him, he could see Freddie and his partner being shown to a table. Megan had not turned up after all. The flicker of annoyance was only momentary. The conversation he'd just had at the bar was too exciting to dwell on minor irritations. Cascione had almost exactly the same ideas for development as he had. He'd promised Ellery sight of plans and specifications. He'd also made it clear that he had the right local connections to make it happen. They'd arranged to meet the next morning outside the Institute. Ellery could then go straight to Megan to show her how their future would be assured. Anticipation built in his chest. He had to contain it. This dinner was important. Straightening his tie, he walked forward, prepared to impress Freddie De Stefano.

'Good evening.' Freddie half rose to greet him. Ellery waved him and Giancarlo, his partner, back into their seats. The waiter was fussing with a bottle of red wine, opening and pouring, and then there was the business of ordering from the menu. Ellery made sure his choices were discerning but not extravagant. He tasted the wine. It was excellent. He said so, raising his glass.

The two men responded with nods and smiles. Freddie replaced his glass on the table with careful precision then looked up. 'I'm glad we can have this meeting, Dottore Peters. I'm sure there is much to discuss.' He smiled encouragingly. 'But first, you can perhaps enlighten me – I am intrigued – why was my stepmother so insistent you be invited to lecture at the Institute?'

Megan sat on the loggia, sipping from a glass of the estate wine. It had been a crowded day. *Starting with a bullet and ending with a kiss.* She could have invited Gideon to stay for dinner, but she was glad she hadn't. She needed space to think. Whatever this was between them, she didn't want it to grow too fast. She'd been swept off her feet by Ellery, and she didn't want that happening again. She frowned at her glass. She'd spent too much of the day thinking about Ellery, but he was going to keep intruding until she finally had things out with him. *And he was part of your life for a long time.*

She stared out at the darkening garden. She could just hear the sound of the sea, far below the villa. Ellery had come into her life when she'd still been coping with the loss of her parents and her gran. She'd needed someone and Ellery had seemed right. An academic, older, with an established and clear path to his future – upwards. She'd thought she belonged with him. She had been sure that her parents would have approved, that he was the right man for her. When had she realised that, instead of walking beside him into that future, her place was always to walk behind? She wasn't entirely sure that she *had* ... until Ellery found someone who fitted the role better.

Now she could see things that had drawn him to her – her parents' reputations and the attention attracted by their premature deaths. She'd been the tragic heroine, ripe for very public rescue. He might have expected an inheritance too – except that her parents put every penny they had into funding their various digs all over the world. Gran had specified in a letter of wishes that her small legacy was to help support Megan's PhD studies and her solicitor had made sure that it did.

Megan's shoulders hunched as her thoughts took shape. It was not an edifying picture, but she was sure it was the correct one. Although he hadn't been her academic supervisor, she'd sat at Ellery's feet for four years. Gradually her status as tragic heroine faded. Now she was emerging tentatively as an academic in her own right – no longer a protégée but a potential rival? And then along came Julia, with the right connections, some money of her own and no academic pretensions.

Megan put down her glass, pulling her feet onto the chair so that she could wrap her arms around her legs and rest her chin on her knees. Ellery had taken the future they had planned, along with everything she'd thought was fixed in her life. She'd touched rock bottom again, but she'd recognised it – and known that she had to make it back up by herself. She'd never in her wildest dreams expected Olwen's gift of a whole new life. And she was going to make it work.

It would be foolish not to acknowledge that money and security gave her confidence. It wasn't just the money though; it was the villa itself. The place was *hers.* Her parents had been nomads at heart, renting a succession of houses, their thoughts always on the next dig. The most settled home she'd known growing up had been her grandmother's council house, where she spent the school holidays while her parents moved from one archaeological site to another. Now she had somewhere to belong. She had to make something of that. She wasn't Sleeping Beauty waiting to be awakened with a kiss. *Although a kiss from Gideon is always welcome.* She smiled in the gathering dusk. *Very welcome.*

She'd thrown herself into renovating the villa, but now she had to think about her career as well. And she had something to work on. Her heart started to beat a little faster as she remembered. The legend of the poems could be linked to the tower on the headland, and she had a whole new raft of possibilities to explore. If she talked to people and sought out storytelling traditions, where might that take her? While she did that, she might also trace the history of her own family. People who knew about the tower might also know things about her aunt. Excitement stirred her. She had to put some effort into planning. All she had at present were confusing contradictions, but surely there was someone out there who knew the real story?

She picked up her glass again, taking a thoughtful slip, letting the wine rest on her tongue. The taste took her back to lunch – with Gideon. She couldn't help a soft laugh at the shiver that ran over her skin. *Pure lust, my girl.* She leaned back in her chair. The man was worthy of lust, but he was more than that. He was someone who might be a friend as well as a lover. That afternoon in the bookshop, checking through dusty paperbacks – that was friendship. Ellery would never have done that. She grimaced. *There he is again!* She had to keep Ellery out of her thoughts. Comparing and contrasting the two men was not the way to go.

Gideon made her feel safe. The shiver that ran over her skin now was totally different. That was a trap she *mustn't* fall into. She'd leaned on Ellery at a time when she deeply needed support and got stuck in a relationship that ultimately gave her nothing. She understood that now. *Just because Gideon West is the size of a house, kisses like an angel and prunes a mean rosebush does* not *make him the answer to a maiden's prayer.* She wasn't going there again. *Stand on your own two feet this time, my girl.*

Whatever she had with Gideon would be flirtatious and fun.

And over when it's over.

On that resolution, she drained her glass and stood up. She'd just remembered the book she'd brought back from the shop. She'd abandoned it on the hall table, diverted by the flowers. She padded inside to retrieve it. Carrying it to the library, she pulled down a few hardback volumes, finding those with bookplates in them and comparing them with the remnants left in the Capote.

The bookplates matched.

The main course had been served and eaten. Ellery was sweating a little under a polite but relentless inquisition. He was holding his own. On a couple of occasions he knew that Freddie had been impressed by his answers. That first question had almost thrown him though. *Gabriella De Stephano had asked for him?* He'd dredged up a memory of an article in a popular magazine in which his name had been mentioned and that she might have read. It had been enough. Once he made it onto firmer ground, he'd been able to put forward ideas and arguments he'd used before in similar circumstances. He was *good* at this.

At last, the interrogation part of the evening seemed to be over. Whatever Freddie had in his mind, Ellery sensed he'd passed the test. *More good news to share with Megan.* With dessert on the horizon, conversation became lighter and more general.

'It is a pity Dottoressa Morrison could not join us this evening.' Freddie snapped the dessert menu closed and gave his order. 'The property she has inherited must be taking up a lot of her time. It is quite a change of circumstances from the academic life.'

'It is,' Ellery agreed, declining dessert in favour of coffee. 'Things will move faster now I'm here, of course. Such a large estate.' He shook his head. 'We want to keep the villa itself, naturally, to maintain Megan's family connection—'

'But the rest will be sold?' This was Giancarlo, looking curious.

131

'We haven't fully discussed it, but it's the obvious course of action,' Ellery agreed expansively. 'Funnily enough, I just had a very positive discussion with Antonio Cascione – he's a developer with some interesting ideas.'

Giancarlo leaned forward. He'd been polite but clearly bored through the academic talk. Now there was interest in his eyes. Ellery remembered that the man was an architect. It might be useful to know his opinion.

'We were talking about dividing the garden into small plots for sale, and on the headland, luxury villas ...'

Chapter Twenty-Eight

'So. How *was* lunch?'

'Very good. It was just lunch, Alcinda,' Gideon said placidly, declining to elaborate.

After a couple of days working in the studio, when she hadn't needed him, they were back on the beach. Alcinda was teasing him, as usual, when she wasn't hissing at him not to move, which she was doing now. He settled back into the pose. Alcinda carried on for another fifteen minutes, before putting down her brush. Gideon heaved a sigh of relief. The sun was coming up and the coat he was wearing was warm and heavy. He shrugged it off and dumped it on the rock. Alcinda cleaned her brushes, critically surveying the canvas.

'You know, I'm beginning to wonder whether I should be paying you modelling fees.'

'Really?' Startled, he walked round to look at the painting. 'Why?'

'This—' she pointed at the canvas '—is going to be *huge*. Women will queue around the block to try to buy it. And a few men too.' She tilted her head provocatively. Gideon just laughed. She ought to know that she wouldn't get a reaction. 'I may have to sell prints.' Her expression now was pensive. 'I want more. A whole series of paintings.'

Gideon looked curiously at the picture. To his untutored eye, it looked almost finished, although Alcinda said there was more to do. She'd captured a man, *him,* Perseus, standing on a rocky beach with the dawn just breaking behind him – head down, lost in thought, half shadowed, enveloped in his greatcoat. At his feet an indistinct swirling shape was washed by the receding tide – a jellyfish, or the snake-haired head of the Gorgon? It was powerful and disturbing – a modern take on an ancient legend. It was difficult to believe that it was him. *It isn't a portrait, it's Alcinda's vision.* 'You think it's *that* good?'

'It *is* that good.' She flipped him the finger, knowing he was getting his own back for her teasing.

They set off up the beach, Gideon carrying the canvas, suitably protected, and Alcinda with her painting gear.

'I heard about your visit to the gallery. I'm sorry I wasn't there.' There was genuine regret in her voice.

'It was a spur of the moment thing.'

'Dottoressa Morrison has excellent taste.' They'd paused to cross the road from the beach.

'Because she chose the biggest painting?'

'Because she wants expert advice on where to hang it,' Alcinda reproved. She looked thoughtful as they passed slowly up the street to the building that housed her studio. 'That, I assume, is her academic nature – to seek out expertise when she needs it.'

They'd reached their destination. Alcinda pushed open the outer door for Gideon to bring the painting through. When they reached the top of the stairs with his awkward burden, he was breathing a little more heavily than he would have liked. Manhandling it carefully into the studio, he got a surprise; it seemed Alcinda had begun another painting, almost the same as the one he was carrying, but this one was life-sized. 'Wow!'

'You like?' Alcinda's grin was very smug.

'It's ... powerful,' he said hesitantly.

'Mmm.' Alcinda nodded and came to stand beside him, her face unusually tense. 'I'm serious, Gideon. This piece—' she gestured at the picture '—there's something there that even I don't quite understand.' She looked up. 'This is taking me to a whole new level. That's why I want to do a series, with you. I have things here.' She tapped her forehead. 'Achilles, Theseus, Apollo.' For a moment her eyes clouded, perhaps seeing visions. *Uncomfortable visions.* Then, abruptly, she was back and seeing *him* again. 'You're built on heroic proportions, Gideon West. You stir my senses.' Now her expression was wicked. 'In a totally artistic way, of course.'

'Of course,' he agreed, laughing. 'Well, as long as I'm here.'

'Be nice to Signora Morrison,' Alcinda instructed. 'Make her a beautiful garden and make beautiful love to her too – then she will keep you and I can have you also.'

Gideon decided it was time to leave, before the blush that threatened to ambush him took hold. He said a quick goodbye and escaped to the street. Alcinda was uncannily perceptive, or maybe she just took the time and trouble to look? She knew how things were between him and Megan. *How you want them to be.* She'd also seen something else. Megan Morrison recognised expertise and employed it. He was an expert.

Just passing through.

The flowers were quite lovely. Gabriella surveyed them with approval. Even better was the delightful note that accompanied them from Dottore Peters, expressing his thanks for her hospitality and for helping reunite him with Megan. Gabriella sighed in satisfaction. She would respond in due course with an invitation for them to lunch with her. When his lectures were delivered, Ellery would naturally be carrying his reclaimed fiancée back to the UK and the nonsense of restoring Il Giardino delle Rose would be at an end. Her offer would be renewed – a generous offer no sensible man would refuse. Almost clapping her hands in glee, she jumped when her stepson appeared unannounced in the doorway.

'Sorry, Mama. Didn't mean to startle you.' He came forward to kiss her cheek. 'This is only a flying visit. We're on our way back to Milan.'

Gabriella pursed her lips. No doubt that man, her stepson's folly, was waiting in the car. She pouted. 'We've had so little time to talk.'

'I know, but I promise I'll see you again before your birthday.' He was looking at the bouquet, tapping a careless finger on the petal of a hothouse bloom. 'These are pretty. A secret admirer?'

'Dottore Peters, thanking me for the party.'

'A nice gesture,' Freddie approved. 'I have to say thank you too, Mama, for suggesting him for the lecture spot. Giancarlo and I had dinner with him last night – he has some interesting ideas for ways that we might develop the Institute. He's going in to talk to the Director about some of them this morning.'

Gabriella was conscious of the smallest pulse of alarm. 'He will be returning to England with his fiancée, once the lectures are done,' she said carefully.

'Oh, yes.' She relaxed a little at the casual reassurance, but the relief was short-lived. 'He's interested in an ongoing relationship though, and I must say it has possibilities, and of course she has the property. We were speaking about that too.' Freddie was studying something on his phone. 'He's making a deal with a developer, to split most of the land off from the villa and sell as small building lots.' He looked up, oblivious to the way Gabriella's spine had gone rigid. A spasm that was close to pain coursed through her as he kept speaking, 'You know, you could think about downsizing. There will be luxury villas on the promontory, once the old tower is gone. Much easier to manage than this place. I know you like that location and the views will be fabulous.' He turned to her, grinning. *Grinning*, while her heart trembled. 'You really should think about it.' He looked at his watch. 'Must go, darling.' He kissed her cheek again. 'See you soon.'

Gabriella's chest constricted. She couldn't breathe. She wanted to scream, but nothing came out. Black dots flashed in front of her eyes. *No, no, no.* The denial ricocheted silently inside her head. Peters was supposed to take the Englishwoman away, to sell *her* the land. Not this!

She put her hands to her mouth, slowly bringing the room back into focus, drawing breath into her lungs. This had to be stopped. Slowly, she rebuilt her composure. She had to have a plan. She had to see Peters before he made any agreements. He *had* to take her offer. He *would* take it. She needed to speak to him *now.*

Keeping her panic under rigid control, she surveyed the room. For all the magnificence of her apartment she was trapped here. If she called for the car, they would *know.* There would be questions. She pulled in a deep breath, calming herself. She had to *think.* She could still drive. They all kept up a polite pretence that problems with her eyesight prevented it, but there was nothing wrong with her eyes. Her sight was perfect. It was just a device to keep her here, where she could be watched and her movements monitored. So – she could drive, but what? The vehicles in the garage were under the vigilant eye of the chauffeur.

She bit her lip for a moment, then almost laughed aloud. There *was* another car here on the estate. No one knew that *she* knew about it – a small, non-descript vehicle, parked in a distant garage on the edge of the grounds. The car her husband had used when he visited his mistress. It was meant to be discreet, considerate – as if a wife did not know when her husband was visiting his whore. The keys to the garage and the car were still in Giovanni's desk.

She looked out of the window. It was a fine day. No one would question her decision to take a book and sit in the summerhouse. Ellery Peters would be at the Institute; Freddie had said so. She would find him there. All she needed was a few moments to speak with him. With a satisfied sigh for a plan made, she headed for her late husband's study.

Megan knelt on the small lawn beside the loggia steps, considering a large rosemary bush. She had just given it a careful haircut. She had a pile of clippings to be bunched and dried. Her hands smelt pleasantly of the astringent herb. *Getting the hang of this.* She'd intended to spend the morning looking through decorating samples, but the lure of the sunshine was too strong. She'd thought about the rooms that would get attention first as she snipped, particularly the small sitting room where she hoped to hang the garden painting. *The room you dragged Gideon into yesterday.* A little shiver of memory warmed her skin, tinged with guilt. *He wasn't unwilling!*

She knew she couldn't take anything for granted. She'd been surprised this morning when he'd casually mentioned seeing Alcinda, and that she was looking forward to installing the picture. Surprised and a little disturbed. And disturbed that she was disturbed. *And isn't that a tangle?* She hadn't fully taken in that Alcinda was using Gideon as a subject for a painting. And now there was going to be a whole series. She leaned back on her heels. *A little twinge of green-eyed jealousy?* Possibly, she agreed to herself. Then she laughed, scrambling to her feet and tucking the vibrant secateurs carefully into their case then into the pocket of her loose cotton trousers. If Gideon was going to pose for a series of paintings he'd be around for a while, which was good. She pushed jealousy out of her mind

Just a little summer fling, remember?

Ambling through the garden to where there were sounds of activity, Megan found herself in the old rose garden. The arbour was gone, with only a foundation and the climbing rose, now twining around a sturdy obelisk, to mark where it had been. Gideon and Matteo had formed a pruning party, dealing with the bushes in the side beds. Bushes in the central section were beyond help, even she could see that. When Gideon noticed her, he left what he was doing to come over. 'Have you got any ideas?' He gestured to the bedraggled bed.

'More roses?'

'We can do that – be wise to dig out the soil first – or you could have something different. An old-fashioned knot garden might work, or I was wondering …' He hesitated and she was intrigued.

'What?'

'I was wondering about a labyrinth.'

'Oh!' She was fairly sure her face must have lit up as she took in the idea. 'That's awesome.' She moved to pace along the edges of the bed. 'A labyrinth, as opposed to a maze. Used as a tool for meditation or prayer. *Caerdroia.*'

'I'm guessing that's Welsh?' He was grinning now.

'Troy Town – that was what the very old labyrinths were called, after the walls of Troy.'

He nodded. 'It's not a big space, but we can do something with it – turf and stones maybe.'

'I'd like that.' She nodded her head decisively. 'What made you think of it?'

'Oh, we did one for a guy in Cornwall who was opening a meditation centre ...' His voice tailed off. Megan looked up, surprised. He'd shifted so she couldn't see his face. 'Er ... that was a very big one,' he said, rather awkwardly.

'Well, I'll take whatever you can fit in.' She decided it was better not to notice his discomfort, even though her curiosity was aroused. *What had happened in Cornwall?* They'd been talking quite easily, and then he'd remembered – what? Something that happened when "we" were creating the labyrinth? It really wasn't her business. He'd tell her if he wanted to. She wasn't going to pry. 'Hey, I pruned a whole rosemary bush this morning,' she declared, showing off. 'Want to come and look?'

Gabriella let out a triumphant sigh. She'd done it. She was here, sitting in the car within sight of the Institute. She had been nervous, naturally, but it had all gone smoothly. No one had questioned her desire to visit the summerhouse, although no doubt one of them would be there in half an hour or so, to bring her coffee that she hadn't ordered. She'd left a crumpled blanket and a book to suggest that she was walking somewhere nearby. Her heart was beating fiercely when she got to the garage, but the door had opened easily, the car had started without trouble and the tank was full. The chauffeur, a conscientious man with too little to occupy him, no doubt did what was necessary to keep it in order. Perhaps he too used it when he needed to be *discreet*.

Her heart pounded uncomfortably again when she pulled out from the service road at the back of the palazzo, but she had made the journey without trouble, even enjoyed the sense of freedom and the late morning sunlight. She'd parked at a distance at the end of the street, not too close, but where she could see the entrance.

She sat for a moment, slightly at a loss. Getting to the Institute had been the first hurdle. Was Peters there? Could she walk in and ask for him? She bit her lip. What if he had already left? No. She shook her head. That could not happen, not now she had come so far, but she needed to move closer, even if she risked being seen. In a swift decision she reached for the ignition. She would move to where she could be sure of catching Peters as soon as he left the building.

It had been a very successful meeting. Ellery hummed softly under his breath as he jogged down the stairs to the reception area. His lectures on the English Romantic poets on the Ligurian coast would be the culmination of the Institute's current lecture series, and the Director had been receptive to several other ideas.

With a small bound, Ellery reached the bottom of the stairs, regaining his balance and looking at his watch. If Cascione came up with proposals, as promised, he could be at the villa in time for lunch. Satisfaction made him smile as he pushed through the doors into the street. And there was Cascione, carrying a cardboard tube of blueprints and a hefty brochure. Its glossy cover showed an artist's impression of a handsome villa with the sea behind it. Ellery acknowledged him with a smile and an outstretched hand. Cascione shook it warmly and passed over his burden. 'Here you go. Sorry I don't have time to talk – site meeting – but I'll catch you this evening. Hotel bar?'

Ellery received the bundle eagerly, confirming that they would meet in the bar. Cascione walked away with a wave. Ellery tightened his grip on the folder and strode towards his car. If Megan came with him this evening, they might even be able to get an agreement in writing; a letter of intent or something. He really could see a bright future unfolding. He walked along the pavement, lost in delightful plans. He'd had to park right at the end of the road as the street had been busy with parents dropping children off at nursery. Now they were gone and the street was quiet and empty, giving him space to think.

As Gabriella started the car, a movement further down the road caught her eye. Peters, emerging through the swing doors of the Institute to greet a man who was crossing the road. A man holding plans and papers. The developer! She could hear the blood thundering in her ears over the noise of the engine, as the papers were handed over with nods and smiles. Nods and smiles and a *handshake*. The deal was done. Peters would convince his fiancée to take that man's money. *No!* The blood pounded louder, drowning the screaming in her head.

Her hands clenched on the wheel.

She stamped her foot down on the accelerator.

Chapter Twenty-Nine

After Gideon had expressed suitable appreciation, the trip to inspect the
rosemary bush turned into an expedition to the library to look up information
on labyrinths. Megan thought she'd seen a copy of Matthews' classic work,
Mazes and Labyrinths, published in the 1920s. Gideon stood back as she
searched along a shelf.

'Here!' she pronounced in triumph. As she pulled the book out, another
slimmer volume came with it. 'Oh! Look.'

Gideon picked the book up from the floor. It was an American
publication – a guide to creating labyrinths and mazes in domestic gardens.
Megan was looking at him with wide eyes. 'Aunt Olwen was thinking about
that too?' Her voice was hushed. *Awestruck.*

'Looks like it.' He flipped it open 'There will be diagrams – maybe some
ideas. Ahh!' Pressed between the pages was a thin sheet of blue paper – a half
written letter. Silently, he held the open pages towards Megan.

With fingers that trembled a little, she lifted the paper, turning it in her
hand, revealing the sender's address at the top of the page – *Il Giardino delle
Rose.*

'Dearest Mary Jo,' she read. 'I have been nagging Cosimo for days to
write to thank you for your birthday gift, but the boy still has his head full of
poetry and not much room for anything else!! Already he is talking of a
second volume of translations!!! I will continue to nag and you *will* get a
letter, but do not be surprised if it consists of half a page of verse!! Then we
will be turning the house upside down to find out what he has done with it!!!'
Megan looked up, her face pale in the cool light of the library. 'This must
have been written by my aunt. She writes just like my great grandmother –
my gran had a few old letters from when she was at university, with all the
exclamation marks.' She turned the page to show him. 'Cosimo was Olwen's
son – but the references to translations and poetry ...'

Putting her hand to her head, she sat down abruptly on an ornately carved
chair. 'Do you think that *he* was the one who translated the poems? He was
only a teenager when he died.'

'That doesn't make it impossible. He would have been the same sort of
age as the poet,' Gideon pointed out. 'It would explain the expensive binding
and the connection to the villa.'

Gently he took the letter, scanning the remainder. The birthday present to Cosimo was the copy of the book. 'The wretched boy *was* pleased, although he is too distracted to tell you so himself.' The undertone of loving and indulgent pride caught at something in Gideon's chest. 'In between his studies, he is plaguing me to make a labyrinth, like the one you have in the yard at the beach house. Apparently, there is something in one of the verses. He wants it on the cliff, beside the tower, but I keep telling him the ground is too uneven. I think we can manage something smaller.' Beneath was an outline drawing of a labyrinth. The letter ended there.

Maria opened the door and stuck her head in. She came into the room when she saw their expressions. 'What's the matter?'

'Letter from the past.' Megan gestured for him to show Maria. She was looking less shell-shocked, he registered with relief. He could see the academic cogs beginning to whirr. Had her cousin translated the poems – and were there more?

'Ah.' Maria was scanning the letter. 'This is the Marchesa's handwriting – you found it in the book?' She looked puzzled for a moment. 'I wonder why it was never finished and posted? Oh.' Her face crumpled as she noticed a date at the top of the letter. 'I am not certain, but I think it was around that time that the Marchesa's son died.'

Chapter Thirty

Gabriella walked slowly along the path to the summerhouse. Everything looked normal; the quiet sunlit garden, her book and the blanket – now neatly folded on the chair – and yes, a cup of cooling coffee.

She couldn't remember much about the drive back, after ... after ...

She had simply kept her foot on the accelerator and kept going. The car was back in the garage, the door locked, the keys in the pocket of her dress. Her limbs had stopped trembling and her heart no longer raced. In fact, she felt quite calm, calmer than she had for several days. There was really nothing to worry about. In a while she would telephone the lawyer again and push him to resume her offer for Il Giardino delle Rose. She would double— triple the price. Everything would be fine.

She sat at the table near the open door of the summerhouse and picked up her book, stretching out for the cup. The coffee was still warm. And here was the girl who had brought it hurrying along the path. Her expression was strained, but her face cleared when she saw the table was now occupied.

'Signora! I wondered where you were!'

'Just a short walk.' Gabriella picked up the cup with a smile. 'It is such a beautiful day.'

Megan stood beside Gideon, feeling the sun on her face. They were back at the rose garden, looking at the patch in the centre.

'You still want to go ahead?' Gideon asked softly. 'Finding the letter hasn't creeped you out?'

'A bit,' she admitted. 'On the other hand, it's a connection.' She turned around, looking at the whole of the garden, plants bursting into bloom, birds singing in the trees, bees blundering past in search of nectar. 'I've felt it ever since I came here. That it was all – I don't know – that I was part of something?' She shoved a hand through her hair, brushing it off her face. 'Not ghosts or anything like that, just that there was a pattern and I could fit into it ... if I wanted.'

She turned away, looking at the gap where the arbour had been. That all sounded ... odd. *Go on, admit it, it sounds as if you've cracked.* She turned back, knowing that she was giving Gideon a sheepish smile. He wasn't looking at her as if she was crazy. He looked ... as if he understood.

'It's this place.' He gestured the garden. 'The way I kept coming back, even though I knew I was trespassing, and Alcinda came here to paint. Even Tommaso and Maria didn't want to leave.'

They'd established that Maria didn't know anything more about Cosimo Rossi's death. She'd only suspected, from chance remarks and Olwen's sadness around that time of year, that it was a significant date. Tommaso, wrapped up in the garden, hadn't been aware of anything. The investigations Megan had asked Signor Agnello to set in motion were not yet complete. *It's like getting a jigsaw puzzle, one or two pieces at a time.*

She straightened her shoulders, aware that Gideon was watching her. He was right. This place had a hold on all of them. 'Yes.' She nodded decisively, her heart suddenly lighter. 'We will have a labyrinth and I'm going to learn how to use it for meditation. A memorial for Cosimo,' she added softly.

'That sounds good.' Gideon took her hand, squeezed it gently and let her go. 'I'll take some measurements.'

She nodded again and turned to go back to the house. That letter held parts of the jigsaw – but the reference to another volume of translation and a poem about a labyrinth? There was no labyrinth in anything she had seen so far. Her heart kicked up a little. Were there more poems? Where were they? She sighed softly. Would the villa show her, in its own good time?

She was crossing the hall, her hands full of samples of wallpaper and fabrics to spread on the big table in the library, when the doorbell sounded sonorously through the ground floor.

Ellery!

It had to be. She looked at her watch. It was gone three. She'd expected him on the doorstep first thing, demanding to know why she'd stood him up. She really didn't want to see him, but she knew she must. With a heavy heart, she called to Maria that she would answer, dumped her burden onto the nearest chair and went to open the door. It was a few seconds before she recognised the elderly man standing there.

'Dottore Marchiano?' The Director of the Institute's shoulders slumped and his hair was in disarray. His skin was an unhealthy grey colour. He looked as if he had aged ten years since the party.

'Dottoressa Morrison, I ... I am sorry to intrude, but I felt that I must come, personally, to tell you ...' His face crumpled. 'I'm afraid I have some very bad news.'

Chapter Thirty-One

'Ellery is dead.' Megan found her way around the house to the kitchen garden. Gideon and Tommaso were there, putting up a frame to protect soft fruit bushes from depredation by the birds. Maria was sitting in the sun in her grandfather's old canvas chair, supervising.

'What?' Gideon and Maria spoke at the same time. Tommaso stood with his mouth gaping, holding the net. Then Maria was on her feet, guiding Megan to the chair. Megan sank into it gratefully. She felt very cold, despite the sun.

'What the hell happened?' Gideon moved to stand beside Maria.

'It was a car – outside the Institute – a hit-and-run. He died in the ambulance on the way to hospital.'

Maria muttered a shocked blessing, crossing herself. After a second Tommaso followed suit.

Gideon was frowning. 'Did the police come to tell you?'

'No, it was the Institute Director. He looked dreadful ... I really should have made him come in – but he needed to get back because of the police.' She put her hand to her head. 'I can't believe it.'

She'd opened the door expecting to face Ellery.

It was all ... unreal.

Gideon's hand, a quick warm clasp on her shoulder, called her back to the sunny garden. He was speaking to Maria in a low voice. 'Do you have any brandy?'

Maria hurried into the house, returning with a bottle and four glasses, pouring one for each of them. Megan started when Maria shoved a glass into her hand and coughed when the raw heat of the spirit hit the back of her throat. She drank the rest of the glass and handed it back to Maria, who was watching anxiously. 'I'm all right. It was just a shock.'

She turned, putting out her hand. Gideon took it. She curled her fingers around his palm – strong, warm, calloused – *safe*. She shut her eyes and then blinked them open again. 'The Director said it was deliberate. There was a witness, a delivery man – but who would want Ellery dead?'

In the following week, it became clear that, in the opinion of the police, the most likely place to look for the answer was Il Giardino delle Rose. They were all questioned, politely but exhaustively, and all the vehicles examined

– even Tommaso's decrepit old truck. Thankfully neither her bright blue Fiat nor Gideon's SUV matched the witness description of a small black car and everyone questioned had alibis, backed up by the gardeners and the builders.

The confirmation that Ellery had been in discussion with a developer brought a high-ranking officer back with a new set of questions. Megan realised too late that her vehement denial that Ellery was acting on her behalf might not have done her any favours, except perhaps to prove her honesty.

'I don't know what the hell Ellery had in his mind.' She was leaning against a stone balustrade, looking down on the part of the garden that they'd taken to calling the sculpture court. Gideon was leaning beside her, his hand just brushing hers on the warm stone.

An expert from one of the museums in Florence had arrived to inspect the statuary and was excited by a headless and armless torso in one of the small pavilions. He hadn't been much interested in Gideon's goddess – dismissing it as modern, although well executed. It would be cleaned, along with the others.

Megan clenched her fingers on the rough surface of the balustrade. 'From something the policeman said, I think they suspect the driver was a woman – which puts me in the centre of the frame. Ellery must have thought he could persuade me to sell.' That realisation made her angry, which also made her uncomfortable. She didn't want anger. She didn't want *any* strong emotion. She mourned Ellery as someone from her past, and as a life that should not have been cut short, but her heart wasn't touched. *Maybe I did my mourning when he dumped me?*

She squinted up at Gideon, closing one eye against the sunlight. Their nascent relationship was still holding, but that was all it was doing. He'd clearly not been sure how Ellery's death and the investigation would affect her, until she'd shown him, but they'd still not exchanged more than kisses and the occasional touch. Megan wanted more, but, somehow, she hadn't been able to imagine Gideon in her bed – or she in his attic in Portofino.

'You might be the most obvious suspect, but unless this is the plot of an Agatha Christie novel and we're all in it together, the police are not going to break your alibi – oh hello—' Gideon paused. The expert had finished his inspection and was making beckoning signs. 'Looks like we're wanted.'

In the next week the police visits decreased. A report arrived from the solicitor's office, with an apologetic note about the paucity of the material but a promise of continued inquiries. Megan was sitting in the library reading it

145

when Gideon came up to the house with the news that the specialist who would be doing cleaning and restoration had begun work on the statues. He was also looking for a plaster for a cut to his hand, delivered by the headless torso, which had made a spirited attempt *not* to be disturbed. Megan made disparaging noises about Gideon's efforts to tend the cut himself, did it for him, pressed a kiss into his palm and dragged him into the library.

'There's not much – mostly information from official records about births and deaths.' She showed him the report. 'They traced Uncle Eduardo's birth certificate, which was a bit of a surprise. He and Aunt Olwen were much closer in age than I realised, only a few months between them. He must have only been about fifteen when he enlisted. Her birth will be registered in Cardiff, and there's no record of their marriage.'

'Happened abroad – in the States?'

'I'm wondering.' She tapped the paper. 'The details of my aunt's will I already knew. The office of the lawyer who looked after my uncle's affairs before he died burned down and the lawyer himself died a few months later, so the records are gone and there's not much for the last twenty years. Uncle Eduardo passed in 1997.'

'And your aunt began to withdraw from the world.'

'Yes.' Megan nodded sadly. The clerk's report was a catalogue of heartbreak. She took a deep breath and pointed to the last paragraph. 'This is about Olwen's son. He was born in 1970, the year before my mother.' For a second, her face clouded and Gideon registered with a pang that both those children were now gone. 'Olwen was forty-two. He must have been a shock.'

'Or a gift.'

Megan thought about that half-written letter. 'A gift,' she decided. There was sadness again for a young man, a cousin, whom she had never known. 'Maria was right, he died in 1988. Apparently, it was the result of a fall.' She saw a shadow pass across Gideon's face. 'You're thinking maybe suicide?' she interpreted, on a long sigh.

'It crosses your mind. It's one of the biggest causes of death for young men. But why?'

'A question many families must ask themselves.' She stared out of the window. 'If he was entranced by the poems – the story of lovers who killed themselves because they couldn't be together ...'

'Adolescent angst over a girl that his parents disapproved of?'

Megan brought her attention back to the room. 'Who knows? This is only an interim report. I hope I can find someone who will be able to tell me more, but there seems to be so much speculation and rumour. And if it was suicide ...' She found that she couldn't finish the sentence. A wave of tiredness washed over her – Ellery's death and, in those dry sentences on the page, the loss of a young man with his whole life ahead of him. She put up her hands to brush her hair from her face, letting them fall as Gideon moved to frame her face with *his* hands.

The kiss was warm and deep. Life affirming. *He always seems to know.* She nestled into his body, seeking the reassurance of touch. He dropped his hands to hold her.

She shifted restlessly in his arms. Ellery's death was inexplicable. It could only be a grotesque case of mistaken identity. Ellery had died in someone else's place. *We might never know who or why.* There was an ache too under her ribs for the cruel loss of her great-great aunt's only child, that late born boy. No wonder Olwen had retreated, closing herself into the sanctuary of Il Giardino delle Rose – a place of pain but also lost love. *Whose walls are currently closing in on her great-great niece.* 'I wish ... I'd like to get away.' Impulsively, she voiced her thoughts.

'Why can't you?' He tipped her chin to look into her face. 'Why can't *we*?'

'We,' she confirmed. She didn't want to be alone.

'Then how about taking a day out? We could go and visit a garden somewhere – research.'

Megan found herself laughing. 'Busman's holiday?'

'Why not? We can go all the way to the border, to the Hanbury Gardens – La Mortola. That's another garden created by a British ex-pat, but that was in 1867. It was badly damaged in the war, but there's been a lot of work done since. It's bound to give you ideas.'

Megan put her hands flat on Gideon's chest. He was giving her ideas already. With the shadow of murder – she managed to get her mind around the word – hanging over them, and *between* them, she and Gideon had been skirting around each other. Careful. Circumspect. She knew what was in his mind – not giving the police any more grounds for suspicion. He was caring for her by keeping his distance, but when they did touch or kiss the heat was still there. She *wanted* that heat.

'Let's do it. Let's go tomorrow. To La Mortola.'

Chapter Thirty-Two

Gabriella De Stefano adjusted the parasol arranged over her chair so that none of the sun's rays touched her complexion. The day was warm and the small terrace outside the summerhouse was sheltered from any breeze. She'd taken to sitting here for an hour every morning before walking for a while in the grounds. Should they be asked, she doubted if the staff would remember any specific day with certainty. Of course, there had been no questions. Ellery Peters' body had been returned to his family in England, the schedule of lectures at the Institute had been adjusted and the matter had faded from interest. The … incident … had been unfortunate but necessary. It was now best forgotten.

Gabriella put down her cup of coffee and dabbed her mouth delicately with a small linen napkin. She had given the chauffeur a large bonus and a week's leave and arranged with Freddie that he would not return. His replacement knew nothing of that *discreet* car, garaged in the grounds. She had walked that way just yesterday. No one had been near the place.

She tapped a finger against the bone china cup, admiring the newly applied polish in pale rose, then frowned a little. The Morrison girl was digging into the past, trying to find out about the old woman and her son. For a disconcerting second, Gabriella's hand trembled. She rested it flat on the table. *All that was a long time ago.* It was fortunate that her manicurist was engaged to one of the clerks in the fool solicitor's office and that the girl was a gossip. All it took was a few well-placed solicitous-seeming questions. Gabriella admired her nails once again. Her hands had always been beautiful and she knew how to take care of them.

She picked up the cup to drink the remains of her coffee. If Megan Morrison was asking the solicitor to make enquiries, then the old woman had not left any papers behind. A small cloud of worry lifted. No letters or diaries. It *was* all a long time ago. Even so, Gabriella's hand, returning the cup to its saucer, still trembled slightly. Her memory of the time before her darling Giovanni whisked her away to their beautiful home in the Caribbean was hazy in places … and there were other occasions, before her marriage …

Her fingers convulsed on the delicate cup. She unclenched them with an effort. She had been *ill*. Giovanni had said so. He had cared for her and kept her safe, away from all the things that might disturb her. *The injustices.* They hadn't seemed to matter there, in the beauty of the Caribbean with her beloved husband. Now … now he was gone and she was back here where she belonged, ready to claim her proper inheritance. Her mind was very clear on that. She hoped that the unfortunate accident and the attentions of the police would convince Dottoressa Morrison to accept her very much increased offer. She folded her hands in her lap.

Il Giardino delle Rose *would* be hers before the summer was out.

'This is lovely.' Gideon watched Megan breathe out, visibly relaxing as she took in the historic garden and the view over the sea. 'I'm so glad you suggested it.' She looked around her with a critical eye. 'I can see how it influenced Olwen – the statues and the cypress trees and the loggia up at the villa. She created Il Giardino delle Rose from a bare site just like Hanbury did. And that!' She gestured to the Tempietto – the Temple of the Four Seasons – where they were standing, a dome supported by stone pillars. 'She *completely* stole that.'

Gideon laughed. 'To be fair, I've seen similar things in other places, but I think maybe she did copy this one.' He could see Megan taking in that she was following in her aunt's footsteps. 'It's really coming to mean a lot to you isn't it – that connection?' he asked impulsively.

'Yes, it is.' Megan turned, shading her eyes from the sun. 'Leaving me the villa was a gift at a time when I really needed it. I want to do right by her and the garden.' They fell into step, descending one of the paths, and Megan pointed. 'That's something we don't have.' She indicated a large agave. 'Or the cacti and the aloes. We could try them on the undeveloped part around the tower,' she suggested.

Gideon didn't respond at once, disconcerted by her confident use of "we". *Did she realise?* When she looked quizzically at him, he hurried to nod. 'Worth a try.'

When she grinned, Gideon felt a strange sensation, as if the sun had come out, except that the sun was already shining quite hotly. 'Shall we find a drink and maybe something to eat?' he proposed to cover his confusion. They'd started out early and food seemed a good idea.

'Sounds good,' Megan agreed. 'And there's something else here that I want too – a citrus grove.'

They spent the rest of the afternoon companionably exploring all the planting. Their research into the grove idea included a long conversation with one of the staff tending the citrus trees that were a hallmark of Hanbury. Gideon was aware of tension building in him. He thought he was picking up something from Megan too. Soon they would have to leave for the drive back, unless ... He hadn't had an ulterior motive when he suggested the trip to the border, but he couldn't deny that when they'd set out this morning, he'd wondered ...

When Megan put a hand on his arm and looked up at him, clear-eyed, he wasn't entirely surprised. 'I don't want to go back tonight. Can we stay?'

Megan was getting nervous. She'd rung Maria and they'd found a small hotel in Ventimiglia, with a simple but welcoming room and a view of the sea. After some essential shopping, there was dinner in a busy restaurant that specialised in seafood. Gideon had kept everything light and made no demands or assumptions. *Not that kind of man.* Now she was standing on a tiny balcony, watching the stars come out over the water and wondering exactly what she was doing.

She wanted this, wanted Gideon – but she hadn't been to bed with anyone but Ellery for over four years. She flinched away from thoughts of Ellery, but couldn't avoid them. She'd slept with him on their third date. It hadn't really been a conscious decision. He'd expected it – and she'd convinced herself that she was falling in love. Now she recognised that the decisiveness she'd seen in him, that she thought she needed, was really only entitlement. It wasn't just familiarity either; Ellery had teased her on occasions that she was restrained when they were in bed. Had he been suggesting she was frigid? It was true that she didn't always make it over the line. More often than not actually, but Ellery had been satisfied even if she wasn't.

Her stomach was churning now, and she was getting cold in a way that had nothing to do with the night air. Desires and worries seethed about, making her feel slightly sick. She wasn't in love with Gideon, but she did want him, or she thought she did. Just kissing him turned her inside out, but when it actually came to it—

'We don't have to do anything.' Gideon stepped behind her on the balcony, folding her very gently into his arms, so that she was leaning back against his chest. 'Just watch the stars and cuddle a bit.'

'Is that ...' Her voice was husky. 'How can I ... *I* asked you ...'

'You said you didn't want to go back tonight, that's all.' She could feel his breath, warm on the side of her neck. Suddenly she very much wanted him to kiss her there. And she wasn't feeling so cold. *How can you be cold with this warm man engulfing you*? 'I know this is pretty strange, being here like this with me,' he said simply.

'I haven't—' Abruptly, she turned in his arms, putting her palms against his chest. Her body was telling her that this was *good*. That it felt good to be enfolded by a man whose muscles came from hard work, not an expensive gym. He was big and warm, and she could tell from the way that he pressed against her that he wanted her. *But he isn't going to push you into anything.* 'There was no one but Ellery for a long time.' She almost baulked at the name, but she had to say it. 'And no one since Ellery.'

'It's been a while for me too,' he admitted softly. His lips touched her forehead briefly. 'There was someone, a year ago …' His voice tailed off, and in a heartbeat Megan knew what she had to do. She put a hand up swiftly to cover his mouth, shaking her head.

'No more. Tonight, there's just us. No one else here. Just us.' The balcony was dark and shadowy, but she saw the glitter of Gideon's eyes as she dropped her hand. She tilted her chin up to meet him.

The kiss was long and sweet, with a dragging undertow that put ripples of awareness into her nerve endings. When his hand gently cupped her breast, she was ready. *This* didn't feel cold. This felt like she *wanted* Gideon West and she was going to have him. A full body shiver went through her.

He pulled away instantly. 'What?'

'Nothing. Anticipation,' she clarified.

'I like that.'

He guided her back through the French doors into the room, warmly lit by the shaded bedside lights, and to the bed. And they did cuddle, just for a while, shedding garments bit by bit. Gideon touched every piece of skin as it was revealed, stroking and kissing her wrists, her inner elbows, her collarbone, her throat.

A restless need was building inside her. In the back of her mind, she understood the control he was exerting to give her this. It was soft and slow and languorous, and she could stop right here. Suddenly, like a switch being flicked, she didn't want slow and languorous – she wanted heat and sparks.

She turned to run her hands over him, feeling as much as hearing a soft laugh as she explored his rib cage and down, and the quick in-drawn gasp as her hand reached his zip. 'Oh, sweetheart.'

His breath was warm on her neck again. She shifted, inviting the kiss, inviting his hands on her breasts, feeling the throb of his heart and the rapidity of his breathing. Clothes peeled away until skin met skin. She *wanted* this.

'Gideon.' She pushed back a little, so that she could look into his face. 'Make love to me.'

It had been ... like nothing she had ever experienced before. They'd teased and touched, and Gideon's mouth and hands had gone places and done things she'd only ever imagined before, until she was panting and moaning and wanting and, yes, begging. She'd given as good as she got, putting her hands and mouth on him in return, moving instinctively, wanting to please him, to make him desperate.

Restrained – like hell!

By the time he'd reached for a condom, his hands had been shaky. *I did that.*

When he slid inside her and she felt his weight, she was just about ready to detonate … and in a few short moments, she did. She hadn't been sure that she hadn't died. Blissfully. The room had come slowly back into focus.

And now they were cuddling again, her head on his shoulder, and everything was amazing.

'That was—'

'Stupendous, awesome, mind-blowing,' she suggested, before a tiny thrill of apprehension caught her. What if he hadn't felt—

'All of those.' His arm tightened around her, and she knew he'd picked up on what she was thinking. 'It was also rather fast ...' He settled his chin on her hair and she felt his heart beating under her ear. 'Maybe next time we can take the ending just a little slower?'

'Next time?' She wriggled to prop herself up on one elbow. She traced a pattern on his chest with one finger, letting it wander down through the light furring of hair to the treasure trail that led to well – treasure. Interesting and interested treasure. 'How about now?'

Chapter Thirty-Three

When they got back to the villa, mid-morning, Maria greeted Megan with a knowing grin and telephone messages from Signor Agnello and Dottore Marchiano. While Megan disappeared inside to change and return calls, Gideon loped off down the garden to check on progress during his absence.

Everything there was on schedule. Matteo made an excellent deputy when Gideon wasn't around. *Maybe Megan will offer him the post of head gardener when I go?* The thought brought Gideon up short. At the end of the summer, when the contract ended, he would leave. Something cold and spiky settled behind his ribs. Of course, he would leave. Megan was amazing, and last night ... his mind wandered off when he thought of last night. He'd never—

'*Scusi!*' Gideon jumped. One of the gardeners was barrowing a load of stones to the rose garden for the outline of the labyrinth and he was standing in the middle of the path staring into space. *Probably with a stupid grin on my face.* He shifted out of the way and went to look at the perimeter where the formal garden met the headland. Megan's idea about planting here would work. He could imagine aloes and agaves, although there might be some losses in winter storms. Some elements of a gravel garden might work too, with grasses and flowering plants that preferred dry conditions? It would change the look of the tower – give it a whole new slant – an old warrior sleeping in the sun rather than an abandoned ruin from a fairy tale?

He approached the building, taking care over the rough ground. He'd not really done more than give it a cursory look. Uncertain about the stability of the structure and how much specialist work might be needed to make it safe, they'd agreed to leave an exploration until the main garden was in better order. There had been plenty of work there to tackle first, and Megan had accepted that for the moment it was better to admire from afar – but as he was here ...

He considered the uneven ground. There needed to be a proper path for a start. You could easily turn an ankle with an incautious step. He made a mental note to get a crew out here to do some basic clearing and levelling.

He was surprised when he reached the structure. It was much less derelict than he'd thought – the tumbledown look was cosmetic. It had been made that way. The branches of an overgrown rose waved in the breeze off the sea.

Curious and cautious, he ducked through the arched entrance. It opened into a semi-circular space. Slit windows in the walls and the turret, open to the sky, flooded the place with light. The wall closest to the sea was flat with a stone staircase that ran up steeply, twisting to reach a narrow ledge at the top that circled the curve. The steps at ground level were old and worn and deep – slippery looking and splattered with bird droppings.

Gideon stepped over to investigate. The floor was gritty with small stones, but under the rubble were wide flagstones. Standing in the centre to look round, Gideon could see that part of the base of the tower and the back wall *were* old. There was a distinct line where the original structure gave way to new construction. An aged ruin had been built up to create a folly. With an effort, he quelled the impulse to climb the staircase, resisting the lure of what he suspected would be an awesome view. He needed to schedule a visit from a surveyor. He reached towards the nearest wall. The brickwork seemed solid, but he wasn't going to risk a broken leg or worse.

He ducked back out, retracing his steps towards the main garden, deep in thought. Megan was coming to meet him, picking her way carefully over the uneven ground. She'd changed into a pale yellow blouse and white jeans. The sun was shining lights into her hair and making her skin glow. Something heavy and solid thumped briefly in his chest.

Last night you held that vibrant woman in your arms ...

He wanted to do it again, right here, right now, but they'd decided on the journey back from Ventimiglia that everything that had happened stayed just between them. 'No one's business but ours,' Megan had said decisively. It didn't stop him wanting to touch, to kiss. He could still *look*.

'Hi!' She waved and waited for him to reach her. They turned back towards the main garden, falling into step. He reported on what he'd found in the tower and outlined the possibilities for the planting she wanted. 'It all sounds great.' Her forehead wrinkled a little. 'I wish we had records for the tower – I wonder how old the bottom part is? Maybe the Institute knows someone who specialises in that kind of thing.' They'd reached the garden proper. 'I'll ask Dottore Marchiano.'

'You got hold of him? What did he want? The questions were out before Gideon was able to clamp down on them. *It's really not your place to ask.*

Megan didn't seem to be worried about him interrogating her. 'I don't know whether to be scared or flattered.' The lift in her voice suggested the latter. 'He wants me to deliver a lecture in their summer programme.'

'About the poems.'

'Yes.' Her excitement was clear in her sparkling eyes and flushed cheeks. 'Maybe someone who comes along will know something about the legend. Or the villa.'

'It's also a professional compliment?' he suggested, grinning.

'It is. That's the scary bit. I've never done anything quite like that – a few conferences and peer presentations, but no public lectures.' Her mouth turned down for a moment, then she rallied. 'I'll just have to make sure I give them their money's worth.' She dived into her pocket and produced the pink secateurs. 'But for the rest of this morning, I'm going to prune roses.'

'Sounds like a plan,' Gideon approved, aware of a sinking feeling under his heart. The glow around her was as much about her career as about the night that they'd spent together. *And that's good. It's good that she's being recognised. Suck it up and be happy for her, you idiot. This is who she is.* 'If you want to practise your talk, you can do it on me.'

'I'll take you up on that,' she promised. She'd spotted her chosen bush and was stalking towards it. 'The lawyers have yet more paperwork for me to sign, so I have to go to Genoa.' She turned to walk backwards for a few steps. 'And one of the people trying to buy the property has repeated their offer.'

'Persistent.'

'Very. I suppose it's that developer, giving it another go. They'll get the message in the end.' She offered Gideon a heart-stopping smile. 'Il Giardino delle Rose is mine now.'

Megan drove to Genoa in the afternoon, diverting to Portofino and the gallery on impulse on the way back. Both Bianca and Alcinda were there. She'd been a little nervous, but she was welcomed enthusiastically.

Bianca unearthed a bottle of Prosecco left from the reception and turned the sign on the door to "Closed". 'Ah!' she collapsed into one of the couches at the back of the space, kicking off her heels with a sigh of relief and pouring the wine into glasses that Alcinda had retrieved from the tiny kitchenette. Megan found herself telling them all about the visit to La Mortola – the garden, not the overnight stay. Alcinda told tall tales about her experiences painting in the open air. There was a lot of giggling.

'Now you're painting Gideon,' Megan noted. He'd spoken of the early morning sessions quite casually, and Megan had to admit she was curious.

'Yes.' Alcinda's eyes took on a faraway look. 'He's actually a brilliant subject, intelligent and intuitive, better than some professional models I've worked with.' Her eyes focused again and she grinned. 'For God's sake,

155

don't tell him I said that! I don't want to give him ideas. Nothing worse than an uppity model.' Megan joined in the laughter. At the same time there was also a surprising little flicker of pride, hearing Gideon praised.

Oh – possessive much?

Conversation moved on. They'd avoided it so far, but it was probably inevitable that Ellery's death would come up when she told them that she'd been invited to lecture at the Institute. Both women expressed their condolences. 'Have the police found out anything?' Bianca asked, leaning over to dribble the last of the Prosecco into their glasses.

Megan shook her head. 'I'm not sure that they'd tell me if they had. If they have to have a suspect, the villa is the place to look.'

'Not a very nice situation.'

Megan could see that Bianca was uncomfortable at having raised the subject. She hastened to reassure her, 'They've stopped coming round asking questions now. I think they've reached the conclusion that it was essentially an accident. Someone wasn't paying attention, then panicked and drove away.' She shrugged. 'There really is no other explanation.'

'And you're not planning to sell up and leave?' Alcinda looked at her over her glass, narrow-eyed.

'No, I'm not.'

'Good.' Alcinda clearly approved. 'I want to come and see the garden.'

'Which probably means she wants to paint it,' Bianca suggested. Alcinda waved a hand in a "what else?" gesture.

'You would be very welcome. Both of you. And to the lecture. If you want to come, that it is.'

'I'll hold you to that.' Alcinda was laughing now. 'And we will both come to the lecture.' Her eyes went dreamy again. 'I'd like to know about the poems.'

'She'll be moving in, wanting to paint the tower,' Bianca warned.

They were giggling again when Gideon appeared unexpectedly at the door. Bianca got up to let him in. His eyes widened when he saw Megan and the glasses. 'Sorry, I don't mean to break up the party. I just want to know if we're on for tomorrow morning?' he asked Alcinda.

Alcinda confirmed that they were. Megan uncoiled herself from the seat. 'I must go. I really enjoyed this. And you do have to come and see the villa.'

There was a flurried exchange of telephone numbers. Megan followed Gideon out of the gallery, stumbling a little as the warm evening air hit. 'Oh – Prosecco.' She laughed as he touched her arm to steady her, then dropped it

156

quickly. 'I'm not sure I should be driving for a bit.' She treated Gideon to what she hoped was an encouraging sideways glance.

'We could have dinner?' he suggested. That was not what she had in mind. It took him half a second to get with the programme. 'Or I could show you my apartment and cook you an omelette.'

'An omelette sounds perfect. Thank you.'

Chapter Thirty-Four

Alcinda was waiting for him when he reached the studio a little later than usual. She treated him to the usual evil grin. Was it his imagination that there was also a knowing gleam in her eyes? She waved her brush to indicate that he should take up position on the dais, with the early sun behind him.

Returning her grin, he shook his head and walked over to her side of the canvas. The portrait of the mourning Achilles was almost finished – a man pictured against a sketchy, desolate background that suggested rocks and sand. Half sitting, half lying, slumped over an indistinct bundle clutched in his arms, this time the heavy coat lay beside him. In the few days since the last sitting, she'd added a line of gilding to the vaguely fan-shaped edge of the bundle and a more distinct shape to the coat.

Gideon felt the hairs rise on the back of his neck. It was still a figure, *him,* with a bundle and a coat. But it was also the grief-stricken Achilles, slumped over his war helmet with the tumbled body of Patroclus lying beside him.

'Is it good, or is it good?' Alcinda stood next to him, head tilted.

'I think it's brilliant.'

'Thank you, kind sir.' She bobbed a curtsy, then waved an imperious brush. 'So – get on that dais and give me more brilliance.' Grinning again, Gideon did as he was told, shifting position until he was back where Alcinda wanted him. She began to attack the canvas with small stabbing strokes. 'I want to do you in Megan's garden.'

'What!' His head jerked up.

Alcinda hissed until he repositioned himself. '*Stupido*! I want to *paint* you in the garden of the villa. Apollo – in one of those temples with the columns and the domes,' she explained. 'But first, Theseus,' she declared.

More paintings. He'd known she'd been thinking of what came next. It had been disconcerting to find sketches of his face, body or just body parts, pinned up around the studio, but he'd got used to it. Now that the decision was made, they were gone. Alcinda had signed two head studies with a flourish and made him a present of them, along with an assurance that she still remembered her promise of a painting of the garden.

He shifted slightly to reclaim the pose. If Alcinda wanted to paint him in the garden, it would be convenient for work. *And other things.* He wasn't sure how it would go down with the crew though. And there was definitely one gun he was sticking to. 'I'm not posing naked.'

All he got in response was a grunt, and an instruction to move his right leg. Point made, he settled back to being Achilles, mourning his dead lover.

'We need to shift this lot.' Alcinda had put down her brush and was looking around the studio. Gideon moved cautiously, checking for limbs that might have gone dead without him being aware. He wasn't sure furniture removal was part of a model's duties. 'Spring cleaning?'

'Party, Friday,' she responded. 'Bring Megan.'

Gideon decided he wasn't going to unpack that one. 'What do you want moved, and where?'

When he later mentioned Alcinda's abrupt invitation to Megan she frowned. 'Friday?'

'Would you like to go?'

'Yes and no,' she said honestly. 'It might be interesting, but ...'

'Yeah. I know,' he agreed. 'But ...'

After a moment she straightened her shoulders. 'Yes – let's go.'

The noise was already drifting down the stairs when they arrived, and the studio was full of people. Gideon put a protective arm around Megan. *Protective not possessive.* He knew that she was still nervous about meeting Alcinda's artist friends. *And truthfully, so am I.*

They'd tentatively agreed that if either or both of them felt like a fish out of water they'd make a discreet exit and find a place to have a quiet dinner. In the event, plan B wasn't needed. The evening flew by in laughter, conversation, argument and more laughter. Many of the guests were intrigued by what Alcinda was currently working on. Gideon was amused at various attempts to find out. He'd been warned to keep quiet and Alcinda gave nothing away. Megan, also warned, became heavily involved in a discussion about the various generations of foreign writers, artists, musicians, royalty and aristocrats who had gravitated to the Riviera. He spent a long time simply studying her face as she talked.

As midnight approached, the crowd thinned, Alcinda sent out for pizza and the remaining guests perched on an assortment of prop chairs, couches and thrones to eat. A middle-aged couple who sculpted in metal were prodding around the space at the end of the studio where they had corralled Alcinda's equipment and the ongoing art.

'Oi! Come out of there!' Alcinda waved her pizza, scowling.

'Not doing any harm, darling.' The female half of the partnership, who had eyes like a startled doe and shoulders like a prop forward, whisked the sheltering cover off one of the paintings, like a conjuror unveiling a rabbit. 'What have we – oh – darling!' The doe eyes widened to an even more enormous size at the sight of the smaller version of the Perseus. Her husband came up to stand behind her.

'*That* is incredible. It's you, isn't it?'

He turned to Gideon, who found the mouthful of pizza he had just swallowed had lodged in his throat. He'd got used to the sight of the picture. He'd never really thought about the fact that the object of paintings was that people *looked* at them – the reaction that they might provoke. Alcinda, who seemed to understand, patted his knee and shoved a can of Coke towards him. He closed his fingers on it, blindly, his eyes on Megan. She was sitting with a piece of pizza drooping in her hand, staring at the painting.

'It's awesome,' she breathed out softly, looking from the canvas to Gideon and back again. Alcinda leaned over to pat *her* knee. Some sort of look passed between them before she turned back to the sculptors. 'Right, you've had your preview, now cover it up again and have another drink.'

They were both very quiet in the SUV on the return journey. Gideon glanced over at Megan and then back to the road. It could be that she was all talked out – it had been a very noisy party – but the stunned look he'd caught on her face when she saw the painting was still echoing in her eyes. His hands tensed on the wheel. He made himself relax them. A movement in the undergrowth beside the road and eyes lit in the momentary wash of the headlights reinforced the need to keep his mind on his driving, but he couldn't help his thoughts straying. Unwelcome thoughts.

He'd never considered that anyone might connect him to the pictures – the figure on the canvas was Perseus or Achilles, not him. Doe-eyes and her husband had recognised him because he was *there* – in front of them, that was all. No one else was going to realise. Even so, worries gnawed. He didn't want … *that* … in his past, to mess up work that was clearly taking Alcinda to a new level. *Really? A local scandal in a small town in the north of England?*

Did he need to tell Alcinda or just let it go?

Megan stared out of the window at the dark road swishing by. She felt ... well, she didn't know how she felt ...

Yes, yes, she did. It was the same feeling as when a manuscript in an archive opened up a whole new avenue of exploration. Excitement, anticipation, maybe a little trepidation. *Can you handle this?* She didn't really know a lot about art, but she knew when she was in the presence of something special. *That painting of Gideon is special.* It had been a privilege to get even a glimpse of it.

Alcinda understood her subject – latent power in a moment of stasis. She'd painted Perseus, but she'd painted Gideon too. What she'd seen in the painting had made Megan's heart trip against her ribs. She turned to look at the man beside her, studying his profile as he focused on the road. She knew now, without doubt, that their casual flirtation, fling, whatever, had the potential to turn into so much more. She could tell herself that she was crazy to decide that based on a depiction in paint that wasn't even really *him.* Crazy or not, she *knew.* She and Gideon ... risks and possibilities. She felt the excitement.

Gideon West, you are bloody dangerous ... and I didn't see it coming.

She was on the brink of something. She didn't quite know what. Maybe what they had *would* just fade at the end of summer. The thought sent a strange forlorn shiver through her.

But if it doesn't fade – then it has the power to hurt.

She made up her mind in an instant. Being alive was about feeling things, and she wanted to *live* and she wanted to *feel.* She'd chosen safe and predictable once for stability, because she was afraid. She knew she wasn't in love with Gideon. *Not yet.* Maybe she never would be, but she could see the possibility. And she was going to take the chance. The Megan Morrison who owned Il Giardino delle Rose was a whole new woman, and she was going to *be* that woman.

Even if heartbreak is part of the package.

They'd reached the top of the drive. The building was a silhouette against the sky with a soft-focus half-moon. All the windows were dark. Gideon brought the SUV to a stop at the bottom of the front steps. She knew that she could lean over and kiss him, then open the door and slide out. He would drive away with a wave. He didn't push or expect. It was up to her and the thought was exhilarating.

Turn the page, see what's written.

She released her seatbelt with a clatter, turning to rest her hand on Gideon's shoulder. 'Come inside with me.'

Megan sat on the loggia with her second cup of breakfast coffee. The book on labyrinths was open on her lap, but she wasn't reading. She was chewing her lower lip and thinking. Not the high-flown thoughts of the journey home last night. Common sense came with a sunny morning and the hangover headache behind her eyes that indicated consumption of more red wine than she was used to. Both suggested that last night she'd been a trifle overdramatic. But only a trifle. She could fall for Gideon West. Whether she would, whether she wanted to …

She screwed her mouth into a pout. She wasn't entirely sure whether you could control stuff like that. She was an academic who relied on order, method and logic. This was about emotions. Whatever this was, she was going to have to live with it. That had not changed from last night. Gideon was gorgeous. He was also intelligent, talented and generous – in all sorts of ways. She was glad there was no one here on the loggia to see her. She was sure her reminiscent smile was making her look incredibly smug. They were involved in a relationship and she was going to enjoy it.

She laid the labyrinth book on the chair beside her and stretched, registering the small and mostly pleasurable aches in her muscles. Megan took a deep breath, then jerked against the chair, her nose prickling. What the hell was that peculiar smell? She stood up, darting down the steps and around the house. Her nose led her to where Gideon and an excited Tommaso were supervising delivery of a truckload of pungent manure. Apparently, it would be stored at a safe distance, behind the kitchen garden, until well rotted down and suitable for use.

'It is very good, Signora Megan.' Tommaso was practically dancing with delight. 'For the roses.'

Megan met Gideon's eyes over the old man's head. Warm and amused. Something in her stomach settled. *You just put one foot in front of the other and see where it takes you.*

Right now, that was back to the house to close some windows.

High summer eased in slowly. Megan revelled in sunlight, uninterrupted blue skies and short, warm starlit nights. Gideon reorganised the rotas so that the crews worked in the cool of the morning, returning for a couple of hours in the late afternoon. Alcinda was currently painting a female friend as Helen of

Troy, her face shaded by a beach parasol. There was another offer to buy the property, which Megan refused. The labyrinth was taking shape

Megan polished her lecture and tried not to chew her nails. She picked out a dress from her wardrobe, pale grey linen – cool and authoritative. *Yeah, keep telling yourself that.* Her career was currently on hold, but somehow she wasn't worried. Everything felt breathless, poised on the edge of something. She wasn't sure what the something was, but it didn't seem to matter. Days and nights with Gideon were like nothing she had ever experienced before. She was drifting, but that was fine. One perfect summer; a gift from Il Giardino delle Rose. She didn't want to breathe too hard on the bubble, making it stretch and shatter. The villa was holding secrets; she could sense it. There were so many puzzles and maybe she'd never know all the answers. In the autumn, when the restoration work was finished, when Gideon moved on – she shied away from the thought – then there would be time enough.

Right now, she had sunshine and starlight.

Chapter Thirty-Five

'And that concludes my talk, ladies and gentlemen. Thank you for coming this evening, and for your attention. I'm ready to take questions now.'

Megan looked over the sea of people seated in orderly rows, filling the Institute's main hall. It was gratifying when a number of hands shot up, but also a bit scary. This was the tricky part. She knew some questioners tried to tie a speaker into knots, demonstrating their own intellectual superiority; she'd seen Ellery do it often enough. She wrestled her mind away from that thought. The Director, sitting beside her on the stage, as chair of the event, was beaming, thanking her and organising a running order for questions.

Megan took a deep breath. Most of the people here were strangers. Gideon, Bianca and Alcinda were out there somewhere, and she'd spotted Signora De Stefano in one of the front row seats. *Not that she was a friend, exactly.* The first questioner was on his feet. Megan summoned up what she hoped was an encouraging smile.

'Dottoressa Morrison, first I'd like to thank you for a stimulating and thought-provoking lecture – can you tell us a little more about the various archives you consulted?'

'Oh. Yes. Thank you.' *No problem.* She could handle this.

Just like a swan, Gideon thought, as Megan stepped down from the stage. She was immediately engulfed in a crowd of well-wishers and questioners who had not managed to get themselves called. She glided through it, just like the swan, but he knew about the nerves and frantic paddling going on under the surface. None of that showed. He'd heard the talk before, several times, making good on his promise that she could practise on him, but it had still captured and held his interest. Realising that many of the audience would be members of the public, not academics, she'd structured it like a treasure hunt, detailing how she'd pieced together the discoveries that made up her thesis, garnished with enough technical stuff to keep the professionals happy. It had worked. In just a few minutes she'd had the audience eating out of her hand.

The Director of the Institute stood alongside her, beaming at everyone. By the look of it, he was getting ready to extract his successful speaker and carry her off to the reception being held in the Institute's small rear garden. Gideon stepped forward, as instructed, to join them. He would have been quite content to catch up with Megan later, letting her have her solo moment of academic glory, but she'd insisted. He moved slowly, in no hurry to break up the enthusiastic gathering around her, but the Director was intervening, clearing a path for someone to come forward – Signora De Stefano and her stepson. Gabriella offered her hand. From where Gideon was standing, it looked as if she'd intended to begin a conversation. Instead, a young woman, presumably the latest secretary, and the stepson steered her away towards the garden.

Through the small gap in the crowd caused by this manoeuvre, Megan caught sight of him. Her face lit up with a smile of welcome tinged, he could see, with residual relief that the talk was over. Warmth bloomed in his chest. She no longer looked like that dreamy Alma-Tadema heroine from the first morning on the loggia. *She's just as beautiful, but now she's mine.*

The garden of the Institute was nothing special; raked gravel paths, lumpy grass and a few trees, but someone had taken trouble to dress it for the occasion. There were lanterns in the lower tree branches and a canvas gazebo housing an outdoor bar. The air hummed with academic talk and Megan was flushed and pretty, accepting compliments and fielding yet more questions. Gideon found a number of people, too, who wanted to talk about gardens.

After about an hour, people began to drift away. Alcinda wandered up to make a date with Megan to visit the villa, giving him a warning look.

'Yeah, I know,' he acknowledged. 'Apollo. And I'm still not taking my clothes off.' *That* earned him a surreptitious middle finger, before Bianca dragged her sister away.

Once the crowd started to ease, Gideon looked around, vaguely surprised that Signora De Stefano had not reappeared, but strangely pleased that she hadn't. There was an uncomfortable coldness about the woman, although he still couldn't really believe Alcinda's allegation that she was a murderer. The stairs at the palazzo had appeared pretty lethal for the unwary.

'You're looking very fierce.' Megan put a hand on his arm and leaned in. The weight of her body pressed close and the scent of her skin warmed him.

'Trick of the light?' he suggested blandly.

'Hmm.' Megan gave him a sceptical glance. He could see, from the sparkle in her eyes, that she was high on success. 'It went well,' she breathed. 'They actually liked it.'

'Why wouldn't they? It was interesting.' Gideon scanned the surroundings. No one else seemed to want to buttonhole Megan. It was safe to leave.

Knowing that Megan had eaten very little during the day, and trusting that there would be cause for celebration, Gideon had made a reservation at a small restaurant overlooking Portofino. They were led to a table for two on an intimate terrace, with a view of the lights of the village below them. The food was as good as the surroundings – a garlicky fish soup, followed by large sharing platter of stuffed vegetables. Megan tasted and exclaimed and fed him slivers of what she had on her plate. Gideon watched her face in the dancing candle light and tried not to notice the way she was licking herb-infused sauce off her fingers.

When they had eaten their fill and were settled with fruit and coffee, Megan delved in her bag, pulling out a clutch of business cards.

'Networking,' she announced, spreading them out on the table. 'A couple of invitations to events, a conference and two post-grads looking for a co-supervisor – and the Director wants more talks for the Institute,' she finished breathlessly. 'I was wondering how I was going to re-start my career, but it looks like it's coming to me.'

She sounded bemused by the attention, but he was not surprised. She blushed delightfully when he told her so.

'Snap.' He drew his own collection of cards from his pocket. 'A couple of people want to discuss work on their gardens, here on the Riviera.'

Megan was looking up at him, her eyes shining with excitement and encouragement. 'That's wonderful.'

The look on her face made his heart jump. *Can you do this? Rebuild your career? Make a fresh start here?*

Megan bent her head. 'And there's this.' She prodded a folded piece of paper towards him. He picked it up. Her eyes were still shining, but there was a different edge to her excitement. The candle on the table between them flickered.

'Edith Moreau?' He frowned. 'And the address – it's a nursing home?'

'Assisted living, in Nice,' Megan confirmed. 'The tall woman in the red dress, with the earrings shaped like parrots, suggested I visit her. She's some sort of second cousin, and apparently she's nearly a hundred. According to the woman, she was a friend of Olwen's,' she said, with a slight quiver in her voice. 'Will you come with me to see her?'

If she'd wanted to go alone, that would have been fine, but it felt good that she had asked. He pushed away the idea that there was something unsettling about how good it felt.

166

He grinned. 'As it happens—' he indicated one of his own cards '—these people who want to talk about their garden are based in Nice.'

'That's great!' She reached across the table to take his hand. 'I've never been to Nice. Maybe we can stay over, give ourselves some time?'

She freed her hand to pick up the paper and stow it safely in her bag again.

He didn't want to kill her excitement and her hope, but he knew he had to say it. 'If she's nearly a hundred and in a care home – she may not remember,' he warned gently.

Megan gave him a clear-eyed look. 'I know. I'm trying not to expect too much. But if there is another piece of the jigsaw in Nice, I have to find it.'

Gabriella massaged the cleansing balm slowly into her face, careful not to stretch the skin. She considered her reflection in the mirror over the dressing table, picking up a cotton pad to begin removing the cleanser. The familiar ritual calmed her but did not entirely quell her feeling of irritation. She smoothed her fingers between her brows, teasing away the frown. Her visit to the Institute had *not* gone as she'd intended.

She had been received appropriately by the Director and found the lecture interesting. She had been presented, naturally, but there had been no time to speak, what with the crowd milling around. She'd expected to have the opportunity later. She pursed her mouth. Her lawyer was prevaricating, as usual, claiming not to have received a response from Dottoressa Morrison's lawyer. She had made up her mind, finally, on a direct approach. She was willing to pay whatever the woman asked and her lawyer knew it – this pose of hiding behind an anonymous offer in order to negotiate the price had gone on long enough.

She had made up her mind to speak, either at the reception or afterwards at the restaurant. But there had been a problem. Freddie, flustered and full of apologies, had miscalculated the timing of the lecture. If they did not leave immediately after it ended, they would lose the restaurant reservation.

It was of course quite foolish of him – as if they would not have held the table for *her* whatever time she chose to arrive, but the boy had always been a worrier. Even so, he might still have escorted her to the reception. He could have sent the secretary he insisted should accompany her to functions – really, the boy was as protective of her as his father had been – to wait at the restaurant. Before she could suggest it, they were in the car and on the way there.

The meal had been excellent and the service attentive, but while the Director had joined them the Morrison woman had never arrived. Gabriella's hand tightened on the pot of cleanser. She relaxed her fingers to release it. The whole thing had been a catalogue of mistakes and mismanagement. Despite that, she *had* enjoyed herself. She went out in the evenings so infrequently these days – only when Freddie was available to escort her. The deference shown by the waiting staff at the restaurant had been everything she required, and the maître d' had remembered her favourite dishes, pointing them out to her on the menu.

She tilted her head, regarding herself in the mirror. Perhaps after all, it was for the best. Maybe she had been too impetuous? It was one of her failings. Her darling husband had chided her on it. A public restaurant, however elegant and discreet, might not be the best place to approach such a matter?

She studied her reflection in the glass, satisfied that she had removed every trace of make-up. She needed to meet Megan Morrison face-to-face, without distractions. *Also, you need something to confirm your agreement.* She sat still, much struck by the thought. Why had she not realised that before? The lawyer must draw up something. She should have paperwork – then she would be *sure.* She would send an invitation when she had a document.

Chapter Thirty-Six

'This place has style.' Alcinda surveyed the entrance hall to the villa with approval. 'I'm glad I didn't wait until you finished the decorations.' She grinned at the debris of paper hanging equipment and paint pots. 'Seeing work in progress is interesting.' She looked around slowly. 'Same goes for the garden.'

'Coffee first,' Maria spoke decidedly from the door of the kitchen. 'I have pastries also.'

They sat at the kitchen table. By the time the mugs were empty, Megan realised why Maria had been so definite about the coffee. There was a distinct and mutual spark of interest between the two women. It also explained why, while being appreciative, neither had made any moves on Gideon. Megan grinned. That was fine by her.

They spent the morning prowling the garden. Alcinda was particularly interested in a pavilion she hoped to use as a setting, and the statues; she gave Justice a friendly pat on the rump in passing. She was nostalgic for the brambles and enthusiastic for Megan's schemes for planting on the promontory. 'That would make a fabulous background for something.' She got the unfocused look that Megan was coming to recognise. 'Something soft, in contrast. Aphrodite maybe? Can we go out to the tower?'

Megan hesitated, 'Well, just a quick look. The surveyor says it's basically sound, but there's work to be done.'

They picked their way carefully towards the building. The area had been partially cleared but was still quite treacherous underfoot. It was a perfect day, with deep blue sky and circling gulls. Once inside, Alcinda revolved slowly, taking in the rough walls and the staircase. She ran her hands over the old stones. 'If these could talk …'

'I wish they could,' Megan agreed. 'Oh!' She put out her hand in a restraining gesture, pulse speeding up in alarm as Alcinda hopped up onto the first step of the staircase. 'I'm not sure it's safe—'

'Seems all right to me.' Alcinda was already halfway up. Gingerly, heart in her mouth, Megan followed. The risers were uneven and worn, with only the wall on one side to hold onto. Alcinda had already reached the top. 'Hey!' she called down. She'd stepped onto the ledge that circled the tower. 'The view is awesome. Oh shit! Look out!'

Megan flattened herself against the wall as a handful of stones plummeted past her, landing with a clatter like hail on the tower floor. 'Sorry.' Alcinda was coming back down, looking contrite. 'It was some loose stuff, I accidentally kicked it. The rest seems pretty solid.'

'No harm done.' Megan edged down the steps. Her heart was still thumping in an uncomfortable fashion. The debris had only been pebbles, not enough to do damage, even if they had hit her, although she might have lost her balance on the stairs. 'I need to move that work up the to-do list.'

Alcinda was quiet for a while, apologising again but perking up when they completed a circuit of the villa and she found a section of the grounds at the back of the house that Gideon and his crew had not yet reached. She was more cautious this time, pushing a little way into the undergrowth. 'You've got a terrace here.' She held up a bramble, showing steps and flagstones. 'What's on the other side, inside the house?'

Megan led the way in through the side door to the large salon that spanned the villa. One wall was almost completely taken up with French doors and the room had the same shifting, underwater quality that the library had before the foliage was cleared. 'Hey, this is an awesome room!' Alcinda announced. 'Look at the floor and that ceiling.' The floor was dark parquet and the ceiling had ornate plaster mouldings. Megan knew they must be reproductions – the house wasn't old enough for them to be genuine – but they were still impressive. Alcinda was craning her neck, head flung back. 'Looks like there might have been chandeliers.'

'There were,' Maria spoke from the doorway, coming further into the room. 'Venetian glass. I think Signor Rossi had them made, but I don't know when they were taken down. They may be in one of the attics.'

'You need to look for them.' Alcinda made an expressive gesture. 'This would be a terrific space for a party – warm summer nights, doors open to the terrace.'

'It would.' Megan remembered that the idea had crossed her mind but hadn't been a high priority. Now that she was making friends and gathering acquaintances, though … 'Another thing for the list.'

'You have to do it,' Alcinda asserted. 'Bring the place alive again.'

'This is good.' Maria gave an enthusiastic nod. 'And now I have lunch ready.' She was looking at Alcinda as she spoke.

Megan decided that there must be something upstairs that she needed to fetch before she could have lunch. Whatever it was, it would take a while to find, to give the two women a chance to talk. *Maybe exchange phone numbers?* 'Er ... I have to ... upstairs,' she mumbled. 'I'll see you in a few minutes.'

When she got upstairs, she walked the corridor to reach the rooms that were over the salon. She'd looked before, but her attention had been on the other side of the house. There were two bedrooms here with a bathroom between. She hadn't included any of them in her improvement plans.

The first bedroom was an ordinary square space. The second, when she looked in, was a much larger room. French doors, like those in the salon below, opened onto a narrow metal balcony, smothered in creepers. The vegetation and the partly closed shutters made the room dim. She walked over to push them aside, her steps echoing on the bare floor. This wasn't really the back of the house, although she always thought of it that way. The loggia was at the back. This was at the side, with west-facing windows which would get the evening sun.

Suddenly, she had a mental image of sitting in a high-back chair here, next to the windows, watching the sun go down. She turned slowly. The bed would go there. A unique designer creation made by the company owned by Cassie's friend, Nadine. She breathed in, anticipation running down her spine. As she headed for the door, she made up her mind. This was going to be her new bedroom.

A bigger space – more room for two people?

She banked the thought.

She needed to talk to the builders again.

Chapter Thirty-Seven

The nursing home was a sprawling white building in extensive and well-kept grounds. The notice board beside the staffed gatehouse had a welcome in French and English. Megan turned to look up at Gideon. 'I never thought … despite the name, I wonder if Edith Moreau is English?'

'Could be that was why they were friends. Lots of ex-pats on the Riviera, even now.'

Megan nodded, thinking it over and surreptitiously admiring Gideon as she did so. They'd both opted for smart-casual summer dress, in deference to what a lady of nearly one hundred might expect. Gideon wore a cream linen jacket and dark trousers. Megan's slim-fitting white dress had a red belt and buttons. She was glad of the choices they'd made when an elderly gentleman in a summer-weight suit, collar and tie walked towards them. He was leaning heavily on a stick but was still making brisk progress towards the main gate. 'Good afternoon.' He raised his Panama hat as he spoke.

'Ah! Monsieur Grey!' A dark-haired girl in the smart red tabard of a care worker was hurrying down the drive after him '*Non*! No, Monsieur Grey.' She caught up with her quarry, gently turning him towards the building while throwing a grin back at them over her shoulder. 'We do not want to go walking now. There is afternoon tea on the lawn in just a few moments.'

The old gentleman agreed that he could drink a cup of tea and allowed himself to be piloted back to the house.

They had also been invited to tea. Megan had telephoned, more nervously than she'd expected, to ask if a visit was possible. She'd made no secret of the purpose of the request. The administrator had been welcoming but had a warning. 'I am sure she will enjoy entertaining visitors, but her memory …' She had sighed. 'We will hope it is a good day.'

Megan was sincerely hoping that.

Madame Moreau received them in a cheerfully sunny ground-floor room with French windows opened wide to the garden. The tea things were already set out on a low table. Megan recognised the delicate china with its gilding and overblown pink roses. 'My grandmother had that pattern, inherited from her mother. Royal Albert, American Beauty,' she said softly.

'Quite right, my dear.' Edith Moreau, small and fragile, gave an approving smile, although there was puzzlement in the faded blue eyes. 'Come in and sit down, please,' she invited them in English. 'I've had that china since just after the war, when I married my Pierre. I'm nearly a hundred years old, you know? I like to have my things around me,' she explained.

Megan could see that from the ornaments and knickknacks arranged about the room. She could also hear the Welsh accent, which explained a few things.

'You're Eluned's girl,' Edith said decisively. 'You've got the look of her. Rosalind, is it?' She looked so pleased to have remembered the name that Megan didn't have the heart to tell her that Rosalind was actually her grandmother. 'Is this your husband?' Edith looked up at Gideon, a long way up, with a distinctly roguish twinkle.

'Oh, no … he's just a friend.'

'Hmm. Friend.' Edith turned her attention back to Megan. 'I wouldn't let this one get away if I was you, my dear. Not always easy to get a handsome one. My Pierre was a handsome one. That's why I married him.' She gave a wicked giggle, then her face fell. 'He's been gone now—' her face creased in an effort of memory '—I forget. I'm nearly a hundred years old, you know? Please do have some tea.'

With care, they negotiated the intricacies of afternoon tea with a nonagenarian. Megan decided not to confuse things by explaining that she was not her grandmother. That small snippet alone confirmed that Edith Moreau had known both Olwen and Eluned.

The tea and the food were excellent; small sandwiches, macaroons and tiny éclairs – the sort of thing to tempt an old lady's appetite. The conversation was frustratingly elusive. Time and again, Megan steered the talk to Edith's old friend, Olwen, only to have it revert to Edith's childhood in Swansea. She sat back when she found that the old lady responded slightly better to Gideon's probing, addressing him with an arch coyness and references to gentlemen callers. Twice he got her talking about the rose garden at the villa, by way of the roses on the tea set. She'd obviously seen the garden planted, but each time she veered away again. Megan had to consciously loosen her hold on the fragile handle of her cup, afraid that she'd snap it off.

'Three musketeers we were,' Edith said suddenly, when Megan had all but given up hope. 'Olwen, Eluned and me. Three English roses on the Riviera. Welsh roses, more like. We planted three of them, one each.' She nodded to the cups. 'American Beauty roses, in the garden.'

Megan was almost afraid to breathe. 'The roses are still there. I'd love to hear more about how you planted them.'

Edith made a tutting noise. 'Long time ago. I'm nearly a hundred, you know? I was the eldest, but the other two went first.' There was distinct satisfaction in the old eyes. 'Long time ago. I'll tell you though, there was a tale …'

Megan leaned forward, conscious that beside her Gideon had done the same, and found that she was hearing the story from the poem, about the lovers and the tower, but told as if it had happened when the garden was being laid out. She let out a disappointed breath as the account came to an end. They were reaching the limit of their allocated time. Very soon one of the care workers would be here to show them out. She could see that Edith was tiring. Her eyelids drooped. Suddenly, she blinked and sat up.

'She came back with a gun, you know. Cosimo's girl.'

Megan jumped as if she'd received an electric shock. 'A gun?'

'Waving it around like a mad woman. We were having tea together, just like this, in the arbour.' Edith made a dismissive gesture 'But that was later. I get mixed up.'

Megan could hear footsteps in the corridor outside and the sound of voices. Praying that the carer on her way to see them out had been waylaid by another resident, she gently touched the papery skin of the old woman's hand. 'What happened? To Cosimo's girl?' She didn't know if that was the right question, if they were still talking about the poem, or something else.

Edith's eyelids had drooped again. They snapped open suddenly and her voice, which had been fading, took on a renewed strength. 'I helped her when he'd gone, you know? With the papers. She couldn't destroy them, but she couldn't bear to have them near. We did it at my bank here in Nice. Kept them safe.' She took in a gulp of air, shook her head and smiled. 'Such a long time ago. I'm nearly a hundred years old, you know? So nice of you, Rosa, to visit an old lady. And so like your mother.' She looked up as the carer bustled into the room. 'Isn't that nice, Valentina? These young people coming to visit an old woman.'

'Very nice. I'll just show your visitors out and I'll be back for the tea things.'

'I think she enjoyed herself,' Valentina commented as she led them along the corridor. 'I'm glad it was one of her good days.'

'Does she have them often?'

'Not so much now. She can be very confused, asking for her husband over and over, and she tires easily. She *is* nearly a hundred.' The girl grinned as she opened the front door to let them out. 'Ah! *Non*, Monsieur Grey.' She dived past them to intercept the gentleman with the Panama hat, on his way to the gates again, tucking her arm in his. 'Monsieur Dubois is putting out the croquet hoops. He is waiting for you to give him a game.' She waved her hand as she and her charge disappeared behind the building.

Megan and Gideon walked slowly down the drive to the gate. 'What did you make of that?' Megan asked as they reached the car.

'Honestly – I have absolutely no idea.' Gideon unlocked the doors. 'The bit about the gun – it sounds as if it might have been how those bullets got in the arbour – but it could just as easily have been something she saw on TV.' There *had* been a seemingly brand-new sixty-inch screen in the corner of the room. 'And the references to Cosimo's girl?'

'I know.' Megan let out a deep, frustrated sigh as she slid into the passenger seat. 'We were so close a couple of times. She definitely knew Olwen *and* Eluned – but the rest? And the stuff about the bank? Was she talking about Olwen, or something else entirely?'

'Gut reaction?' Gideon prepared to pull out into traffic. 'It was something to do with Olwen, but God knows what. Will you try to see her again?'

'Not sure. I'll maybe leave it for a few weeks, then phone and find out how she is. I'd like to know anyway.' It was disconcerting to talk with someone who had been friends with her aunt when she was creating the garden. She opened her handbag to look for her sunglasses. 'Remind me, what time is your garden appointment tomorrow?'

'Ten o'clock.'

'We'll have time for breakfast.' Megan put the glasses on. 'Then I'm going shopping.'

After a bit of Internet juggling, Gideon had found them an amazing last-second two-night deal. They'd landed up in a suite in a luxury hotel on the Promenade des Anglais, full of antiques, art and the most marvellous rugs, for less than the cost of a night in more modest establishments further away from the beach. Their room had an awesome four-poster, a tiny balcony and a view of the sea. The bed had cemented Megan's resolve to get herself something equally fabulous, and also made her look more critically at the oversized T-shirts with cute animals on the front that were her current nightwear. After a quick trip through the Cours Saleya market to admire the colourful displays of flowers and produce, Megan headed for the main shopping area – a woman on a mission.

She found exactly what she was looking for in a small boutique – a long nightdress in navy blue lace that clung modestly high at the front and plunged daringly low at the back. It had a matching robe and fitted as if it'd been made for her. She added two strappy, silky camisole sets, in rose pink and eye-popping scarlet, picking up matching lipsticks in the cosmetic hall at Galeries Lafayette. They were meant to be kiss proof. Accepting a sample of a fragrance that the advertisers promised would make her smell like an orange grove at dawn, she sniffed and found that it did – or something pleasantly citrusy anyway – and added that to her purchases.

Main mission accomplished, she set out to wander back to the hotel, exploring narrow streets with small specialist shops. The slim facade of one that was displaying luxurious bedding caught her eye. She pushed open the door and stepped in, finding herself surrounded by shelves of pillowcases, sheets and duvets of every colour. Everything was high thread count in plain colours, with the occasional discreet stripe. The shop smelled of lavender and linen, and she knew without a shadow of doubt that she would not be leaving until she found the perfect set.

With a happy heart, she began rummaging.

In the end, she'd had to arrange to have her purchases delivered to the hotel – duvet covers in deep turquoise, dark grey, a pale grey stripe and duck-egg-blue, with matching pillows and sheets. A smiling proprietor rang up her haul, which came to a slightly staggering total. Megan hesitated for a second – could she really justify spending all that? With a deep breath, she backed her penny-pinching conscience into a corner and told herself that she could. She had money now. Quality like this would last for a long time. She left the shop with only a slightly guilty grin on her face.

It hadn't escaped her that everything she'd bought today seemed to be related to beds.

Gideon stood looking out over his potential clients' garden, checking that he had done everything that needed to be done. It was a commanding corner plot, sloping down to the sea, in a small retirement community outside Nice. The garden, laid out at the same time as the villa was built, was well kept but bland. He'd spent the morning taking a brief of what the clients wanted, needed, liked and disliked. He had everything now to create the three potential new layouts that they'd asked for. He could feel the old familiar excitement of a new design project stealing through him. *You can do this.*

He *wanted* to do it. There was a quick stab of regret for the portfolio he'd lost, but that was gone. There was no reputation any more, only what he could build – but he could start here. The clients had a realistic budget and an open mind about suggestions. He was sure that he could come up with something they would love. They'd be contacting other designers, so it was up to him to be the best. *You were that once.*

He turned and walked slowly back to the house, knowing that the excitement wasn't just about the challenges of the garden. If he got this contract – if he could get others – could he develop a new design business here on the Riviera?

A fresh start – and the chance of a future with Megan?

The thought made his heart beat faster.

Chapter Thirty-Eight

Dusk was falling over the Promenade Des Anglais. They'd dined early at the hotel's restaurant, then been drawn outside by a spectacular sunset. The evening was warm. Palm trees shifted in a tiny breath of wind and waves lapped the pebble shore. The lights of ships out to sea were emerging as pinpricks in the gathering darkness. Looking up, Gideon could see the glow from the window of their room on the top floor of the hotel – their room and that amazing bed. There was a tug on his hand. Megan was smiling, her eyes bright. 'Shall we go in?'

He didn't answer, just let her lead the way.

Gideon dragged a chair to the open window, sitting to watch the lights and the strollers still promenading below. Megan had retreated to the bathroom. Something was going on. Something to do with the carrier bags stacked in the suite when he got back from his appointment. He grinned. He was a patient man. He could wait.

It was worth waiting for. When he at last heard the bathroom door open and close, he turned – and found his mouth drying on whatever he was going to say. He couldn't remember what it was. In the soft light of the room, Megan was a remote and mysterious goddess, swathed in dark blue lace, part of the night and the shadows – until the mirror behind her gave him the view of her back, all of her back … right down …

He managed to swallow at the second attempt. He found that he was standing as she glided towards him. The delicate fragrance of sweet citrus washed into the space between them. When she reached him, she wound her hands around his neck, pulling his head down to hers. The lace was whisper-soft under his hands, with soft flesh beneath it, and warm skin where the lace stopped. He realised, dimly, as he parted his lips for the kiss, that he was wearing far too many clothes. Then he ceased to care.

He wasn't really sure where the magic came from – whether it was from the blue lace, the room, the bed. Making love took a long time, full of kisses and slow exploration. The gown had a thigh-high slit and tiny buttons fastening it under the arm. It took a forever of kisses and caresses to unfasten them and strip the lace away and equally long to rid him of his clothes, one fastening at a time. Megan's breath came out as a long exhale when he cupped her breast, a muffled moan when he took the erect nipple into his

178

mouth. When he finally slid inside her he thought his control was at breaking point, but he was wrong. They rose together to an inexorable, engulfing high.

In the aftermath, she curled against him, head on his chest, her hair tickling his chin. Her even breathing told him that she had fallen asleep. He inhaled that citrus scent and watched shadows flitting across the drapes of the bed. He'd traced the disturbing source of magic. *Megan magic.* He'd thought she was a cool, remote goddess, but the woman he held in his arms was focused, warm and passionate.

And he was on the brink of falling in love with her.

Megan was glad they'd made an early start as they navigated their way out of Nice. The city was already busy with traffic. Gideon was preoccupied, his attention on the road. They'd talked over breakfast about the commission he was hoping to win. Some of his ideas sounded exciting. She'd suggested he ease back on the active gardening at the villa to concentrate on working up his proposals, using one of the smaller salons as an office. Last night was still humming in her veins. If he got this commission he'd be staying, at least for a while longer. Carefully, she disconnected from a thrill of anticipation. First, he had to get the job. Right now they were together, she was relaxed and happy – and that buzz still lingered. She daydreamed whilst looking out of the window, enjoying the sunshine.

They were unpacking the SUV and Gideon had laughingly grabbed her for a swift kiss, when a small hire car pulled up on the drive. Megan frowned, trying to place the woman getting out. The severe black dress emphasised the young woman's thinness and pallor. A black hair-band held fine blonde hair away from a strained face. It took Megan a moment to recognise her.

'Julia!'

'Dr Morrison.' The stiffness of the greeting jerked Megan out of her surprise and out of Gideon's arms. She hoped she wasn't going to blush. Not in front of *this* woman.

She turned to Gideon instead. 'Gideon – this is Julia Metcalfe – Ellery's … fiancée.' She turned back to the woman, who was watching them with a confused expression. 'I'm sorry for your loss,' she said formally. 'But I'm not quite sure why you're here.'

Julia Metcalfe still looked confused. *As if she's come here for a purpose and somehow the wind has been taken out of her sails?* Megan watched as the woman visibly collected herself. 'I came to Italy because the police don't

179

seem to be getting anywhere. Ellery's parents —' she gestured '— they're distraught.'

'I'm sorry. They have my sympathy,' Megan said simply. She recalled the aloof elderly couple who had found it hard to welcome a Welsh girl with no family and no pedigree as Ellery's chosen wife. *Julia probably suits them much better.* But whatever they'd felt about *her,* they'd loved their son. Looking at Julia's drawn face, Megan realised something that she hadn't been sure of. *You loved him too.* Ellery hadn't just represented an advantageous marriage for the Vice Chancellor's niece. A strange mix of relief and anger welled inside her. Relief, which was disconcerting, that she hadn't been pushed aside simply for expediency. There had been feeling involved, at least on Julia's side. The anger was at how Ellery had cultivated that feeling for his own ends, and had then been prepared to throw it all aside when he thought that *she* was the better bet. *And indirectly that duplicity resulted in his death.*

Realisation quelled the anger. She hoped none of those emotions showed in her expression. 'I'm still not sure why you're here.'

Julia visibly gathered herself together. 'I came because you saw Ellery, before he died.' The pain, uncertainty and confusion that Megan could see in the other woman's eyes took on a tinge of suspicion.

'We met, briefly, at a party, the night he arrived.' Megan felt a sigh forming that she couldn't let out. Her deepest and nastiest instinct was to tell this woman to go to hell, that she owed her nothing, but she couldn't give in to it, which meant she had to deal with this thing as tactfully as she could. 'I think you'd better come in.' Now the sigh did escape. She freed her hand from Gideon's. She hadn't realised that she was still holding it as he stood beside the SUV, in silent support.

'I'll go and see how it's going on-site.' He shut the door of the vehicle. 'We can empty this later.' He nodded to Julia. 'My condolences, Ms Metcalfe.' He leaned forward with a swift, light kiss to Megan's mouth and strode off down the path. Megan took her time watching him go before turning back to Julia, noting her curious expression. 'Mr West is the consultant supervising the remodelling of the garden.' *Plenty of food there for gossip on the campus.* She waved to the open front door. 'Will you come in?'

Half an hour later Megan saw Julia Metcalfe out again, waiting until she got back in her car and drove away. The woman had refused offers of refreshment, sitting stiffly on the edge of a chair while Megan described meeting Ellery at the party. She'd made it as light as she could, playing down the supposed mix-up over them still being engaged and Ellery's interest in the redevelopment of the villa. 'He was trying to help, as an old friend.' She emphasised the last few words. 'He didn't realise that I had decided to make my home here.'

'You have?' Surprise and suspicion were back on Julia's face. 'You're not coming back to the UK?'

'Not to live. My home is here now.' Repetition of that word, *home,* helped settled her ruffled nerves. 'I would have made that quite clear to Ellery, if I'd had the opportunity.'

Julia was chewing her lip. 'You didn't invite him here?'

'Certainly not. Seeing him again was a complete surprise.'

'Oh.' Julia digested that. 'You're with Mr West now?' The question was an imposition, but Megan was prepared to answer it, given the circumstances.

'I am,' she confirmed.

Abruptly, the other woman stood up. 'I think I should leave.'

Megan certainly wasn't going to make any move to stop her, seeing her to the door and leaning limply against it as the car disappeared down the drive. An uncomfortable and unnecessary thirty minutes. She suspected that Julia Metcalfe had come to the villa looking for a fight, believing that Megan had somehow enticed Ellery here, trying to win him back. Seeing Megan with Gideon had confused her.

Running her hand through her hair, Megan peeled herself away from the door. She hoped she'd done enough to defuse any other accounts that Julia got about the party, and that the woman did not stir the police into looking in this direction again. The visit had all but killed her relaxed and happy mood of the morning. She took herself off to the garden, and Gideon, to see if she could retrieve it.

Chapter Thirty-Nine

Gabriella looked down at the lawyer's letter. Her hands were shaking and the single typed sheet quivered in her hold, but she could still read the words.

Dear Signora De Stefano,

I write to respectfully advise you that I have again approached the owner of Il Giardino delle Rose, through her legal representative, reiterating your request to purchase the property. Signor Agnello indicates that his client has no desire to sell and intends to make her home at the villa. He therefore requests that no further approaches be made. He is, of course, aware of your interest, should the situation change, but this is not anticipated. In view of this, I regret I am unable to pursue this particular matter further on your behalf and enclose our account for services provided ...

Gabriella crunched her fingers on the paper, crumpling it in her fists.

No, no, no! Could no one understand! Il Giardino delle Rose was *hers.*

After a moment, she put the letter down carefully, willing her hands to stop shaking and controlling the impulse to tear the sheet across, along with the bill. *A bill!* The fool had not even done as she'd instructed and prepared a document for Megan Morrison to sign!

A scream was clawing at her chest. She held it in. If she let it go, people would come running. Gradually, with effort, she got herself under control. Just because that spineless idiot of a lawyer thought it was time to stop didn't mean that she should. She rose to pace the room in hurried footsteps. She had not yet formulated the right invitation to secure her face-to-face meeting with Megan Morrison. She would do it. She would take control. Then they would see. Her pacing was interrupted by the telephone. With an exclamation of annoyance, she lifted the receiver.

'Signora De Stefano?'

'*Sì.*' It took a second to place the voice. Marchiano, the Director of the Institute.

'I wondered ... Signora De Stefano ... if it was convenient ...'

She controlled the urge to yell at the man to stop stuttering and spit out whatever it was he wanted. 'How may I help you, Signor Marchiano?'

'Ah.' *A note of relief?* 'I was wondering if it might be possible for you to come here to the Institute, or maybe if I sent her to you ...' Gabriella held her temper as the man rambled. 'Only, I have Dottore Peters' fiancée here. She wanted speak to you.'

'Dottoressa Morrison? At the Institute?'

'No. It seems we were mistaken.' He gave a nervous laugh. 'This is Dottore Peters' ... er ... *present* fiancée, from England.'

Calling for the car to take her to the Institute, rather than the beauty salon or the house of one of her acquaintances, caused a small flutter among her watchers, which pleased her. She didn't want this Julia Metcalfe at the palazzo, but she did want to see her. It seemed that Peters had been playing a deeper game than she'd suspected – *and a callous one* – coolly pursuing Dottoressa Morrison without informing his new fiancée that her services were no longer required. *Securing one prize before relinquishing the other.* The man had clearly been despicable in his dealing with women. Really, one could almost say that his greed and deceit had called down a kind of justice.

The thin, washed-out girl who confronted her at the Institute did not impress her. Megan Morrison was far superior to this pale child. The large square-cut diamond on her hand *was* convincing, however. After conventional expressions of regret, Gabriella arranged her features into an appearance of attentive sympathy and waited for the girl to talk. When she had, running down like an unwound clockwork toy, Gabriella considered the situation. Megan Morrison had prepared the ground, she had to reluctantly admit. It was clear that Ms Metcalfe had come here not just to talk to the police, but also to accuse Dottoressa Morrison of enticing Peters to Italy to try to revive their engagement, which Megan had firmly refuted.

Gabriella had no doubt that Peters would quickly have dropped this pathetic child in favour of the woman who had unexpectedly come into property, if Dottoressa Morrison had welcomed him back – which it seemed she had not. Gabriella noted this with a flicker of annoyance. The plan had been a good one, though the execution had failed as a result of Peters' blind avarice. It really *was* better that he was out of the picture.

Speaking quietly, in measured tones to suggest sympathy, Gabriella smoothed over the unfortunate circumstances of Ellery's visit. 'Dottore Peters was invited to speak at the Institute, but it was not at the instigation of Megan Morrison.' *That much was certainly true.* 'I regret that my misunderstanding about their relationship may have caused you distress.' *But I regret even more that my plan did not work.* She brought herself to pat the girl's cold hand in what she hoped was a reassuring manner.

Julia Metcalfe was giving her a wide-eyed rather glassy stare. 'Ah. Now you've explained, I can see it was a mistake. I was confused. Of course, Dr

183

Morrison is with Mr West now. They were … they looked very happy together.'

The girl was blinking, close to tears. Gabriella inferred that she had surprised Megan and the gardener in some compromising position and that their "happiness" was what was making her look pale and cry. Frankly she had expected more from Morrison. A liaison with her gardener!

Maybe there was something here …

She had learned all she could. It was time to leave.

On the return journey, Gabriella considered her plans. That pallid child with the grotesque diamond had given her useful information. It had been worth the effort to see her. Now she needed to review her next steps. She had, of course, considered and discarded the ultimate solution – that Megan Morrison should be eliminated. Her death would simply create bureaucratic turmoil while another heir was found. Gabriella needed a sale – a clean and final transfer. Killing Morrison would not achieve that object – but to give her a distaste for her inheritance? To make her *want* to sell? If things became difficult …

Another approach to the contractors working on the villa was called for. The old woman must have left more money than expected, but it had to be running out soon. But, also, something more personal …?

Gabriella alighted quickly from the car when they reached the palazzo, extracting her phone from her bag as she hurried to the privacy of her apartment.

Megan Morrison was involved with her gardener. She was happy.

When you care for someone, that has power, the power to hurt.

Sitting down at her desk, Gabriella took a moment to compose herself before tapping in the number. The phone rang once, twice, then it was answered. 'Mr Brown?'

'Eh?' There was a garbled noise from the other end. 'Signora De Stefano?'

'I have another assignment for you. I want you to find out everything you can about a man called Gideon West.'

'But … Signora …' The man's unease came clearly over the phone. There was the sound of a door closing and the background noise faded. 'I'm an heir tracer, not a private detective. And with just a name—'

'I will double your fee. The man is a landscape gardener and I have a photograph.' A guest at the party had sent her copies of pictures he had taken. She hadn't known what she was expected to do with them, but now …

Gideon West was in one of the photographs.

'Well—'

'*Double* your fee.'

'All right.' The capitulation came as quickly as she expected. 'Send me the picture. I'll see what I can do.'

Chapter Forty

Gideon stood back from the drawing board that he'd set up in his improvised office in the smallest of the salons. The last plan was completed and it was good. He was confident of that. But was it good enough? Cat's paws of tension skittered over his skin. The proposal was ready to send to Nice. One last look in the morning and it could be dispatched.

He stretched, easing out the kinks in his shoulders. In a few moments he would change and go for a run. *Thinking time.* He'd met an architect at the reception at the Institute who'd followed up with a visit to Il Giardino delle Rose. As a result, Gideon had requests from a family extending a house in San Remo who wanted to remodel the garden, and an ex-pat couple who were converting an old farmhouse in the hills into retreat for creatives and were excited by the idea of a labyrinth. He was getting prospective clients simply by word of mouth.

He leaned against the table, aware of something that felt like hope. Could he reclaim his career – with no reference to the past? Was there a future here with Megan?

You need to tell her.

The voice in his head was getting more insistent as the days passed and he was becoming more aware … *more aware that you're falling in love.* He had to do it and do it soon, but he wanted … just a little more time.

If he got the commission in Nice, if he had the prospect of a future, then he would tell her.

Gabriella turned the packet over. It had a UK postmark. The return address was a jeweller in London, but that wasn't where it came from. Freddie and the staff treated her forays into Internet shopping with amusement and indulgence. As a cover-up, it was an excellent device. She weighed the envelope in her hand as she carried it to her private sitting room – light, containing only papers. Brown had rung back much quicker than she'd expected, furtive and excited. She hadn't let him tell her what he had found, insisting that he post it. Knowing it was significant, she'd wanted to handle the evidence in tangible form, to savour it.

And here it was.

She sat at the desk, slitting the seal on the envelope with a small gold paper knife. The blade was dull, but it did the job. She shook the contents free and spread them out. Newspaper cuttings from a local paper in a place in England she had never heard of and a short typed note. Her breath quickened as she read the bold headlines and saw the photographs. She'd been looking for a lever, something that would convince West to return to England. She hadn't been sure what that might be. A stellar job offer perhaps, or the rekindling of an old romance? This … this was better than she might ever have hoped.

She sat for a long while, thinking, then with a decisive gesture she reached for the telephone, punching in a number. 'Mr Brown, the package arrived. Yes, very pleased. You have earned your fee, but now there is something more. I need you to come here, to Italy.'

Nest building. Megan grinned as she looked around the empty space that was soon to be her bedroom. She was nest building. It was a new and heady experience, and she was enjoying every moment. The walls had been painted in a rich midnight-blue, and the floor gleamed where the boards had been sanded and sealed. The sound of hammering confirmed that work had begun on the bathroom. She had commissioned her new bed – pale wood with four delicate finials marking the corners, and a headboard with a stylised design of a rose that she'd found in an old book in the library.

She walked to the open window. The terrace below had been cleared. High summer at the villa, and she was happy like she'd never been happy before. It was a shock to realise that. It took her by surprise every time she woke in the morning to rediscover it. That the happiness was bound up with the man occupying the bed beside her had not escaped her. For the moment she was tiptoeing around the idea that Gideon West might be part of her future. She'd thought that about Ellery. She wasn't ready to probe what was between them. *Why take a risk with something this good?* There would be plenty of time when Gideon established himself in business here on the Riviera. He would, she was sure of that.

She ran her finger down the windowpane, chasing the smoothness of the glass. He hadn't told her much about his life back in the UK – the occasional story from his training, small glimpses of projects he'd worked on, some of the assignments he'd done for Jake, but nothing at all about his family. It could be that, like her, he didn't have one – but she didn't think that was so.

There was more, she sensed it, but she hadn't felt the need to ask. It wasn't important. He'd tell her when he was ready.

She crossed the room, checking on the state of the bathroom. It was being remodelled to install a walk-in shower and a massive tub, with a new doorway giving access to the bedroom. When she'd commissioned the extra work, she'd anticipated a request for an upfront payment. Signor Agnello was still indignant about that, but it didn't bother her as long as the work was done.

She wandered down the stairs. Gideon was standing at the bottom.

'Hi.' She leaned in for a quick kiss.

'Mmm.' He hummed appreciatively, but he was looking at his watch over her shoulder. 'I have to go. Another potential client in Genoa.'

'That's great. Word is spreading.'

'Yeah.' He shrugged himself into a jacket. 'I'm not sure about it though. It's a construction company – grounds of an industrial building being turned into apartments. The woman who called didn't seem to know what was wanted, but I suppose I'll find out.' He stole another kiss. 'See you later.'

The sun was hot and the house and garden were quiet, all the various workmen having knocked off for a few hours. Megan was resting her eyes over a book on the loggia. She didn't envy Gideon driving to Genoa, but if there was work involved ...

'Er ... excuse me, Miss?' Megan jumped, her eyes jerking open at the unexpected voice. The book fell to the floor. 'Oh, sorry. Here let me.' The man addressing her was middle-aged and non-descript, sweating in a suit that was too heavy for the day, and obviously English. He picked up the book and handed it to her. 'I'm sorry to disturb you, only I was told I might find West here – Gideon West?'

Megan hesitated. The man didn't look like a potential candidate for a garden project, but who knew?'

'I'm sorry but you're out of luck. He would normally be here, but not this afternoon. I could give him a message – Mr ...?'

'Brown. Jack Brown.' He shifted from one foot to the other, clearly uncomfortable. 'Thing is ... look, I know this is a bit of a cheek, but you've got a nice place here, Miss ...?'

'Morrison,' she answered automatically. For a second she thought there was a flicker of recognition in his eyes, but they definitely didn't know each other.

'Can I ask … what's this bloke, West, doing here?'

Megan's instinct was to respond that it was none of his business, but something made her stop. *What does Brown want?*

'He's a consultant, supervising the restoration of the garden,' she answered stiffly.

'Oh hell.' The man put his hand to his head. 'I was afraid of that. Look, I've got to level with you. I'm a reporter – my paper's doing a follow-up on a lot of recent fraud cases – exposés, you know? West's is one of them. I guess he hasn't told you.' Again, there was that tiny flicker, as if he was checking her reaction. 'Yeah, well, why would he? It's not a pretty story. I'm supposed to doorstep him – get an off-the-cuff reaction.' He ran his hand over his thinning hair. 'This really isn't my usual sort of thing and you seem like a nice lady—'

'You're accusing Gideon of fraud?' she interrupted. 'You think he's defrauding me?' She shook her head. 'You've got the wrong man, Mr Brown. There's no way Mr West is taking money from me.'

'Yeah, well, that's what his family thought. Tried to diddle them, didn't he? Didn't get away with it as it happens, but that kind, they don't stop.'

Megan found she was on her feet, looking down at Jack Brown standing on the lowest step, sweating in his too-heavy suit. 'It's a mistake. You've confused Gideon with someone else. I think you should leave now.'

'All right. All right.' He began to back away, shaking his head and waving his hands. 'Sorry I spoke. But you seem like a nice lady,' he repeated, raising a finger to point. 'You want to check it out. Look at the newspaper. *The Brickhaven Herald* – April and May, last year. It's all there, online – Brickhaven Nurseries. He didn't get away with it, but a lot of people lost their jobs because of him. You just check it out. *Brickhaven Herald* – April and May.'

He walked away, around the side of the building. Megan heard a car start. She was standing still, but she found that she was shaking. It was a mistake. Somebody's idea of a joke. A nasty one.

Megan sat down, reaching for her book. Best put it out of her mind. When Gideon came back, he'd explain – put the reporter straight if *he* came back. The guy had admitted he was here to stir up trouble. What had he said – to doorstep Gideon? *But how can a stranger stir up trouble if there is nothing to stir?* It *was* nothing. Some misunderstanding that the newspaper was trying to make into a story. She fiddled with the corner of her book. If she just checked online, she'd see how stupid it was. Maybe there wouldn't even *be* anything. It was a mistake. When Gideon came back, he'd laugh and she'd feel foolish for even thinking ...

She settled in the chair and opened the book. The author was arguing a complex point concerning Italian poetry. After ten minutes, having read the same paragraph three times, Megan put the book down. The words weren't making sense. The point was too abstruse, or the writer wasn't expressing himself clearly, or both. *Or you're not concentrating because you're wondering exactly what is in that newspaper.* With a huff of irritation, she got to her feet and went to find her tablet.

It took fifteen minutes, because she typed Brickholm the first time and found nothing. Relief spilled through her. She was about to put the device down when something caught her eye. The menu was offering her alternatives to the thing she'd typed. *Brickhaven Herald.* With a shaky hand, she selected it. The news pages opened on screen. She tapped to find the archive editions for April last year, and there it was.

It was a brief report, full of speculation, but one that was unhappily all too common – a local business that was a landmark in the area was rumoured to be experiencing financial difficulties. An old family firm, established before the First World War, Brickhaven Nurseries occupied what were now two prime development sites; a retail outlet at the centre of the small town and fields and glasshouses on the outskirts. If the business was wound up and the sites sold, nearly fifty people would lose their jobs. No one from the firm's management was available for comment. There was a picture of the Nurseries' gates. Just visible getting into a car on the other side was a familiar figure. There was no mistaking, even though she couldn't see his face clearly. It was Gideon.

Megan took a moment to control her trembling. All right, Gideon was there, but what did that prove? This was a sad but familiar story in a provincial newspaper. Megan's skin prickled a little when she read the words "development potential", but there really wasn't anything there. In the following week there was no report. The matter had slipped out of the news, ousted by the marital problems of a locally born soap star.

Megan leaned back, relieved. The story was distressing. She could understand Gideon not wanting to talk about it, but if it was a family business, he wouldn't have borne all the responsibility if it had gone under.

They would talk when he got back.

She was about to close the search when the reporter's voice echoed in her head. *April* and *May*. Her hand, acting as if it had a will of its own, scrolled again.

This time there was a banner headline, *Landmark Local Business – Shock Closure Follows Covert Deal*, over a photo of the Nurseries with employees standing outside holding placards, some visibly distraught, others clearly belligerent. There was a shot of Gideon caught on a doorstep, as Brown had said, one hand up to shield his face, and a small picture of another man, captioned *International Businessman, Justin West.*

It was a grim, sordid story of family deceit, occupying two inner pages. Justin West was again pictured, wearing a smart suit and a pained expression, with two of the Nurseries' employees and the firm's designer, Lucy Wallace. When interviewed by the paper's staff reporter, a shocked and saddened Justin had reluctantly described returning to the UK from managing his business interests in Spain, a few hours before his father Phillip's death, to discover his younger sibling about to close down the family business, having sold the sites using paperwork signed by Phillip West in the last few weeks of his life. Gideon West had claimed to be the firm's chief designer, the paper reported, taking the credit from Ms Wallace. *In reality, Gideon West was only a site manager constructing designs under her direction.*

It was too late to stop the sale, but Justin West pledged to make provision for the workers, out of his own pocket if necessary. The name of Brickhaven Nurseries would continue as a landscape design studio under the direction of his fiancée, Ms Wallace. Gideon West was unavailable for comment.

In a small tragic coda at the end of May, the paper recorded the death of talented young garden designer Lucy Wallace, fiancée of local company director, Justin West, in a road accident.

Megan scanned through subsequent editions but that was it. *Isn't it enough?* Gideon had tried to cheat his brother, selling prime sites for redevelopment and putting all those people out of work. The words burned off the screen. Was that what he was planning here? Romance the gullible owner of this prime development site?

The gullible owner – me.

A few miles away, Jack Brown parked his hire car in a lay-by and fumbled for his phone. The call was answered immediately.

'It's done. You were right, she didn't know. Yeah – didn't really think he would have told her. She brazened it out, but you should have seen her face. I doubt if West will be around much longer.'

At Il Giardino delle Rose, Megan sent the newspaper pages to print, hearing the machine in a corner of the library whir into action. She crossed the room to pick up the sheets. Gideon West, fraud and fake, not even the award-winning designer he claimed to be. No wonder he'd never spoken about his family! For a moment Megan's thoughts wavered. Cassie's husband, Jake, had vouched for him. *Yeah, but Jake's not infallible.* Why wouldn't he fool Jake? He'd fooled her, all the way into her bed. She snatched the papers from the printer tray, carrying them with her to sit on the front steps.

To wait.

Chapter Forty-One

There was a headache hovering behind Gideon's eyes. He'd just wasted hours driving to Genoa and then around the city, looking for a property that didn't exist. The address he'd been given turned out to be a church in one of the suburbs. There was no industrial building anywhere around being converted. None of the few people on the street in the shimmering heat had been any help. When he tried the number that had called him to make the appointment, it went to an automated voicemail. He left a message in case the mix-up had been their end, but he must have scribbled down the wrong address. *Not likely to get a contract out of this. Just chalk it up to experience.* He pulled in through the gates, his heart lifting when he saw Megan sitting on the steps, waiting for him. He could murder a cold drink, and then they'd laugh about him driving around getting suspicious looks when he tried to ask for directions. He shut off the engine and got out, beginning to walk towards Megan. *Coming home.*

The thought made his step falter slightly. *Coming home, not to the villa, but to Megan.* Except that now he was close enough to see, her expression wasn't one of welcome. She was frowning, scowling in fact. Her eyes were red, as if she'd been crying.

'Darling – what is it?' He cleared the remaining space to the steps, arms outstretched as she stood up. She didn't come into them. There were papers in her hand, and that hand was trembling. She held them out. He could see what they were. Computer printouts. Newspaper headlines. His stomach dropped with a sickening thud. *You should have told her.*

'There was a man, a reporter, looking for you.'

'Williams?' It was an instinctive question, but he saw it register in her eyes. Damned and double damned.

'He said his name was Brown. His paper is doing a follow-up. He wants your reaction.'

His reaction was a bone-shaking desire to punch something. He shut his eyes, drawing in a deep, ragged breath, then opened them.

'Can we talk about this?' He had to ask, but he already knew the answer.

'I don't think so. I'd appreciate it if you'd collect whatever things you have in my ... home ... and leave. I don't want you to return to the estate. I'll arrange for Signor Agnello to forward what you're owed—'

'Sod the money! Megan, please, talk to me. Let me explain.' She'd winced at his expletive. *Good call, buddy.*

'I don't think we have anything to talk about. You tried to defraud your *family*. I can imagine what you had in mind here.' The red-rimmed eyes skittered around the garden.

'That's not—' His words died when her eyes came back to him, full of anger and pain. Defending himself wasn't going to work. The newspaper reporter had hung him out to dry and she'd seen it all. All he could give her now was his absence. He brushed past her up the steps and through the open door. 'I'll be gone in fifteen minutes.' He headed to the small salon and his drawing equipment.

So much for coming home.

Megan trailed into the house and then into the kitchen, hunting in the cupboards until she found the bottle of brandy. She slopped a large measure into a mug, gulped it down and choked at the fire in her throat. It felt better than the burn of tears, but not much. She stood, sipping more slowly, and listening. A distant clatter, footsteps on the stairs. He really was leaving. *Which is good.*

She'd been prepared for surprise and confusion when she confronted him, something to tell her that it was all a mistake. She would have listened. *She would.* But he'd known straight away, asked the name of the reporter, made no attempt at denial. She took another slug of brandy. She had been a complete and utter fool.

She looked around the kitchen, at the view through the window. This place – she'd thought it was a home, a chance to belong, to rebuild. All it had brought her aunt was tragedy, and all it had brought *her* was men trying to persuade her to sell, so they could take a cut of the proceeds. Her stomach heaved in horror as much as because of the brandy. She'd known what Ellery had had in mind: the revival of an old relationship. But Gideon – how deep a game had he been playing? Would he have asked her to *marry* him?

Her head jerked up. There were footsteps in the hall. It had to be Gideon; Maria was out for the day, on a date with Alcinda. She held her breath as he passed the kitchen door. If he came in, if he called her name—

He didn't.

Reverberation of the front door slamming echoed through the house. Faintly, she heard the sound of the SUV starting up. Now he really was gone.

She was completely alone. Again.

She wiped her face on her sleeve, rubbing away tears that she really didn't want to shed. The printouts, with their screaming headlines, lay on the kitchen counter. She screwed the whole lot into a ball and pitched it into the bin. She should go out to the loggia and find her book and thank her lucky stars for her timely escape.

She knocked back the rest of the brandy, feeling her head swim. Maybe it would be better if she went upstairs to lie down. She'd need to change the sheets before she could sleep. Feet dragging, she left the mug on the counter and went into the hall. She needed to sleep, so she wouldn't have to think. She'd done that, sitting on the steps in the sunshine, waves of pain biting into her chest, pain that was almost physical. Thoughts about belonging, about lucky escapes and about the disturbing, crushing suspicion that she might have fallen in love with Gideon West.

Fallen in love and not understood that ... until it was over.

Chapter Forty-Two

'Lovers' tiff?' Gideon tried giving Alcinda a blank stare, knowing all the time that it wouldn't work. She wasn't daunted. 'Word is that you haven't been seen at the villa in over a week.'

Word is – meaning Maria's word? At least Megan had someone with her in that big house. He hoped that Matteo had stepped up to manage the garden. He wanted to ask, but he knew he mustn't. He looked away, shrugging. 'Do you want to do this painting or not?'

Alcinda gave him one of her assessing looks, then nodded. 'Let's get to it.'

It was a small canvas, his back view only, as if he was looking out over a harbour, once she'd put that into the background. He was Theseus, looking out at the ship that would take the tribute from Athens to Crete – seven young men, seven young women, sacrifices to a half man half beast. He, Theseus, son of the king, would be one of them. She'd stopped talking about Apollo, which was a relief

He settled into position, hearing the small familiar noises of Alcinda at work. There was only one thing about posing – it gave him time in his own head. He was trying hard to think only the thoughts Theseus would have. A lot of the time it was working. Alcinda hadn't complained anyway.

Over a week since he'd seen Megan. He'd thought that she might come looking, giving him a chance to explain. *Yeah, like why you didn't tell her any of it?* Even that would be enough to make her doubt him. He'd never really thought the thing would follow him. The story might have been big in Brickhaven but was hardly front-page news anywhere else. *But you still should have told her.* He had intended to.

And the road to hell ...

Who would have thought that bloody reporter, Rod Williams, would have followed him here? Megan said he had given the name Brown, but it had to be Williams. Who else could it be? Every day since his visit to the villa, Gideon had expected the guy to pop up, demanding to speak to him. Strangely, that hadn't happened. If and when it did, he wasn't going to say anything. He certainly wasn't going to give in to what the darker parts of his mind suggested – which was ram the grinning bastard's teeth down his throat. Jake had warned him to keep his temper in check.

Pent-up frustration made him shift restlessly before he remembered where he was. With a muttered apology, he fell back into the pose. Megan hadn't told Alcinda – but *he* would have to at some stage. It was up to her then what she did about the paintings. She was clever; she could make him look different, change the colour of his hair or something, so that he wouldn't be recognised.

He stared grimly at the wall and thought of ships with their human cargo of sacrifice.

He needed to sort his life out. He'd hoped—he shut down on his hopes. He was going to stay here on the Riviera, he knew that much. With nothing else to do, he'd delivered the proposals for the garden in Nice in person, instead of e-mailing them. He'd walked the clients through the plans and got that contract *and* the labyrinth and some other work at the creative retreat. A solid start to a new business – the irony of the universe.

He could base himself further along the coast, San Remo, or over the border in Nice, and maybe look into the formalities of changing his name. *New place, fresh start.* That was what he had to concentrate on now. Working to cover the gaping hole carved in his chest when he thought of Megan.

No thinking. Keep moving. Keep working.

When Alcinda at last dismissed him, he slouched moodily back to the SUV parked in a side street. Now he didn't have to be Theseus, his mind and emotions were churning. He stood beside the car, keys in hand, arrested by the searing claw of anguish in his chest. He braced his hands on the roof of the car, head down, looking at nothing.

Who the hell guessed it would be like this?

Most of the time it was fine – well not fine, but just this side of bearable. Then these great sweeping ambushes came out of nowhere when his brain registered, yet again, that it was *over*.

After a few long seconds, the choking darkness faded. He opened the car and got in. He really needed to move on, move away. Staying here, staying in the apartment, sleeping in the bed where they'd made love, waking in the dark from a dream of her. He'd conjure her up, sitting opposite him at the table eating pasta, using her fork to illustrate some point she was making. He'd even gone through the wine glasses, trying to find a trace of lipstick – an imprint of where her mouth had been. That was how sad he was. Sad and needy.

He gripped the steering wheel, resisting the temptation to rest his head on it. He had nothing much to do and all the time in the world to do it. If he

197

hadn't held off from telling Megan, if that bastard Williams hadn't come stirring it all up again – *if, if, if.*

He couldn't really blame anyone. This was on him. Do the crime, do the time – except that he hadn't done the crime. Not the first crime, the one he'd been tried for in the press and found guilty of. But this wasn't just about what happened in Brickhaven. *You didn't tell her.*

Too late now.

Anguish was building up in his chest again. He swallowed it down. He had to move on. Leave Portofino. He was in a much better position than he had been when he'd arrived here all those months ago. He had an embryonic business. He needed to find a new place to live, somewhere cheap in an unglamorous part of one of the coastal towns, a room with a bed and a table and good light, so he could work. He started the SUV. A job for the day. Hunt for a room.

Gabriella pushed aside this month's choice from her book club – a dreary tale about small people doing small things in a small dreary town. She wouldn't read any more. She would wait, as she always did, until others had made their comments, then parrot them with a gentle smile. It always worked. Each month she toyed with the idea of giving up the whole charade, but she knew that she would not. It was one of her few chances to leave the apartment – safe, respectable, time-limited.

Sometimes, after the dreary book was dispatched and the wine began to flow, there was gossip that was useful or that she could manipulate. A small start of surprise, a sympathetic look if the new owner of Il Giardino delle Rose was mentioned – poor girl, inheriting such a rundown place with so little money to fund repairs. Gabriella had seen the garrulous wife of one of the local building contractors absorb that one. The book club served its turn.

She sat back in her chair. Brown had done well. Her plan was working. West had returned to the villa from his wild goose chase to Genoa and had left again almost immediately. Brown had seen his SUV speeding past while he was still sitting in the lay-by. According to casual conversations, struck up with workmen in various local bars, West had not been seen at the villa since. Tomorrow Brown would call again, in the guise of the reporter, to make certain. After that he would disappear back to England, his work complete.

Gabriella traced a finger over the lettering on the cover of the dreary book. Breaking up a potential romance and leaving Megan without her chief gardener was progress, but she knew she needed more. The ideal would be a series of accidents of increasing severity, giving the place a bad reputation, but she had no means of achieving that – no one on whom she could rely. Brown would only go so far. There was another way though – an incentive. An offer to Dottoressa Morrison of a position back in the UK? Perhaps it was time the Institute had an outpost in London, or perhaps Oxford?

An outpost that would need a director.

Megan sighed, putting a bookmark into the volume she had been consulting and adding it to a similarly annotated pile on the library table. With considerable effort, she was focusing her attention on an article she was writing for one of the professional journals, but it wasn't easy. Anger, betrayal, pain, loss. The emotions marched relentlessly through her thoughts. She looked out of the window. There was a rosebush that needed attention, but she didn't have the heart to go and find her tools. The pink gloves and secateurs reminded her too painfully of Gideon.

Everything reminded her of Gideon.

He'd wound his way into her life. *Into your heart?* She was very afraid that was true. She'd wanted to keep it light, just a casual affair, but it hadn't worked out that way. All the things they'd shared – working together, laughter, long glorious nights. Had he been secretly mocking her, unable to believe his luck? All she had now were questions and a cold void of loss under her ribs.

At least things in the house and garden were going smoothly. Everyone had accepted her mumbled excuse that Gideon had been called away on urgent business. Maria had looked at her with slightly narrowed eyes, but hadn't commented. Megan leaned back in her chair and stared at the ceiling. *You could have given him the chance to explain.*

'Let him explain, or fill me up with lies?' she retaliated to the voice in her head with a snarl. It was getting better. She only heard from the voice five or six times a day now. By the end of the month, it would hopefully have dwindled to nothing.

Absently she rubbed her chest, realised what she was doing and forced herself to stop. The hollow feeling would not be cured by rubbing, any more than the chill in her limbs was helped by putting on a cardigan. She wasn't sure what the feeling was, whether it really was love or simply betrayal. She'd thought she was in love with Ellery and had been crushed when he dumped her, but this was nothing like that. This was pain. A dull ache of loss that began when she woke up in the morning and didn't leave as she dragged herself through the day.

A couple of times when it was really bad, and when the voice was hammering in her ears, she'd almost reached for the phone to call Jake, to ask him what he knew. She'd stopped herself in time. Calling Jake wasn't going to make the facts go away. She wasn't going to embarrass her friend's husband by pointing out that he'd been taken in by a fraud, or herself by admitting that she had too. She'd talk to Cassie when she next went back to Bath. She stared some more at the ceiling, letting her eyes drift shut. She wasn't sleeping very well.

She came back to herself with a jerk, forced awake by a familiar commotion. *Someone at the door.* She got up, straightening her skirt and smoothing down her hair. In the hall, Maria was attempting to turn away a familiar figure – Jack Brown, the reporter.

'It's all right, Maria.' Megan stepped forward, looking the man up and down. He was wearing a lighter suit today but still looked uncomfortable. 'Good afternoon, Mr Brown.' Maria, seeing that Megan knew the man, took herself back to the kitchen, although with a curious look over her shoulder. 'What sort of story do you have for me today?' she enquired tartly.

'You looked then, at the newspaper.'

'I did. Your write-up was interesting, if colourful.'

'Not mine.' He made a repudiating gesture, then seemed to collect himself. 'Like I said before, you seem like a nice lady. West's a crook. He didn't get away with it, but he's still a crook.' He gave her a sideways look. 'He's gone then.' He must have got that from Maria.

'He has,' she confirmed. 'And I don't think I have anything more to say to you, Mr Brown. If you want to speak to Gideon West, you'll have to look elsewhere for him.'

'Oh, no ... well ...' he stuttered. 'If he's gone, then there's nothing more ...' He stumbled to a stop.

Megan stood silently. After a second of hesitation, Brown turned to leave. Megan watched him go, leaning against the door frame for support, aware of something odd about the conversation, but not sure what it was. As Brown reached his car and opened the door, a hire car drew up and parked on the other side.

'Oh, great,' Megan muttered, as Julia Metcalfe got out. Julia walked towards the house, giving Brown a puzzled look as she passed. He slid hurriedly into his vehicle and drove away.

'Who was that?' Julia asked as she reached the steps.

'Reporter, looking for a story.' Megan dismissed Brown from her mind to deal with her second unwanted visitor. 'You'd better come in.' Realising she sounded ungracious, Megan stepped back, summoning up a smile.

She led the way to the small salon and indicated a chair, dropping onto the sofa opposite. 'What can I do for you? Would you like a drink?'

'No, it's okay.' Julia brushed her hand over her skirt. 'I'm not going to stay. I just wanted to apologise for my attitude the last time I was here.' Long, thin fingers plucked at her sleeve, then stilled. 'I spoke to the police and the people at the Institute. I also had time to think. When I came here, I believed that you'd invited Ellery here. That you were trying to take him away from me – and that somehow it was your fault that he was dead.' She let out a gusty breath. 'I understand now. It was the other way around, wasn't it? You didn't want him here.'

'Well …' Megan hesitated, then decided on the truth. 'I didn't,' she admitted. 'He came because he wanted to revive our engagement. I'm sorry,' she said quietly. 'I will always regret that coming to see me resulted in Ellery's death, but none of it was orchestrated by me.'

'It's all right. I realise that now.' Julia bowed her head, before looking up again. 'I get it – Ellery was tempted by all this.' She looked round. There was a sad, crumpled stoop to her shoulders. After a moment she straightened, rising to her feet.

Megan scrambled to follow as the woman held out her hand. 'Thank you for listening, I won't be bothering you again. I'm flying home tomorrow, but I felt I had to see you first.'

'Thank you for that,' Megan said, accepting the handshake.

Ushering her out, Megan was reaching to open the front door when Julia stopped, giving a muffled exclamation. 'Sorry,' she apologised as Megan swung the door open. 'I just realised why that man looked familiar. You said he was a reporter? Is his name Jones or Brown – something like that?'

'Brown,' Megan confirmed, her senses suddenly alert. 'You've seen him before?'

'Yes, I'm pretty sure. No – I *am* sure. It was at Ellery's office at the University.' Her face creased into a pleased smile at having remembered. 'He was the one who told Ellery about your inheritance – he wanted to talk to you, to do a story. What a persistent man to come all this way.'

'He's persistent all right,' Megan agreed. Her thoughts were revolving like a merry-go-round. Somehow, she bade Julia goodbye in a coherent fashion.

Shutting the door, she returned to the salon to sit down. Brown was a reporter. A reporter who had followed Gideon to Italy to do a story on him for a provincial newspaper in the north of England? A reporter who had also sought out Ellery in Bath because he wanted to do a story about *her*? Something wasn't adding up. Would a local reporter be covering two fairly minor stories in different parts of the country? And while he was here, why hadn't he asked for the story of her inheritance? On his first visit he hadn't been certain about who she was. She remembered all that, "you seem like a nice lady" stuff that he'd spouted.

She took in a long breath. Whatever else was going on, the report in *The Brickhaven Herald* existed. Gideon was still implicated in that.

And someone wanted you to know about it.

The realisation hit her like a blow to the chest. Somehow, for some reason, she was being played. She leaned back against the sofa, trying to put her thoughts in order. There was always the possibility that Julia Metcalfe was wrong about Brown. *But you don't think so.*

She needed to dismantle this thing very carefully. She sat for a moment, assessing her feelings. Instinct told her where she needed to start.

Give Gideon the chance to explain himself.

Was that instinct or hope? She really couldn't tell, but she had to start somewhere. Pulling her phone from her pocket with unsteady fingers, she thumbed Gideon's number.

Chapter Forty-Three

In a few moments she would see him.

Megan found a parking place and got out of the car. She'd chosen a small café in Chiavari for the meeting. Neutral ground. She still didn't know if she was making a mistake. *You didn't give Gideon a chance to explain.* Newspapers didn't always get things right. She leaned against the car, remembering the bleak look in his eyes when she'd told him to go. Would a practised fraudster have tried to talk her around? Gideon never spoke about his family. Should that have been a red flag? Might he have told her eventually?

Someone made sure you found out.

And that was another can of worms. Just because someone wanted her to know, it didn't make any of it untrue. She had to keep her critical faculties sharp. She couldn't let her feelings, physical or emotional, get in the way. Just because she *wanted* him didn't mean she could trust him. *And if you can't trust him, nothing else matters.*

She pushed away from the car and set off around the corner to the café.

He was there before her, sitting at one of the tables on the tiny forecourt. He hadn't seen her. For a moment she just stared, drinking him in, feeling a juggernaut of desire and a gaping void of need. She wanted to run, but she really wasn't sure if that was towards him or away from him. *Gideon West has the power to hurt you more than you have ever been hurt before.* And she was letting him in, giving him the power.

No – he already has it.

She couldn't let that colour her judgement. She'd come here to listen. Pulling her shoulders back and holding her head up, she walked forward.

Gideon kept his hands very still. He'd thought that ten days without her was bad enough. Seeing her after that ten days and not being able to touch her was worse. Pure longing was clawing holes in his chest and stamping on the raw results. When he'd heard her voice over the phone, he'd thought his heart or his head might explode.

Now she was sitting across from him, a cup of coffee in front of her, expecting him to talk – and his tongue had swollen into cotton wool just looking at her. *How long would she let you look, if you just sat silent?*

Her face was pale and the skin under her eyes had a bruised quality, but the bright red lipstick and the scarlet scarf she'd looped around her neck said quite clearly "Don't mess with me". She was giving him a hearing. Now he had to make the most of it. All he could give her was the truth. Then it was up to her.

You should have told her.

Those words had been beating a tattoo in his head for all of the ten miserable days. Pride had stopped him. And respect for the memory of three people who had loved him and whom he had loved. Now, what he felt for Megan – that was on a completely different planet. He saw her shoulders twitch with the rise and fall of an in-drawn breath. She was tired of waiting. 'You defrauded your family – your brother and your father – in order to sell land for development.'

Ah – there it was, the pain and the betrayal. Would she even accept that none of it was true? He took a sip of bitter black coffee to unglue his tongue.

'Justin West isn't my brother – not even a step. Phillip West was my father in everything that mattered, except biology. Brickhaven Nurseries was a family business, but it wasn't *my* family.' In a second he saw that he'd missed his footing by the flare of emotion in her eyes.

'So, it didn't matter if it went to the wall?'

'No!' Urgent denial made him reach across the table. He recollected himself just seconds and inches away. 'It's a complicated story.'

His voice sounded tired in his own ears. Tired and defeated. The realisation jabbed at him. To hell with it. He had to pull himself together. He had one crack at this, so he had to take it. Jake and Cassie believed him, even if no one else did. It seemed that Megan hadn't called them yet. Was that a good thing or a bad thing?

He took another gulp of coffee, emptying the cup. She was watching him, her eyes dark and questioning and so very lovely that it broke his heart. He took a deep breath. 'I don't remember my real father. He walked out when I was about three years old, left my mother and me and a pile of debt. His name was Rob West. My mother sold up everything we had to see off the bailiffs. She didn't have any family she could ask for help, it was just her and me. We were homeless and more or less penniless. Job opportunities for a single mother with a young child were limited, but one of the neighbours had a friend in Brickhaven who'd just lost his wife to cancer and left him with a twelve-year-old son. He needed a housekeeper and my mother needed work where she could live in, so we moved from London to Brickhaven. The widower and his son were Phillip and Justin West, a complete crazy coincidence. People who didn't know thought we were family and, after a couple of years, we were. Phil fell in love with my mum and she with him, but they never got around to getting married. She didn't know where my father was to start divorce proceedings and didn't want to know. She didn't want contact and reminders. And it didn't matter anyway. She was Mrs West and I was Gideon West and we *were* family. Phil was everything a kid could want in a father. Justin …'

He stopped, looking down. When had he finished all his coffee? Silently, Megan pushed her untouched cup towards him, signalling the waiter for a refill. Gideon took a sustaining mouthful from it, placing it carefully back on the table.

'Justin and I were never brothers. Sometimes we got on okay, but the age difference was too big. Mostly he just ignored me. He was grieving for his mother when we arrived, and we were cuckoos in the nest. His big ambition was to get out of Brickhaven. Once he left for university, he never really came back. He had one of those finance jobs that took him all over the world with a lifestyle to match, no interest in the family business at all, while I was following Phil around the Nurseries within days of moving in. He taught me about plants and about the business and paid for my training. He did everything for me that he would have done for his own son. My mother died when I was twenty – also cancer – and we mourned her together. We both chucked ourselves into work. The business was doing well – we had major displays at horticultural shows and we won medals.'

A quick stab of loss jabbed at his ribs. 'Some of the best memories I have of him are trying to put together a show garden in the pouring rain when half the plants were refusing to flower because it was too cold, or had gone over because it was too hot. And standing beside him when the judges came round, the first time we won a gold medal ...' He was choking, damn it. Thankfully, the waiter arrived with more coffee. The pause gave him chance to get himself together.

Megan sat silently as the waiter removed the used cups and substituted fresh ones. The strength of her emotions as she listened to Gideon's story shook her. If these were lies, it was an Oscar-class performance. *But it could be that he's simply convinced himself that it's true.*

'Brickhaven Nurseries were thriving.' Gideon's voice made her start. 'Justin blew in from time to time – all fancy cars and fancy suits and looking down his nose at transit vans and overalls. He'd splash his cash for a few days and then he was off again.' Gideon looked up with a faint grin. 'It was quieter once he'd gone.' The grin faded. She saw him grip the coffee cup. 'Three years ago, it seemed like the Nurseries couldn't go wrong. I was doing a lot of design work and getting noticed for it. Phil never said anything, but it was sort of understood between us that the Nurseries would come to me.' He took a very deep breath. 'Then there was Lucy.'

Megan sat up a little straighter. *His brother's fiancée*. Had there been something between her and Gideon? Yes, there had been; she could see it in the set of his shoulders.

'She was the daughter of an old friend of Phil's wife. I'd known her since she was a baby, knew that she was … fragile. She'd had a bad time with her first job, encountered a very persistent office bully. It damaged her confidence. She had anxiety issues. She was getting help and her mother suggested gardening as a sort of extra therapy, so she came to work at the Nurseries. It was good. She worked with me on the design side too. She had an eye for colour and plant combinations. She came to the shows to help set up and she even worked the stand. She was shy, but she had a way with people.'

Megan saw the faraway look in his eyes. *And you were just a little in love with her?* She pushed the painful thought away. She couldn't be jealous of a dead woman. Gideon had stopped talking, staring down at his hands. 'What happened?' she prompted.

'Phil got sick. Cancer again. It's hideous disease. He had treatment and everything seemed fine. Justin came home for a few weeks. I found him poking around in the office a couple of times but didn't think much about it – too worried about Phil and keeping the business going. We were busy. It was coming up to Christmas, and then the New Year was going to be a fresh start. Phil was talking about making the Nurseries over to me.' He looked up, his mouth twisted. 'I wouldn't let him. It seemed as if I was writing him off. He knew better than I did. The cancer came back and so did Justin. Phil was in a hospice by then. We knew it was only going to be a couple of months at most.' His voice got gruffer and speeded up. 'That was when I was supposed to have made the deal with the developers, convincing Phil to sign the papers.'

'It wasn't you, it was Justin,' she said softly. She put out a hand and felt a jolt as Gideon's fingers closed over it.

He nodded. 'Phil lasted nearly three months, but by then the sale was all but complete, although I didn't know it – and whispers were circulating that the business was in financial trouble. A couple of suppliers suddenly couldn't fill our orders and one or two of the staff got jobs elsewhere.'

'Rumours spread by Justin?'

'I assume. It was a lie, but it justified closure and disposal of the sites.' He paused. Megan could see the pain in his face. This was true and this was real. Gideon had loved the man who had taken him and his mother in. Emotions were shifting and sliding inside her. Sympathy, remorse, anger ... love?

'Phil was dying and my attention wasn't on the business.' Gideon grimaced. 'The last weeks, when Phil was fading, I spent most of my time at the hospice and it all got beyond rumour. The staff were asking questions. I think ... I think Justin had counted on his father being dead before the full story got out. I think he panicked. The Nurseries were a big thing in Brickhaven – not good for his image to be the man who closed them down.' Gideon shrugged. 'Maybe he always intended to put it all on me. He went to the press, claiming he'd just got back from Spain and passing himself off as the good guy trying to do the right thing. You saw the newspaper.'

Megan thought of the photographs and Gideon's picture, his blank stare. Not guilt but exhaustion and grief.

'There was a very old will, dating from when Phil's wife was still alive,' Gideon continued. 'Under that, Justin inherited everything. He could have waited and sold the sites legitimately, but that risked the chance of a last-minute new will, so he did a fast deal. If I'd let Phil have his way, the business would already have been mine. Justin knew that. He didn't intend to share.'

Gideon ducked his head, then looked up. 'There *was* a new will, leaving the Nurseries to me and a small legacy to Lucy. The house and everything else went to Justin. One of the hospice nurses found it when she was clearing Phil's things. It was one of those DIY forms. Phil didn't hold much with lawyers.' He gave a wry smile. 'That was one of the things I played on to dissuade him from signing over the business. Whether the form would have stood up if Justin had challenged it is anyone's guess, but it didn't matter because it wasn't signed or witnessed.'

Gideon gave her a level look. 'I think, but I can't prove, that Phil thought he was signing *that* when he signed the papers for the sale. He said a couple of times that Justin had made sure that things were all right, but I didn't get what he was talking about. I thought Justin had told him he was helping to keep the business going or something. As it was, that will had no legal standing – it was just a piece of paper. And I wasn't family. Phil never married my mother or adopted me. I had no legal claim and I certainly didn't have resources for a legal dispute, but I think Justin was rattled. He was skating on thin ice over the sale, so he pushed the story even further – I was only ever an under-manager, working to Phil's direction, and the landscape designs were done by Lucy. He'd browbeaten Lucy into going along with it. None of the other employees contradicted him.'

Megan could see that betrayal had hurt. He shrugged. 'They had their own troubles, and Justin is a persuasive guy who was promising compensation. He and Lucy had a whirlwind engagement, and there was all that stuff about the business carrying on with her as designer. Whether he would actually have married her I don't know, but the question didn't arise …'

'Because Lucy died.' Megan had a hideously cold feeling in the pit of her stomach. She remembered their conversation, about Olwen's son. 'Did she take her own life?'

'It crossed my mind, but I honestly don't know. Her car went off the road and into a tree. It was raining heavily, the road was slippery and Lucy was a nervous driver at the best of times. The official view was that she lost control because of the weather. Whatever it was, she's gone.' He exhaled. 'It cut off any real chance I had of proving anything against Justin. He had the local press on his side. He was at school with Rod Williams, the reporter. I couldn't deny all that stuff about her being the real designer without tarnishing her memory, and Phil made me promise not to tell that he'd never married Mum. He kept coming back to it when he was dying. There wasn't anything I could do without betraying the memories of a lot of people. I didn't have any money to sue, even if I'd wanted to, and the articles are very carefully written – all based on interviews with Justin. He wasn't going to involve the police – and that made him look magnanimous towards his conniving brother.' Gideon exhaled, pushing his hand through his hair. 'I don't know what sort of case there would have been to answer anyway, as Phil had signed all the papers – undue influence maybe? Justin got the money, so he hadn't been cheated. The only people who lost out were the employees.'

And you. You lost.

Megan heard the words loud in her head. She knew with bone-deep certainty that what Gideon had told her was the truth. With the clarity of an outsider, she could see the holes in the edifice that Justin West had constructed – holes the reporter might have found, if he'd dug deeper. Justin was clearly a clever and persuasive man, but he couldn't have done it alone. There had to be other people involved – were they friends and cronies? She could also see the vindictiveness that had driven Justin to destroy the cuckoo in the nest who'd taken his father's time and attention ... *and love?* Gideon attributed it to panic, but Megan recognised jealousy. *At least Justin drew the line at revealing they were not related.* And Gideon – exhausted and deep in grief, sideswiped by events, protecting people he'd loved, even after death, shocked and mourning and unable to see the way forward ... *I know a little about that.*

Gideon leaned back in his chair. Some of the tension had left him now that the story was told. 'I walked away with virtually nothing – much like my mother, all those years before. I went back to Bristol where I'd studied. I just wanted to get away. I picked up a few odd jobs gardening and security work for Jake. I'd worked for him when I was in the city as a student. He knows all of it. He believed me.'

'But I didn't.' Their hands were still clasped across the table. Not quite holding hands. She tightened her fingers so that they were. 'I'm sorry.'

'Not your fault. The story in the newspaper is convincing. And it touched a nerve – Ellery was trying to sell Il Giardino delle Rose, wasn't he?'

'He was, but I shouldn't have let that influence me. I should have let you speak, talked to Jake—'

He shook his head. 'Doesn't matter – not as long as you believe me now.'

'I believe you,' she confirmed softly.

'Thank you.' He lifted her hand, pressing a kiss to her knuckles. 'Oh God, I do love you.' There was a sudden heart-stopping pause. Colour flooded into Gideon's face. 'Sorry, I shouldn't have said that. Wrong thing. Take no notice.' He was trying to pull his hand away but she wouldn't let go.

'It's only wrong if you don't mean it.'

He was looking at her wide-eyed, as if she'd said something earth shaking. Maybe she had.

'Do you ... I mean ... Oh hell!' He tunnelled his free hand into his hair, pulling at it. She wondered if he was checking to see if he was awake.

'I would like it if you thought you were in love with me … because I think I may be falling in love with you,' she said carefully. 'I'd like to work on it, if that's okay.'

'Okay! It's brilliant, awesome, amazing—'

'Shh!' Laughing, she put up a hand to cover his mouth. 'I'm not making any promises – and I don't expect any from you,' she warned. 'I don't really know what I feel, except that I feel something. Can we go on as we were before, and see what happens?'

Gideon's heart was turning over in his chest. How could he say no? She was looking at him so earnestly, checking that he understood. He wanted to gather her up and kiss her until neither of them could remember their own names. Instead, he settled for nodding his head. She'd given him hope, and it was all that he could ask for. She'd been hurt in the past. He got that she wanted to be careful now. And she'd just accepted his account of what really happened in Brickhaven. That was huge. If she needed space, he would give it to her.

She'd made the first move, to contact him. He had to credit her for that. The newspaper articles were damning. As soon as he knew that she'd seen them his only option was to walk away. Williams had spun a convincing story – or had it fed to him. People Gideon considered as friends, and employees who'd known him for years, believed it. Why wouldn't Megan? And the guy had come looking for him. A flicker of alarm tinged some of the hope. *What more does Justin want?*

'What is it?' She'd obviously been watching his face.

'Just … the reporter, Williams, came here. I'm wondering why.'

'I was wondering exactly the same thing. The man gave his name as Brown,' she said thoughtfully. 'What does Williams look like?'

'Six-foot, fair hair, early forties?'

'Brown wasn't that tall and his hair, what there was of it, was grey. I'd put him in his sixties. It wasn't Williams.'

Gideon wasn't sure if that was a relief. 'Then who the hell was he?'

'Someone who was sent to make sure I saw that newspaper story,' she said with certainty.

Gideon listened, in growing confusion, as Megan described Brown's visits and the connection that Julia Metcalfe had made. 'Brown was pretending to be a reporter?'

'Unless Julia is wrong and I don't think she is. And that's not all – you talking about false rumours put an idea into my head – about the difficulty I had getting workmen and them demanding money upfront. I thought it was because I was a stranger.'

'Someone put the word out that there was a danger they wouldn't get paid?'

'Exactly.' She looked around, ducking her head as if she felt a cold draught on her neck. He'd felt one on his. 'Someone is trying, very subtly, to get me out.'

'Someone who wants to buy Il Giardino delle Rose?'

'It's the only thing I can think of. The big question is who?'

'And how can we find out?' He reached to take her hand again. An uncomfortable tremor ran down his spine. Someone was targeting her. The thought gave him a cold, dark ache in the pit of his stomach.

Chapter Forty-Four

Gideon sank his spade into the soft ground. Digging out the dead stump of a rhododendron gave a man time to think. It wasn't the way he'd expected to do it – telling a woman that he loved her for the first time in his life. He hadn't expected the words to come tumbling out like that; the product of relief, joy, hope. And then to have her say them back.

Or almost say them.

She was being careful. He understood that. He'd willingly give her time, space – blood – whatever she needed. She knew the worst about him and she'd accepted what he told her. Whoever had tried to use his past to break them apart hadn't succeeded. The thought made him a little uneasy, wondering what the consequences of that might be, but mostly he was just, well ... happy.

One day at a time. They'd agreed that, and he could live with it. As long as there was hope. She cared. He knew she cared. It was in her eyes, in whispered words when they made love, in the touch and taste of her mouth. The sight of her just walking towards him down the garden path, like she was now, could lift the day so it was brighter, the sun stronger, the sky bluer.

Megan walked along the path, enjoying the day, the sunshine and the sight and scent of the roses, but with her thoughts wandering. *Are you really falling in love?* Was it stupid that she couldn't tell? She knew that there was a part of her that was afraid to let go, to trust. Trust mattered. She was in lust with Gideon, no question about *that.* She was almost sure about the love thing. The way she'd felt when she thought she'd lost him, and the way she felt now ... was it enough to show her? She sighed. She wasn't getting anywhere by trying to analyse her feelings for Gideon minute by minute. *Can you overthink love?* She rather thought it might be possible. Much better to concentrate on something specific, like the idea that she'd had this morning, or the sight of Gideon with a spade in his hand. *That will do too.*

'When we're finished, I'd like to open the garden for visitors – organised groups perhaps to start with,' Megan announced as she reached him.

Gideon paused from attacking the stump to wipe sweat off his face with his arm. 'It's a garden – what makes you think it will ever be finished?'

His grin curled her toes. *Every damn time.* Megan poked him in the ribs. 'You know what I mean!' She looked around. 'I think I should share it, social responsibility and all that. I'm not prepared to let the land be developed, but it's not right to keep it to myself.'

'Sounds good to me.' He leaned on the spade. Megan took a moment to appreciate the fit of the T-shirt that at some stage had been white but now sported decorative streaks of soil. Things between them had been awkward at first. She'd felt as if she was walking on egg shells – they both did, it seemed – moving carefully around each other. Now, after three days, it all seemed more or less normal again.

She knew her nerves were on edge though, and she was trying not to keep looking over her shoulder for some anonymous threat. The only place she felt really safe was in Gideon's arms, which should probably tell her a lot. *Except that you're not going there yet.*

She'd cornered the owner of the building firm yesterday and he'd admitted reluctantly that there *had* been rumours that there was no money to pay for work. When she pushed harder, he'd dredged up that it was gossip his wife had passed on from a friend. He was vague about whom. Megan suspected he didn't know and didn't really care. She put him right about the money and let him off the hook. Brown hadn't come back, and she had no idea about how she might find him, so there had to be another way.

'I was wondering ...'

'Yes?' She could see caution in Gideon's eyes.

'The work on the house is nearly done. When it is, I'm going to throw a party – inviting friends and neighbours to my new home. We could announce the garden visiting plans then.'

'Make a statement that you're here to stay, basically.'

'Yes. Whoever it is who is hoping to get rid of me will *have* to get the message.'

He nodded in support, but she could see the flicker of doubt in his eyes. She clamped down on the same flicker in her own heart.

Megan looked with satisfaction at the documents on her computer. There were two articles for literary journals that she had just completed and a proposal for an address to an international symposium being held the following year in Boston. She'd be *really* lucky if she was invited to attend something that prestigious, but what the hell – go big or go home.

The post had been delivered, including a copy of a new gardening magazine with Gideon's article on Riviera gardens flagged up on the cover. His name was only a by-line in small type on the article inside, which was something of a relief. After a quick look, he'd left it with her to read. He already had four new enquiries about garden designs and was hoping for more off the back of it. *As long as no one connects him to Brickhaven.* There was a brochure and a letter from a company in Bath that ran garden tours for small groups. Cassie had put her in touch with the owner who was interested in including Il Giardino delle Rose in her itineraries for the following season. Last but not least was the embossed invitation card. Megan picked it up and went to look for Gideon in his impromptu office.

She stood for a moment in the doorway, watching him work, dark head bent over a plan. The well of feeling that came over her in a rush was too complex to analyse the separate components. All she knew was that it felt *right.*

'Are you going to hover, or are you coming in?' he spoke without looking up.

Megan laughed, aware of a fizz of happiness, padding over to brush her lips on the back of his neck. Of course, he turned and grabbed her, dragging her into his lap for a very thorough kiss.

'Sorry to interrupt.' She rested her forehead against his.

'Are you?' He moved back to squint at her. 'Really?'

'No.' She reached to pull his head down to hers. 'Kiss me again.'

It was some moments before she remembered what she had come for. The invitation, slightly crumpled now, had fallen to the floor. Megan retrieved it and waved it under Gideon's nose. 'My friend, Nadine Wells, is getting married in Nice. Would you come with me to the wedding?'

'Happy birthday, Mamma.'

'Freddie!' Gabriella allowed her cheek to be kissed before her stepson sprawled into a chair opposite her. 'Did I expect you today?'

'I wanted to bring you this.' He gestured to an ornately packed parcel on the table. 'I know your birthday is next week, but there was some Institute business to take care of, so I thought I could take you out to lunch and then head over there.'

Gabriella smiled as she unwrapped the coffret of exclusive perfume and bath products – Freddie had excellent taste and knew her so well. 'Lunch would be delightful. And I will come with you to the Institute. I have a matter that requires attention.' She had telephoned *twice* and *twice* been promised that Marchiano would be in touch.

'Yeah, the administrator said you'd left a couple of messages. Not urgent, though, is it?'

With an effort, Gabriella held onto her composure. *Yes, it is urgent. Vital in fact.*

Her stepson's whole demeanour, including the casual way he'd picked up the newspaper from the table in order to scan it, told her that her enquiries to the Institute were not being treated seriously. She relaxed her spine, careful not to show emotion as she meticulously folded wrapping paper. If Marchiano would not come to her, then she must seek him out. She needed to finalise her strategy so that she could invite Megan Morrison to meet. She needed the right incentive to offer her. She *needed* to speak to the Director.

She hesitated for a moment. Should she let Freddie know her plans? He must see the benefit. When she was installed in her rightful place at Il Giardino delle Rose, the Institute could be relocated to the palazzo as her dear husband had wished. In the proper setting, its scope would be so much wider – dramatic performances, recitals, even opera. She would, of course, still act as hostess ...

She surfaced from her enjoyable fantasy to find Freddie standing over her, looking down with a quizzical expression, waiting for her reply as he offered his arm. He had dropped the newspaper on the table in an untidy heap that made her wince inwardly. The boy could be so careless. She would not confide in him. It was better that she played the hand alone – show him what she could achieve, that she still had that power. The result would be a happy surprise. She stood, smiling over her irritation.

'Merely some ideas I wanted to share with the Director.' She waved a calculatedly casual hand.

'I'm sure he'll be glad to hear them when he gets back.'

'He is away?' she asked sharply.

'In Padua for some sort of meeting and then on leave for a few weeks,' Freddie confirmed blithely. 'Are you ready – shall we go?'

Gabriella took Freddie's arm, seething inwardly. The girl who had taken the message might have told her that! *To be dependent on lackadaisical fools!* She controlled her temper with an effort.

She *would* send Megan Morrison back where she belonged. She just needed to be patient.

'This really is an amazing room.' Gideon looked around the newly decorated salon. Outside the vegetation had been cleared from the terrace, revealing a balustrade and a small statue of Venus presiding over shallow steps that led to the front garden. Tall French doors, now free of obstruction, let afternoon sunlight spill over the dark wood floor. Megan had chosen wallpaper with a pattern of birds and trellis for the wall with the windows, so that it looked like an extension of the exterior. Additional wall lights had been installed, which just left the chandeliers.

They stood looking up at the empty ceiling fittings. 'Maria thinks they might be in one of the attics,' Megan said. 'Want to come and look?'

'I will if you will.'

'Good. I need someone to deal with the spiders.'

'If there are spiders, I wish to reconsider my offer,' Gideon said solemnly.

'It's an attic! There are bound to be spiders.' She put out her hand to draw him to the door. 'We can be brave together.'

The chandeliers *were* in the attic, carefully stored in three large boxes. Gideon walked around them, keeping a wary eye open for arachnids. Megan rummaged in the packing peanuts that filled the boxes, uncovering fragile tissue-wrapped Venetian glass.

'Can we get them down?' she asked, scooping the packing back.

'We'll sort something out.' From the glimpse that Megan had uncovered, it would be worth it. Gideon considered the size of the crates. 'It must have taken effort to move them up here, plus the specialist packing. Why?'

'Another of the mysteries of Il Giardino delle Rose.' Megan looked round. 'You know, this is not what I expected to find.' There was a faint note of disappointment in her voice. 'You think of attics as being full of old junk and lost treasures.'

It was dusty and there were spider webs, illuminated by the sun coming through a skylight, but except for the chandeliers, the attic was empty.

'I suppose as the house was newly built it hasn't accumulated clutter.'

'Could be,' Megan answered absently. Gideon turned to look at her. Her attention was focused on a door in the corner of the space. 'Where do you think that goes?'

'Just a cupboard, isn't it? Although—' he swung round slowly '—this probably isn't the whole of the roof space. Another attic?' For some reason, his heart had begun to beat a little faster. 'That's the one with the treasure?'

Megan crossed over to try the door. 'Whatever it is, it's locked.'

'And no key.'

Megan scanned the room. 'And no sign of one.'

She frowned, clearly frustrated by the locked door. He moved to stand beside her to kiss the frown away. 'You can get a locksmith. It looks a pretty substantial affair, but they should be able to get it open.'

'Unless we can find the key.' She was still looking at the door. Then she straightened her shoulders and took his hand.

'Unless we can find the key,' she repeated softly as they walked back downstairs

Megan huffed in frustration as she closed the last drawer in the bureau with more force than was strictly necessary. She'd gone through every set of keys and every drawer and cupboard that dated from her aunt's time, with no success. The key was missing and the door remained stubbornly closed. She was beginning to think that she *would* have to resort to a locksmith. *Or an axe.* She couldn't say why finding out what was behind the door mattered so much. The sense that there was something hidden nagged at her. She was unhappily aware that the furniture still left from her aunt's time was only a fraction of what had once been here. The idea that an item had been disposed of with the elusive key *inside* it made her huff some more. She lay back in the desk chair with a grumpy sigh. After a few seconds, her sense of humour got the better of her and she laughed. 'It probably *is* just a cupboard or another empty room!' She got up and went to the kitchen in search of a drink.

Maria was washing salad leaves. 'I was thinking, about that key,' she said as soon as she saw Megan.

'Yes?'

'Have you tried Grandfather's shed? He has all kinds of stuff in there.'

Megan helped herself to a bottle of water from the fridge and took it with her to the shed, one wall of which was covered in narrow shelves. There were tins full of nails and screws, boxes of nuts and bolts, glass jars full of pencil stubs and old table knives, washers and mysterious pieces of metal. She wondered if Tommaso himself remembered what half the stuff was for. There were boxes of seed packets, lengths of string, drill bits and small plastic flower pots. There were also five bundles of assorted keys. Triumphantly, she gathered them up and went in search of Gideon.

They were on the last bundle, and she was on the point of giving up hope. Gideon sorted through them, selecting two and holding them out. 'These are the only ones for that sort of lock.' She met his eyes, knowing that what she could see in them was probably mirrored in her own – curiosity, anticipation, maybe a little apprehension.

'I don't think we're going to find the skeleton of the madwoman in the attic,' he said softly.

'No,' she agreed, wishing he hadn't put the idea in her head.

He leaned over to gather her close to his side. 'Sorry.'

'It's okay.' She weighed the final two keys in her hand. 'Bet neither of these works either.'

She was wrong.

The very last key slid home and turned.

The lock clicked open.

Chapter Forty-Five

With fingers that trembled slightly, Megan turned the handle. The door swung inwards with a faint protesting creak. Gideon's hand rested, warm and reassuring, on her shoulder. *I'm big and brave, of course I am, but I'm glad he's here.*

It was another room, not a cupboard, and it wasn't empty. She peered in, dust tickling her nose. At the far end, a window set in the roof let in a shaft of sunlight, illuminating a square of floor, but between the door and the sunshine, shrouded in shadows, were a series of mysterious humps. Gideon reached over to flip the light switch, but nothing happened.

'Bulb must have gone.'

Megan's eyes were getting accustomed to the light, making sense of the shapes. 'Luggage. It's a luggage store. Cabin trunks.' She stepped into the room.

'So it is.' Gideon followed her.

There were four trunks and some smaller items – suitcases and an old-fashioned hatbox. Gideon examined the closest trunk by the light of his phone.

'These are old. Look.' He indicated colourful labels from a famous transatlantic shipping line. 'Someone travelled in style with these.'

'Aunt Olwen and Uncle Eduardo.' Megan pointed to a ripped label bearing their names. Much of the address was gone, but not the city. 'Boston. They came from Boston.'

'That's why people assumed your aunt was an American.'

'It makes sense. Are there more labels? Are they empty?' Megan was aware of a strange feeling inside. Excitement and reluctance. Someone had hidden these cases away behind a locked door. *Or were they just put in storage when they were no longer needed and the key simply lost?*

Gideon looked over at the other trunks in their pools of shadow. 'We need a more powerful torch, or a lamp.'

It took a moment to rig up two bedside lamps on a long extension cable from the landing. Megan opted for that rather than lugging a stepladder up the stairs to replace the bulb. 'If it's only empty suitcases, we don't really need to go to that much trouble.'

Gideon clicked on the second light. She could see the glitter of anticipation and understanding in his eyes. 'You ready?'

'After the big build-up they're *bound* to be empty. Or full of spiders.'

'*Earch*! Don't!' He gave a theatrical shudder which made her laugh.

The first one opened from the side. It *was* empty. Megan wasn't sure if her dominant emotion was relief or disappointment. She inspected the fittings. 'Look at this.' The trunk was like a cupboard, with rails for garments to hang. 'I think they were used like wardrobes on long voyages.'

The second trunk, opening from the top, wasn't empty. The fragrance of lavender hit her as she raised the lid.

'Clothes.' Megan stirred the carefully folded heaps. Old-fashioned men's clothes – a teenager she realised, seeing the jeans and T-shirts. There were oversized jackets in pale pastel linen and denim, a military style tunic with gold braiding and a couple of bracelets of beads and feathers. Her stomach lurched. She quashed an impulse to slam down the lid. 'I think these belong to Cosimo – Olwen's son.'

Gideon moved to stand beside her. 'Stuff from the eighties. When he died, it was just put it away.'

'That's … sad.'

Now she could understand the locked door. *Impossible to throw or give them away, impossible to keep them in sight.* Her hand closed over the bracelet, feeling the roughness of the wooden beads and the softness of the feathers. Cheap and garish but fun, worn by a cousin she would never know. A strange muffled grief welled up inside her. She let the bracelet drop, looking around. 'I suppose the rest of the stuff is his too.'

Gideon moved to another trunk, looking at her enquiringly. When she nodded, he raised the lid, quickly closing it at her in-drawn breath. One glimpse was enough. Toys, books, stuffed animals – the relics of a childhood and a lost child. 'Do you want to leave the rest alone?' he asked softly.

'No.' She swallowed. 'Let's look at everything.'

The suitcases and the hatbox were empty, but behind them Megan pounced on a familiar shape, pulling it into the light – a writing slope.

She'd fallen to her knees. Gideon stooped over her. 'It's just like yours, the one in the library.'

'That belonged to my grandmother and she had it from her mother. Their grandfather made them. My great great great grandfather.' She looked up to meet Gideon's eyes. 'I don't think Olwen would have been able to take hers when she ran away. Eluned must have kept it.'

'Which proves that they were in touch.'

Megan nodded, too full up to speak. Her hand hovered over the lid. It would probably be empty. Without thinking, she put up her free hand to find Gideon's. His fingers were warm and his grip firm. She lifted the wooden lid.

'Oh!' It was a long, drawn-out sigh. 'Gideon!'

'I can see.' The slope was full with notebooks and stationery. An old-fashioned fountain pen nestled in a slot especially made to hold it. Megan lifted the cover of one of the books. 'These are journals.' Her heart was beating so hard she could feel it in her throat. 'Olwen's. They must be.'

'We'll take it downstairs.' He reached past her to lift the box. 'It's heavy. There's a lot of stuff in here.' He turned as he reached the door. 'Oh – what about the last trunk?'

It was another one that opened from the side. Megan eased it open, backing away as its contents came to meet her – an avalanche of slim leather-bound books.

'What the hell!' Gideon put the slope down by the door and came back as she picked up one of the volumes – pale blue leather and gold lettering.

'It's the poems. There must be hundreds of copies.' She gathered up those that had spilled. 'The English and Italian versions.'

'Published privately – like Signora Bertolo said.'

Megan nodded. 'What we would call vanity publishing – the author would pay for their own print run, but that's all it was. The writer would just get boxes of books. There are all sorts of sad stories of authors with boxes in the garage. They had to try and sell them themselves. Very few bookshops would take them. It's different now, with the Internet.' She held up one of the books. 'These must be most of the copies that were printed.'

'Translated by Olwen's Cosimo and stored here when he died.'

'I think so.'

'Why not put his name on them? If his parents paid for them to be printed, why not give their son the credit?'

Megan stroked a hand down the fine leather. The book was pristine, its pages untouched.

'Who knows? Maybe they weren't intended for public distribution. Just copies to be given to friends with a handwritten message? Maybe they thought they didn't need to?' She gestured to the name on the title page. 'Cosimo – the name of the poet and his translator?'

Gideon considered the volume in her hand and the piles on the floor. 'The books you inherited – Olwen must have given copies to her sister straight away. Or sent them.'

'And the habit of secrecy was ingrained, even though their father was gone – so there was no message inside.' Megan stroked the book in her hand again. *Not been touched for so many years – but the poems are out in the world now, at last.*

Together they picked up the books, carefully restacking them to shut the trunk. Megan made a circuit of the attic to make sure they hadn't missed anything while Gideon carried the slope down to the library, then came back to dismantle their makeshift lighting system.

Once it was done, Megan closed the door. After a second's thought, she turned the key in the lock and pocketed it.

Megan realised she was feeling slightly nauseous. *Excitement and apprehension.* Had she found the story of the villa and her aunt's life or was the contents of the box simply a random collection of junk, or maybe worse, just tantalising fragments? *And do you really want to know?* Part of her wasn't sure.

Gideon had set the slope down on the library table. Hers was sitting in the window seat where she'd been working yesterday. They were identical – plain dark varnished wood. *Made with love for twin granddaughters.* Gideon stood by the table, watching her. 'I think you need to be alone to look through this stuff.'

She felt a spike of relief that she hadn't needed to ask. Gideon must have been as curious as she was, but he understood her wish to do this by herself. 'Thank you,' she said quietly.

'I'll be in the kitchen garden with Tommaso. He's keen to have a poly tunnel and wants to show me where.'

'Have fun.'

Gideon rolled his eyes, kissed her cheek, and left.

Megan sat for some time in the window, just staring into the garden, before she fetched the slope and opened it for the second time. The contents looked like the sort of stuff that was always in her grandmother's box – stationery supplies, letters awaiting a reply, the occasional formal invitation, a bill to be paid or queried, a few keepsakes. *But this box hasn't been opened for maybe thirty years?* Since Olwen had slowly begun to retreat from the world, after the death of her son?

With a convulsive swallow, Megan reached into the box.

In a few minutes, she had organised the contents into piles – half a dozen mismatched books in various states of repair, a small heap of assorted correspondence, another of miscellaneous items. Nothing in the last pile had any sort of date – scraps that had found their way into the box as mementoes, reminders, maybe even by accident. She would begin with the books.

She picked one up at random. The brownish-red cover was worn and faded in irregular patches with a circular stain from a cup carelessly placed. She flicked through the pages – columns of figures, lists, some with items crossed out, a note about a dress pattern, a scribbled recipe for jam with a stain that suggested it had been tried.

She sat back and let the book close. Not diaries as she had thought but household journals. In another era they might have been called commonplace books – kept by a careful housewife to record matters relating to her home and kitchen. A quick skim showed that a few did have dates.

Megan's fingers hovered over one that was different from the rest, with a royal blue leather cover. The writing, when she opened it fully, was clear but faded. Written with a fountain pen, maybe the one that remained in the box.

Megan curled her feet under her and began to read.

20 January 1969

My brand-new journal. A present this morning from my Darling E. He said it is for me to write down everything that I want to record for the new life that is coming and that it is mine and that he will not look, so that if I want to write down all the curses for the trouble he is causing, I may do so! As if I would! But he is right. It is exciting but also frightening, what we are doing. Writing my thoughts might help with the loss that is to come and the changes that are before us – as well as the lists I will need for such another journey! This time there will be a whole houseful of possessions to move with us, that we have accumulated in our life here in Boston, not just one small bag.

So here we are – I will begin now.

Chapter Forty-Six

23 January 1969, Boston

America has a new president, a Republican, Richard Nixon, and official confirmation has come from Italy. Eduardo's father is dead and Eduardo inherits – the younger son. Despite what lay between them, the Marchese has not simply left an empty title, as we expected. He has left my Eduardo everything – the family house in Genoa, the land in Portofino, the olive groves and the vineyard. We do not need any of it. My Eduardo is clever. He has made himself a rich man by his own efforts, but still I know how much it means to him, despite what the old man did. And now Eduardo wants, at last, to go home. His home, not mine. After all these years, we have made a good life here in Boston. His uncle, his mother's brother, welcomed us when we had nothing. He is gone now but we still have friends, a life.

In Italy ...

But I love Eduardo today just as much as I did when I looked up from tending Aunt Myra's grave and he was standing there, with a hoe in his hand, smiling at me. He loves me, and never a word of reproach or blame, although he feels the same sorrow as I that we have no child. So – we will go to Italy and start once more to make a new life. This time it will be easier. Money always eases the way.

Megan turned the pages. The next few sheets had lists and notes – the preparations of a woman making ready to begin a new life in another country. Emotions churned inside her. It was as if her aunt was speaking to her, although she had never heard her voice. She leafed forward, finding the next block of script.

30 March 1969, Boston

Tomorrow we travel to New York to join the ship for England and then to Italy. Eduardo has business in London. He asked me this morning if I would like to journey to Wales to see my home again. For a moment longing overwhelmed me, then I shook it off and told him no. All that was long ago – almost a quarter of a century. How much might have changed – or nothing at all? If my parents still live, my father will be well past his three score years and ten, my mother sixty-nine. And the boys and my sisters? Would they even remember me, except of course for Eluned? No. We shall turn our faces to the future.

There were numbers in the margin where Olwen had worked out her parents' ages. For some reason, the scribbled note brought a lump to Megan's throat.

29 May 1969, Genoa

So much to do! The house here in Genoa is a mausoleum! It reminds me of the front parlour at home – dark drapes, heavy furniture and settees too hard and stiff to sit on properly. Eduardo hates it more than I do. It holds bad memories. His father lived here alone until nearly the end. And well deserved, the miserable old sinner. I know our dad would say that a good Christian forgives the past – not that he practised that himself, mind. I do not forgive easily. Eduardo rarely speaks of it, but his uncle told me the story, many years ago. He knew Eduardo would not return while the old man still lived.

The only things that I have found of interest in this house are the family photographs. They were in the room that belonged to Eduardo's mother. The silver frames were sadly tarnished. I got the girl to polish them.

If anything could belie the old man's conviction that Eduardo was not his son, they do.

There are Eduardo's parents, stiff and formal in a studio portrait – his father, Cesare, upright and dour, his mother, slim and delicate with a wealth of dark hair. There are pictures of Vittore, the heir, very good-looking but with a look. We would have called him a jack-the-lad. In one, he is standing with a well-dressed young woman on his arm. Eduardo says it was the girl he was engaged to. He was killed, fighting with the partisans, before they could wed. She seems very young. And in one picture is my Eduardo, not much more than a boy, but as handsome as he was when I first set eyes on him in Cathays Cemetery, gardening as a prisoner of war. He is with his brother and his father, and all alike as peas in a pod!

It was Uncle Joe who told me the story, when we got to America. He was a good man, the brother of Eduardo's mother, who welcomed us into his home and made Eduardo more like a son than a nephew. His own two sons died on the beaches of Normandy and he had no other relatives. The story was a miserable one – a shameful slander to Cesare's younger son and to his wife, Joe's sister. The fantasy of a stiff, unyielding man caught up in his own superstitious imaginings. That was my Eduardo's father.

For years – decades – the Rossi family had produced few children. For the last generations, back to Eduardo's great-great grandfather, there had been only one child that survived in each generation, fortunately a male heir.

*In Eduardo's generation, there was the heir – Vittore. The pattern was
fulfilled. When Eduardo arrived five years later, Cesare was convinced that
he was not the father. Joe suspected that he hoped Eduardo would die in
childhood. When that did not happen, Eduardo was sent away to school,
although Vittore begged that he be educated at home. The matter came to a
head when Eduardo was fifteen and his mother died. He came home for the
funeral. After his mother was buried, Eduardo's father repudiated him and
turned him out of the house. Vittore was probably told that Eduardo had
returned to school. Confused and desperate, unable to contact his brother,
Eduardo enlisted. He ended up in Wales as a POW and Vittore died. Eduardo
became the heir, but it was too late. He had made up his mind not to return
while his father lived. And he stuck to it. A miserable story and the source of
much pain, all for one man's stupid obsession. But if he had not disinherited
Eduardo, we would never have met, so I suppose I ought to attempt
forgiveness in my heart.*

*Genoa is an interesting city with much history, but neither Eduardo nor I
wish to live here. It holds painful memories for him. As soon as possible, this
house will be sold. Eduardo plans to build a villa on the land at Portofino.
There was a farmhouse there many years ago. It is a shell now, only fit to be
demolished, but the site is good and with a ruined tower!*

*Eduardo has dreams. I also have plans. Eduardo teases me about flower
power and being a romantic hippie and I don't have an answer, because he is*
right. *The place is beautiful and now I am dreaming of a garden.*

The next pages were more notes and lists, mainly about flowers and
garden plants and some notes on expenses for the house in Genoa, menus and
guest lists for dinner parties. It would be interesting to examine them when
she had time. Gideon would enjoy the references to the garden. Now Megan
was reading for the story. She leafed through until she found more blocks of
text, skipping household matters.

21 July 1969

*Yesterday a man walked on the moon! We saw it on television! Clearing
the site at Portofino is almost done and building can begin. Eduardo is there
every day, watching the workmen. He wants to make good progress before
winter sets in. And I – this morning I was sick for the third day in a row. I
have begun to wonder – but the move here to Italy ... I am forty-two years old
and I thought beyond hopes.*

Megan flipped past pages of lists.

2 December 1969

It is true – there will be a baby before next summer! Finally, I am letting myself believe it. Eduardo says it is the best Christmas present ever and is chasing the builders to get the house habitable. I am afraid, but hopeful. The doctor is understanding and says I am quite well. I feel quite well. Italy agrees with me. I must believe *that we will raise a family in our beautiful new home in Portofino.*

4 January 1970

Eduardo has done a wonderful thing. He has contacted my sister, Eluned, and she has agreed to come here and be with me for the birth of the baby! I would almost not believe it, but I have her letter. Mam is gone, but Dad is still hale and as upstanding in church as ever, although the congregation is much smaller now. Eluned has been married and widowed and has a daughter, Rosalind, who is twenty-one and at university. The first-ever of the family. Dad must be proud, even though I'm sure he would have preferred that honour for a grandson. My sister is coming to me, but will not tell Dad. Eduardo will pay for it all, of course, but as far as anyone at home knows, Eluned will have had a win on her premium bond and be spending it on a holiday in Llandudno. The villa will be ready by then and the planting in the garden well advanced. I am growing bigger by the day, but Eduardo has hired no less than four gardeners to do my bidding! All I have to do is direct them, although I cannot resist pottering amongst the newly planted shrubs and flower beds. There is to be a kitchen garden and young trees are already planted. I have a vision of a belvedere and roses.

Here there were small sketches of what Megan recognised as the rose garden, along with a note about ordering baby clothes.

7 February 1970

I had a strange encounter yesterday, waddling around the new paths in the garden. Eduardo has commissioned a statue and I had to decide where to put it! I came out at the higher end of the drive, meaning to go back to the house – the day was warm for a whale who has lost sight of her feet! There was a woman standing in the drive, just looking at the house, with the strangest expression on her face. When I asked if I might help her, in my very best Italian – I hardly ever have to search for a word now – she looked at me as if I was a ghost, picked up her skirts – which were old-fashioned long, not a maxi skirt – and simply ran away. Eduardo saw her too. He had just come out of the house to speak to one of the workmen. He did not know who she was, but thought it might be Adriana, the girl who was engaged to his

227

*brother. Not a girl any more, of course, and I must say she looked haggard.
No longer the lovely young beauty in the photograph.*

*Eduardo had more news later over dinner. Our first meal in our brand-
new dining room.*

Here there was a margin note about ordering extra table linen.

*He had been talking to the workmen. I might have guessed he would find
out. He is the greatest gossip, except in financial matters when he will make a
clam seem chatty! It probably was Adriana. Her family home is near here. It
is a sad story. Apparently, when Vittore was killed and his body brought in,
the girl collapsed and then had some sort of nervous breakdown and was sent
away to her older sister to recover. When she was there, she met and married
a much older man, a colleague of her sister's husband. She lives now outside
Genoa but must have been visiting and curious and then embarrassed. It is a
pity, as I am vaingloriously proud of what Eduardo has achieved here and
would have been happy to show her the house and grounds.*

*My darling husband has decreed that the garden shall not extend onto
the promontory. He says that the present size is large enough, with a baby on
the way – I must leave some space for those who come after! Like a good and
obedient wife, I will do as he asks. The tower will be left to its wildness. He
has found some notes about it in the family papers he brought from the house
in Genoa. Part of it is very old but apparently a group of young men – poets
and artists – who rented the farmhouse for a summer in the 1820s, rebuilt the
ruin as a folly and lookout point – meaning, I think, for it to resemble
something from an Arthurian legend. It is certainly romantic. If I am not to
incorporate it into the garden, I will plant a rose to scramble up – La
Follette, perhaps. It will make a pleasant view.*

The next few pages were notes on the purchase of roses and baby
equipment, with a couple of sketched designs for the arbour.

10 March 1970

*The baby is here!! The labour was long, but our son arrived as the sun
came up over the house that Eduardo has built for me. Our son – strong and
complete and perfect. Cosimo. Eduardo said he would have given me
diamonds, but he knew I would prefer rosebushes. I think he has bought up
every rosebush between here and Florence! The villa has a new name – Il
Giardino delle Rose (Eduardo gave me diamond and sapphire earrings too).*

*I am tired but the baby thrives, and it is so good to have my sister with
me. I did not imagine how good. Eduardo is very wise, although I make sure
not to tell him that! Eluned's hair is already white, like our mam's. It started*

228

to go when she lost her David in an accident on the docks. I have to say that time has been less kind to her than to me. She looks much older; I suppose I am the pampered darling of a wealthy man. The family is scattered now and moved away from Cardiff, although Eluned still lives near Dad in the old house in Cathays. Her daughter, Rosalind, is at university in Warwickshire, studying history, with a job in the civil service in prospect. She has a young man in the offing too – and my young man only just born! The world is a wonderful, strange place, made stranger by the people in it! I cannot help but think of those two stiff-necked old men, Eduardo's father and mine, estranged from their children because they had to have their own way in everything.

Megan scanned through the rest of the books but there were no more personal entries. *No time for reflection with a new baby and a new home.* She was about to pick up one of the letters when it occurred to her that she was hungry. She glanced over at the carriage clock on the mantle, registering that it was nearly seven at the same time as there was a knock on the door. Gideon put his head round it with an enquiring look. She beckoned him in. He'd changed out of work clothes into dark chinos and a white shirt that fitted perfectly over a deeply muscled chest. His skin was bronze from outdoor work and his unruly, dark hair was in need of cutting, flopping forward over his eyes.

Megan was conscious of a tingling in her abdomen. She watched him come towards her, emotion welling up inside her. This was not the man she'd ever imagined being with – *that would be Ellery* – but Gideon was the one she wanted to share this with – her aunt's story and everything else. She wanted a love story like Olwen and Eduardo's with *this* man.

This one.

The whispered words in her head made her sit forward, planting her feet on the floor in surprise. His smile washed over her like sunlight. Something inside her settled like a sigh.

'Sorry to interrupt, but if you're hungry I wondered if you'd like to go out to eat?' he asked as he reached her. 'How are you getting on?'

'There's some amazing stuff here – a lot of answers but a lot more questions as well.' She put out her hand to let him pull her from the chair. 'I would like to go out. I can tell you about it then.'

Gideon extracted a succulent prawn from the plate of seafood they were sharing. He offered it to Megan but she declined, smiling. She looked amazing in a dark pink dress with her hair scooped back in a patterned scarf. She'd just finished telling him what she'd found in the journals.

'So, they went to America from Wales at the end of the war – which explains a few things. I wonder how they managed it? They must have been barely more than kids.'

'I'm guessing Uncle Joe organised it. Eduardo must have reached out to him somehow. Cardiff was a commercial port – there were probably ways to get a passage.' She frowned. 'It must have been *mega* scary, for a girl who'd never been out of Wales.'

'But they were in love.'

'They were.' Megan's voice was very soft. 'And it seems they stayed that way.' Gideon slid his hand across the table to entwine her fingers. 'I'd like to make enquiries in Boston, to see if there's anyone who might remember them.'

'Sounds good,' Gideon agreed. 'The father must have been a real piece of work, doubting his wife and rejecting his son for such an irrational reason.'

'I wonder how he would feel now, knowing the property has passed completely out of his family.' Megan's fingers twined more tightly into his. 'We know now about the early years – and about the garden. Eluned came here when Cosimo was born, when the garden was new. She probably came at other times as well. And Cosimo …' She paused to take a sip from her wine glass. 'He was born in March 1970, and my mum was born in April the following year – Olwen's son and Eluned's granddaughter. If they were still alive, they'd both be nearly fifty – and I might never have seen Il Giardino delle Rose, much less inherited it.'

'There's nothing about what happened to Cosimo?'

'Not yet, but there's more stuff to look through. Will you help me when we get back?'

The rush of happiness was warm and unexpected. *Trust.* 'Of course I will.'

Gabriella stood in the window of the dress shop, looking out over the square, the harbour and the brightly lit restaurants. The shop was officially closed, but the owner was always ready to open up after hours for *her*. It was a tradition that she bought a new dress for her birthday. Her choice was being packed in tissue in a shallow box. The owner was clucking and cooing over it with the girl Freddie insisted should act as her secretary. At least she would be useful to carry the parcel to the car.

At last they were done and the shop owner ushered them out, still clucking. *As well she might, the sum that had been spent.* But the dress did look good on her; palest pink with long puff sleeves and pleats. The evening was warm and the square was crowded. More crowded than Gabriella liked, but in a very few moments they would be at the car.

It was interesting *sometimes* to see these people – little lives thinking that they were brushing shoulders with the "jet set". The girl was chattering, but Gabriella let her voice wash over her, concentrating on the faces. There was a young woman in a pink dress seated at one of the restaurant tables, her head almost touching that of a young man sitting opposite her. Even as Gabriella watched, the man leaned in for a kiss before they both sat back laughing.

Gabriella stopped dead as horrible realisation swept over her. The woman was Megan Morrison and the man was West, the gardener. *No!* She could hear the screaming in her head. He was supposed to be gone. Morrison was meant to be alone.

Gabriella's heart was pounding, her fists clenched. Morrison had sent him away. Brown had said so. *Yet here they are.*

The secretary was fussing, all concern. Was Signora De Stefano feeling faint? The evening *was* warm.

In a glaze of rage, Gabriella allowed herself to be led back to the car. She had to do something. This could not go on. *Finally*, she had to take direct action. There was no other way.

Chapter Forty-Seven

The library was quiet, lit only by lamps and the very last glow of the setting sun. Together they were sifting through the remaining items from the writing slope. Gideon had found a few handwritten paragraphs that he identified as passages from the garden brochure, which matched the message on a crumpled pink card announcing the birth of a granddaughter, Amy.

'That was my Mum, so it's definitely Eluned's writing. She *did* write the brochure.' There was a clip with bills, including one for the Justice statue commissioned in 1970. 'You think that was a reference to Eduardo's father – Eduardo finally got justice?' Megan waved the bill, amused to see Gideon engrossed in a folder of garden plans.

'Eh?' He glanced up, clearly not giving the matter his full attention. 'Yeah, maybe.'

Megan looked at him and then at the room and felt an enveloping wave of happiness. Everything here was *right*. She'd found her place.

She picked up a sheet of thin blue airmail paper, part of a letter in Italian. To a friend in Boston? There was a stain like spilled coffee across the writing and below that, on the unused page, the design for a flower bed, which was probably why it was kept. She began to read the lines. 'Oh!'

'What?' This time Gideon's attention was fully on her. She handed the letter over. 'This must be the second or third page of something. Look what it says.'

'Something about the son, Cosimo? My written Italian isn't all that good.'

'It's a little joke.' Megan knew she was grinning. 'About Cosimo translating Cosimo.' The grin faded. 'All these fragments may be proof that he was the translator, but we've found no trace of any papers, no original documents, nothing.'

'We can only keep looking.' Gideon's voice was soft and reassuring. It gave her a flicker of hope, even if it was misplaced.

The last small pile was the miscellaneous items that had been gathered in the bottom of the box – a pebble, a length of gold chain, an invitation to an engagement party, artwork done by a child signed with a flourishing *C*. Gideon picked up a cardboard envelope, decorated in garish colours.

'Photographic prints, from the days when you took film to the chemist to be developed.' He handed the envelope to Megan. She lifted the flap. Pictures of the garden. Roses and more roses, and a close-up of a young man with a wide smile and a mop of artfully disarranged blonde hair, laughing into the camera. Gideon leaned in to take a look. 'Cosimo?'

'It has to be. God, he was gorgeous – he could have been in one of those eighties' bands – Duran Duran or Spandau Ballet?'

Gideon tapped the photograph. 'That's the coat from the trunk – the military one with the gold braid.'

'Taken not long before he died?' Megan sighed, looking at the clock. It was nearly eleven and the shadows in the room were lengthening. There was one item left. She picked up the padded bag and tipped the contents into her hand. Something shiny and metallic bounced onto the floor. Gideon picked it up. It was a key.

The other thing in the bag was a bundle of stiff white cards, edged in black. Megan knew immediately what they were. 'Order of service – Cosimo's funeral.' She held one out. Gideon took it. His warm fingers counteracted the cold choking feeling in her throat. 'Cremation,' she said softly. 'So, there's probably no grave.'

Gideon's eyes widened. He knew her so well. 'You were thinking about that Pre-Raphaelite poet who buried his verses with his wife?'

'Rosetti – and then he regretted it and dug them up again.' She shook her head. 'The poems didn't go to any grave with Cosimo.'

Gideon put the cards and the key back in the bag and dropped it into the slope. 'Look through it all again in the morning. You might find something else on a second look,' he suggested, getting up and pulling Megan to her feet and into his arms.

The kiss was long and soft and healing.

Gideon put out the lamps while she closed the windows. They checked all the doors together. On impulse, Megan took a bottle of wine from the fridge and found glasses. When they reached her bedroom at the back of the house – her new bed was not arriving until next week – she turned on all the lights, chasing away the shadows. They shared the wine and kisses and soft endearments. The heat building inside her drove out the lingering hurts from the contents of the box. When Gideon was at last inside her, she knew that the sense of oneness and belonging was real and total.

The morning sun made patterns on the floor of the palazzo. Gabriella closed the clasp of her bag and pulled on a pair of white cotton gloves, stretching them over her fingers. It was time. She was ready. She'd toyed with the idea of calling for the car. Arriving in a limousine was bound to impress. It would reinforce the seriousness of her offer, but to call out the chauffeur would raise questions. The fools surrounding her might even try to stop her. This was the only way. She would speak directly to Megan Morrison; show her clearly what the correct course of action was.

Gabriella had turned the matter over in her mind all night. Were the lawyers to be trusted? There was no way of knowing if Dottoressa Morrison had even been *told* of her offer. The woman might be delighted to have a way out of her financial predicament. They would settle a price and then they would both sign the simple agreement that she had prepared herself – with no need of lawyers – and it would be done.

Gabriella adjusted the glove on her left hand, settling it more carefully over her wrist. If the girl chose to make difficulties, there were other ways – but she would not think of that. She would walk to the garage and she would drive Giovanni's non-descript car to Il Giardino delle Rose. Then they would see. They would all see.

Chapter Forty-Eight

Megan was just sitting down with the contents of the writing slope spread out on the library table when she heard a car approaching. Curious, and strangely reluctant to begin sifting through the contents of the box again, with all its hopes and sadness, she went out to the hall and opened the front door. A small black car had parked outside. At first, she couldn't place the woman who alighted, then realisation kicked in. Gabriella De Stefano. *What is she doing here?*

'Signora De Stefano, this is a surprise.' Megan tried to put enthusiasm into her voice, but the woman's intense stare disconcerted her. 'How can I help you today?'

'We have business to discuss.'

Gabriella was already making her way into the house. Megan found herself scrambling to show her into the small salon. *Really!* She bit down on an acid remark. The woman clearly believed she was a person of importance, and she *did* have a family connection to the Institute. *And you are hoping for the chance to lecture there again. Is that why she's here?* Megan invited her to sit and offered coffee. The chair was accepted but not the refreshments. The woman seemed, not nervous exactly, but … excited?

'You realise why I am here this morning, Dottoressa Morrison.' The smile that accompanied the words was the coldest thing Megan had ever seen. She shifted uneasily in her seat. She knew she was being absurd, but she wished that Gideon wasn't working down at the tower and that the entire gardening crew weren't attending to some trees on the perimeter of the estate. She gathered her thoughts with a jolt. Gabriella was waiting for a reply.

'Actually, I don't.' She tried a smile of her own, hoping it was a better effort.

'Pah!' Gabriella made an irritated gesture. 'Lawyers! Negotiations!' She drawled the words as a sneer. 'I am glad I came to speak to you myself.'

Totally confused, Megan found that she was not at all glad and her feeling of unease was growing.

'I can't imagine—'

Gabriella waved her imperiously into silence. 'I am here to purchase Il Giardino delle Rose. You will name your price and it will be met.'

'What!' Megan almost let out a bark of nervous laughter but managed to stifle it with a hand over her mouth. The woman was … Megan wasn't sure what the word was to describe her, but the intense quality of the dark eyes boring into her made it quite clear that this was no joke. Gabriella was deadly serious.

Megan swallowed hard. This was going to be difficult. 'I'm sorry,' she said as gently as she could. 'I think you have somehow been given the wrong impression. I have no intention of selling to *anyone,*' she emphasised. 'I intend to make my home here. I'm sorry,' she repeated, although she wasn't quite sure that she was. Indignation at the woman's arrogance was beginning to stir. *But not wise to let it show.* 'The villa is not for sale.'

'I am here to purchase the property. It should be mine by right, but I am prepared to pay whatever you ask,' the woman repeated her demand as if she had not heard Megan's refusal.

A cold knot of alarm was forming in Megan's stomach. She got to her feet. 'I'm afraid you've had a wasted journey. I'm not open to offers. I have nothing more to say on the matter. I think it would be best if you leave now.'

The woman was fiddling with the clasp on her bag, eyes still focused on Megan's face. 'You *must* want money. I will pay. I have an agreement for signature.'

'I'm not signing anything. I don't need money.' *And I wouldn't take yours, even if I did.* 'Thank you for your offer. Obviously, you're disappointed but I'm not selling. I'll see you out.'

There was a split second of relief when Gabriella surged to her feet, but her expression had not changed, Megan realised with alarm. 'No! You will sell. I—'

'Dottoressa Morrison.' Maria's voice, at its most formal, jerked Megan's head around to the open doorway. She wondered how long Maria had been standing there. She suspected it might have been for a few moments. 'I apologise,' Maria continued, bobbing what was very nearly a curtsy. 'I did not realise that you had a guest, and I have not brought you refreshments.'

'That's quite all right.' Megan hoped that she was signalling "thank you" and "I don't know what the hell is going on here" with her eyes. 'Signora De Stefano was just leaving.'

She stepped back, indicating the door. Gabriella gulped in air, her hands still clutching at her bag, then abruptly her shoulders dropped and her bravado crumbled as she looked at Maria and then back at Megan. 'I will leave.' She pulled her head up and stalked to the door.

Maria was across the hall with the front door open by the time she got there. There was a heavy silence as the woman walked through. Maria closed it with a loud click. Megan put her finger to her lips as they waited. After a moment there was a sound of a car engine and tyres on gravel.

'What was all *that*?' Maria demanded.

'She just swept in here demanding to buy the place.' Megan sagged against the back of the sofa, feeling limp now that confrontation was over. 'Thanks for the rescue. I was having trouble convincing her to take no for an answer.'

Maria tapped her forehead in a suggestive way. 'Alcinda says she's crazy.'

'Going by today's performance, I'd certainly say weird.'

'Coffee,' Maria decided. 'We need something, and it's too early for gin.'

Gabriella brought the car to a halt at the bottom of the drive, where she was out of sight of the house. She sat for a moment, composing herself. Her body was shaking and her breath coming in erratic gasps. With an effort she brought both under control, but there was still fury raging inside her.

The arrogance and insolence of the Englishwoman, denying her, Gabriella De Stefano, what was hers by right. If there was any justice, the villa should be hers. It *was* hers. Could no one understand? She smoothed her hands down both sides of the steering wheel, noting that they were now steady. She had followed the reasonable course, made her offer, had it rejected to her face. Now she would have to use other means to secure justice. She picked up her bag and got out of the car.

The grounds were quiet, but she could hear the sound of voices and machinery in the distance. She set off into the garden, nodding with approval as she walked the gravelled paths. The young man, West, had done good work. It was him she was looking for.

She stopped at a junction where three paths met, uncertain which to choose. The tower was that way. For a second, her eyes clouded. The image of a beloved laughing face, that absurd military jacket and the feathered bracelets rose in her mind, so vivid she almost reached out to touch ...

Love welled up in her heart, followed by the stab of remembered pain. It had been just such a day as this, sunny and quiet, when she had found *him* and it had all gone wrong. He had not understood either.

'*Merda*!' Gabriella jumped at the sound of a voice. A scruffy old man emerged from one of the flowerbeds and looked her up and down, growling something in a thick accent.

'I am looking for Signor West.' Inspiration struck her. 'I wish to discuss a commission.' The old man was still eyeing her suspiciously. After a moment he spat, then jerked his head. 'That way.'

Gabriella nodded. It was a path she knew.

Towards the tower.

Gideon stood up straight, wiping his hands on his jeans. He had the terrain on the point marked out. Now he could get to work finalising the selection of plants and preparing the ground. Once it was finished, he was pretty sure it would look good. He turned and shaded his eyes. The sun was very bright. There was a figure making its way towards him, a dark silhouette. Female. His heart lifted. *Megan.* He walked forward to meet her.

It was West! There was no mistaking his height, although for a moment, in the glare of the sun ... Gabriella brushed her hand over her face. That was just a trick of memory. Cosimo. *Her* Cosimo ... he hadn't understood. But this time, it would be right.

She opened the flap of her bag and drew out the gun.

Gideon stopped beside the tower. It wasn't Megan coming towards him but Gabriella De Stefano. *What the hell is she doing here?* Something metallic in her hand caught the light briefly. Gideon swallowed. It couldn't be. The woman couldn't be holding a gun.

Except that she was.

'Signora De Stefano?' He moved forward again, cautiously. The barrel of the thing was wavering and there was a sudden sweat dampening the back of his shirt. *This cannot be happening.*

'You were supposed to leave. If you were gone then the Englishwoman would go also,' Gabriella asserted. 'This would not have been necessary.'

She brandished the weapon, obviously intent on herding him back towards the cliff. He took a step back, then another, his mind working furiously. He had no idea what was going on, but the woman was clearly dangerous. *You need to do something.*

He tried to look around for a rock that he might throw. Yelling wouldn't be any good; the work gang was too far away to hear. Tommaso was somewhere about, but he wasn't going to get the old man mixed up in this.

'Signora De Stefano ...' He raised his voice. 'I don't know what it is you want, but can we talk? If you could explain—'

'No!' She shook her head emphatically. Then an expression he couldn't read crossed her face. She put up her free hand, as if to brush something away. 'Cosimo.' It was a low-pitched moan, but she was still coming forward.

Gideon had no choice but to retreat.

Megan strolled down the path, swinging the carrier with the water bottles. Gideon would be ready for a drink and these were fresh out of the fridge. She wanted to hear his final plans for the exotic garden and tell him about her weird encounter with Signora De Stefano. Maria was going to tell Alcinda about it, so she could speak to Gabriella's stepson. *Could the woman be suffering from early-onset dementia?*

Megan had almost reached the point. She could see the top of the tower, and there was Gideon, almost at the edge of the cliff. Dangerously near the edge. Dropping the carrier with the bottles, Megan began to run. *What the hell is happening?*

There was another figure standing between them – dark hair and a pale blue dress. 'Signora De Stefano!' Megan yelled the woman's name before she saw it – and then she couldn't believe it.

The woman was holding a gun.

Megan's shout made Gabriella look back over her shoulder. Gideon was gesticulating now, motioning for Megan to run in the other direction. She shook her head, looking around frantically for a weapon, a stick, something to sweep the gun out of the woman's hand. If she hadn't dropped the bottles …

'Stop! Leave him alone!' Megan didn't understand any of this, but she knew it was real, not a nightmare.

With a dismissive shrug, Signora De Stefano turned back and took aim. The sound of the shot was a sharp crack in the quiet air. Seagulls rose up from the tower in a squawking cloud. Gideon swayed for a second, a red stain blossoming across his white shirt. Then he fell backwards over the edge, towards the sea.

Chapter Forty-Nine

'*No!*' Megan ran, desperate to reach the cliff. 'Gideon!' Her anguished cry was all but lost in the keening wail from the woman standing between her and the edge.

'Cosimo!' The wail echoed over the cries of the gulls. 'You don't understand.'

'*I* understand.' Megan reached the woman. Now she could see that her face was wet with tears. 'You just *shot* him.'

In an instant she realised that Gabriella wasn't talking to her, wasn't even *here*. She was somewhere inside her head. There wasn't time to figure it out. Megan moved to push past, intent on the spot where Gideon had dropped. *He can't be dead. He* can't *be dead.*

'Stop!' Megan had got too close. Gabriella grabbed her wrist, back in the present, waving the gun in her face. 'I will have the villa. You will sign. You *will* sign.' She lowered the gun, attempting to reach into her bag which was still hanging incongruously from her arm, at the same time as holding on to Megan. 'The agreement—'

With a massive heave, Megan wrenched herself out of the woman's grasp, but she was still between her and Gideon. And the gun had steadied, pointing directly at her. Gabriella's face had settled into a mask, the tears dried. 'You will sign or I will shoot you.'

Megan took a step back, although everything in her wanted to run to the cliff edge. 'Shooting me won't get you Il Giardino delle Rose. You will be charged with murder.'

'No.' A slow, chillingly cold smile stole over the older woman's face. 'The tower. Two lovers.' She glanced briefly upwards. 'No one suspected before.' For a second the smile crumpled into pain. '*You will sign.*'

This time she reached into the bag, pulling out a sheet of paper. Megan knew, without any doubt, that no matter if she signed or if she didn't, this woman was going to shoot her and drop her body over the cliff.

There was only one thing she could do.

She turned and ran.

She'd taken Gabriella by surprise, but she wasn't going to make it to the main garden and the work crew. Even as the thought came, there was the sound of a shot and a bullet whistled past her head. There was only one slim chance. She changed course and headed to the tower.

She was nearly at the top of the staircase, slipping and sliding on the steep old stones, when Gabriella reached the doorway. Another bullet ricocheted off the step below Megan. She scrambled higher, then turned. Gabriella was advancing behind her, waving the paper. *'You will sign.'* The words were a screech.

Megan looked up to the ledge around the top of the tower. She'd bought herself a few seconds and the advantage of height. With both hands full, Gabriella's ascent was slow and uncertain.

If there was something to throw – if Gabriella could be induced to expend all her bullets – Megan clambered onto the ledge. The sudden strength of the breeze off the sea took her by surprise, making her wobble. She grabbed the crenulated wall as her foot slipped away sideways, missing the steps to dangle into space. Her hands bit into the brickwork, scrabbling before she found a handhold.

Gabriella was halfway up the stair, muttering softly. Megan hung, half suspended, her heart racing and her breath surging in panic. She heaved to get both feet onto a firm surface. Relief flooded through her as she almost got her balance, but as her foot settled, loose stones lying on the ledge shifted. Instinctively, she kicked back, sending them flying away and down.

The cry from below made Megan turn. Gabriella's hands were up, shielding her face as a hail of tiny pebbles pattered around her.

There was a terrible second as Gabriella swayed, arms raised, knuckles white, as one hand clutched the gun and the other the paper.

Then, with a scream, she was gone.

The gun fired again as her body hit the stone floor with a sickening thud and lay still, arms outstretched.

Megan clung to the turret, head spinning, bile in her throat. Slowly, she unpeeled her fingers and sank onto the top step.

Gabriella's eyes were open, but she had not moved. The gun lay a few feet away against the wall. Megan could just see the edge of the paper under Gabriella's body.

She wrapped her arms around her knees, shaking, knowing she had to get to Gideon but unable to move.

She was still sitting like that when Tommaso and the rest of the garden crew poured in through the doorway.

Chapter Fifty

There was a machine somewhere close by, beeping out a regular rhythm. This one didn't seem to be attached to him, although he thought there had been machines when he'd woken up before.

Gideon kept his eyes closed while he decided if he was staying around this time. It seemed like a good guess that this was a hospital. It smelled like a hospital and there was that machine, still bleeping. His left side felt kind of stiff and strange. His arm was too heavy to lift and his mouth was dry. He'd felt better, but, on the whole, it didn't seem too bad. *If you open your eyes, someone might give you a drink.* But then there would probably be prodding and poking and possibly needles. He wasn't ready for that yet, so the eyes were staying closed.

He wanted to figure out what had put him here, before any new stuff started. His mind was fuzzy with sleep. He concentrated. He'd been working, and then there was a woman waving her arms and calling him by someone else's name, and then something thumped him and he'd stumbled back over the cliff.

Hell! He jerked, wincing at the memory as his body protested. The woman hadn't just been waving her arms. She'd been waving a gun. She'd shot him!

The next bit was hazy. He'd been lying on something uncomfortable. There had been a lot of blue sky above him, and his arm and his head hurt, so he'd just looked at the sky, trying to figure out what colour blue it was to take his mind off things. He vaguely thought that there had been people and shouting and noise and then this place. His thoughts were foggy and this was exhausting, so he was glad he hadn't bothered to open his eyes. Maybe he'd just drift off again for a bit. He took a deep breath and inhaled something that was not hospital. *Lemons and honeysuckle.* He opened his eyes in a rush.

'Megan!'

'You're awake.' Her voice sounded shaky. She was standing by the bed, leaning over him. Her face was pale, her eyes red-rimmed, but she was smiling.

'I love you.' It seemed important to say that, but he wasn't sure how distinct the words were because it felt as if he'd eaten a pillow full of feathers.

'I love you too.' She *did* understand and she was reaching for something. Water, to give him a tiny sip.

'Marry me?' He wasn't clear where that came from, though it seemed like a good idea, but her eyes filled with tears, so maybe it wasn't.

'Ah!' Another voice, brisk and business-like. 'Our patient is awake.' A nurse loomed into view. Gideon resigned himself to the prodding and the poking.

Megan sat on a hard plastic chair in the hospital corridor, tears of relief running down her face. The nurse had called the doctor and Megan had been shooed out while she conducted her examination. Megan didn't know why she was crying. Gideon's wrist was broken, there were stitches in his upper arm where the bullet had grazed him and he'd lost some blood. He'd been incredibly lucky, landing on a flat grass-covered outcrop rather than plummeting down to the sea below.

Like Cosimo?

She shivered, wiping her nose on the back of her hand. Gideon was alive and would mend. *And he just asked you to marry him.* He'd still been half asleep though, on the edge of awareness. *He probably won't remember.* She certainly wouldn't be reminding him.

She'd realised, in the confusion and terror of the rescue, that there was no doubt about it any more. She loved this man. It hadn't come as a thunderclap or a sudden revelation, and it wasn't just a reaction to the drama of nearly getting killed. It was a deep, inexorable knowledge that if Gideon had died, part of her would be gone forever. He was woven into her heart now. She didn't need a ring to make it so.

'Dottoressa Morrison?' Someone was standing beside her. A large man, offering her a handkerchief. After a second, she recognised one of the policemen who had arrived with the medical first responders.

'Thank you.' She took the handkerchief and scrubbed her face.

'Signor West, he is awake?'

Megan nodded, waving vaguely at the door to Gideon's room. Of course, the police would want to talk to him. They were investigating attempted murder. Gabriella De Stefano hadn't died in the fall. She was here, in another part of the hospital somewhere. She'd never walk again and there was a possibility of more extensive paralysis. *But she didn't die.*

Megan hadn't yet decided how she felt about that. She thought that she might eventually settle for acceptance. At present, the desire to find the woman and put a pillow over her face was still uncomfortably close to the surface. There were a lot of questions that needed answers. *And probably some that will never be answered.* Smothering Gabriella wouldn't provide any answers at all, so she would wait for acceptance.

The policeman, having confirmed that she was fit to be left alone, turned towards Gideon's room. Megan sighed and leaned her head against the wall as he went in.

Chapter Fifty-One

The sun was shining and a light breeze was coming off the sea, enveloping her in the scent of late flowering roses. It felt like a good omen. *As if the garden is listening.* Megan held the two lockets, Olwen's and Eluned's, chains entwined, the gold warm in her hand. She was walking the labyrinth for the first time, not so much for meditation as to order her thoughts. *And to let the villa and its old ghosts know what really happened.*

It was fanciful, and there were still gaps in the story, but what she was doing felt right. Gideon was sitting quietly on the turf seat that had been constructed to overlook the labyrinth, in silent support. His arm in its cast rested on his knee. In the three weeks since the terrifying encounter on the point, they'd put a lot of pieces together – from recollections, from snippets that the police let fall and from an unexpectedly illuminating visit from Freddie.

Megan paced slowly, starting at the beginning of the labyrinth and of the story. That was the part that was most speculative, but she was sure in her heart that it was true. Gideon's fall from the cliff hadn't been the first. The policeman who'd given Megan his handkerchief had confirmed that was where Olwen's son had met his death, with a question mark over whether it had been an accident or suicide. The question mark was gone now as far as Megan was concerned. She and Gideon had put their recollections together last night in the library by candlelight over a bottle of wine.

'Signora De Stefano had mixed me up with Olwen's son.' Gideon sipped from his glass, leaning back against his chair. 'She was back in the past, seeing him.'

Megan sighed. 'It seemed that way to me too, but nothing can be proved, unless she opens up and speaks of it.' The woman was apparently turning her face to the wall and refusing to speak to anyone, including the police. 'I think …' Megan stared at the flame of the closest candle. 'I think there was something between her and Cosimo – remember Edith Moreau spoke about "Cosimo's Girl"? Maybe it was more on her side than his. They *were* only kids. I think she acted out the same scenario with the gun – trying to get him to admit that he loved her and to agree to marry her. She fired, maybe just to scare him, and he went over the cliff. He wasn't as lucky as you.' She reached to clasp Gideon's free hand, feeling and holding the warmth. 'If Cosimo had married her, that would have made the villa hers.' Megan stared

245

at the flame, the scene unfolding itself in her mind. The windswept point, the gulls, the desperate girl and the confused, uncomprehending boy, not understanding what was at stake.

She paused now, in the sunshine, letting that piece of the story loose to the breeze, before she moved on. Most of the rest of what they knew came from Freddie. He'd turned up yesterday, embarrassed and apologetic and clearly seeking some sort of absolution. Megan hadn't been keen to give it at first, but in the end she had. Maybe he'd been careless, but he really wasn't responsible for his stepmother's actions. *And it all started a very long time ago.*

Obsessions from the past, handed down and nursed in secret, until they finally erupted. 'Which could have got both of us killed,' she pointed out to Gideon when they'd finally seen Freddie on his way, after a fraught hour of explanations. Gideon had pulled her into a one-armed hug, planting a kiss on the top of her head. 'It didn't though. And it's a hell of a sad story about wasted lives.'

Sad and complex and going all the way back to the war, Freddie had explained. 'My stepmother's grandmother, Adriana, was the girl Eduardo's older brother was meant to marry.'

'Vittore, the son who was killed fighting with the partisans?'

Freddie nodded. 'Gabriella's mother, Paola, believed that she was actually Vittore's daughter. It became an obsession that she passed down to *her* daughter.' He grimaced. 'It wasn't true. The dates didn't fit. Paola was the daughter of the man Adriana actually married. A DNA test that my father eventually arranged for Gabriella proved it, though Gabriella wouldn't acknowledge it. As far as she was concerned, she was a Rossi – the true heir and owner of Il Giardino delle Rose.'

'The illegitimate heir,' Megan pointed out.

'Yes,' Freddie agreed. 'Apparently she looked for a long time for some evidence that there had been a marriage. In the end, she accepted that there hadn't been, but it didn't change her conviction that she had a moral right to Il Giardino delle Rose – that she was seeking a form of justice. That was why she planned to buy the place once the Marchesa was gone.'

'And then I happened along and wouldn't sell.' Megan heard the cool note in her own voice. She couldn't help it, but she saw Freddie wince.

'Believe me, I had no idea that things were as bad as they were. My father explained it to me before he died, but I thought … I thought he was exaggerating.' He looked down for a moment, then raised his head. 'There

was an incident when I was away at university. My stepmother came here.
She had the gun – a relic of the war—'

'But in remarkably good order,' Gideon said, his hand going
automatically to the healing scar on his upper arm. Freddie winced again.

Was it kept that way by your father? Megan wondered, seeing guilt in his
expression. *Well – the police have it now.*

'Shots were fired,' Freddie said.

'The bullet holes in the arbour,' Megan said softly, shaking her head and
waving for Freddie to continue when he paused.

'My father followed her, but not fast enough. It was all hushed up. Papa
took my stepmother to live at the family property in the Caribbean. It's a
beautiful place on a remote island with many loyal staff ...' He let the
sentence hang.

Megan saw the picture – a woman transported to paradise – but a remote
paradise where she could be watched.

'That was when he had the DNA test done, to be sure. Time passed. They
were very happy. Everything was fine. The old obsession seemed forgotten.'

'And my aunt became more and more of a recluse.' *And how much did
the invasion of her home by a deluded woman waving a gun contribute to
that?* She would never know.

Megan stopped again on the labyrinth, letting breeze and sunshine wash
over her. 'I'm sorry, Aunt Olwen. Sorry you had to suffer that.'

A sudden gust of wind sent a flurry of rose petals to settle at Megan's
feet. She stooped to pick one up and carry it with her, going back in her mind
to Freddie's narrative. The bit he'd found difficult to tell.

'My father knew that he was dying. He wanted to come back to Italy.
That was when he explained to me about Gabriella. It all seemed...' Freddie
stopped. Megan saw the honesty in his eyes and the cold inside her melted a
little. 'It all seemed like something out of an old Gothic novel, but I promised
to keep an eye on my stepmother. There was always plenty of staff ... I did
what my father asked, but it all seemed ... ludicrous.'

'Except that it wasn't,' Gideon pointed out in a flat tone.

'I realise that now.'

And back in Italy, when Olwen finally died, Gabriella had her chance. It
hadn't been too difficult to piece her campaign together. The rumours that
Megan had no money, the man Brown, hired to stir up trouble and whom the
police had yet to trace, the repeated offers through the solicitors to buy the
villa.

'She did everything she could to tempt me and then to drive me away,' Megan said. *Including murder.* That thought sent a hard shiver through her. The police had removed the small black car that had been found on the lower end of the drive for forensic testing, but the visible damage to the vehicle had told its own story. 'She brought Ellery here to convince me to go home, then killed him when she thought he was making a deal with a developer.' Freddie looked pale at the statement, and Megan found herself softening again. 'She was still trying to *buy* the villa. She offered me whatever I asked for it.'

Freddie's face twisted. 'Yes. Her lawyer admitted that, and that he'd been trying to stall her.' *Which may have compounded the problem.* Megan didn't say it. She had refused and would have kept on refusing.

'The thing is—' Freddie's expression was a complex mixture of disbelief, contrition and a kind of rueful regret '—she couldn't make that kind of offer. The lawyer knew. My father was a very rich man, but my stepmother doesn't have access to any of that money. She is the beneficiary of a very generous trust and has the lifetime use of the palazzo, but my father's fortune was left to found and run the Institute.' He gave a small helpless shrug. 'My stepmother could not have purchase Il Giardino delle Rose, even if you had accepted her offer.'

'It was all based on nothing,' Gideon said as they stood on the front steps watching Freddie leave. 'All of it.'

Megan nodded. She'd managed to thank Freddie and bid him a civil goodbye, but her emotions were raw. 'Tainting so many lives.' The grip of Gideon's good hand on her shoulder sent reassurance through her. 'And *he* bears some of the blame.'

'And his father before him. The woman needed help, not to be shunted off to some Caribbean bolt-hole.'

'But issues relating to mental health still carry a stigma for many people.' Megan sighed as they turned to go back into the villa.

'It's over now.'

'Yes.' She leaned against Gideon, gripping his hand. 'It is.'

'So that's it, Aunt Olwen.' Megan had reached the centre of the labyrinth and the end of her aunt's story. Gideon had been called away by one of the workers installing cacti and agaves on the point. They'd agreed it was best to press forward with the work – to reclaim and recreate the area. 'There was a lot of sadness in your life, but you were happy here too.' For a moment Megan closed her eyes on a vision of a woman tending a rosebush while a laughing golden-haired boy and handsome dark-haired man walked down the path to find her. They were all together again now. 'And now you have the whole story as well – as much as we know. And it *is* over. Il Giardino delle Rose is mine and I'm so grateful for that.' She opened her eyes and stood absorbing the sunshine. She was sure that it wasn't just imagination when a sense of peace settled around her like a cloak.

She turned. The way back would be hers. The future was hers. She had plans and a man she loved, who had plans of his own. *But not for marriage?*

Megan walked slowly forward. After that breathtaking question when he woke in the hospital, nothing more had been said. *He was medicated, more asleep than awake. He doesn't remember.* She had no intention of speaking about it. She loved Gideon. It was enough. She would make it enough. She was on the last stretch of the winding path.

Time to make those plans.

There was plenty for her to do. First would be sorting out the papers and journals that her aunt had left. She knew that Gideon was keen to find references to the making of the garden. It was a good time to do it, when his arm prevented physical activity. *Not all physical activity.* She laughed when a breeze stirred the bushes again, scattering her with petals.

She would scour the commonplace books to see if there were any references to the originals of the poems. Was the key to unlocking their mystery somewhere in those journals? She was nearing the end of the labyrinth. Ahead of her something white lay on the path. She bent to pick up the gull's feather. She assumed it was from a gull, although there were no birds around. She put the feather in her pocket.

She'd been thinking about a key. Why did that strike a chord …?

Gideon stood looking out to sea, the tower at his back. Behind him Matteo and Tommaso were wrestling with an oversize aloe. He was pleased to find his breathing and heart rate were normal. He had come here the day he was released from hospital, forcing himself to stand on this spot, so now he could do it without wanting to throw up. The cast on his wrist would be a reminder until it was removed, but the threat that hung over the villa was gone. And in five days' time, he and Megan were travelling to Nice, to her friend's wedding.

Wedding.

He bit his lip. He couldn't be certain, but he *thought* that when he'd woken up in hospital he'd asked Megan to marry him. He wasn't sure and she'd said nothing. *Which means that you didn't, or that the answer would be no.* Absently, he scratched his arm around the top of the cast. It was probably for the best. She believed him, but as far as the world was concerned, he would be offering her a name mired in scandal. She had a new life and a new career opening up. He loved her, and he was sure that she loved him. They didn't need more.

'Gideon!' He turned to see Megan making her way towards him. She was smiling. 'I've had an idea.' The words were spilling out before she reached him. 'The key in the writing slope, it had a number on it. When we visited her, Edith said something about a bank. Do you think it could be the key to a safe deposit box?'

Chapter Fifty-Two

Megan's heart was thumping so loudly she was sure the bank official would be able to hear it. Signor Agnello had worked miracles, finding the correct bank in Nice and confirming that there was indeed a safe deposit box registered in the name of Olwen Rossi, as well as getting official sanction for Megan to open it while they were in Nice.

Now they were on their way to the vault. Megan squeezed Gideon's fingers, remembering not to grip too hard. Things were awkward enough without putting his other hand out of commission. She looked up at him and he grinned down at her. He was as excited as she was. *You mustn't expect too much.*

The bank had confirmed that the box had not been opened since her aunt had rented it thirty years ago, with a large down payment to cover the fees. *Locked and forgotten. Or locked and hidden?*

The doors of the small lift serving the vault slid open. The official gestured for them to exit. The air was cool, with the tang of a permanently air-conditioned space. They were ushered down a short corridor. The official unlocked a door and the box was waiting on the table inside the small room.

Heart beating harder than ever, Megan handed over the key. She'd made up her mind that whatever was in there she would take nothing away with her today. She just wanted to see. She nodded to the official to use the bank's key and then hers. He unlocked the box and prepared to leave. Megan touched his arm.

'Please stay.' The gleam in the man's eye told her that he was as interested in the contents as she was.

'Would you like me to open it?'

Megan nodded, finding that there was a lump in her throat too big for her to speak. *Aunt Olwen, what did you hide here?*

The lid swung open. The official gently tipped the box so that the contents were visible – papers. Megan reached forward, lifting out the top layer and spreading it on the table. It was a horde she recognised. Notebooks and folders, drafts and typescripts. A researcher's working papers, and under them a thick blue file. With a shaky hand, she took it out and folded back the cover.

These papers were old. The sheets were yellowed and fragile but the crabbed writing was legible.

'Verses by Cosimo,' she read the words with a voice that wobbled. She looked up at Gideon, remembering what Edith had said. 'She couldn't keep them, but she couldn't throw them away,' she said softly. 'These are the originals of the poems – and her son's papers for the translation.'

'This place is fabulous.' Gideon waved his free hand to take in the immaculate grounds surrounding them. They were sitting beside the pool of the villa where Nadine and Ryan had been married the day before. The ceremony and the party that followed, organised by Cassie, had been the fanciest wedding he'd ever attended. *Not that you've attended that many.* The service in the flower-filled chapel, where the couple had eyes only for each other, had brought an ache to his chest that had still not quite dissipated, despite the revelry that followed.

Now the newlyweds had departed for their honeymoon and the other guests had said their goodbyes. Jake had asked that he and Megan stay over in the cottage in the grounds that they'd been allocated as guest accommodation. Jake hadn't disclosed why, but Gideon assumed Cassie wanted to know about the contents of the mysterious safe deposit box. They hadn't shared any information about the trip to the bank, this being Nadine and Ryan's time, but now they were sitting by the pool as dusk fell with a couple of bottles of wine from Megan's vineyard. Cassie, visibly pregnant, was drinking lemonade. Megan had just finished the story. Her eyes glittered like stars. 'It was all there – the original poems – including some new ones and some of the poet's letters *and* my cousin's notes for the translation.'

'That poor woman must have just scooped it all up when her son died and dumped it,' Cassie said.

'When her son was murdered,' Jake put in softly. They'd shared the details of that story too. 'And now you can uncover it and bring his name out into the open.'

'Yes,' Megan agreed with the long, contented sigh of an academic with a brand-new research project. Gideon identified it with a smile.

'The villa had more than one gift,' Cassie observed. She was looking speculatively from him to Megan. He'd noted that look a couple of times over the last few days. *Well, we are sharing a cottage.*

Jake had just topped up his wine. He leaned forward now. 'I suggested you stay tonight so that I could show you this.' He retrieved a folded newspaper from under his chair.

Gideon saw the masthead – *The Brickhaven Herald* – and stiffened. 'What is it?' he asked warily.

'Rod Williams' latest investigation. Read it.'

Reluctantly, Gideon did as Jake asked, conscious of Megan sitting beside him, alert and vibrating with curiosity. He shifted so she could see over his shoulder. It was a short paragraph, indicating that police were investigating the activities of a prominent local businessman. The piece was circumspect, with no names mentioned, but Gideon knew that if he'd been hooked up to one of those hospital machines right now, it would be bleeping furiously. 'This is Justin.' He could hear the tremor in his voice.

'It is,' Jake confirmed. 'With more to come. I think we can safely say that you will be completely vindicated before the end of the year.'

Gideon raked his hand into his hair, his mind spinning. 'How ... why is Williams doing this?'

'I can be very persuasive.' Jake's grin had a wolfish cast. 'Although, to be fair, Williams was already having second thoughts about that piece he wrote on you.'

'Pity he didn't have them *before* he wrote it,' Cassie said, chasing an ice-cube around her drink with her finger. 'Jake suggested the man dig a little deeper, with a few hints about where.' She granted them a pussy cat smile. 'You were too wiped out at the time to think straight, but it was fairly clear to those with a little experience—' she raised her glass to salute her husband '— that this was not Justin West's first rodeo. You need a few dodgy contacts to make a scam like that work. Turns out the guy has a trail of crooked deals and confidence tricks behind him. He'd made Spain too hot to hold him. The police there were already on his track. Once he got to Brickhaven, he couldn't leave well alone.' She fixed Gideon with a steady gaze. 'The chance to bring you down was too much to resist – and that vindictiveness made him take risks that a man with his experience really should have avoided.' She smiled again. 'I doubt he'll be very popular at the local golf club when it all comes out.'

'Williams will make sure that the true picture regarding the Nurseries will be fully reported, although that will probably take a while,' Jake added.

Gideon was almost too giddy to take it in. He was, or would be, vindicated. Williams was probably keen to cooperate to avoid a lawsuit, but suing Williams and his newspaper would tie up his time, emotions and money for years to come. He wasn't ready to go there. He'd rather close the door on it – the guy *had* been taken in by an old school friend. The sudden relief was massive. More than he would ever have expected. He looked over at Jake. 'Thank you.'

Megan went one better and leaped out of her chair to kiss Jake. Gideon wasn't even jealous. He didn't need to be, as soon she was throwing herself into his arms to kiss him too.

Megan turned her face up to feel the sun on her skin. She'd enjoyed the excitement of the trip to Nice and the wedding, but it was good to be back at the villa. Gideon was at work on the exotic garden and Alcinda had just arrived unexpectedly, mid-morning, asking to look at the little temple with the headless statue. She'd been away in New York, but was still pondering her plans for a painting of Apollo, using the temple as a setting. During their amble through the garden, Megan shared what they'd learned and suspected about Gabriella.

'The woman was obsessed. Self-absorbed ... and evil,' Alcinda said, when she had finished.

They walked on in silence for a few moments before Alcinda spoke again, 'Freddie offered me the paintings back – the ones of the garden and the legend that Gabriella bought. I don't want them – I just want them to be *seen*. We've agreed that they should go on display at the palazzo, when the Institute takes over and moves in.' She shot a sideways glance at Megan. 'Maria said you were opening the garden to the public. I wondered if you'd like to show them here for a bit, if we can find the right space. Bianca would help with the arrangements.' She looked around at the vibrant plants and the distant tower. 'They should be here ... at least for a while.'

'That would be amazing.' Megan hoped her voice conveyed her pleasure as well as her surprise. 'Will Freddie be okay with that?'

'Yes,' Alcinda said uncompromisingly. 'He feels guilty.' She kicked a small stone a short way down the path. 'Gabriella should have been stopped. A long time ago.'

The flatness of Alcinda's voice stirred Megan's memory – something Gideon had told her. 'You're thinking about your friend?' she asked carefully. 'The one who was Gabriella's secretary?'

'Battista.' Alcinda nodded. 'And your cousin – Cosimo. Gabriella killed them.' Megan heard her inhale. 'There will never be any proof. Not after all this time.' They'd reached the temple. Alcinda put her hand on one of the pillars, staring at the statue. 'But two young people, both falling like that? No one ever really explained why Battista was on that staircase that morning when the staff were always expected to use the service stairs – and why would Cosimo go right to the edge of a dangerous cliff unless something forced him to? It can never be proved,' she repeated. 'But I *know*.'

She turned, and for a hair-raising second, Megan saw in her friend's eyes the cool, otherworldly certainty that drove Alcinda's talent. Then, in another second, it was gone and Alcinda grinned. She gestured to the statue. 'Let's go and find Gideon. I know now what I want for the Apollo. I'll let him keep his clothes on.' The grin got wider and wickeder. 'Well, some of them.'

Epilogue

Gideon quietly let himself out of the French doors onto the terrace, glad that he'd stashed a sweater with the clothes he'd hidden in the downstairs cloakroom the previous evening. The autumn days were still warm, but now there was a chill in the pre-dawn air. The sky was just showing the pearly glow of first light. His fellow conspirators were already sitting on the wall of the terrace, smoking. He padded over for a silent greeting. Tommaso and Matteo responded with wide grins, stubbing out their cigarettes.

Matteo rubbed his hands together. 'Okay, let's do this,' he breathed, nodding to the row of small potted orange trees that he and Tommaso had manhandled up the steps after dark last night. They'd worked out the plan for positioning the birthday surprise over a bottle of wine in Tommaso's shed. Now all they had to do was move the pots into place. These were small trees that could stay on the terrace. The citrus grove proper was ready for planting behind the kitchen garden. They'd had a scare yesterday when Megan had wandered that way. Luckily, Gideon had been on hand to stage a diversion. *A very satisfactory diversion.*

Matteo, seeing the reminiscent grin, nudged Gideon in the ribs and pointed to the nearest tub. Gideon nodded and got to it. The cast had been removed, but he still had a brace on his wrist. He could never have shifted the pots without help, even with two fully functioning hands. They soon had a rhythm going, using a trolley with well-oiled wheels to manoeuvre the trees.

When they were half done, Gideon stood up and stretched, assessing the effect. It looked good. He hoped that today would be a good day. He would never have guessed how much could happen in the month since Nadine and Ryan's wedding. Megan had retrieved the papers from the bank and now had an office at the Institute and provision for them to be safely stored. The Director was delighted with the find and with Freddie's suggestion that her work should take place under the Institute's auspices. There was talk of a research assistant and a long-term plan for an international conference. The poems were going to put Megan and the Institute firmly on the literary map.

Gabriella had recovered sufficiently to be released from hospital. The specialists that Freddie brought in were in agreement that she would never walk again and had approved a discreet transfer to a long-term care facility in the mountains. With the results of forensic tests on the car, the police had confirmed that it was the one that had killed Ellery, although proving who was driving would not be an open and shut case. Megan had met with Julia and Ellery's parents on a short visit to Bath, using Jake's private plane. They seemed to have achieved a degree of closure, whether or not the police were able to go forward.

And he – he was doing fine. With the publication of a couple of articles in the *Herald* concerning Justin's activities he'd felt renewed confidence in reaching out to old contacts and promoting his new business. He'd come across as Justin's dupe – but he wasn't alone. Justin had left a trail of high-flying financiers around the globe with egg on their faces and holes in their portfolios. He'd dismantled his father's business just because he could, and had unwittingly brought himself down by setting McQuire on his case. Jake hadn't disclosed much, but Gideon knew he'd been instrumental in uncovering Justin's past. There would always be people who only remembered part of the story, or believed that there was no smoke without fire, but Gideon could live with that. Megan knew who and what he was. That was what really mattered.

The last pot was in position. The sun was higher in the sky. They fastened the sign reading *Happy Birthday* to two of the trees, and, with silent high-fives, Tommaso and Matteo left. When Gideon was sure they were gone, he unrolled the second and third signs. Fastening them with his braced hand was tricky, but he got it done in the end. He told himself that the light sweat on his face was the result of exertion, not anticipation. This was it. *Everything or nothing.* He gave the closest banner a final tweak and sat on the wall to wait.

Megan rolled over, putting out her hand, then opening her eyes with a jerk. Gideon's side of the bed was not only empty, it was cold. Was he out running? She sat up, collecting herself. Today was her birthday. They'd agreed to spend the day looking around the aquarium in Genoa, which was apparently worth seeing. Tonight there would be a party, just a few friends. The terrace room, with the re-installed chandeliers would be too big, but she really did want to use it, to help grow the feeling of happiness she sensed pervading the villa. *Happiness and love.*

She slid out of bed, grabbed a robe and crossed the room to do what she did every morning – open the windows, lean over the tiny balcony and see what the day was doing. She leaned out, then stopped dead, her breath caught in her throat. Gideon was down there, looking up. He wasn't smiling as she would have expected. Then she saw the trees positioned around the terrace and the banners. *Happy Birthday*, *I love you* and *Will you marry me?*

'Oh!'

'For God's sake, don't fall.' Gideon stepped forward, his face creased with concern. She realised that she had stretched precariously far out over the railing.

'No … I mean I'm not going to fall. Yes. The answer is yes! Stay there,' she ordered. Now he was laughing, and she was too. Without bothering to find her slippers, she pounded down the stairs to the terrace room, out of the doors and into Gideon's arms. He swung her up, so that her bare feet didn't touch the cold floor.

'Yes.' She found his mouth and kissed him. 'Yes, I will marry you.' The sun was coming up, pink and gold. The villa stood behind them, solid and strong and enfolding.

'Happy birthday.' He nuzzled her hair. 'I thought we could maybe look at jewellers, in Genoa … for a ring? And you need to see the rest of your present.' He held her away, looking down at her feet. 'You need shoes. We watered the ground last night, ready for planting.'

For a second, she was puzzled, then she got it. 'More orange trees – an orange grove.'

'Oranges and lemons.' He was smiling in a way that nearly tipped her heart out of her chest. 'They might even be established enough for a wedding ceremony, maybe next spring? Once Cassie has the baby and can organise it?' he suggested hopefully.

Laughing, she reached up to pull his head down for another kiss

'I love you, Gideon West. I will marry you, next spring, with or without the citrus grove. And this is the best birthday ever.'

Thank You

Hello,

I really hope you have enjoyed *A Villa in Portofino*. This is the third book in the "Riviera" series, and once again I've loved the chance to mix romance with mystery and suspense, this time on the Italian side of the border. It was both fun and challenging to create a villa and a glorious garden and to juggle the strands of a family story that stretched right back to the Second World War.

I like to think that my books are pure escapism – excitement and love in the Riviera sunshine. I'm currently working on book four of the series and hope that you will be coming with me to the Riviera again before too long.

Before we get to travel together again though, I have a request. If you have enjoyed *A Villa in Portofino*, it would be great if you could leave a review on any or all of your favourite sites, or mention the book on Twitter or Facebook. You can follow me on both and read my blog to keep up with my news (details on my 'About the Author' page next). I really would appreciate a review, if you have a few moments to post one.

Thank you for reading *A Villa in Portofino*, and here's to our next trip to the Riviera sunshine.

Evonne

About the Author

Evonne Wareham was born in South Wales and spent her childhood there. After university she migrated to London, where she worked in local government, scribbled novels in her spare time and went to the theatre a lot. Now she's back in Wales, living by the sea, and has just completed a PhD in history. She still loves the theatre, likes staying in hotels and enjoys the company of other authors through her membership of both the Romantic Novelists' Association and the Crime Writers' Association.

Evonne's debut novel, *Never Coming Home* won the 2012 Joan Hessayon New Writers' Award, the 2013 Colorado Romance Writers' Award for Romantic Suspense, the Oklahoma National Readers' Choice Award for Romantic Suspense plus was a nominee for a Reviewers' Choice Award from RT Book Reviews. Her second romantic suspense novel *Out of Sight Out of Mind*, was a finalist for the Maggie Award for Excellence, presented by the Georgia Romance Writers' chapter of the Romance Writers of America.

For more information visit:
Twitter: www.twitter.com/evonnewareham
Facebook: www.facebook.com/evonnewarehamauthor
Blog: www.evonneonwednesday.blogspot.com

More Choc Lit
from
Evonne Wareham

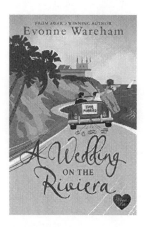

A Wedding on the Riviera
Riviera Series – Book 2

A return to the Riviera on the trail of a runaway groom ...
When out-of-work actor Ryan Calder attends a wedding as the plus-one of
successful businesswoman, Nadine Wells, he doesn't expect to get in a
scuffle with the groom.

But Ryan has a good reason. He recognises the groom from another wedding
where the same man made a quick getaway, taking the wedding money and
leaving a heartbroken bride in his wake. It seems he's struck again, and
Nadine's poor friend is the target.

Ryan and Nadine decide they can't let it happen to another woman, so with a
group of friends they hatch a plan that will take them to the French Riviera,
hot on the heels of the crooked groom. But could their scheme to bring him to
justice also succeed in bringing them closer together?

Visit www.choc-lit.com for more details.

Summer in San Remo
Riviera Series – Book 1

Anything could happen when you spend summer in San Remo ...
Running her busy concierge service usually keeps Cassie Travers fully occupied. But when a new client offers her the strangest commission she's ever handled she suddenly finds herself on the cusp of an Italian adventure, with a man she thought she would never see again.

Jake McQuire has returned from the States to his family-run detective agency. When old flame Cassie appears in need of help with her mysterious client, who better than Jake to step in?

Events take the pair across Europe to a luxurious villa on the Italian Riviera. There, Cassie finds that the mystery she pursues pales into insignificance, when compared to another discovery made along the way ...

Visit www.choc-lit.com for more details.

Never Coming Home

Winner of the 2012 New Writers' Joan Hessayon Award

All she has left is hope

When Kaz Elmore is told her five-year-old daughter Jamie has died in a car crash, she struggles to accept that she'll never see her little girl again. Then a stranger comes into her life offering the most dangerous substance in the world: hope.

Devlin, security consultant and witness to the terrible accident scene, inadvertently reveals that Kaz's daughter might not have been the girl in the car after all.

What if Jamie is still alive? With no evidence, the police aren't interested, so Devlin and Kaz have little choice but to investigate themselves.
Devlin never gets involved with a client. Never. But the more time he spends with Kaz, the more he desires her – and the more his carefully constructed ice-man persona starts to unravel.

The desperate search for Jamie leads down dangerous paths – to a murderous acquaintance from Devlin's dark past, and all across Europe, to Italy, where deadly secrets await. But as long as Kaz has hope, she can't stop looking …

Visit www.choc-lit.com for more details.

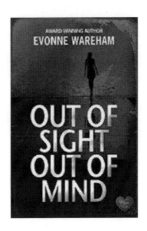

Out of Sight Out of Mind
Finalist for the Maggie Award of Excellence

Everyone has secrets. Some are stranger than others.
Madison Albi is a scientist with a very special talent – for reading minds. When she stumbles across a homeless man with whom she feels an inexplicable connection, she can't resist the dangerous impulse to use her skills to help him.

J is a non-person – a vagrant who can't even remember his own name. He's got no hope, until he meets Madison. Is she the one woman who can restore his past? Madison agrees to help J recover his memory, but as she delves deeper into his mind, it soon becomes clear that some secrets are better off staying hidden.
Is J really the man Madison believes him to be?

Visit www.choc-lit.com for more details.

What Happens at Christmas

A Christmas to remember

Lori France and her four-year-old niece Misty are settling in to spend the holidays in Wales after unexpected events leave them without a place to stay. Best-selling author Andrew Vitruvius knows that any publicity is good publicity. His agent tells him that often, so it must be true. In the run-up to Christmas, she excels herself - talking him into the craziest scheme yet: getting himself kidnapped, live on TV.

Little do they know they're about to make a discovery and experience a Christmas they're not likely to forget …

Visit www.choc-lit.com for more details.

Introducing Choc Lit

We are an independent publisher creating a delicious selection of fiction.
Quality stories with a romance at the heart.
See our selection here:
www.choc-lit.com

We'd love to hear how you enjoyed *A Villa in Portofino.* Please leave a
review on the store where you purchased this novel or
visit **www.choc-lit.com** and give your feedback.

Choc Lit novels are selected by genuine readers like yourself. We only publish
stories our Tasting Panel want to see in print. Our reviews and awards speak
for themselves.

Could you be a Star Selector
and join our Tasting Panel?
Would you like to play a role in choosing which novels we decide to publish?
Do you enjoy reading women's fiction? Then you could be perfect for our
Tasting Panel.
Visit here for more details:
www.choc-lit.com/join-the-choc-lit-tasting-panel

Keep in touch:
Sign up for our monthly newsletter Choc Lit Spread for all the latest news
and offers: **www.spread.choc-lit.com.**

Follow us on:
Twitter: **@ChocLituk**
Facebook: **Choc Lit**
Instagram: **ChocLituk**

Where heroes are like chocolate – irresistible!

Printed in Great Britain
by Amazon